Praise for the novels of #1 *New York Times* bestselling author Debbie Macomber

"Macomber is known for her honest portrayals of ordinary women in small-town America, and this tale cements her position as an icon of the genre."
—*Publishers Weekly* on *16 Lighthouse Road*

"Debbie Macomber [has a] gift for understanding the souls of women—their relationships, their values, their lives."
—*BookPage* on *Between Friends*

"Macomber is a master storyteller."
—*Times Record News*

"With first-class author Debbie Macomber, it's quite simple—she gives readers an exceptional, unforgettable story every time, and her books are always, always keepers!"
—*ReadertoReader.com*

"No one writes better women's contemporary fiction."
—*RT Book Reviews*

"Macomber has a gift for evoking the emotions that are at the heart of the genre's popularity."
—*Publishers Weekly*

DEBBIE MACOMBER

Texas Home

mira

ISBN-13: 978-0-7783-6988-2

Recycling programs
for this product may
not exist in your area.

Texas Home

Copyright © 2019 by Harlequin Books S.A.

The publisher acknowledges the copyright holder
of the individual works as follows:

Nell's Cowboy
Copyright © 1998 by Debbie Macomber

Lone Star Baby
Copyright © 1998 by Debbie Macomber

For questions and comments about the quality of this book, please contact us at
CustomerService@Harlequin.com.

Harlequin.com

Printed in U.S.A.

Also available from Debbie Macomber and MIRA Books

CONTENTS

THE PEOPLE OF PROMISE

Nell Bishop: Thirtysomething widow with a son, Jeremy, and a daughter, Emma. Her husband died in a tractor accident.

Ruth Bishop: Nell's mother-in-law; lives with Nell and her two children.

Dovie Boyd: Runs an antiques shop and has dated Sheriff Frank Hennessey for ten years.

Caroline Daniels: Postmistress of Promise.

Maggie Daniels: Caroline's five-year-old daughter.

Dr. Jane Dickinson: New doctor in Promise.

Ellie Frasier: Owner of Frasier's Feed Store.

Frank Hennessey: Local sheriff.

Max Jordan: Owner of Jordan's Town and Country.

Wade McMillen: Preacher of Promise Christian Church.

Edwina and Lily Moorhouse: Sisters; retired schoolteachers.

Cal and Glen Patterson: Local ranchers; brothers who ranch together.

Phil and Mary Patterson: Parents of Cal and Glen; operate a local B and B.

Louise Powell: Town gossip.

Wiley Rogers: Sixty-year-old ranch foreman at the Weston ranch.

Laredo Smith: Wrangler hired by Savannah Weston.

Barbara and Melvin Weston: Mother and father to Savannah, Grady and Richard; the Westons died six years ago.

Richard Weston: Youngest of the Weston siblings.

Savannah Weston: Grady and Richard's sister; cultivates old roses.

Grady Weston: Rancher; oldest of the Weston siblings.

NELL'S COWBOY

To Anita and Allen Greenstein, who love the Florida sunshine and good wine as much as Wayne and I do.

One

Nell Bishop barreled down the highway, heading home, racing against the approaching storm. The March winds whipped against the pickup as she hurried toward Twin Canyons Ranch, thirty-four miles south of Promise, Texas.

Her mother-in-law was with the children, but Jeremy and Emma would have difficulty getting the animals into the barn without help. Ruth would do what she could, but the older woman's heart wasn't strong and... Nell didn't want to think what might happen if she didn't make it back in time.

Her life had been on a fast-moving treadmill for the past three years, ever since her husband died in a tractor accident. Storms were the least of her worries, considering the financial challenges she'd faced working the ranch without Jake. Not a day passed that her husband wasn't in her thoughts. Twenty years from now, *forty* years from now, he'd still be a part of her.

Ruth and others had encouraged her to remarry, at least to date, but Nell had resisted. She never expected to love again—not the way she loved Jake. Their love was the kind that happened only once in a lifetime, and no other man could compare to her Jake.

Nell had always known she wasn't any candidate for homecoming queen, but Jake had made her feel like one. He'd understood what it was to be big-boned and just plain big. Dainty or elegant would never describe her; at six feet, Nell was as tall as most men. Jake had been six feet four inches by the time he was a high-school freshman, and the only boy in school taller than Nell.

They'd lived in the same town all their lives, but it wasn't until high school that she'd noticed him. The very first day of high school, as a matter of fact. She was a freshman to his senior, and the minute his eyes met hers as she walked down the hall, she knew she'd found her life's mate. He was the only boy she'd ever dated. When he enlisted in the army and became an Airborne Ranger, she'd written him every day. He served his time in the army and was discharged a week after her graduation. Despite her family's protests, she'd married Jake while still a teenager.

Neither was to know that ten years was all the time they'd have together. It was Nell who'd found her husband trapped beneath the tractor, Nell who'd held him in her arms as the life flowed out of him, Nell who'd screamed in anguish, helpless to do anything to save her husband's life.

Now it was Nell who struggled to hold on to Twin Canyons Ranch, tended what remained of the herd, raised their children and cared for Jake's aging mother. The ranch had been Jake's dream—and hers; it was a small spread that they'd bought together, shortly after their marriage. But she was so very tired, weary to the bone with her financial struggles and other worries. The past three years had drained her mentally, emotionally and physically. For that reason she'd sold off most of the herd and started a new venture. A dude ranch.

Bless Jeremy's heart. Her son had been the one to give her the idea. Last year, she'd promised him a reward for acing his spelling test and he'd chosen to rent a movie. Of all the movies available, he'd picked *City Slickers,* and to Nell it was like a revelation.

After seeing the movie, Nell hadn't been able to sleep all night. She was certainly familiar with dude ranches, but it had never occurred to her that this might be a solution to her own dilemma. She couldn't say she understood it, but people actually paid for the opportunity to eat food cooked in a chuck wagon, ride around on horses and drive cattle. Why these people would prefer to live in primitive circumstances when they could experience the luxury of some fancy resort for basically the same price was beyond her. Apparently she had a lot to learn—but learn she did. After months of research Nell was convinced that a dude ranch really was the answer. With a portion of her profits from the sale of last year's herd, she'd had brochures printed and she'd contacted several travel companies. Now she was almost ready for business, and in a couple of months she'd be entertaining her first bunkhouse full of greenhorns.

In many ways she was a natural for this kind of work. After these few years without Jake, there wasn't a ranching chore she couldn't accomplish with the speed and dexterity of a man. At this point, she knew as much about ranching as any cowboy. Not only that, she'd heard the great stories of Texas all her life—stories about the state's settlement and the Alamo and the early cattle drives and many more. She'd always loved those stories, and if she could make money telling them now, romanticizing the Old West, all the better.

Heavy black clouds darkened the sky. Pushing thoughts of Jake from her mind, Nell focused her attention on the highway. Driving well above the speed limit, she rounded a turn in the road and saw a sports utility vehicle parked along the side.

Some damn fool had stopped to take pictures of the approaching storm. The man obviously wasn't a local. Anyone from Texas would know to take cover, and fast. Like the state of Texas itself, storms tended to make an impression, especially spring storms like this one.

Despite her hurry, Nell applied her brakes and pulled over. With the engine running, she leaped down from the cab. The wind slapped her long braid against her face as she raced toward the stranger.

The greenhorn lowered his camera. "Howdy," he greeted her cheerfully. He was taller than she was and clean-cut. His clothes were new-looking but rumpled.

"Listen, I don't mean to be rude, but any idiot knows to head for cover in a storm."

His smile faded to a frown.

"I don't know where you're from or where you're going," she went on, "but if I were you I'd get my butt back into that fancy car of yours and drive into town as fast as those tires will take you." Having done her duty, she started back to her truck.

"Hey," he said, "got a minute? I have a few questions."

"I have to go." Nell didn't mean to sound abrupt, but she didn't have time to waste. She'd said her piece and whether or not he took her advice was completely up to him.

"Are you from around the area?" he called after her.

"Yes! Now listen, we get hail the size of golf balls and if you don't want to pay to have the dents removed, then I suggest you make tracks for town."

"This will only take a minute…"

"I don't *have* a minute, I've got horses and calves to worry about," Nell shouted into the wind. "And I don't have time to convince you a storm is about to break." She raised her hand toward the threatening sky. "It's going to cost you plenty if you don't get that vehicle under cover."

"I'm insured."

"Hail is an act of God." Whether he caught her last words or not she didn't know. Nell leaped into her truck and put the pickup in gear. One glance in the rearview mirror proved that giving this stranger advice had been a wasted effort. He hadn't moved. Furthermore, he wasn't snapping pictures of the dark horizon anymore; he was taking pictures of her!

Shaking her head in wonder, Nell dismissed him from her thoughts, and drove home at breakneck speed.

When she pulled into the ranch yard, she saw Jeremy chasing chickens in a futile attempt to lure them into the coop. Emma and Ruth led the horses toward the barn, yanking on the reins as the two geldings battled the wind. The scene right before the tornado in *The Wizard of Oz* flashed through Nell's mind.

She parked the truck near the barn, where it would be protected, and hurried toward her family. With her help, Ruth and Emma managed to secure the animals before the storm broke.

By the time they scurried into the house, the rain had started and they were breathless and excited.

"We did it!" twelve-year-old Jeremy said, exchanging a high five with his sister. Unlike most siblings, Jeremy and Emma rarely fought. Sure, they squabbled now and then—all kids did—but these two were close in age and temperament. They'd also been through the devastating experience of their father's death, which had created a strong bond between them.

Jeremy was large for his age, like his father and Nell, too—big-boned, muscular and tall. Two years younger, Emma was small and delicate, resembling Ruth, her grandmother.

"I'm glad you made it home in time," Ruth said, pouring Nell a cup of hot tea before filling a second cup for herself.

Nell gazed out the kitchen window at the ferocity of the storm. The wind propelled the rain at an almost horizontal angle, pelting the trees and flowers. Smaller trees were bent nearly in half. Many a new crop would see ruin this afternoon.

Sighing, she turned away from the window. "I would have been a couple of minutes earlier if it hadn't been for some greenhorn," she said. "The silly fool stopped at the side of the road to take pictures."

"Anyone you recognized?" Ruth asked.

"Never saw him before in my life." Nell would have remembered him if she had. He was big like Jake, sturdy and broad-shouldered. Unfortunately—unlike Jake—he didn't seem to possess an ounce of common sense.

Ruth shook her head. "Probably one of those tornado chasers."

Nell frowned. "I don't think so." He wasn't the type. Too soft, she decided, and although it might sound unkind, not all that bright. Anyone with brains knew to seek shelter in a storm.

"What's for dinner?" Jeremy asked.

"Not chili," Emma pleaded.

Despite herself Nell laughed. "Not chili," she assured her. Her family had been good sports, sampling different variations of her chili recipe for the past few months. Nell was perfecting her recipe and had used her family as taste-testers.

The Chili Cook-off was being held that weekend as part of the Promise Rodeo. These festivities launched spring the way the big Cattlemen's Association dance in June signaled the beginning of summer.

Nell held high hopes that her chili might actually win this year. Her talents in the kitchen were legendary, and she believed she made a great pot of chili. For weeks she'd been combining recipes, adding this, subtracting that. After feeding her family chili twice a week, she was finally satisfied with her recipe.

"Are you going to win the cook-off?" Emma asked.

"Of course she is," Ruth answered before Nell could respond. "I don't see why she shouldn't, seeing she's the best cook this side of the Rio Grande."

Both children nodded enthusiastically, and Nell smiled. "How about porcupine meatballs for dinner?" she suggested. The meatballs, made with rice and cooked in tomato soup, were one of the children's favorites. Jeremy and Emma instantly agreed.

"I'll peel the potatoes," Ruth said. As usual her mother-in-law was willing to lend a hand.

The lights flickered just then, and the house went dark.

"That's okay," Jeremy said. "We don't need electricity. We can roast weenies in the fireplace, can't we?"

"Yeah," Emma seconded. "We could have hot dogs."

"Sounds like a good idea to me." Nell reached for a candle, grateful her children maintained a sense of adventure. They were going to need it when the first dude ranch guests arrived.

Cal Patterson shook the moisture from his jacket as he stepped inside out of the driving rain. He removed his Stetson and placed it on the hook just inside the porch to dry. He'd done what he could to protect his herd, gotten his horses into the barn and battened down the shutters where he could. Glen, his brother and business partner, had left for town early in hopes of beating the storm. Cal had worked alone, listening with half an ear for his wife's arrival. He didn't like the idea of Jane driving all the way from town in this kind of weather.

"Cal, is that you?"

His heart rate accelerated at the sound of her voice. "Jane? What the hell are you doing here? Where's your car? I didn't see it."

"I live here, remember?" she teased, joining him in the kitchen porch while he removed his boots. She'd obviously just had a bath and now wore a flannel bathrobe, belted loosely about her waist. "And I didn't park in my usual place because Glen's truck was still there."

"You should've stayed in town," he chastised, but he was delighted she'd managed to make it home. He didn't relish the idea of a night spent without her. Two months of marriage, and he'd grown accustomed to sharing his home and his heart with this woman.

"The clinic closed early," she informed him, "and I've got my beeper. Anyone can reach me in case of a medical emergency."

Cal shed his jacket and slipped his arms around her

waist, pulling her close and urging her into the kitchen. His wife was the town's only physician, so there were constant demands on her time. "I don't know if I'll ever be able to stop worrying about you."

"Hey, I'm a big girl."

"Sure you are!" He was about to kiss her when the lights went out. Not that he minded. A romantic interlude wasn't unwelcome.

"I've got a fire going in the fireplace," she whispered, pressing against him, reminding him of the benefits of married life. She looped her arms around his neck and kissed his jaw.

Cal shut his eyes and inhaled her fresh sweet scent. This was about as close to heaven as he expected to get in his lifetime. "I don't suppose you're wearing that seethrough nightie of yours?"

"No," she said, "but that could be arranged."

"Now you're talkin'."

Cal felt her smile against his skin. "I love you, Rebel."

Growling, he swung her into his arms and carried her into the living room. Sure enough, a small fire flickered in the fireplace. This had become their favorite room; he'd lost count of the number of times they'd made love in front of the fireplace. The room had a special significance for him, since it was here that he'd first realized how much he'd come to care about her. It was here in this very room that Dr. Texas, as he was fond of calling her, had taken his freeze-dried heart and breathed life into his lonely existence.

Cal was happier than he'd ever thought possible. With each passing day he loved Jane more. Their love had demanded plenty of adjustments on both sides. Sacrifices. But for everything he'd given up, he'd gained so much more.

The storm raged outside and a fair one was building on the living-room carpet when Jane's beeper went off.

Cal groaned and rolled onto his back, inhaling several deep breaths. "That damn well better be important," he muttered.

"Cal!"

"I want someone *real* sick."

Giggling, Jane scrambled for her beeper and read the message. "It's Laredo Smith," she said.

"Wanna bet he's phoning about Savannah?"

"She's just over eight months," Jane said, sounding concerned.

"But Laredo's acting like she's three weeks overdue."

"He's worried, that's all."

Cal figured he would be, too, in Laredo's situation. This was the Smiths' first child, and Savannah was over thirty; as well, Cal knew there'd been some minor complications with the pregnancy. Despite that—and unlike her husband—the mother-to-be remained calm and confident. Savannah had insisted on a home delivery, overriding Laredo's protests.

"This shouldn't take long," Jane promised. She hurried over to the hall phone.

Cal cupped his hands behind his head and watched his wife move through the room, bathed in firelight. Her hair was mussed and her bathrobe hastily tied—and he couldn't recall a time she'd looked more beautiful. It never ceased to amaze him that Jane had agreed to be his wife.

Cal had begun to wonder if someone had spiked the water supply last summer. In less than a year most of his friends had married. First, Savannah Weston had met a stranger to Promise named Laredo Smith and subsequently married him. His own brother had married Ellie Frasier, owner of the local feed store, last September. No sooner had *that* wedding taken place when Grady Weston asked the postmistress, Caroline Daniels, to marry him—all within the space of a few short weeks. Even Sheriff Hennessey had married his longtime sweetheart, Dovie Boyd.

It hadn't been long before Cal fell in love himself.

At one time Cal, Glen and Grady had been confirmed bachelors. With Cal, it had been a form of self-protection, he realized now. He'd been jilted by a former fiancée and the experience had left him bitter, determined never to fall for a woman again.

But that was before he'd met Jane. Their first date was arranged by Ellie. At the time Cal had been annoyed and frustrated that his brand-new sister-in-law was matchmaking. By the end of the evening, however, Jane had managed to pique his interest. To his surprise he discovered he was looking forward to seeing her again. Before he could help himself, he was deeply in love with her.

A city girl. Worse, one from California. If anyone had told him six months ago that he'd marry a woman like Jane, he would have run screaming into the night. Now he couldn't imagine living two minutes without her.

With the phone against her ear, Jane caught her husband's eyes and blew him a kiss. He grinned, content to wait. Relaxing on the rug, he listened to one-half of the conversation.

"Don't worry," Jane was telling Laredo, "you didn't interrupt anything important."

Cal sat upright at that, raising his eyebrows. *Didn't interrupt anything important?* He saw that his wife could barely hold in her laughter at his expression.

But her smile faded as she continued to listen to Laredo. "No...no you were right to phone. How long ago did you say her water broke?"

The smile left Cal's face, too. This was more serious than either of them had anticipated.

"How far apart are the contractions?" Jane reached for a pad and pencil and noted the information.

Cal had delivered enough calves to know the signs of imminent birth. Savannah and Laredo were about to have their baby during the worst storm of the year.

"I'll be there within the hour," Jane promised, and replaced the receiver. "Savannah's in labor," she told Cal.

"So I heard." He stood and she walked over to him and caressed the side of his face.

"Looks like we'll have to put our romantic interlude on hold."

"I'm a patient man," he reminded her. He caught her fingers and pressed a kiss into her palm. "What time are we leaving?" he asked, snapping his shirt closed as he spoke.

"We?" Jane asked, arching her brows expressively. "I'm perfectly capable of delivering this baby."

"I never doubted it for an instant." He opened her bathrobe, kissed the valley between her breasts and refastened it.

"I can drive in a storm, too."

"I realize that," he said, "but how good are you at keeping two strong-willed ranchers out of your hair?"

"Two?"

"Laredo and Grady." Cal knew his best friend, and Grady would be as nervous as Laredo at the birth of his first niece or nephew. Jane was going to have her hands full, and it wasn't with Savannah or the baby, either. It wouldn't surprise him if father *and* uncle made damned nuisances of themselves. "Trust me, darlin', you'll thank me later."

"Oh, all right, Cal Patterson, you can tag along, too. Now I'd better go change."

He grinned, pleased he'd been able to convince her she was going to need him. Truth be known, he wouldn't miss this birth for anything. It was about time something good happened in that family, especially after Richard Weston's trial and sentencing.

A baby was just what the Westons needed to put their troubles behind them. Cal was determined to celebrate the blessed event with his friends.

Travis Grant rolled into Promise at precisely the moment the storm struck. He drove down Main Street, peering out between the constantly beating windshield wipers, but he couldn't locate a single hotel. Seeing as his last meal had been aboard a plane and hadn't amounted to much, he decided to stop for dinner and inquire about a place to stay. By the time he found a parking space and raced to the restaurant through the pounding rain, he was soaked to the skin.

He gulped down a glass of water and started on a bowl of tortilla chips with salsa before he even looked at the menu. His stomach growled and he ordered *arroz con pollo,* his favorite Mexican dish.

Gazing out the window, he decided the town was

just the way Richard Weston had described it. This was something of a pleasant surprise. Men like Weston weren't exactly known for their truthfulness. Travis had interviewed him shortly after he was sentenced to twenty-five years in a New York prison. No possibility of parole, either. He wouldn't have talked to him at all if it hadn't been for his ex-wife, who'd been Weston's state-appointed attorney. As far as Travis was concerned, Weston was the ultimate sleaze—an opinion that the interview only reinforced.

Knowing his interest in Western ghost towns, Valerie had told him about Weston, a man who'd hidden from the law in an abandoned town buried deep in the Texas hill country. Weston had agreed to an interview—in exchange for certain concessions. The warden of the prison, however, hadn't approved of the idea that Weston should have a TV and sound system in his cell. Weston had consented to the interview, anyway—because it was another opportunity to be the center of attention, Travis figured. Their meeting continued to leave a bad taste in his mouth. If it hadn't been for Valerie, Travis would have abandoned the entire project, but his ex-wife seemed to have a way with the man.

Valerie. Travis frowned as he thought about her. She'd dumped him and their marriage for another man five years earlier. His lack of malice seemed to disappoint his friends. Frankly, he considered life too short to waste on ill will. He'd loved her, still did, but as she'd so eloquently put it, she'd fallen out of love with him.

She'd remarried as soon as the ink was dry on their divorce papers and seemed content. For that matter, he was, too, although it had taken him longer to achieve peace and he hadn't become involved in another serious relationship. Also, to his friends' surprise, he and Valerie had stayed in touch.

The waiter, a kid of maybe eighteen, delivered a plate heaped with rice and chicken and covered with a thin tomato sauce and melted cheese. "Could you give me directions to the closest motel?" Travis asked him.

"Brewster's got a motel."

"Great." Travis reached for his fork. "How far away is that?"

"About a hundred miles."

He laid his fork back down. "You mean to say a town the size of Promise doesn't have a motel?"

"We've got a bed and breakfast."

"Fine." A bed was a bed, and at this point he wasn't picky.

The waiter lingered. "You might have trouble getting a room, 'cause of the big festivities this weekend."

"Festivities?"

"The rodeo's coming, and then there's the big chili cook-off. I thought that was why you were here."

Apparently the town was small enough to recognize him as a stranger. "Where do the rodeo cowboys stay while they're in town?"

The youth stared at him as if the answer should be obvious. "Motor homes."

"All of them?"

"Unless they got family close by."

"I see," Travis murmured. He hadn't considered that there wouldn't be a motel—but then that was one of his problems, according to Valerie. He didn't think ahead.

"If you'd like, I could write you out directions to the Pattersons' B and B."

"Please." Famished, Travis dug into his meal, devouring it in minutes. He'd no sooner finished when the waiter returned with a hand-drawn map listing streets and landmarks. Apparently the one and only bed and breakfast was off the beaten path.

Thunder cracked in the sky, followed by flashes of lightning. No one seemed to pay much heed to the storm until the lights flickered. Everyone in the restaurant paused and waited, then sighed with relief when the lights stayed on.

The storm was bad, but he'd seen worse off the New England coastline five years before. Holed up in a rented cottage in order to meet a deadline, Travis had watched storms rage as he fought his own battles. It'd been shortly after the divorce.

He thought of that sassy ranch woman who'd spoken to him today and wondered what she'd say if she knew he'd stood on a rocky bluff overlooking the sea, with the wind and rain pounding against him, and openly defied nature.

Remembering the way she'd leaped out of her truck, eyes flashing with outrage, brought a rare smile to his lips.

She'd been an attractive woman. Practically as tall as he was and full-sized, not some pencil-thin model. A spitfire, too. Definitely one of a kind. Briefly he wondered if he'd get a chance to see her again and rather hoped he would, just so he could tell her he'd managed to survive the storm.

Following the directions given him by the waiter at the Mexican Lindo, Travis drove to Pattersons' Bed and Breakfast, which turned out to be a large older home. He rang the doorbell.

Almost immediately a tall gray-haired lanky man

opened the door and invited him inside. "Welcome to Promise." The man extended his hand and introduced himself as Phil Patterson.

"Travis Grant. Do you have a room for a few nights?" he asked, getting directly to the point.

"Sorry," Phil told him. "We're booked solid."

Travis had left New York early that morning and didn't relish the thought of traveling another hundred miles through a storm to find a bed for the night. "I'm tired and not difficult to please. Isn't there any place that could put me up for a few nights?"

Phil frowned. "The rodeo's coming to town."

"So I understand."

"I doubt there's a room available in Brewster, either." Travis muttered a curse under his breath.

"Phil." A woman's voice called out from the kitchen. "You might try Nell."

"Nell?"

"Nell Bishop."

Phil sighed. "I know who Nell is."

"She's opening her dude ranch in a couple of months, so she's probably got rooms to rent."

Phil's face relaxed. "Of course, that's a great idea." Travis's spirits lifted.

"I'll give her a call." Phil reached for the phone, punched in the number and waited. After a minute or two he covered the receiver. "Nell's busy, but her mother-in-law's there and she said you'd be welcome to drive out, but she feels obliged to warn you there's no electricity at the moment."

"They have a bed and clean sheets?"

"Sure thing, and Ruth—that's her name—said she'd throw in breakfast, as well."

He named a price that sounded more than reasonable to Travis. "Sold."

Phil relayed the information, drew him a map, and soon Travis was back on the road.

Patterson had told him that the ranch was a fair distance out of town; still, by the time Travis pulled off the highway and onto the gravel drive that led to Twin Canyons Ranch, he suspected he was closer to Brewster than Promise. Approaching the front door, he felt as though his butt was dragging as low to the ground as his suitcase.

A kid who looked to be about twelve answered his knock and stared blankly at him while Travis stood in the rain.

"Hello," Travis finally said.

"Hello," the boy answered. A girl two or three years younger joined him. Good-looking children, but apparently not all that bright.

"Most people come to the back door unless they're selling something, and if you are, we're not buying."

Despite feeling tired and cranky, Travis grinned. "I'm here about a room."

The two kids exchanged glances.

"Who is it?" He heard an older woman's voice in the background; a moment later, she appeared at the door. "For the love of heaven, young man, come out of the rain." She nudged the children aside and held open the door.

He stood in the hallway, which was all gloom and shadows except for the light flickering from a cluster of candles. Travis glanced around, but it was impossible to see much.

"Mom's in the barn," the boy said.

"I know that," the older woman told him. She put the candle close to Travis's face. "You look decent enough."

"I haven't eaten any children in at least a week," he teased, eyeing the two kids. The little girl moved a step closer to her brother.

"I'm Travis Grant," he said, turning his attention to the woman.

"Ruth Bishop, and these two youngsters are my grandchildren, Jeremy and Emma."

"Pleased to meet you." He shifted the suitcase in his hand, hoping Ruth would take the hint and escort him to his room. She didn't. "About the room…" he said pointedly.

"You'll need to meet Nell first."

"All right." He was eager to get the introductions over with so he could fall into bed and sleep for the next twelve hours straight.

"This way." She led him through the house to the back porch, where she pulled on a hooded jacket. Then she walked down the back steps and into the rain, holding her hand over the candle to shield the small flame.

Travis wasn't enthusiastic about clumping through the storm yet again, but didn't have much choice.

"Ruth?" a new voice called into the night. A low pleasant voice.

"Coming," the grandmother answered.

They met halfway across the yard in the pouring rain. "I got us our first paying guest," Ruth announced, beaming proudly. "Travis Grant, meet my daughter-in-law, Nell Bishop."

It took Travis no more than a second to recognize Nell as the woman who'd called him an idiot.

He liked her already.

Two

Nell located an old-fashioned lantern for Travis Grant. It had probably been in the family for fifty years and was nothing if not authentic. Next she gathered together fresh sun-dried sheets, a couple of blankets and a pillow. She tucked everything inside a plastic bag and raced through the storm, holding the lit lantern with one hand. When she arrived at the bunkhouse, Nell discovered Travis sitting on the end of a bed, looking tired and out of sorts.

The initial group of tourists was scheduled to show up the first week of May, and almost everything in the bunkhouse had been readied. It was primitive, but then this was the real thing. A genuine ranch, complete with enough cattle to give would-be cowboys the experience of dealing with a herd, horses for them to ride and plenty of land. Nell was as determined as Curly in the movie *City Slickers* to make real wranglers out of her guests. It was what they were paying her big bucks to do, and she firmly believed in giving them their money's worth.

"Thanks," Travis said when he saw her. He stood up

to remove the bag from her arms, and she placed the lantern on a small wooden dresser opposite the bed.

"I realize this isn't the Ritz," she said as she spread the crisp sheet across the thin mattress.

"Hey, beggars can't be choosers," her guest reminded her. "I'm grateful you're willing to take me in at all."

Actually no one had thought to ask her. It was her mother-in-law who'd agreed to put him up for the night when Phil Patterson phoned. But to be fair, Nell suspected she would have agreed herself.

"With the rodeo coming, the Pattersons didn't have any vacancies," he explained unnecessarily, leaning over to help her with the top sheet and blanket.

The lantern actually gave a fair amount of light, much to Nell's chagrin. She chose to pretend she didn't recognize him. And either he was too tired to remember the way she'd harangued him at the side of the road or he'd decided to forget. Whatever the case, she was grateful.

"Does the Texas hill country generally get storms like this?"

"This one's worse than some," she told him, lifting the edge of the mattress to tuck in the covers. Given his size, she wondered if the bunk would be big enough for him. Well, there was no help for it, since this bed—or another exactly like it—was the only one available.

"What about losing your electricity?"

"Happens now and then," she said, not looking at him. She reached for the pillow and stuffed it inside the case, then plumping it up, set it at the head of the bed. "Is there anything else I can get you?" she asked, ready to return to her family.

"Nothing. I appreciate your putting me up," he said again.

"No problem."

"Mom." Breathless, Jeremy burst into the bunkhouse, his face bright. He carried a blue-speckled tin coffeepot in one hand and a matching cup in the other. Emma followed with a covered plate.

"Grandma sent us over with hot chocolate and—"

"—one of Mom's cinnamon rolls," Emma finished for her brother. Travis could see a black-and-white dog waiting patiently at the door.

He took the pot and cup from Jeremy and set them on the nightstand. "Hey, no one said anything about room service. How'd I get so lucky?"

Emma handed him the plate. "My mom's the best cook in the world."

Nell grinned and put an arm around each of her children. "Now probably isn't the time to mention we roasted hot dogs in the fireplace for dinner."

"Are you staying for the chili cook-off?" Emma asked their guest.

"I wouldn't miss it for the world." Travis sat on the side of the bed and poured himself a mug of steaming cocoa.

Nell wasn't sure how Ruth had managed to heat the cocoa—the fireplace, she supposed—but was pleased her mother-in-law had made the effort.

"Mom's going to win. Her chili's the best."

"Emma's opinion might be a little biased," Nell said, steering the two children toward the door. "Let us know if you need anything."

"I will. Good night," Travis said as they left to go back to the house.

Nell turned and smiled when she saw that he'd already started on the cinnamon roll with the appreciation of a man who rarely tasted anything homemade.

The children ran across the yard ahead of her. Lucky, their border-collie mix, followed at their heels. Ruth waited for Nell in the kitchen, holding the candle and looking inordinately pleased with herself.

"Travis Grant seems like a nice young man," she said the moment Nell entered the kitchen.

"He's from New York City," Nell said, wanting it understood right then and there that he was a big-city boy and only drifting through Promise. It just so happened that he'd ventured into a strange town and needed a place to sleep; there'd be plenty of guests just like him in the months to come.

"We have a big day tomorrow," Nell said. "It wouldn't hurt any of us to get to bed early for once."

As she'd expected, her children put up token protests, but they didn't argue long. Both were tired and, without electricity, there was little to entertain them. The lights probably wouldn't be coming on soon, especially with the rain and the wind still so intense.

"Did our guest mention what he's doing in Promise?" Ruth asked. She held her hand protectively in front of the flame of the candle she carried and led the way across the living room.

Nell wondered, too. "He didn't say."

"You could've asked."

"Well, I didn't. That's his business, not mine."

"Weren't you curious?"

"A little." A lot actually, but Nell wasn't willing to admit it.

"He's probably here for the rodeo," Jeremy suggested, heading up the stairs, Lucky at his side.

"Maybe, but I don't think so." Nell wasn't sure why she thought that, but she did. Her guess was that when morning came Travis Grant would pack up his bags and leave.

"He reminds me of someone," Emma said, and yawned.

"Me, too," Jeremy murmured.

Jake. Nell had seen it, too, not in looks but in build. Travis Grant was a lumberjack of a man, just the way her beloved Jake had been. Sadly the children's memories of their father had dimmed with time into vague recollections.

The family stood at the landing at the top of the stairs, where they exchanged good-night hugs and kisses. Even Jeremy let his mother and grandma kiss him tonight. Ruth guided the children to their bedrooms while Nell retrieved a candle for herself.

Once everyone was in bed, she undressed and put on a full-length white cotton nightgown. She unbraided her hair and brushed it out, the thick dark tresses reaching halfway down her back. Jake had loved her hair, had often gathered it in his huge hands and run it through his fingers. Nell missed those moments, missed everything about Jake.

Time, she'd discovered, was a great healer, just as Pastor McMillen had told her. The grief became duller, less acute, with every month and year that passed. But it was still there, always there. Now though, her grief shared space with all the good memories, the happy moments they'd had together.

Nothing would ever erase those ten wonderful years she'd shared with the man she loved.

Setting her hairbrush aside, Nell pulled back the covers and climbed into bed. She leaned against the headboard, her back supported by two pillows, and opened the drawer in her nightstand. She took out a pen and her journal.

By the light of a single candle, she wrote down the events of the day, pausing now and then to collect her thoughts. When she'd finished, she reread what she'd written, something she rarely did, and was surprised to note she'd mentioned Travis Grant in the first line. It didn't take her long to figure out why.

It was because he was like Jake and meeting him had shaken her. Not the first time on the road into town, when she'd stopped and read him the riot act, but later. It hadn't hit her until they stood across from each other to make the bed. He was the same height as Jake.

Nell reached for the framed photograph of Jake taken on their wedding day. It was a rare shot of him without his Stetson. Fresh from the military, his hair had been cropped close. He looked strong, capable—and oddly vulnerable.

Her heart clenched as it always did when she studied the photograph, but the usual tears didn't come.

"Good night, my love," she whispered, and placed the photograph back on her nightstand. As she did, Nell saw a light come on outside the window. Tossing the blankets aside, she peered out and noticed a bright, even glow coming from the bunkhouse. The electricity was back on.

"I don't know how much longer this is going to take," Laredo Smith said as he reappeared to give another update on Savannah's progress. He'd practically worn grooves in the carpet from the bedroom to the living room where the men had gathered. Rain continued to beat against the window and there were occasional flashes of lightning, although the storm had begun to let up.

Grady smiled indulgently at his brother-in-law, grateful that the electricity was back on. "Babies take as long as they take," he said wisely. He reclined in the leather chair and laced his fingers behind his head, rather pleased with his insight.

"That's easy for you to say," Laredo snapped in a rare display of temper. "It's not *your* wife in there giving birth to your child. Let's see how calm you are when Caroline delivers."

The grin faded from Grady's face. Laredo had a point.

"Birthing babies is a whole lot different from bringing calves into the world," Cal said. Grady's best friend leaned forward and rested his arms on his knees, then glanced at his watch.

Grady was surprised when he checked the time. It was already past midnight, and it could be hours more before Savannah's baby was born. Not one of the assembled group showed any sign of being tired, much less leaving. Caroline and Jane were with Savannah, and his daughter was in bed upstairs. Six-year-old Maggie had tried to stay awake but fell asleep in his arms around ten.

Laredo had been with Savannah from the first, but returned to the living room periodically to make his reports. Grady watched his brother-in-law with interest. Laredo was so pale he looked in danger of passing out.

"I had no idea it would be like this," Laredo mumbled, ramming all ten fingers through his hair.

"That it'd take this long?" Grady asked.

Laredo vigorously shook his head. "No—that I'd feel this scared, this nervous. Savannah and I must've read ten books about pregnancy and birth, and I thought I was ready. Hell, man, I've been around horses and cattle all my life, but this is nothing like I expected."

Those books were the very ones Grady and Caroline were reading now. His wife was two months pregnant. Grady had been walking on air from the moment she'd told him. He'd thought about the baby a lot, his excitement building as he watched his own sister's pregnancy progress. He and Caroline had told only a few people, since she was months from showing.

To Grady, his wife had never looked more beautiful. Maggie was pleased and excited at the prospect of becoming a big sister. What Grady hadn't considered was this strange emotion Laredo exhibited.

Fear.

He hadn't thought of his child's birth as a frightening event. He'd imagined himself a proud father, holding his infant son or daughter. He enjoyed the prospect of people making a fuss and giving their opinions on which parent the baby resembled. Friends would come to visit and it would be a time of celebration and joy.

But tonight Laredo had destroyed his illusions. In his imaginings, Grady had glossed over the actual birth. Until now. Beyond any doubt, he knew that when it was Caroline's time to deliver their child, he'd be as bad as Laredo. Pacing, worrying, wondering. Praying.

"I'm going back in there," Laredo announced as

though he couldn't bear to be away from Savannah a moment longer.

Grady stood, slapped his friend on the back to encourage him, then sank into his seat again.

"We're going to be just like him, you know," Cal said.

Grady nodded in agreement. "Worse, probably."

Cal grinned. "When's Caroline due?"

"The end of October."

"You two certainly didn't waste any time, did you?" Cal teased.

"Nope." Their wedding had been the last week of October, and Caroline was pregnant by the first week of January. They'd hoped it would happen quickly, seeing as Grady was already well into his thirties and Maggie was going on seven. It made sense to start their family early.

As the wind howled, Cal looked out the window. "Why is it babies are always born during a storm?"

"It probably has something to do with barometric pressure."

Cal scratched his head. "You think so?"

The hell if Grady knew, but it sounded good. The phone pealed in the kitchen and the two men stared at each other.

"It's probably Glen and Ellie again," Cal said.

Cal's brother and his wife lived in town and would have been with them, Grady suspected, if not for the storm.

Grady answered the phone. "Nothing yet," he said, instead of his usual greeting.

"Why didn't anyone phone me?" Dovie Boyd Hennessey demanded. Dovie and Savannah had been close since the death of Savannah's mother, Barbara, seven years earlier. Dovie owned and operated the antique shop, which sold everything from old scarves and jewelry to valuable china cups and saucers, all arranged around antique furnishings. The women in town loved to shop at Dovie's; she was universally admired and treasured by the town.

"Savannah's in labor and I only *now* find out," Dovie said, as though she'd missed the social event of the year.

"Who told you?" Grady asked. The women in Promise had a communication system the CIA could envy.

"Frank, naturally," Dovie told him. "I guess he talked to Laredo earlier this evening. He just got home." She paused for breath. "Has the baby come yet?"

"Nope, and according to Jane, it could be hours before the blessed event."

"How's Savannah?"

"Better than Laredo," Grady said.

Dovie's soft laugh drifted over the line. "Give her my love?"

"Of course."

"And call me the minute you hear, understand? I don't care what time of day or night it is."

"You got it," he said on the tail end of a yawn.

"Don't let me down, Grady."

"I wouldn't dream of it," he assured her.

By the time he returned to the living room, Cal had picked up a magazine and was flipping through the pages.

"You read that one an hour ago," Grady reminded him.

"So I did."

A few minutes later Caroline came into the room, and Grady leaped to his feet. "Sit down," he urged his wife. "You look exhausted." She should have been in bed hours ago, but he knew better than to suggest it. Caroline was as stubborn as they came, but then so was he. They understood each other, and he could appreciate her need to be with her best friend.

"It won't be long now," she told him as she slid her arms around his waist. "The baby's crowned."

Grady nodded. "Wonderful. How's Savannah?"

"She's doing well."

"And Laredo?"

"He's holding Savannah's hand and helping her with her breathing." Grady sat down, pulling Caroline onto his lap. She pressed her head against his shoulder, and he kissed her temple.

Grady glanced in Cal's direction and found he'd folded his arms and shut his eyes. Caroline's eyes were closed, too, and Grady decided to rest his own. Just for a few minutes, he told himself.

An infant's cry shattered the silence. Grady jerked awake and Caroline jumped to her feet and shook her head. "Oh, my goodness!" she gasped.

Grady hadn't a clue how long they'd been out. Cal straightened and rubbed his eyes with the heels of his hands.

"The kid's got one hell of a pair of lungs."

A few minutes later the bedroom door opened and Laredo emerged, carrying a tiny bundle in his arms. Grady noted that his friend's eyes were bright and his cheeks tear-streaked.

"We have a daughter," he said, gazing with awe at the baby he held. "Laura Rose, meet your family," he whispered to the newborn. "This is your uncle Grady and aunt Caroline."

"Hey, don't forget me," Cal said, stepping over to gaze down at the baby.

"That's Cal," Laredo continued. "His wife's the one who coaxed you into the world." Laredo gazed at the small group gathered around the baby. "Isn't she beautiful?" he said. "Doesn't she look like Savannah?"

Grady studied Laura Rose carefully and decided she looked more like an alien, but he certainly didn't say so.

Another hour passed before Grady and Caroline were in their own home and their own bed. Fortunately the rain had ended. Grady had carried a sleeping Maggie from Savannah's place to the car and then into her room; she never did wake up. He was exhausted, too. This had been a night to remember. His sister was a mother, and for the first time in his life he was an uncle. Damn, but it felt good.

Caroline pulled back the covers and joined him. She sighed as her head hit the pillow. "Did anyone phone Dovie?" she asked.

"I did," Grady said as he reached for the light.

"Good." Caroline rolled onto her side. "I think I could sleep for a week," she mumbled.

Grady drew his wife close, cuddling her spoon-fashion. His arm went around her and he flattened his hand against her stomach and grinned, feeling extraordinarily happy. Soon Laura Rose would have a cousin.

Travis awoke and lay in the warm bed, unwilling to face the bright morning light. Not just yet, anyway. Something warm nestled against his feet, and he was content to stay exactly as he was for a few more minutes.

Despite his exhaustion, he'd had a hard time falling

asleep. It didn't help that his legs stuck out a good six inches over the end of the bed. Those cowboys must've been pretty short guys, he thought wryly.

His eyes flew open as his toes felt something damp and ticklish. He bolted upright to find a goat standing at the foot of the bed, chewing for all it was worth. It didn't take Travis long to realize that the animal had eaten the socks clean off his feet. All that remained were a few rows of ribbing on his ankles.

Obviously, once he'd fallen asleep, he'd slept deeply—the sleep of the jet-lagged. He laughed and wiggled his toes just to be sure the socks were the only thing the goat had enjoyed. So far, so good.

"Yucky, what are you doing in here?"

The door flew open and Nell's boy—Jeremy, if Travis remembered correctly—rushed inside.

The boy planted his hands on his hips and glared at the goat.

"Morning," Travis said.

"Hi." Jeremy smiled and must have noticed Travis's feet for the first time because he burst out laughing. "Yucky ate your socks!"

"So I noticed."

"Sorry," Jeremy said, sounding anything but. He covered his mouth to hide a giggle, which made the situation even more amusing. "Mom said to tell you breakfast will be ready in twenty minutes if you're interested."

Travis didn't need a second invitation. His stomach growled at the mere mention of food. If the cinnamon roll the night before was any indication, Nell Bishop was one hell of a cook.

Travis dressed, showered and shaved, entering the

kitchen just as Nell set a platter of scrambled eggs and bacon on the table.

"Morning," he greeted her.

"Morning," she returned, and poured him a mug of coffee.

Travis gratefully accepted it and pulled out a chair. Nell joined him and the children, and the three bowed their heads for grace. The instant they were through, Jeremy reached for the platter.

His mother sent him a warning glance and Jeremy immediately passed the platter to Travis. "Here," the boy said. "You're our guest. Please help yourself."

Travis was impressed with the boy's manners. So many children didn't seem to have any these days. He forked some fluffy scrambled eggs onto his plate and took a piece of toast from a bread basket in the center of the table. He gave Nell a sidelong glance as she buttered her own toast. She was obviously doing her best to be a good mother. The owner of the B and B had told him Nell was a widow, and he admired her for the loving manner in which she schooled her children.

"You collected all the eggs?" Nell asked Emma, interrupting his thoughts.

"Yes, Mama."

"Did you check under Bertha?"

The little girl grinned and nodded.

"I understand," Nell said, turning to Travis, "that we owe you a pair of socks."

He glanced up from his plate and saw that her mouth quivered with the beginnings of a smile.

"Best darn pair I owned."

"Your feet must've been pretty ripe to attract Yucky's attention," Jeremy said.

Travis couldn't help it; he burst out laughing. Nell, however, didn't take kindly to her son's comment. Jeremy read his mother's look and mumbled an apology.

Breakfast was wonderful, the food even better than he'd expected and the company delightful.

As soon as the kids had finished, they excused themselves and set their plates in the sink, then rushed out the back door.

"The children have animals to tend before they catch the school bus," Nell explained before he could voice his question.

"I see."

"Jeremy's got rabbits. Then there's Yucky, whom you've already met."

"We have a close and personal relationship," he said, leaning back in his chair, savoring the last of his coffee.

"Currently we have twelve horses, but I plan on buying several more. Jeremy feeds them grain and alfalfa, and Emma makes sure they have plenty of water. I'll be mucking out the stalls later this morning."

Travis could see that they had their chores down to a science and admired the way they all worked together. Briefly he wondered about Ruth, but guessed she reserved her strength for later in the day.

Nell cleared the remaining dishes from the table. "Take your time," she said as she put on a sweater and headed toward the door.

"Can I help?" he asked.

"Not at all. Just enjoy your coffee."

Travis did as she suggested and watched from the window as Nell and the children worked together. They were a real team, efficient and cooperative. Half an hour later Jeremy and Emma raced into the house and grabbed their lunch boxes from the counter.

"We gotta go to school now," Emma said, staring at Travis as though she'd much rather spend the day with him.

Jeremy was on his way out when he paused. "Will you be here tonight?"

Travis had to think about that. "Probably."

"I hope you are," the boy said. "It's nice having another man around the place." And with that, he flew out the door.

Travis rinsed his mug and set it beside the kitchen sink. He met Nell as he left the house. "Do you mind if I plug my computer into an outlet in the bunkhouse? I want to get some work done while I'm here."

"Not at all," she said, her smile congenial.

Whistling, Travis returned to the bunkhouse and retrieved his portable computer from his bag. With a minimum of fuss, he located an outlet and set up shop. The computer hummed its usual greeting as the screen saver reminded him that he was one hell of a good writer—a message he'd programmed in to battle the deluge of self-doubts all writers faced.

The note was just the boost his ego needed before he dug into his latest project. He'd achieved indisputable success with his series of Western stories for preadolescents and young teens. The book he planned to write next might possibly be his best; he could feel that even before he wrote the first word. A mainstream novel set in a Western ghost town—his editor had been ecstatic over the idea.

Travis never did the actual writing while he was on the road, but he wanted to document facts about the storm from the night before. One of his characters was sure to lose his socks to a hungry goat, too. He prided himself on the authenticity of his details, although in his past books, most of that background had come from research.

Rarely did anything happen to him that didn't show up in a book sometime, one way or another. He used to think he kept his personal life out of his work, but that was a fallacy. Anyone who really knew him could follow his life by reading his books. The connections weren't always direct. Take the end of his marriage, for example. Of the two books he'd written the year of his divorce, one took place in Death Valley and the other on the River of No Return. Those locations had corresponded to his emotional state at the time.

He didn't want to stop and analyze why a ghost town appealed to him now. Maybe because his life felt empty and he struggled with loneliness. Travis realized without surprise that he envied Nell her children.

He entered notes about Texas, the drive from San Antonio, his impressions of the landscape and the people. The storm was described in plenty of detail. He made notes about Nell and her children. Ruth, too.

The next time he glanced up, he was shocked to discover it was midmorning. He stored the information onto a computer file and headed for the kitchen, hoping Nell kept a pot of coffee brewing during the day. He didn't expect to see her, since she had stalls to muck out and plenty of other chores, many of which he knew next to nothing about.

He was pleasantly surprised to find her in the kitchen.

"Hello again," he said.

"Hi."

The spicy aroma of whatever she was cooking made him instantly hungry, despite the fact that he'd enjoyed one of the finest breakfasts he'd eaten in years.

"What are you making?" he asked. He noticed a can of beer sitting by the stove at—he glanced at his watch—10:35 a.m.! He wondered with some concern if she was a drinker...but then he saw her add it to whatever was in the large cast-iron pot.

"It's chili," she said. "Would you like a taste?"

"I'd love it."

Nell dished up a small bowl and brought it to the table where Travis sat. "This might sound like a silly question, but did you happen to mention to Ruth how many nights you intend to stay?"

He delayed his first sample, wondering if Nell was looking for a way to get rid of him. He'd be keenly disappointed if that was the case. He happened to like Twin Canyons Ranch. His visit would add texture and realism to his novel. And being here was so much more *interesting* than staying at a hotel, or even at a bed and breakfast.

"I'm not sure yet," Travis said in answer to her question.

He tried the chili. The instant his mouth closed over the spoon he realized this was the best-tasting chili he'd ever eaten, bar none. The flavors somersaulted across his tongue.

"What do you think?" she asked, her big brown eyes hopeful.

"If you don't win that prize, I'll want to know why." He scooped up a second spoonful.

"You're not just saying that, are you?" Her eyes went from hopeful to relieved.

"If I was the judge I'd award you the prize money without needing to taste anyone else's. This is fabulous."

Nell's freshly scrubbed face glowed with a smile. Travis had seen his share of beautiful women, but he felt few would compare with Nell Bishop and her unspoiled beauty. The kind she possessed didn't require makeup to enhance it. She was as real as a person could get.

"I made a terrible mistake when I saw you on the road yesterday," she said, suddenly frowning a little.

"How's that?"

"I implied you were…not too bright." She pulled out a chair and sat across the table from him. "I was wrong. You're obviously very bright, indeed!"

Three

"How come *you* were asked to be one of the judges for the chili cook-off?" Glen asked Ellie as they walked toward the rodeo grounds. The air was charged with excitement.

"Just clean living," his wife replied, and did her best to disguise a smile. Actually it had more to do with her participation in the Chamber of Commerce. But her husband had done nothing but complain from the moment he learned she'd been asked to judge the chili. It was a task he would have relished.

"I'm the one who happens to love chili," he lamented—not for the first time.

Unable to help herself, Ellie laughed out loud. "If you want, I'll put your name in as a judge for next year," she said, hoping that would appease him.

"You'd do that?" They strolled hand in hand toward the grandstand. Luckily the ground had dried out after the recent rain. The rodeo was one of the most popular events of the year, along with the big summer dance and the Willie Nelson Fourth of July picnic. The town council always invited Willie to the picnic, but he had yet to accept. With or without him, it was held in his honor, and his music was piped through the park all day.

"Sure will. I'll let Dovie know you want to be a judge next year," Ellie promised. "Consider it just one of the many benefits of marrying a local businesswoman."

Glen wrapped his arm about her waist and gave her a squeeze. "I know all about those benefits," he said, and kissed the top of her head.

He raised his hand so that it rested just beneath her breast. "Glen," she warned under her breath.

He sighed and lowered his hand to her waist.

Ellie saw Jane and Cal and waved. Dr. Texas immediately returned her wave, and the two couples sauntered toward each other.

"So you're going through with it," Glen said when he saw his brother.

"I can't talk him out of it," Jane said, rolling her eyes.

"I've competed in the bull-riding competition for ten years," Cal argued. "Besides, if I'm injured, I know one hell of a fine physician who'll treat me with tender loving care." He winked at his wife.

From the look Jane tossed her husband, Ellie suspected she'd be inclined to let him suffer. Grinning, she reflected on how well her matchmaking efforts had worked. She gladly accepted credit for pairing Cal with Jane; the match had been brilliant, if she did say so herself. Jane had moved to Promise as part of a government program in which she agreed to work for three years at the community health clinic in exchange for payment of her college loans.

Cal, of course, had been burned in the romance department several years earlier when his fiancée had dumped him a few days before their wedding and skipped town. In addition to the hurt and rejection he'd suffered, Cal had been left to deal with the embarrassment and the questions that followed. For years afterward he'd refused to have anything to do with women.

Until Jane.

She'd moved to town after living her entire life in California. Poor Jane had been completely and totally out of her element until Dovie took charge. One of the first things Dovie had done was introduce her to Ellie.

In the beginning Ellie wasn't sure it was possible for them to be friends. Jane had an attitude about all things Texan, and it rubbed her—and just about everyone in town—the wrong way. Everything she said and did had an air of superiority.

Jane's start had been rocky, that was for sure. Ellie smiled as she remembered that first lunch in which she'd suggested Jane take her wine-sipping, quiche-eating butt and go back where she'd come from. She was grateful now that Jane had decided to stick it out.

When Ellie set up the date between her distrustful brother-in-law and the doctor-with-attitude, she knew she was taking a chance. It would have been just like Cal to take one look at the setup and walk out of the restaurant. He hadn't. In fact, he'd shocked both Glen and Ellie when they discovered that he'd agreed to give Jane horseback-riding lessons.

They were married within six months and Cal was happier than she could ever recall seeing him. He hardly seemed like the same person.

"I have a feeling I could win this year," Cal said.

"He's been claiming that every year since he first entered," Glen muttered just loudly enough for everyone to hear.

"I'm gonna win," Cal insisted, defying his brother to challenge him.

"This is a man thing," Ellie explained to her sister-in-law. "Glen competes in the calf-roping event."

"I have the *blue* ribbons to prove it."

Cal winced at the small dig. "Ouch, little brother."

"Calf roping I can tolerate, but watching Cal on those huge bulls is something else again." Jane looked at her husband, and Ellie saw a spark of genuine fear in her friend's eyes. She had to admit she was grateful Glen wouldn't be competing on the bulls.

"I've done everything I know to talk him out of this," Jane confided as the two women made their way to the grandstand and found seats in the second row. Both men were by the chutes, chatting with their friends and making small talk with the professional rodeo riders.

Jane clenched her hands in her lap.

"It'll be fine," Ellie assured her. "Cal's no fool."

"How can you say that?" Jane said, biting her lip. "Only a fool would risk his neck riding an ill-tempered beast who weighs as much as the state of Texas."

Ellie laughed.

"If...if Cal happened to get hurt, I don't know if I'd be able to treat him."

"You love him that much?" Ellie asked.

"Yes, but that's not the reason. I don't think I could stop myself from clobbering him for worrying me like this."

Ellie laughed outright, although she understood.

The grandstand quickly filled to capacity as the competition time neared.

"I heard a wild rumor," Ellie said, hoping to distract Jane from her worries. "Someone told me Willie

Nelson might make a surprise appearance at the dance later this evening."

"You're joking!"

She shook her head. "I don't know if it's true, but that's what people are saying."

"That would be wonderful. What brought it about?"

"I've heard he likes surprising people now and then." She gave a slight shrug. "He knows this is Willie country and he's never been able to come to our Fourth of July picnics. Maybe that's why."

"My parents went to hear him recently," Jane said. "They said he isn't going to replace the Beach Boys in their eyes, but the music was entertaining."

"Give 'em time," Ellie said.

The calf-roping event was one of the first on the program, and Ellie wasn't surprised when Glen took first place. She loved the way he raced after the calf, roped him on the first try and maneuvered the animal onto its back. He made it all look so easy. But when he tied the animal's legs, then tossed his hands in the air and leaped back, his eyes didn't go to the time. Instead, they zeroed in on Ellie and he'd smiled that secret little smile meant for her alone. Only then did his gaze go to the clock.

When his time was announced, Ellie jumped to her feet and applauded loudly. Pursing her lips around her index finger and thumb, she released a piercing whistle. Jane stood with her and the two of them made several victory punches in the air.

"How long before Cal rides?" Jane asked after they sat back down.

"Pretty soon."

Jane placed her hands between her knees and took

several deep breaths. Ellie gently patted her shoulder. "Hey, it's only eight seconds."

"A bull like that could kill him in one."

Ellie let the comment slide. "Cal knows what he's doing."

Jane nodded, but she looked pale. Ellie realized how difficult this was for her. Not having been raised around cattle ranches, Jane must view these competitions as barbaric. Ellie decided she hadn't given her sister-in-law the credit she was due for marrying into this whole new way of life.

When the competition had begun and Cal's name was announced, Jane bit her lip and closed her eyes. Cal sat high in the chute on the bull's back, his concentration intense. The door opened, and man and beast plunged forward. The bull snorted, shaking his massive head, determined to dislodge his rider.

Jane leaped to her feet and covered her mouth with her hand. Ellie had just stood up, too, when Cal went flying off the bull's back. There was a collective drawing in of breath as the crowd waited for him to jump out of the bull's way. The clowns diverted the bull's attention, but Cal remained on the ground.

"Dear God!" Jane cried. "He's hurt. I knew it, I knew it." She was already stumbling past everyone in the row, Ellie right behind her. "I swear if that fall didn't kill him, I will."

By the time they made it down to the steps, Cal had been carried off the grounds on a stretcher. Just as they reached him, they heard the final contestant's name being called.

Glen, who was with his brother, took Ellie's hand. Jane knelt beside her husband, tears in her eyes.

"It's all right, honey," Cal said, clutching his ribs. He gave her a smile but was clearly in pain.

"He's had the wind knocked out of him," Glen said.

Jane began to unfasten Cal's shirt.

"Jane—not in front of all these people," Cal said in a feeble attempt at humor.

"Be quiet," she snapped.

"Best not to cross her in this frame of mind," Cal said, then groaned when Jane lightly pressed her fingertips against a rib.

"I'll need X-rays, but my guess is you've broken a rib."

"It won't be the first."

"But it'll be the last one you'll ever get riding bulls," Jane said in a voice few would question.

"Whatever you say."

"You might want to take this with you." Max Jordan, a local business owner, hurried over to join them.

"Take what?" Glen asked.

Max grinned broadly and handed Cal a blue ribbon. "Congratulations, Cal! You stayed on longer than anyone."

Despite the pain it must have cost him, Cal let out a loud triumphant cry.

Travis had been writing for years. He'd researched rodeos and even written about them—but this was the first one he'd actually attended. Jeremy and Emma had volunteered to be his guides, and he welcomed their company. Nell was busy adding the final touches to her chili; judging would take place later in the afternoon. The last time he'd seen Ruth, she'd introduced him to two friends, Edwina and Lily Moorhouse, sisters and retired schoolteachers. One of them had mentioned something about cloves—cloves?—a special cordial, and the next thing he knew, all three women had disappeared. Made no sense to him.

Now that the rodeo was over, Jeremy and Emma decided it was time to show Travis the booths. It seemed everyone in town had something on display. All new to Travis. The closest thing New York had to this was the farmers' market, in which everything from rip-off brand-name running shoes and "real" French perfume to home-grown vegetables and spicy sausages was sold.

Travis and the kids wandered by the long tables where the chili was being cooked. "Hi, Mom," Emma called.

At the sound of her daughter's voice, Nell turned. She wore a pretty blue cotton dress with a white bib apron over it.

"I wondered where you two had wandered off," she said.

"The kids are playing tour guide," Travis explained. "They're doing a good job of showing me the ropes." He ruffled Jeremy's hair, and the youngster grinned up at him.

"I hope they aren't making a nuisance of themselves."

"On the contrary." They were likable kids, and seeing the rodeo and other festivities through their eyes had been a bonus.

"I'll get my purse so you can buy your lunch," Nell told her children.

"That's all right, Mom," Emma said. "Travis already fed us."

Nell's gaze briefly met his.

"We didn't ask," Jeremy added, apparently recognizing the look in his mother's eyes.

"It was the least I could do," Travis said, not understanding why she'd be disturbed about something so minor.

"My children and I pay our own way, Mr. Grant," she said before he could say anything else.

"It was my pleasure, Nell—honestly. Without Jeremy and Emma, I would've been lost." Both kids had taken delight in tutoring him in each of the rodeo events. They'd also shared tidbits about the community and its traditions, and the education he'd gained had been well worth the price of a couple of hamburgers and ice-cream bars.

"When are the judges going to be here?" Emma asked.

Nell glanced at her watch. "Not for another hour."

"You're gonna win," Jeremy said with confidence.

"I'm crossing my fingers for you, Mom." Emma held up both hands to show her.

"Good luck," Travis tossed in.

"We're headed for the carnival now," Jeremy said. "I promise I won't spend all my allowance."

Nell nodded and glanced at Travis. "Listen, everyone, I'm sorry, I didn't mean to snap at you earlier. I guess I'm more nervous than I realized about this contest."

"That's all right, Mom."

"No apology necessary," Travis said, thinking it was unusual these days to find anyone willing to apologize. It was a sign of maturity and inner strength, and he admired her for it. In fact, there seemed to be quite a bit to admire about Nell Bishop...

"Have fun at the carnival," she said, stirring her chili.

"We will."

"If they don't mind, I'll tag along just for the fun of it," Travis said to Nell. He couldn't recall the last time he'd been on a Ferris wheel—probably when he was younger than these two; and maybe he could convince Jeremy and Emma to go on it with him.

He'd never spent much time around kids, although his books were geared to them. Life was full of ironies such as this, he reflected. Valerie used to say he related to children because he'd never grown up himself, and he supposed it was true. She'd meant it as an insult, but Travis had considered it a compliment.

They had a wonderful afternoon on the midway, and he loved every minute. He let Jeremy and Emma spend part of their allowance, but he paid for most of the rides. They went on the octopus, a ride he remembered from his boyhood, and Emma covered her eyes, screamed the entire time, then insisted they do it again.

"Don't spend all your money on us," Emma said when he bought them each a huge cotton candy.

Travis was half-tempted to say there was plenty more where that came from, but decided it would be a crass comment. "Don't worry..." he began.

"Be happy," Jeremy completed for him.

"Right," Travis said, and chuckled. He enjoyed children, always had. That was one reason he'd chosen to write for the age group he did. His overwhelming success had surprised even him.

"In that case, could I have some popcorn, too?" Emma asked.

Laughter bubbled up inside him. Both of these children were forthright and honest, hardworking and appreciative—and they had a sense of humor. It would be unfair to compare them to children in New York, since he knew so few, but he was sure these two were special. As special as their mother.

"Have you met Dovie?" Emma asked a short while later between mouthfuls of popcorn.

Dovie—not dove. A name. "No, I haven't."

"You gotta meet Dovie," Jeremy said, directing him away from the carnival rides.

They led him to a large booth set up close to the chili cook-off area. A friendly slightly rotund older woman stood in front of a colorful patchwork quilt.

"Hi, Dovie," Jeremy said.

"Hi, Dovie," Emma echoed.

"Hello, Dovie." Travis figured he didn't want to be left out.

Dovie looked at him and blinked, as if she was afraid she should've recognized him and hadn't. Jeremy and Emma burst out laughing.

"This is Travis," Emma said, and reached for his hand. It was an innocent gesture, but it tugged at his heart.

"He's staying at the ranch," Jeremy added.

"From what I hear, I'm the first paying guest," Travis explained.

"Pleased to meet you," Dovie said, holding out her hand. "I don't mean to be rude, but I'm wondering if I could interest you in a raffle ticket for this fine quilt."

"Of course." Travis reached for his wallet.

"The Dorcas Group at church is raffling it off to raise money for missions."

"How much?"

"A dollar each, or six for five dollars."

Travis pulled a ten from his wallet. "Give me twelve tickets."

Dovie flashed him an appreciative smile.

"He's a good guy," Jeremy said proudly.

"I like him, too," Emma added.

Travis tucked the ticket stubs securely into his hip pocket and wished Dovie luck with the quilt.

"Thank you. How long will you be in town?" she asked.

It'd been a common question all day. "I'm not sure yet."

"I hope you enjoy yourself."

Emma took his hand again. "You ready?" she asked. "For the chili judging?"

"Sure," he returned.

"Is it time?" Jeremy asked.

Emma nodded.

A crowd had gathered around the chili cook-off area and the judges, five of them, stepped forward to do their taste tests. The samples were numbered so it was impossible to tell who had cooked which chili.

"That's Ellie Patterson," Jeremy whispered. "She owns the local feed store." A pretty brunette sampled the first taste and nodded in approval.

"I hope that was Mom's," Emma said.

So did Travis. The taste she'd given him the day before was fabulous and nothing like any chili he'd tasted before. He'd accidentally discovered her secret ingredient was beer but had been sworn to secrecy.

In his short visit he'd learned quite a bit about Texas chili, which was different from anything he'd tasted in New York City or on his previous travels. In Texas the chili was thick with meat and spices and it wasn't made with beans.

"That's Mr. Jordan," Jeremy said, identifying the next judge. "He owns the Western-wear shop."

Someone called Billy D, owner of the local tavern, and Adam Braunfels, a restaurateur, tasted next.

The last one to try the chili samples was a large rancher type.

"Who's that?" Travis asked.

"Pastor McMillen," Jeremy whispered back.

That surprised Travis. The man looked like he'd be more comfortable on a horse than in a pulpit.

After all the judges had sampled the entries, they cast their votes. The crowd grew quiet with anticipation as the town sheriff, Frank Hennessey, stepped forward with the results of the voting.

Emma stood next to Travis with her eyes tightly shut, her hands raised and fingers crossed.

Sheriff Hennessey cleared his throat. "It was a difficult decision this year, but it appears that one entry stood out as the most flavorful. The voting is unanimous. The winner is—" the faint sound of a drumroll could be heard in the background "—number five."

Travis frowned, not knowing who the winner was until he noticed Nell. She stood there as though in a daze.

"Nell Bishop," Frank Hennessey shouted cheerfully as a stunned Nell moved slowly toward the microphone. "It gives me a great deal of pleasure to present you with this check in the amount of five hundred dollars."

Nell might be in shock, but Travis noticed that she snapped out of her stupor fast enough when it came to reaching for the check. The crowd loved it.

Following the competition, spoonfuls of chili, dished up in small paper cups, were left for the crowd to taste. People surged toward the table that held the samples labeled "number five."

"Yay, Mom!" Emma said, rushing forward and hugging her mother.

"This is really cool," Jeremy said. He exchanged a high five with his mother.

Travis barely knew Nell Bishop, but he was as thrilled that she'd won the cook-off as if the success had been his own.

Nell was exhausted. Exhilarated but exhausted. Adam Braunfels, one of the judges and the owner of the Chili Pepper, the best restaurant in town, pulled her aside when the competition was over. He told Nell her chili was the best he'd ever tasted and that he'd like to talk with her later about the possibility of buying her recipe. He wanted to serve it in his restaurant. Nell could hardly believe her ears.

Following their conversation, Adam handed her a ticket for a free meal and suggested she stop off at his booth for dinner. Nell sat at one of the picnic tables at the far end of the rodeo grounds and savored a barbecued-beef sandwich and a heaping cup of coleslaw. It was the first time she'd eaten all day; she'd simply been too nervous before.

Jeremy and Emma were with their grandmother, who'd taken them home. The kids had chattered incessantly about Travis Grant. Apparently he'd shown them the time of their lives and they sang his praises to all who'd listen.

"Do you mind if I join you?"

Her thoughts seemed to have conjured up the man. Travis stood directly across the table from her, holding a cup of coffee.

"Please." Nell gestured toward a chair, and Travis sat down.

"Congratulations again," he said.

"Thank you." She was dying to tell someone about her conversation with Adam Braunfels, but held her tongue. Nothing was definite, and she didn't want to say anything until the details were settled.

"From what I understand, I owe you a debt of thanks," Nell said. "The kids told me this was the best rodeo of their lives, and all because of you."

"I was just about to thank you for sharing them with me. They're terrific kids, Nell."

"I think so, too."

She pushed aside the rest of her dinner and reached for her coffee. After being on her feet all day, she was grateful to be sitting. "Ruth drove them home," she said unnecessarily. She'd stayed to clean up the kitchen area and talk to Adam, but was so relaxed now she wasn't sure she'd find the energy to move.

"I heard someone say Willie Nelson was coming for the dance later," Travis mentioned.

"Don't believe it." Nell hated to be the one to disillusion him. "This is Willie Nelson country. We love him, and we send him an invitation to a picnic in his honor every single year."

"He's never come?"

"No, but then, we don't really expect he will. He's got bigger and better places to perform. We understand that and love him, anyway." Whether or not Willie showed, the people of Promise would continue to enjoy his music. Willie Nelson represented everything they loved about country music.

"Tired?" Travis asked.

"A little." An understatement if there ever was one.

"Too tired to dance?"

It took a moment to understand the question. Travis Grant was asking her to dance with him. She stared at him, unsure how to respond. It was kind of him, offering to be her partner. With anyone else she would have found an immediate excuse to decline. Not with Travis. For one crazy moment she actually considered it.

"Thank you, but no," she finally said.

If she'd disappointed him, Travis didn't let on.

Nell checked her watch, thinking it was time—past time really—to head home. The band, a popular local group, was playing in the background. The stage wasn't in sight, but well within listening range.

"They sound good," Travis said.

They did. Much better than Nell remembered, but then, it'd been more than three years since she'd stayed for the evening festivities.

All at once a crazed cheer rose from the audience and the announcer's voice came over the microphone. "Ladies and gentlemen, it's a pleasure to introduce the good people of Promise, Texas, to *Willie Nelson*."

Nell's gaze flew to Travis. "This has got to be a joke," she said.

But even before the words were out, the opening strains of "Whiskey River" echoed across the grounds.

Her fatigue gone, Nell leaped to her feet and hurried toward the dance area. So did everyone else within shouting distance. Travis was right behind her.

Nell and Travis never did get to see him. The crowd

grew so thick they couldn't do more than listen. Willie sang three numbers to wild applause, then suggested everyone dance. The music flowed, smooth and easy. People around her paired off, even though they weren't anywhere near the dance floor.

Travis smiled down at her. "Shall we?" he asked, stretching out one hand.

Nell couldn't stop looking at him long enough to decline. It wasn't that Travis was a handsome man. His face was too angular, his features too rugged to be considered pleasing.

He took her lack of response as answer enough and slipped his arm around her waist. His hold was loose and gentle. A lifetime ago Nell had loved to dance. Jake had possessed two left feet, but he'd made an effort for her sake.

Travis danced as if he knew exactly what he was doing—and as if he enjoyed it. What surprised her was how well they moved together, how gracefully.

"Don't look so shocked," he said with a laugh. "Big men aren't all klutzes."

"The same applies to big women."

"You're not big," he countered. "In fact, I'd say you're just about perfect." He brushed a stray lock of hair from her forehead, and his fingertips lingered a moment longer than necessary.

Nell didn't know what madness possessed her, but she closed her eyes and allowed herself to indulge in a fantasy. She didn't pretend that the man holding her was her dead husband. That would have been too painful. Instead, she fantasized that she was a different kind of woman, willowy and lithe, petite and beautiful. Like the young Audrey Hepburn of *Sabrina,* a movie Nell had loved all her life.

It was the night for such dreams.

The dance ended almost as soon as it had begun. Too soon. Nevertheless, she didn't dare to continue. Didn't dare to indulge in any more fantasies.

"Thank you," she whispered. "I've never enjoyed a dance more."

"Me, neither," Travis said, his voice low and sounding vaguely unlike him.

Of one accord they turned and walked across the grounds, toward the parking area.

"Nell." He stopped her in the shadow of the grandstand.

"Yes?"

"Don't be angry."

"Angry? Whatever for?"

"For this," he whispered. He turned her around to face him, then lowered his mouth to hers.

Four

His kiss left Nell feeling light-headed, as if she'd been out in the sun too long. His lips lingered on hers, his arms firm about her waist. He would have kissed her a second time, she sensed, if she hadn't moved her head just then. She needed a moment to compose herself, to gain perspective and deal with what had happened— what she'd allowed to happen. At any point she could have stopped him…and hadn't.

"I…wish you hadn't done that." Her voice trembled, shaky with shock and wonder. What astounded her as much as his kiss was how much she'd enjoyed it.

"Are you looking for an apology?"

His voice was close to her ear and she realized that he still held her.

"I could give you one if you wanted," he went on, "but it wouldn't be sincere."

She smiled at his words and eased away from him. There was definitely something in the air tonight that had caused her to behave so completely out of character.

"It's because of today," she said aloud. "The whole

day." One of the best days she'd had in three years of grief and struggle.

"The day?" Travis repeated, walking at her side as they continued toward the parking lot.

She glanced at him, surprised she'd spoken aloud. Since she had, she couldn't very well leave him in the dark. That would be rude and unnecessary. If he was to continue paying for room and board, then she had best set boundaries between them now. Kissing was definitely *out* of bounds.

"Naturally I'm flattered that you'd want to kiss me."

"I'd like to do it again, if you're not opposed."

She shook her head. "I'd rather you didn't."

He was quiet after that, but not for long. "What did you mean when you said it was because of *today?*"

She exhaled slowly. "Winning the chili cook-off. The kids having such a wonderful time. Willie Nelson showing up like that. Dancing in the moonlight... I wasn't myself. I wasn't thinking—otherwise that kiss would never have happened."

"How weren't you yourself?" he prodded.

Nell was much too tired to endure an inquisition. "I just wasn't."

"How?" he pressed.

"I was happy, excited..."

He couldn't seem to leave it at that. "You aren't normally?"

"No," she returned shortly. "Not for the last three years."

A silence followed her words. Nell heard his sigh.

"You must have loved him very much."

She didn't hesitate. "More than life itself. In many ways I died with my husband. Nothing will ever be the same again."

They paused in front of her battered pickup. The Dodge was well past its prime. It'd been ready for the scrap heap when Jake was alive, but Nell had coaxed three more years from it; she prayed the truck would last another year.

"I disagree," he said.

His words cut into her thoughts. She raised questioning eyes to him. "What do you mean?"

"You loved Jake, and it's obvious you two shared something very special. But you didn't die with him. The woman I kissed is alive and healthy. She's vital and lovely and passionate." He raised his hand as if to touch her face, but changed his mind and slowly lowered it. "I felt your heart pound against mine. The woman I kissed is *alive,* Nell. She has a lot to live for."

"I—"

"You might prefer to think of yourself as dead, but you aren't."

His words surprised her more than his kiss. She didn't know how to respond, how to react. Ruth had been saying the same thing to her, but in different words. All this time she'd resisted, afraid she'd lose even more of Jake than she already had. This was dangerous stuff, too dangerous to think about right now. She'd leave it for another time.

"You haven't dated since Jake died?" Travis asked.

She shook her head.

"What's the matter with the men in this town?" he asked in a way that suggested they were idiots.

"Grady Weston asked me to the big summer dance last year."

"And?"

"And I turned him down. Glen Patterson, too."

"Nell, no." He planted his hands squarely on her

shoulders. "Wake up. Look around you. Breathe in the cool night air and let it fill your lungs. Let yourself *feel*."

He spoke with such intensity all she could do was stare at him.

"You don't believe anything I've said, do you? I can see it in your eyes."

Instantly she lowered her gaze. "I'll never have with anyone else the kind of love I had with Jake."

"Of course you won't," he said.

The man said and did the most shocking things.

"Jake was Jake," he continued. "Any relationship you might have with another man will be different from your marriage to Jake because that man will be different from Jake." He paused. "The problem, Nell, is that you haven't seen it this way. The way you see it, any other man is destined to fall short because he can never be a replacement for the original."

She had to admit Travis made sense. It was exactly what Ruth and Dovie and several others, Savannah included, had been trying to tell her. Either she hadn't fully understood or she hadn't been ready to listen.

It hit her then that Travis spoke as if he was familiar with this type of loss. "You lost your wife?" she asked him.

Now it was Travis who looked away. "In a manner of speaking."

"What manner?" He'd prodded and pried, now she did the same.

"I'm divorced."

"You loved her?"

"Very much," he said, "and I assumed she loved me. But apparently I was wrong."

Nell waited for him to go on, and after a moment he did.

"She met someone else." Travis buried his hands deep inside his pockets as though he felt a need to suppress his anger, even now. "Someone who could give her the things she needed, the things I couldn't—and I'm not just talking about money." He sounded philosophical, but beneath his matter-of-fact statement, she recognized his pain. Recognized it because she'd experienced a similar pain.

"Tony, Val's new husband, sets her on fire," he said, his voice dripping with sarcasm. "I didn't."

Nell might have accepted the words at face value if not for one thing. He'd held her and kissed her. There was definitely fire in him, and it was burning strong. Maybe his ex-wife hadn't provided enough kindling, she mused—and felt some amazement that such a thought had occurred to her. "Bitterness wouldn't solve anything, so I decided to do what I could—go on with my life, put the past behind me."

"Have you?"

"I like to think so." He said this as if he expected her to challenge him. "How is it we're talking about me? You're the one who's still living in the past, not me."

"Really?"

Travis chuckled and held up his hand. "Enough. Your point is well taken. We're both among the walking wounded."

Nell smiled. "Perhaps we could learn from each other," she suggested.

Travis nodded. "Perhaps we can."

They drove back to the ranch in separate vehicles. Travis pulled into the yard seconds behind her.

"Good night," she called, offering him a friendly wave as she headed toward the house. A single light shone above the back porch door. In all likelihood Jeremy and Emma were sound asleep; it would surprise her if Ruth was still up.

"'Night, Nell."

Once inside the house, she climbed up the stairs to her room, undressed in the dark and sat on the edge of her bed, reviewing the events of the day. When she turned on the bedside lamp and took out her journal, it wasn't the five-hundred-dollar prize money she thought of. Instead, she found herself writing about Travis's kiss and the discussion that had followed.

Jeremy and Emma had been up for at least an hour by the time Nell got out of bed. Sundays were just as hectic as schooldays because chores needed to be finished before they left for Sunday School and church.

Nell had coffee brewing and was cracking eggs for French toast when the kitchen door opened and Travis strolled casually inside. "Morning," he said, helping himself to coffee.

"Good morning," she said, whipping the eggs into a frothy mixture before adding the milk. The griddle was ready and she had six slices of egg-soaked bread sizzling in short order.

"You coming to church with us?" Jeremy asked as he and Emma dashed in.

"Ah…" Travis glanced at Nell.

"It's the Lord's day," Emma said severely, as if there should be no hesitation on his part.

"You're welcome to join us if you wish," Nell said.

He didn't show any sign of reluctance. "I'd enjoy that."

At breakfast Jeremy sat on one side of Travis, Emma on the other, the children accepting him as easily as they would a much-admired uncle.

"We're lucky Mr. and Mrs. Patterson didn't have any rooms left to rent," Jeremy said.

"Real lucky," Emma agreed.

"With the rodeo over, the Pattersons should have plenty of room," Ruth muttered as she walked into the kitchen, yawning.

The news landed like a bombshell in the kitchen. The children stared at each other as though they'd just learned the horrible truth about Santa Claus. Nell felt an immediate sense of disappointment, but Ruth was right. Phil and Mary would have space available for Travis now, and the accommodations would be far more comfortable than a too-short mattress in the bunkhouse. At Phil and Mary's, Travis wouldn't need to worry about a goat eating the socks off his feet, either.

"That's true. Mr. Grant could move into town," Nell said, trying to sound as though it made no difference to her. It shouldn't, but hard as she tried to convince herself it would be best if Travis left, she hoped he wouldn't.

Every eye went to their guest. "Move into town?" he repeated, glancing at each in turn. "Would anyone mind if I stayed on here? Your goat and I have recently come to terms. It would be a shame to leave now."

She shouldn't be this happy, Nell decided, but she was. She really was.

"What time is it?" Frank Hennessey mumbled as he rolled over in the large feather bed and stretched his arms to both sides.

"Time for you to be up and dressed," Dovie said. "Church starts in less than thirty minutes."

"Church," Frank groaned. "Dovie, you know how hard it is for me to sit through Sunday service." But he eased himself up in bed to enjoy the sight of his wife fluttering about the room, hurriedly dressing. Dovie was a fine-looking woman and he took pleasure in watching this woman he loved.

It'd taken him long enough to make the leap into marriage. Not many men waited until they were sixty years old—maybe that was why the decision had been so hard. He might have remained single all his life if not for a woman as wonderful as Dovie. Their arrangement was perfect, he'd thought. Twice a week he spent the night. Two of the best nights of any week.

Dovie, being the kind of woman she was, had wanted them to get married. He'd led her to believe that eventually he'd be willing, and for ten years he'd believed it himself. Then all at once Promise experienced a rash of weddings and Dovie became possessed by the idea of marriage.

That was when he'd realized he simply wasn't the marrying kind. Painful though it was, he'd confessed to Dovie that he just couldn't do it—and she'd promptly ended their relationship. Those weeks apart had been agonizing for him.

He loved her, but he'd broken his word to her, and although he hated himself for hurting the woman he adored, he couldn't give up the comforts of his life as a bachelor. For instance, the fact that his house was a mess. It was *his* mess, though, and he knew where things were. Dovie wouldn't tolerate the unsightly stack of magazines by his recliner or the pile of laundry beside his bed.

Marriage meant more than making a commitment to her, he'd thought; it meant he'd be forced to alter his entire life. At sixty such a drastic change didn't come easy.

Things had looked hopeless—and grew even worse when he made the mistake of taking Tammy Lee Kollenborn out one evening. That was the night he'd known he could never love anyone but Dovie. Afterward, when Dovie had gone away on a short cruise, he'd been terrified she'd meet another man. It seemed inevitable that he was going to lose her, and the knowledge was destroying him.

The solution had come from an unexpected source. From the man he'd assumed would be the least understanding. Reverend Wade McMillen. Frank owed him big time. The local preacher had suggested that Frank and Dovie get married but maintain separate households, the same as they were already doing. Then they could both have what they wanted. What they needed. Dovie had the commitment she craved, the wedding band on her finger. And Frank was free to eat baked beans out of a can in front of the television, wearing nothing but his underwear, if he so desired.

"Dovie," he whispered softly, watching a silk slip float down over her breasts and hips. "Come here, love."

"Don't you use that tone of voice with me, Frank Hennessey. I'm running late as it is."

"Dovie," he coaxed, and sat up. He held out his arms to her. "How about a good-morning hug?"

"Not now."

"No?" Frank was surprised. Dovie rarely refused him anything, especially when it came to what she called "the delights of the flesh." He'd never met a woman like her. Dovie was a lady to the core, but when it came to lovemaking, she was both lusty and generous.

"It won't stop with a hug and you know it," she chastised.

He did know it, and he sighed deeply.

Dovie disappeared into her closet.

"Where are you going now?" he called.

"Out of sight, out of mind," she called back, giggling.

Frank tucked his hands behind his head and closed his eyes. He didn't bother to tell her it didn't work that way, at least not with him. The time they'd been apart, he'd done nothing but think of her. Thoughts of Dovie had tormented him day and night, until he was sure he'd lost his mind.

"Do that again," he said, savoring these moments in bed.

"Do what?" came her muffled question.

"Giggle."

"That's a silly thing to ask." But she did.

Frank loved the sound of it. He had to smile every time he heard her giggle. Or laugh. Or just heard her, period.

Dovie reappeared a minute later in a royal blue dress that buttoned up the front and belted at the waist. She braced one hand on the bed post as she slipped into her pumps.

"I'm going to do something with my hair and then I'm heading for church."

"No hug?"

One outraged glance answered the question. Frank laughed.

"I'm driving out to see Savannah, Laredo and the baby after church," she said.

"Do you mind if I tag along?" he asked.

Apparently his question caught her by surprise because she abruptly stopped brushing her hair and met his gaze. Her eyes softened. "You want to see the baby?"

Frank nodded. "That surprises you?"

"Yes. Do you like babies?"

"Actually I'm quite fond of children." It was his one regret in life. He'd give anything to have met Dovie as a young man and had children with her. She would have been a wonderful mother, just as she was a fabulous wife. "I would have liked kids of my own," he confessed with a hint of sadness.

She continued to stare at him and he noticed a sheen in her eyes—as though she was about to weep.

"Dovie?" he asked gently. "What's wrong?"

"Oh, damn," she said, sniffling. "I'm going to ruin my makeup and I don't have time to fuss with it now."

Frank climbed out of bed and reached for his robe. "What is it, Dovie?" he asked again.

"I always wanted children," she whispered. "So badly."

"I assumed you and Marvin decided not to have a family," he said. They'd never discussed the subject, and it seemed strange to be doing so now.

"We couldn't have children," Dovie said. "Marvin...had the mumps as a teenager. I never complained, but..."

"Couldn't you have adopted?"

"Marvin wouldn't hear of it. I asked him to reconsider many times, and he refused. As much as I wanted to be a mother, I couldn't bring a child into our home when my husband felt the way he did."

"I'm so sorry, Dovie."

She attempted a smile. "It was a long time ago. I don't even know why I'm crying. But when you said how much you regretted not having children, I realized…why I love you so much."

The hug he'd been longing to collect all morning was now given with spontaneity. Frank held her tight and closed his eyes.

"Perhaps Savannah and Laredo will allow us to be substitute grandparents for Laura Rose," he whispered.

"I was thinking the same thing," Dovie said. She cradled his face and smiled, her eyes bright with unshed tears. "I love you, Frank Hennessey."

"I wish we'd met years ago," he said, voicing his earlier thoughts.

"We met at exactly the right time," she told him. "Any sooner and I would've been married."

"Any later, and you might've been with that judge you met on the cruise. The Canadian guy."

"Perhaps," she admitted, but skeptically. She dabbed at her eyes. "Frank, I really must rush. You know how compulsive I am about being on time."

Frank checked his watch and knew if he hurried, he'd have time to dress and join her.

"I'll go with you," he said.

"Any reason?" she asked.

"Several reasons—but if I take the time to list them, we'll be walking in during the middle of Wade's sermon."

Travis waited until Jeremy and Emma had left for school on Monday morning before he approached Nell, who was in the barn. "Ruth said I'd find you here," he said, feeling a bit awkward.

She was busy tending a newborn calf, but glanced up and smiled when he entered the barn. Kneeling in the straw, feeding the animal with a large baby bottle, she explained that the calf was one of twins and had been rejected by its mother. Once again Travis found himself admiring her compassionate capable nature.

They exchanged a few pleasantries as she worked, and when she'd finished, he opened the stall gate for her.

"Thanks," she said, walking over to the barn faucet where she washed and dried her hands. "So what can I do for you?"

"Do you have time to talk for a few minutes?"

"Why?" she asked bluntly.

"Well, I'm a writer," he explained, "and I'm working on a project that has to do with this area."

"All right," she told him, "but I haven't got time to stop now. I need to go out and check the fence line. Tag along if you want."

"I'd enjoy that."

It wasn't until Nell led a gelding out of his stall that he realized she didn't intend to use the truck. Travis had ridden before—in Central Park. Years ago.

"You're going on a horse?" This probably wasn't the most intelligent question he'd ever asked. But he had to weigh his decision; on the one hand, he wouldn't mind some Western riding experience and it would be a chance to talk to her. On the other, he didn't want to risk looking like an idiot in front of a woman he found *very* attractive.

"You don't ride?" she asked in a voice that suggested

she should have thought of that herself. She expertly placed the saddle on the gelding's back.

He hesitated before he answered. "A little."

"You're welcome to join me if you want. I've got Jake's saddle and you'd fit that comfortably."

"Is Jake's horse still around?" He figured that would have to be an older horse, which could only help his situation.

"Yup."

"Does he take to strangers?"

"Some."

"That's encouraging."

Nell tossed back her head and laughed, her long braid swaying. "Come on. It'll be fine."

Within minutes she'd brought a huge quarter horse out of his stall. Travis watched her saddle him, amazed at her ease with animals.

"Twister, meet Travis," she said, handing him the reins.

Travis found it amusing that she'd introduce the horse to him and not the other way around.

She led the two geldings outside into the sunlight. With a swift graceful motion, she mounted. "Do you need help getting up?" she asked when he stood there, unmoving.

He tried to look as if the question had insulted him; actually he wouldn't have objected to her holding the reins while he swung his leg over the saddle. With a mighty effort he did manage to scramble onto Twister—appreciating the fact that Nell didn't laugh at him.

As they started out, she set a slow easy pace, for which Travis was grateful.

"You wanted to ask me about the area?" she reminded him.

"Yeah," he said jerkily as his butt bounced against the saddle. "Te-ll m-e wh-at you kn-ow abou-t the gh-ost town."

Nell eased to a stop. "Ghost town?" she asked, frowning.

Twister, following the other horse's lead, stopped, as well. "If I remember correctly, it's called Bitter End."

"That's why you're here?" she asked. "Why you came to Promise?" She nudged her horse into a trot. "I thought you were a writer!"

"Yeah." Travis managed to keep pace with her, but not without a price. If he survived this with all his teeth intact… "I am. And I w-want to—"

"Who told you about Bitter End?" she asked, stopping her horse again. The warmth she'd shown him had cooled noticeably. "You're from New York," she said. "You know Richard Weston, don't you?"

"I met him once, yes, but, Nell—"

"What did he tell you about Bitter End?" she demanded. "We were afraid of this," she muttered, not looking at him. "Everyone was."

"Afraid of what?"

"It doesn't concern you."

"Nell, if you'd give me a chance to explain." He shifted in the saddle, wishing he could touch her, reassure her in some way.

"You've already said everything I need to know. You're a friend of Richard's—"

"No, I'm not! Don't even think that. I met the man *once,* Nell. Just once. For a couple of hours. But it only took me a couple of minutes to see the kind of person he is."

That brought her up short. Her gaze returned to him, cautiously, as if she wasn't sure even now. But he could see she wanted to believe him, wanted to trust him. He yearned for that as much as he did her kisses.

"Valerie, my ex-wife, defended him—his state-appointed attorney. Richard mentioned the ghost town to her, and she told me. I was intrigued. A ghost town from the Old West, one that's basically undiscovered and hasn't been commercialized. I wanted to see it for myself, as background for a project I'm working on."

Nell said nothing. Then she said, "So you came all this way because of Bitter End?"

"That's what initially brought me here. Yes." But he liked the people of Promise, especially Nell and her family.

"Now I suppose you're looking for someone to take you there?"

"Yes—I want to see the town." He wanted to learn the history behind it, too. It was more than just a ghost town, if what Weston said was true, and Travis was hoping to unravel its secrets, include them in his book.

"I'm afraid you've made a wasted trip."

Her unwillingness to help him took him by surprise.

"I won't take you to Bitter End. And no one else will, either."

She sounded stubborn about it, but he could be stubborn, too. "I'm going there," Travis said. "I'll find it, Nell. Others have and so will I. But I'd rather we did it together."

"I can't... I won't. You don't understand."

"Then explain it to me."

"That town has done nothing but bring Promise grief. We just want to forget about it."

"What aren't you telling me?" he asked.

His question seemed to catch her off guard. She was silent for a long time; when she spoke again, it was with the seriousness of a woman who knows more than she wants to. "Nothing good has ever come out of that place. Nothing. The best thing for you is to forget you ever heard it mentioned."

"You've been there?"

"No," she admitted reluctantly.

"Then how do you know? Who told you? How many people have actually been in the town?"

Nell shrugged, not answering him.

"Then how can you be so sure if you've never been there yourself?"

"Everyone knows," she whispered.

"But you've found out where it is?"

She hesitated. "I have a vague idea where it might be."

"Where?"

Nell made a sweeping motion with her arm. "It's out there somewhere. Exactly where, I couldn't tell you."

"And even if you could, you wouldn't."

She nodded.

"This is a historic site. Doesn't anyone understand that?"

"Bitter End?" Nell laughed without amusement. "Why is it so important to you?" she asked again.

"Curiosity, mainly," he told her. "Like I told you, I'm a writer and I'm using a ghost town in my book. I wanted to make it as authentic as possible. I'm also intrigued by the mystery."

"Well, you'll have to ask someone else to take you, because I won't."

"Who, then?"

"I doubt that anyone will. But you might try Grady Weston."

Richard Weston's brother, Travis remembered.

"I wish you well, Travis. If you ride back to the house, Ruth will give you the Westons' phone number." Having said that, she galloped off, leaving him to make his own way back to the barn.

"All right, Twister," Travis said, doing his best to sound calm. "It's you and me, boy. We're friends, right?"

He pulled on the reins to reverse their direction. "See the barn, Twister?" He pointed toward it. "Let's walk there…slowly." Apparently the horse didn't care for Travis's tone of voice, because he took off at a gallop. It was all Travis could do to stay in the saddle.

When he reached the barn, he managed to dismount, then, legs shaky, succeeded in removing the saddle; the bridle he left for Nell. He coaxed Twister into the stall with his name on it, then tottered back to the house.

That afternoon when he phoned Grady Weston, he learned Nell wasn't the only one with strong feelings about Bitter End. It took him several hours to reach the other man; once he did, Weston practically bit his head off. In no uncertain terms, he made it clear that he'd have no part in satisfying Travis's curiosity. Travis supposed Grady's aggression could be attributed to his negative feelings about his brother.

Nell sought him out in the bunkhouse an hour or so later. "Did you speak to Grady?" she asked, her mood more conciliatory, or so it seemed.

"Briefly."

"And?"

"And he isn't willing to show me where Bitter End is, either. Just like you predicted."

She nodded. "You'll be leaving, then?"

"No."

It wasn't the answer she'd expected; he could tell by the way her eyes widened. "No?"

"I'm going to locate Bitter End, Nell, with or without this town's help."

Five

Nell was furious with Travis, but she didn't know why. That morning, as she'd ridden across her property, checking the fence line, she'd thought about him. And she'd thought about Bitter End.

Just when she was beginning to like Travis, really like him, she'd discovered that he had an ulterior motive. He'd made friends with her children, kissed and flattered her, pampered Ruth. All this because he wanted her to take him to Bitter End.

He'd been open enough about telling her he was a writer. Now everything was beginning to fall neatly into place. His job was what had brought him to Promise, probably with all expenses paid by his publisher. She should have suspected he had an ulterior motive for befriending her and her family. He was planning to write about Bitter End—although she didn't really know why. He'd told her he was working on a book. What kind of book? she wondered, and what, exactly, did he hope to achieve?

What *really* infuriated Nell was his comment about Bitter End being a historical site. He seemed to be implying that Texans were a bunch of hicks who didn't appreciate their own history. Well, that was the furthest thing from the truth! She knew as much about this state's history as anyone around here. In fact, she thought grimly, maybe she respected history *more* than that...that Easterner. That wannabe cowboy. Because at least she recognized that the past still had power over the present—the way Bitter End had power over Promise.

Everything she'd ever heard about the town had been negative. Her family's roots went back to the original settlement, which had been founded shortly after the Civil War; so did Jake's. Something ugly had happened there, something horrible. Whatever it was, it'd been disturbing enough to cause everyone to vacate the town. No one knew why, and for years and years the town was rarely mentioned. When people did discuss Bitter End, they spoke in hushed whispers. Now some ignorant Yankee wanted to turn it into a historical site!

When Richard Weston was fleeing the authorities, he'd holed up in the town, and that made sense. He belonged there, if anyone did. Richard had figured out where the town was partly because of Savannah. Despite Grady's objections, she'd explored the countryside to find Bitter End in her quest for lost roses.

Nell had asked Savannah about it, and she'd watched a shiver move down the other woman's arms as she recounted her visit. Savannah had mentioned an impressive find in the cemetery—Nell had forgotten what the roses were called. Savannah had gone on to describe the eerie feeling that had come over her; she'd hurriedly taken the rosebush and left.

Later, convinced she'd allowed her imagination to

run away with her, Savannah had returned, hoping to rescue other roses. She'd told Nell the most astonishing fact. Nothing grew inside the town. Not even a weed. The town was completely without life.

Yet all Travis saw was a money-making opportunity. He'd come to Promise to dig up information about a place best forgotten. Despite everything she'd said, everything Grady had told him, he'd insisted he was going to find Bitter End. Then he'd write about it and attract more people, strangers, to the town. Soon tourists would pour into Promise and their lives would no longer be their own. No one here knew why the settlers had abandoned Bitter End—and Nell thought it was better to leave things that way, to let whatever secrets were buried there lie forgotten. She wasn't the only one to feel this way.

She wished now that Travis had chosen to move into town, to the bed and breakfast. Phil and Mary would know better how to handle his curiosity.

Nell closed her eyes and groaned at the memory of how pleased she'd been when he decided to stay on at the ranch. She felt lost and inadequate; worse, she felt foolish for having allowed this man to weave his way into her life.

She understood now that he had his own reasons for kissing her, for encouraging her kids, for staying at her ranch.

Reasons that had nothing to do with *her*.

Savannah had just placed Laura in her crib when someone knocked on the back door.

"Anyone home?" Unexpectedly her brother stepped into the kitchen.

"Grady, come in." Savannah didn't bother to hide her surprise. It was unusual for him to drop by the house on his own. Her home was only a short distance from the ranch house, and while Grady visited often, it was almost always with Caroline and Maggie.

"How are you feeling?" he asked.

"Wonderful." The birth had been the most incredible experience of her life. Savannah had known there'd be pain and had prepared as best she could for labor. What she hadn't known was how she'd feel afterward—that sensation of stunned joy and amazement, that surge of accomplishment and pride.

In her arms she'd held living proof of her love for Laredo. Together they had created this new life, this beautiful child.

"I was just about to have a cup of tea," Savannah said, crossing to the stove. "Would you care to join me?"

Grady removed his hat and set it on the oak table. "Sure."

He'd get around to explaining his visit in his own time. Savannah could see no need to rush him.

She filled two cups and carried them to the kitchen table, then sat across from him. He asked her a few questions about the baby, but she noticed that he wasn't really paying attention to her responses. He was thinking, weighing his next words, wondering if he should approach her about whatever he'd *really* come about. After living with Grady all those years, Savannah knew him well, better than he realized.

"Nell's guest called me," he said casually as he stirred a second spoonful of sugar into his tea.

Nell's guest! That was the reason for this visit. The

sugar had given him away. Grady seldom added sugar to anything, and two teaspoons was particularly telling.

"I don't believe I've met him," she said.

"His name's Travis Grant. Seems nice enough—Caroline and I met him at the rodeo."

"Oh?"

"Like I said, he phoned yesterday."

"Really?" She remained calm, unaffected.

"He knows Richard."

The words hit her without warning and Savannah stared at her brother. A sinking sensation came over her, and a deep sadness. Her younger brother had been sentenced to twenty-five years in prison without parole. It hurt to think of Richard locked behind bars. She'd written him twice, once shortly after he'd been taken back to New York to stand trial and then after he'd received his sentence. He hadn't answered either letter.

"Actually it was Grant's ex-wife who introduced him to Richard," Grady added. "Apparently she was the court-appointed attorney who defended him."

"Did this Travis Grant tell you what he wanted?" It went without saying that if Richard was involved, their brother was looking out for his own selfish interests.

Savannah often wondered what had turned Richard into a man who acted without conscience or compassion. Her heart ached every time she thought about him. *Why?* She would never understand why he'd used his family, why he'd betrayed good people, why he'd exploited the vulnerable.

Twice he'd stolen from her and Grady. The first time had been the day they'd buried their parents. While Grady and Savannah stood beside the grave, Richard was sneaking away with the forty thousand dollars in cash left them by their father. Six years later he'd returned with a hard-luck story, needing a place to stay.

Savannah blamed herself for what happened next, since she'd been the one who convinced Grady to let him stay. But Grady wouldn't let her accept the blame. He insisted they were equally at fault because he'd known what kind of man Richard was and had closed his eyes to the obvious. Both of them felt an obligation to family, and they both wanted to believe their brother had changed.

Within a few months of arriving back in Promise, Richard had charged thousands of dollars at various stores in town, using the Weston accounts, the Weston name. When it was all uncovered, Richard had conveniently disappeared, leaving Grady to foot the bill. Only after he was gone did Grady and Savannah learn the whole truth. Richard had been on the run—from his unsavory creditors and "partners" and from the law. The New York City DA's office had a list of charges long enough to put him behind bars until he was an old man.

What hurt Savannah most wasn't the fact that Richard had destroyed her faith in him; it was learning that her brother was guilty of bilking immigrants. He'd helped get them into the country illegally, then forced them to live and work in deplorable conditions. If that wasn't bad enough, he'd confiscated their money. He'd been one of several men accused and convicted of a crime so heinous she cringed every time she thought about it. That her own flesh and blood had hurt innocent people in this way had devastated her. Men, women and children had suffered because of her brother.

"Richard told Travis about Bitter End," Grady continued.

Savannah exhaled a deep sigh. "So Travis is here to find it?"

"That's what he says."

"For what purpose?"

"I don't know for sure. He's a writer, so I imagine he's doing research for an article about Bitter End."

Savannah thoughtfully replaced her cup. "What did you tell him?"

Grady scowled, then met her eyes.

"Grady Weston, what did you do?"

He gave her a wry smile. "Now I know where Caroline gets that tone of voice. I should have recognized it was from my very own sister."

"You were rude, weren't you?"

He shrugged. "I told him to mind his own damned business. I said there wasn't a soul in this town who'd help him, and advised him to give up his search now."

"Oh, Grady."

"I don't think he's going to take my advice."

Savannah mulled over this information for a couple of minutes. "I'm beginning to think it might be a good idea to put the past to rest."

"What do you mean?"

"No one knows what happened in Bitter End," Savannah reminded him. "No one's sure why the entire town up and moved. It almost seemed to take place overnight. From what Ellie told me, there were still cans on the shelves in the mercantile store. People left furniture, clothing, all kinds of valuables behind. They were in such a hurry to leave they couldn't get away fast enough."

"It was probably some disease or something to do with the water," Grady reasoned.

"Perhaps. I'm sure there's a logical explanation for what happened. All I'm saying is it's time to find out what went wrong and why. And who better than a writer? Someone who knows how to research and how to separate fact from legend. A stranger. Someone who can approach this without the emotions and fears we all have about Bitter End."

Grady didn't look convinced. "As far as I'm concerned, it's best not to disrupt the past."

Savannah considered her brother's words. "A year ago I would have agreed with you."

"But not now?" he asked, sounding surprised.

"Not now," she said. "Having Richard home was a painful and bitter lesson. It taught me that turning away from the truth, ignoring trouble, is a dangerous thing to do."

"It isn't like we're hiding anything," Grady insisted. "No one knows what went wrong in Bitter End."

"Then don't you think it's time we did?"

"Why?"

"Because, as the Bible says, the truth shall make you free."

"I'm free now," Grady said. He stood up and walked over to stare out the window above the sink.

"We aren't free, Grady," she offered gently. "Otherwise we wouldn't be this afraid."

"I'm not afraid," he countered sharply.

She didn't contradict or challenge him, but she knew that wasn't entirely true. Whatever had happened all those years ago in Bitter End still haunted them. In Savannah's opinion, it was time to bring it into the light, expose it and deal with the consequences. Each generation has been influenced by Bitter End, whether they admitted it or not.

Savannah recalled the first time she'd heard about the ghost town. Grady had been the one to tell her. He'd heard their parents talking when he was a teenager, discussing this secret place and its mysterious past. Afterward Grady, Cal and Glen had decided to find the town and, in the manner of boys, went about making it their own private adventure. Savannah had wanted to join them, but they didn't want a girl hanging around.

She would have gone to look for it on her own, except that Grady had said he'd take her to Bitter End once he knew where it was. Naturally she had to promise not to tell anyone, especially the Patterson brothers.

The three boys had eventually located the town. But Grady never did take her there; it was the first and only time he'd broken his word. All he'd tell her was that something horrible must have happened in that place. She remembered how he'd closed his eyes and shivered, and vowed he was never going back.

His words had remained with her for a long time.

About a year ago she'd sought out the town herself. According to an article she'd read, abandoned cemeteries and homesteads were often a good source of nineteenth-century roses. That motivation was strong enough to let her put aside her apprehensions about the place. After weeks of searching, she'd stumbled upon the town, hidden deep in the hills. Only then did she understand what her brother had meant.

The instant she'd stepped onto the main street of Bitter End, a feeling had come over her, an eerie sensation of anxiety and dread. And yet she couldn't have named the reason, couldn't have said what she feared.

Afterward she managed to convince herself that she'd imagined the entire episode. So she returned. But she'd been right the first time. Something was there—not a ghost, but a persistent feeling of intense sadness, a haunting sorrow.

"Let him do it, Grady," she said, releasing a pent-up sigh. "Let him find out what happened in Bitter End. Let Travis Grant expose whatever wrongs were committed there."

"You think a stranger can do that?"

"He can start."

Her brother pondered her words, his face thoughtful. Then he slowly shook his head. "It isn't often I disagree with you, but I do now."

"You're not going to help Travis find Bitter End?"

"No."

She accepted his decision, but deep down, she wondered how long it would take him to change his mind. Grady was having second thoughts already; otherwise he wouldn't have come to her in the middle of the day. Especially during the busiest time of the year.

Savannah knew she was right, and she knew Grady would eventually see it. Beneath his doubts he, too, felt a need to lay this matter to rest once and for all.

Talk about stirring up a hornets' nest, Travis mused as he sat and stared at his blank computer screen. Nell had avoided him all day. And after speaking to Grady Weston, it wouldn't surprise him if the other man was busy rounding up ranchers to tar and feather him. All this because he'd asked a few questions about a ghost town. Why were they so intent on keeping this secret, whatever it was?

He wondered if the people here even knew what had happened in that town. Perhaps they were being influenced by fears and vague suspicions rather than facts.

Travis preferred to face problems, not let them fester. He believed in knowledge and the power of truth. Shutting down the computer, he leaned back in the chair, hands behind his head, reviewing his options. Soon, however, he discovered that his thoughts weren't on Bitter End anymore.

Instead, he was thinking about Nell. Despite her disapproval of his plans, he admired her strength and courage. He was attracted to her, he admitted that, and he sensed she felt the same way. Even if she preferred to ignore it.

Travis decided to get a breath of fresh air and he reached for a sweatshirt. He walked out of the bunkhouse and around the yard, stopping to say hello to Yucky. As he neared the front of the house, he was pleased to find Ruth sitting outside in a rocker, crocheting.

"Travis," she said with a friendly smile. "Come join me."

After Nell's silence and Grady Weston's explosive anger, Travis was more than grateful for a cordial greeting. He climbed the steps and leaned against the porch railing.

"Was that you I saw on Twister yesterday morning?" Ruth asked.

"Yeah," he said, not mentioning that he considered himself lucky to be in one piece.

"That gelding's got a mind of his own."

"So I discovered."

Ruth laughed, and he grinned himself. The older

woman's fingers agilely worked the yarn, never slowing. It amazed him that she could carry on a conversation without disrupting her work.

"What are you making?" It wasn't what Travis wanted to ask—he had questions about Nell. However, any inquiries would have to be a natural part of the conversation. Unobtrusive.

"An afghan," she answered. "I find crocheting relaxes me."

He started to comment, but Ruth broke in. "You're curious about Nell, aren't you?"

Her directness surprised as much as pleased him. "I won't deny that I am."

Ruth nodded. "She's interested in you, as well. I haven't lived with her all these years not to understand the way she thinks. Have you kissed her yet?"

Slightly embarrassed, Travis laughed. "Yes."

"And?"

"And it was very good."

"You plan on bedding her?"

"That's none of your business," Travis said. He wasn't accustomed to discussing his love life with elderly women, or with anyone else, for that matter. However, he'd certainly fantasized about making love to Nell. She was a passionate woman. Their one kiss had given him a glimpse of that. She was also a woman who didn't believe in half measures; it was all or nothing. He knew that when it came to love, loyalty or friendship, she held nothing in reserve.

For that very reason, she was reluctant to become involved with another man. The potential for pain was too great.

That was something Travis understood. The breakup

of his marriage had been one of the most painful ordeals of his life. He'd loved Valerie and been stunned to learn that she wanted out of their marriage, that she'd viewed their lives together as a temporary thing until someone "better" came along.

She'd been intrigued with Travis because he was a writer. Later she'd urged him to give it up and get a real job. Everyone knew there wasn't any real money in publishing. Not unless you were Stephen King. She'd been scornful about his financial prospects.

The irony was that she'd left him too soon. Not long after their divorce, he'd hit it big and his books had been selling almost as fast as the publisher could print them. She laughed about her lack of insight now. Once, a year before, she'd tried to lure him into bed, saying she'd made a terrible mistake and wanted him back. It'd flattered his ego, but in the end he'd told her he wasn't interested in sleeping with a married woman.

In the years since the divorce Travis had rarely dated. Friends had tried to match him up and he knew he was considered a catch. But he preferred the comfort of solitude; being alone was better than being with the wrong person.

The next time he fell in love, it would be with a woman who loved him back, heart and soul. A woman willing to make as strong a commitment to him as he did to her. In the years since Val had left him, he hadn't met such a woman.

Until Nell.

"She's a bit prickly at the moment," Ruth said, and for the first time since he'd joined her, the older woman's fingers paused. "Did you two have a spat?"

"Not really," Travis said. He didn't bring up the ghost

town for fear Ruth would respond the same way Nell and Grady Weston had.

Ruth scowled. "I don't know what's wrong with her, then, but she'll come around. Be patient, you hear?"

Suddenly the screen door burst open and Nell stuck her head out. "Ruth, have you seen—" She stopped midsentence when she noticed Travis.

"Seen what?" Ruth asked, looking almost gleeful at Nell's reaction to him.

"My kitchen scissors."

"Top drawer, left-hand side. Look under the church directory."

"Afternoon, Nell," Travis said.

"Oh-h, Travis."

It shocked him how his heart raced, how exhilarated he was by the sight of her.

"I'm putting a chicken on to roast," Nell said, her voice unmistakably nervous.

"Let me help," he insisted, and didn't give her a chance to object.

"Yes, let Travis help," Ruth murmured, sounding as if she was about to burst into laughter. "Nell's never cooked a chicken in her life."

Nell marched into the kitchen with Travis following, and just the way she walked told him she wasn't pleased. "I don't need any help roasting a chicken," she announced brusquely.

"I didn't think you did. I just wanted to talk to you."

"If it's about Bitter End, there's nothing to say."

"At least explain to me why everyone reacts this way the minute I say the name."

"I already have."

"Tell me again."

"No." She paused. "Bitter End's the only reason you came here, isn't it?"

"Yes." He wasn't going to lie.

"Then there's nothing to talk about."

"There's everything to talk about."

She stared at him, her expression wary.

"I want to know what it is about this ghost town that evokes this type of response. Don't you want to find out what caused everyone to leave? Aren't you curious?"

"I don't need to know—no one does," she said, then dragged in a deep breath. "You don't understand."

"Then explain it to me."

"I'm afraid," she admitted reluctantly. "Afraid it'll be like opening Pandora's box. I really believe that in this case, ignorance might be bliss."

He frowned.

She shook her head. "Leave it, Travis... please?"

"Fine. I'll leave it—but just for the moment." He lowered his voice. "Right now I'm more concerned with settling this matter between you and me. We were on the brink of getting to know each other."

"No, we weren't," she denied vehemently. "You're reading more into one kiss than you should... You caught me at a weak moment."

"I want to catch you again."

"No," she said with such force she appeared to surprise herself. "Don't even try."

It took a moment for her words to sink in, and when they did, a slow satisfied smile appeared on his lips. "You liked it that much, did you?"

"No!" she said. "I... I wish it'd never happened."

"It frightened you half to death, didn't it?"

She shook her head, which sent her braid flying.

"This is the most ridiculous conversation I've ever had. It'd be best if you left now."

"Not on your life. Oh, Nell, sweet Nell, don't you realize I felt it, too?"

"There was nothing to feel, dammit!" She whirled around and headed for the sink. A chicken rested in a pan on the countertop. Reaching for it, she thrust it under the faucet.

"It's only natural for you to be afraid," he said in low soothing tones as he slowly advanced toward her. He rested his hands on her shoulders, but the instant she felt his touch, she jumped.

"Nell, sweet Nell," he whispered, and kissed the side of her neck.

"Don't do that!"

"Then what about this?" He ran his tongue around her ear and felt a sense of triumph at the almost imperceptible sound of her moan.

"Not that, either," she said, obviously struggling to put some starch in her voice.

"And this?" he asked as he wrapped his arms around her middle.

The chicken fell unheeded into the sink.

"No one's going to help you…"

"Help me what?"

"Look for the town."

"Fine, I'll look for it on my own." He spread a series of nibbling kisses along her neck.

"You won't find it."

"That's okay, because I've found you."

A shiver moved through her. "I think you should go."

"Where?" He was far too involved in kissing her neck and her ear to pay much attention. Her words said one thing and her body another. Her hands hung idle at her sides and she let her head fall back, exposing her throat to his mouth.

"Somewhere else…" Her words were barely audible.

He turned her carefully to face him and smiled at her tightly shut eyes. "Open your eyes, Nell," he instructed. "I want you to know who's kissing you."

"I don't want you to…"

He laughed softly and cupped her face with both hands. "I'd expect you to be honest, if not with me, then with yourself."

She opened her eyes, and he knew his words had hit their mark. "Good, very good," he whispered, and gently lowered his mouth to hers.

His lips had just made contact when the phone on the kitchen wall rang. The sound startled them, broke them apart.

Travis groaned. Every nerve, every sense had been readied to enjoy their kiss.

After two rings, Nell answered it. "Hello," she said, her voice trembling, but only a little.

It surprised him how close to normal she sounded. Travis wasn't sure he could have pulled it off nearly as well.

He watched as her gaze revealed surprise. "It's for you." She handed him the receiver.

"Me?" Only a few people knew he was in Promise. "Travis Grant," he said into the mouthpiece.

"This is Grady Weston."

Grady Weston. Travis didn't think victims were normally contacted in advance of a tar and feathering.

"I've changed my mind," the other man said gruffly.

"About what?"

"Taking you to Bitter End. Be ready by noon tomorrow."

"Fine… Great!"

Travis replaced the receiver. Nell stood a few feet away, with arms crossed, her eyes worried.

"Grady's decided to help me find Bitter End, after all," he said.

Six

Only eleven-thirty. Travis glanced at his watch, pleased that Grady Weston had agreed to show him the way to Bitter End. He wasn't sure what to expect once they got there, especially considering people's reactions every time he mentioned it.

Killing time, he walked over to the paddock outside the barn where Jeremy's horse, Dot Com, ran free. Earlier, Jeremy had told him proudly that he'd come up with the name himself. Now Travis stood and watched the young animal racing back and forth, kicking up his hind legs, running for the sheer joy of it.

The air was clear and Travis inhaled deeply. Until now he hadn't spent much time in Texas other than book signing and media tours in cities like Dallas and Houston. He'd written several stories set at least partly in Texas, but his research had been limited to libraries. The greater his success, the tighter his schedule and the less time he had for personal investigations. A shopping center in San Antonio or an airport in Dallas hadn't prepared him for what he'd discovered here in the hill country. He found the vast openness awe-inspiring and the life so dissimilar from his existence in Manhattan he felt as though he were visiting an alien planet.

The silence was perhaps the most profound difference. Without even realizing it, Travis had grown accustomed to city noise. Taxis honking, buses, shouting, street musicians, the clang and clatter of vendors. He'd lived in Manhattan for almost fifteen years now and hadn't realized how loud it could be. These few days in the country with Nell and her family had changed his whole perspective.

To his surprise he'd slept all night, every night. He never drafted his books while on the road, but the tranquility here had both relaxed and inspired him, and he was overwhelmed with ideas. He'd started to jot down a few thoughts on his laptop last night, and before he knew it four hours had passed. It'd felt like fifteen minutes.

His great-grandparents had been farmers, he remembered. He wondered if he'd inherited some of his ancestors' love of the land, though he'd never experienced country living. His parents had divorced when he was young, and he'd lived in New York state for most of his life.

He heard a sound behind him and glanced over his shoulder. Nell. A smile automatically came to his lips. He was convinced she didn't have a clue how beautiful she was. His attraction to her was as strong as anything he'd known; it still surprised him.

Ruth's probing questions of the day before hadn't helped, either. Thoughts of making love to Nell had begun to fill his dreams, and while the physical attraction was intense, he found Nell compelling in other ways. He loved her determination, her sense of family, her pride in the ranch and the sheer grit it'd demanded to keep Twin Canyons afloat.

"Do you have a few minutes?" she asked, coming to stand beside him.

"For you, always," he said.

She rested one arm on the top rail of the paddock fence and studied Dot Com as though she needed to compose her thoughts before speaking.

"Problems?" he asked.

She shook her head, and the long braid swung back and forth.

One day he'd enjoy undoing that braid of hers, letting her hair slip unrestrained through his fingers. He imagined filling his hands with it and drawing her face to his and kissing her.

"I… I don't know if Jeremy and Emma know about Bitter End," she said, her voice low. "Naturally there was some talk after Richard was found, but mostly everyone kept it as hush-hush as possible."

"And you're afraid I'm going to tell them?"

"Yes."

"I take it you'd rather I didn't?"

"Please…"

But as she spoke, Travis noticed the hesitation in her voice, as though she wasn't sure this silence would be right for her children.

"You really feel it's right for them not to know?"

A small smile trembled at the edges of her mouth. "Am I that readable?"

"No." He placed his boot on the bottom rail next to hers and, leaning forward, rested his arms on the top one. "I'm beginning to know you."

She smiled. "You think so, do you?"

Her eyes went serious then, and Travis knew this matter of the ghost town and whether or not her children should know continued to bother her.

"They'll hear about Bitter End one way or another," he said.

"The children and I have never discussed it," Nell told him, "although I'm almost convinced they heard something about it after Richard's accident. But they didn't ask and I didn't volunteer any information. For all I know, Jeremy and Emma know everything there is to know about the town."

"I won't say anything in their presence if that's what you think is best." He wanted to reassure Nell that he was worthy of her trust, that her confidence in him was well placed.

"There's something else," Nell said, her expression growing truly somber now. She turned and looked away, as though she found Dot Com's antics of sudden interest.

"You can speak to me about anything you want, Nell."

"I have no right to ask you this."

"Ask me, anyway," he insisted gently. He suspected she was wondering about his divorce. She glanced at him, and he saw the gratitude in her eyes.

"It's natural to be curious about me," he encouraged. "I feel the same way about you. I like you, Nell, a great deal, and I'd welcome the opportunity to deepen our friendship."

She hung her head, and he was sure he'd embarrassed her.

"Ask me," he urged.

"Travis…please, don't go. That's what I'm asking."

"You don't want me to go to Bitter End?" He couldn't fathom why, after everything that had been said.

"I've never told anyone this—not even Jake." She faced him, meeting his eyes steadily. "Once, as a child, I heard my parents talking about the town. I was young and impressionable, and I've never forgotten it."

"What did they say?"

She shook her head. "I don't recall exactly. All I can remember is they were worried that one day I'd ask questions about it and find it myself. They'd decided not to mention it until I came to them."

"Which is what you've planned to do with your own children."

Apparently she hadn't made the connection because her eyes widened as she recognized the truth. "You don't understand, Travis, my father was a big man. Nothing intimidated him—but he was terrified of Bitter End."

"He'd been there?" Travis asked.

Nell nodded. "Once, with a bunch of his friends. Whatever he saw or experienced disturbed him, and he was anxious to protect me."

"Is that what you're trying to do for me, Nell?"

She nodded, then shrugged. "You're from New York City—what do you know about the Old West? There are dangers you wouldn't understand."

"I'll be with Grady."

"Yes, but…"

"Does this mean you care about me?" He wanted to hear her admit it.

"Of course I care about you," she returned impatiently. "I care about everyone."

"It'd do wonders for my ego if you'd admit you cared

for me in a more…personal way," he said, loving the way her cheeks instantly filled with color.

She frowned, dismissing his remark. "Call Grady and tell him you've changed your mind," she pleaded urgently.

It hurt Travis to refuse Nell anything.

Her eyes held his, and her fingers squeezed his arm.

"I have to go," he told her with genuine regret. "I'd do almost anything for you, but what you ask is impossible." Even as he spoke, he knew he'd disappointed her.

Another woman might have responded with anger. That had been Val's reaction when she didn't get her way. Not Nell's. Instead, she offered him a resigned smile, as though she'd expected him to refuse. He could tell from the closed expression on her face that she'd retreated emotionally.

He was about to argue, explain himself, when the screen door opened and Ruth appeared, holding the cordless phone.

"For you, Travis," she said. "It's Grady Weston."

Travis took the phone and lifted it to his ear. "Hello," he said crisply, damning the other man's timing.

"Problems," Grady said, skipping the usual chitchat. "I've got a water pump down. Which means I'm not going to be able to take you out to Bitter End this afternoon."

Damn, Travis thought. It wasn't Grady's fault, but his time here was limited; not only that, he felt as though he'd just fought—and won—a dreadful battle asserting his need and his right to go there, and now the opportunity had been snatched away.

"Savannah's been though," Grady continued.

Travis was shocked. Surely Grady didn't expect a new mother to go traipsing all over the countryside!

"She could draw you a decent map," Grady said, "and give you some directions. Then you could find it on your own."

Travis's sagging spirits buoyed. "Good idea. I'll give Savannah a call."

"I apologize if this puts you out any."

"I'll find it on my own, don't worry."

They ended the conversation in the same abrupt way they'd started it.

Ruth and Nell were both watching him when he finished. "Grady's got problems with a water pump."

"But you're going, anyway," Nell said, and her lovely face tightened.

"Yes, I'm going, anyway."

Nell nodded sadly, then turned and walked away.

Grady was late getting back to the ranch for dinner, and Caroline found herself glancing out the window every few minutes. Shortly after she'd arrived home from the post office, Savannah had phoned, explaining that a water pump had broken. Both Laredo and Grady were working on it, and neither man was likely to be home soon.

Caroline hadn't been a rancher's wife long, but she'd lived around cattlemen most of her life. Caring for the herd took priority over just about everything. The herd was the family's livelihood and their future.

Savannah had mentioned something else, too, and that was the reason Caroline awaited Grady's return so anxiously. Her sister-in-law had told her Nell's dude-ranch guest knew Richard.

Caroline was astonished by the apprehension those few words could bring her. She hadn't realized Richard held such power over her. It'd been months since they'd last heard news of him. Richard had been nothing but a source of heartache for the family—and for her.

The fact that Nell's would-be cowboy was an acquaintance of Richard's explained a great deal. Grady had been restless and short-tempered the night before, tossing and turning. Caroline had awakened around two and found him sitting on the porch in the very spot his father had once favored. He hugged her close, kissed her, then after a few minutes, sent her back to bed.

Caroline had known something was troubling him, but not what. He'd tell her, as he always did, when he was ready. That was how Grady operated. But now she had reason to suspect that his recent bout of restlessness was somehow connected to Richard.

At six Caroline ate dinner with Maggie and put a plate aside for Grady. Maggie was playing with her dolls in her bedroom when Grady and Wiley, their foreman, rode into the yard.

Caroline moved onto the porch and savored the sight of her husband, sitting his horse with natural ease. His dog, Bones, trotted along behind. Bones was the grandson of Grady's beloved old dog, Rocket, who'd died the previous year. He looked a great deal like his granddaddy. The minute he'd been born, Grady had picked him out of the litter and trained him personally.

Her heart swelled with pride and love as she watched her husband dismount and head into the barn.

"Welcome home," she said when he returned a short time later. His steps were slow and heavy and she knew how tired he must be.

Grady's face revealed his pleasure at being home and finding her waiting for him. Caroline held her arms open. Grady didn't hesitate to walk into them and hold her tight.

"The pump's working?" she asked.

"Good as new," he said as he released her.

"You hungry?"

"Starving," he growled.

"Then wash up and I'll warm dinner for you."

When he came back into the room he seemed revived. Wearing a lazy grin, he said, "Maggie's decided on a name for the baby."

Months earlier Grady had allowed the child to name a newborn colt—which he'd subsequently given her for her sixth birthday—and she'd chosen Moonbeam. When they learned Caroline was pregnant, Maggie had assumed she'd be naming her little brother or sister, as well. No amount of explaining could convince her otherwise.

Caroline could just imagine the name her daughter had chosen. "I'm afraid to ask."

"For a boy, she's decided on Buckwheat."

"Buckwheat?"

"And for a girl, Darla."

"Ah." Caroline understood now. The television had been on earlier that afternoon and Maggie had been watching reruns of *Our Gang.*

"I'll talk to her again," Caroline promised, thinking she'd let Maggie go through the baby-name book with her. She wanted her daughter to feel part of things, but Maggie needed to understand that the ultimate decision rested with her and Grady.

"I don't know," Grady said with a thoughtful look.

He pulled out a kitchen chair and sat down. "Buckwheat has a nice ring to it, don't you think? Buckwheat Weston. And we wouldn't need to worry about any other kids in his class having the same name."

"Grady!"

Her husband chuckled, reaching for his fork.

Caroline poured herself a glass of iced tea and sat down across from him. "I talked to Savannah this afternoon," she said, hoping he'd bring up the subject of Richard.

Grady didn't so much as blink as he took his first bite of pork chop.

If anything bothered him, he didn't show it. Nothing, it seemed, would deter him from enjoying his meal. A man had his priorities, thought Caroline with wry amusement. He'd wait until he'd finished his meal.

"Did Savannah mention that Travis Grant knows Richard?" he finally asked.

Caroline nodded.

"You weren't going to say anything?" He regarded her quizzically, as though her silence had surprised him.

"I knew you'd mention it eventually."

Grady reached for his coffee and held the mug between both hands. "It bothers me knowing my brother's in prison," he admitted. "God knows it's what Richard deserves..." He leaned forward, set the mug aside and reached for Caroline's hand. He looked into her eyes and she felt his love, stronger than anything she'd ever known.

"I couldn't sleep last night," he told her.

"I know."

"I didn't understand it, not at first. Every time I closed my eyes, Richard was there. Dammit, this is my brother, my little brother. Mom and Dad would have wanted me to look out for him, but—"

"No." Caroline shook her head and tightened her fingers around his. She believed that Grady's parents would have wanted Richard to accept responsibility for his own actions. She told him so.

"Deep down I realize that," Grady said, and released a deep sigh. "But last night I realized something else." He lowered his gaze. "I'm afraid of Richard."

"Afraid?"

Grady nodded. "It's idiotic, I know, but those fears seemed very real in the dead of night."

"But why? He's locked away. He can't hurt us or—"

"My greatest fear," Grady said, interrupting her, "is that one day he'd try to take away what is most precious to me. You, Maggie and the baby."

"Oh, Grady, it'd never, never happen."

"I know it doesn't make sense. But remember that one of Richard's great pleasures was grabbing whatever he thought anyone else wanted," he said bitterly. "Especially something that was important to me."

"Grady, don't you know how much I love you?" she demanded. Had the situation been reversed, though, she suspected she'd feel exactly the same. All she could think to do was reassure him.

Standing, Caroline walked to the other side of the table and sat on his lap. She draped her arms around his neck, then lowered her mouth to his. Their kisses grew in length and intensity, stoking fires of need.

"I've changed my mind," Maggie announced as she stepped into the kitchen. She clutched some small stuffed animals in her arms. "Buckwheat is a dumb name for a boy."

Caroline sighed and pressed her forehead against Grady's shoulder.

"I was just getting attached to it," he said, sounding almost like his normal self. "Do you have any other ideas?"

"Beanie," the six-year-old suggested next. "We're gonna have our own Beanie baby."

Caroline groaned and Grady chuckled.

Dinnertime came and went and Travis had yet to return. Nell did the dishes, but kept her eye trained on the dirt road that wound down from the two-lane highway. He'd been gone the better part of seven hours.

"Are you worried?" Ruth asked as Nell dried her hands on a dishtowel.

"About what?" she asked, pretending she didn't know what Ruth was talking about. She hated being this transparent, but she couldn't stop worrying about Travis. He'd gone in search of Bitter End all on his own, despite her request that he give up this stupid search. It hurt that he'd refused to heed her advice. It'd taken every ounce of pride she possessed to ask him to stay away.

Now this.

"You've been looking at the clock every five minutes," Ruth pointed out. "Travis will be back any moment—there's no need to worry."

"How can you be sure?" Nell asked in a rare display of temper. Anything could have happened. Anything. The scenarios that flashed through her mind saw him dead and bleeding at the side of the road. Or inside a collapsed building, like Richard.

"Did you phone Savannah and Grady?" Ruth returned.

In her panic Nell hadn't thought to contact them. It made all the sense in the world that Travis would stop off and discuss what he'd discovered with Grady. She was surprised she hadn't thought of it herself. Foolish, that was what she'd been. Foolish and histrionic.

Her heart leaped with renewed hope. Casting her mother-in-law an apologetic glance, Nell reached for the cordless phone. Caroline answered on the second ring.

"Hi, it's Nell," she announced cheerfully. "I don't suppose Travis Grant is there?"

If Caroline was surprised to hear from her, she didn't let it show. "No, Nell, we haven't seen him."

"Not at all?" Nell couldn't hide the apprehension in her voice.

"Is everything all right?" Caroline asked.

"I'm sure it is," Nell replied, making light of her concern. By sheer willpower she forced her pulse to return to normal. This not knowing was hell. *Hell!* "I expected he'd be back before now, that's all. I'm sure everything's all right."

They chatted a few minutes longer and Nell promised she'd phone back if Travis hadn't shown up at Twin Canyons by nine.

Nine o'clock. Nell glanced at the clock on the stove. Two more hours. The day's light was already beginning to fade. She didn't know what Ruth thought when she said she was going out to look for him herself. But she figured she'd go stir-crazy waiting another minute; another two hours was out of the question.

She grabbed the truck keys off the peg on the back-porch wall and was out the door. A sense of urgency filled her, a combination of anger and fear.

If anything had happened to him, she swore she'd

give every pair of socks he owned to Yucky. The man was a fool to traipse across unfamiliar territory.

It wasn't until she was at the top of the drive, the truck's headlights stretching across the paved highway, that she remembered she didn't know where Bitter End was or how to get there. Making a quick decision, she headed south toward the Weston spread. From what Caroline had just told her, Travis had gone to Savannah for directions.

Nell left the engine running when she arrived at Savannah and Laredo's home. She leaped out of the cab and raced across the yard.

Savannah met her at the door and said, "Caroline phoned and said no one's heard from Travis."

"Not a word?"

"No. But I drew him a map," Savannah said.

"Can you draw me one, too?" Nell asked.

"Of course." Savannah led the way into the kitchen. Nell followed, her heart pounding.

"You're worried, aren't you?" Savannah asked.

Nell nodded, afraid if she said anything, her voice would crack. Dammit, she was beginning to really care about that greenhorn. Which infuriated her, because she didn't *want* to care about him. He'd drifted into their lives and would drift out again. A few weeks after he left, Jeremy and Emma would probably have trouble remembering his name.

Not Nell. It would take her much longer to forget Travis Grant.

"That map took a long time to draw, and I don't want to keep you waiting," Savannah said, reaching for a pad and pencil. "I'll have to give you a rough sketch." She bent to her task, and in a minute the job was done. "You should be able to figure it out from this."

Savannah's hurried map wasn't ideal, but it gave Nell something to go on.

"Would you like me to come with you?" Laredo asked, joining the two women.

"No." Nell couldn't see any reason to drag him into the night.

"You're sure?"

"Positive. Thanks for your help," Nell said. She bounded out of the house and back into the truck.

Savannah and Laredo came to the stand by the back door silhouetted in the light that spilled from the kitchen. Nell realized she hadn't been able to hide her feelings from them any more than she'd concealed them from Ruth. Heart still pounding, she waved goodbye, then turned back up the drive.

In situations like this, she knew she had to face her worst fear. Recognizing what it was came easy because she'd encountered it once before.

Her greatest fear was finding that Travis had been hurt or killed.

"Dear God, no," she pleaded aloud, her mouth dry with horror. *Not again.* Finding Jake crushed beneath the tractor had forever changed her. It had nearly destroyed her, too.

The tears gathering in her eyes infuriated her, and she roughly swiped them away with the back of her hand.

She came to a juncture in the road and checked her map to choose which way she should turn. According to the directions, Bitter End was inaccessible by car.

Which made sense, otherwise the town would have been found and explored much earlier.

If the makeshift map was at all accurate, Bitter End wasn't anywhere close to the road, and the turnoff point was some distance yet. She inhaled deeply, forcing herself to remain calm and in control of her emotions. As she drew near the section of highway where she'd need to drive onto unpaved land, she slowed to a crawl.

Her heart flew into her throat when she saw tire tracks that turned off the road. She was sure they were made by the vehicle Travis had rented.

She remembered again what had happened to Richard. Cal had found him in Bitter End, near death, half-crazed from thirst and his injuries. A stairway had collapsed on him, and he'd been two days without water or medical attention. It was described as a miracle that he'd survived. He'd been airlifted to Austin and hospitalized.

Nell shook off the memory and concentrated on driving. The terrain was hilly and uneven and the truck pitched and heaved first one way and then another. Fortunately it was a clear night and a bright three-quarter moon had risen; at least she could see where she was going.

Why Travis was in such an all-fired hurry to find the town she'd never know. He was probably on deadline. Here she was, desperately worried about a man who was no doubt planning to make a laughingstock out of the entire community.

He'd urged her to see the town herself, and now he was getting his wish. Nell slowed, squinting into the distance, convinced she'd seen a flash of light.

She eased the pickup to a stop and opened the door.

Standing on the narrow running board, she peered in the direction she'd seen the light. It wasn't visible now.

"Travis," she yelled at the top of her lungs. She waited for a response and thought, just for a second that she'd heard one.

Getting back into the truck, she sped ahead, heedless of the terrain. Sure enough the light reappeared.

"Travis! Travis!" She slammed on the brakes when he was caught in the farthest reaches of her headlights.

Jumping out of the cab, she shouted. "Travis?"

"Here!" As he raced toward her she stumbled in his direction.

He held a flashlight, which he dropped when she neared. He threw open his arms. She wasn't sure which to do first, kiss him or slug him.

She fell into his arms with a force that might have knocked a slighter man to the ground. All at once nothing mattered, except that he was alive, uninjured, and she was in the warm security of his embrace.

"What happened? Where were you? Dear God in heaven, did you have any idea how worried I was?"

He shut her up with a kiss, then explained everything in five simple words.

"I ran out of gas."

Seven

"You ran out of gas?" Nell shrieked.

Travis felt foolish enough without her yelling at him, then figured it was what he deserved. He didn't know how he could've let something like that happen. His only excuse was his unfamiliarity with the vehicle—pretty lame as excuses went.

"I'm sorry," he told her.

"Sorry—all you can say is you're *sorry?*"

To her shock and dismay, Nell broke into sobs. She covered her face with both hands and half turned from him. Stunned that he'd driven her to tears, he moved to reach for her, but stopped, not sure how she'd react to being held when she was in such distress. The sight of her weeping was more than he could bear. He gently drew her to him, comforting her, holding her loosely. She struggled at first and he let her.

"You're right, Nell, sorry just doesn't cut it," he whispered soothingly.

"You're a fool," she told him, wiping the tears from her face.

"I know."

"You're not supposed to agree with me."

He cradled her face between his hands. "You were worried sick, weren't you?"

Even in the dark, with only the headlights behind her and the glow of the moon, he read Nell's fear.

"I… I was the one who found Jake," she said. "I was so afraid you…"

She didn't finish; she didn't need to. Travis wrapped his arms completely around her, his heart pounding with an emotion so overwhelming it made him weak in the knees.

"I'm fine. A little chagrined but fine."

"I'm not," she said, and clung to him.

Holding her like this was worth every moment of anxiety he'd endured, every second he'd floundered around, hoping he'd headed in the right direction. Common sense said he should have remained with the vehicle, but he'd felt compelled to make his way back to the road. Back to Nell.

She sniffled and raised her head to gaze up at him. Their eyes met, and something warm and wonderful passed between them. A recognition, an acceptance, a consent.

It was a profound moment.

Travis lowered his mouth to hers, and when their lips met, he barely managed to stifle a groan, it was that good. His lips lingered on hers as he prolonged the kiss, not wanting it to end.

She slipped her arms around his neck. He'd been the one to initiate the few kisses they'd exchanged to this point. She'd allowed his kisses, even enjoyed them, but she'd always remained slightly aloof, tentative.

That restraint was gone now. Her fingers were in

his hair and her mouth clung to his, warm, demanding, erotic. By the time the kiss ended, Travis felt weak, drained—and at the same time exhilarated.

"Nell...sweet Nell." His voice was barely audible.

As she buried her face in his shoulder, he closed his eyes and breathed in her scent, the scent that belonged only to her. Equal parts soap and hay...and Nell. A cool breeze rushed against his face, and he silently prayed it would clear his head. At the moment all he could think about was making love to Nell. Not here, he told himself. The timing, the location, everything was wrong, but his body seemed intent on convincing him otherwise.

"Let's talk," he murmured.

"What do you want to talk about?"

"I have a few thoughts I want to discuss with you."

"Now?"

He nodded. "It won't take long."

He slid an arm about her waist and they walked toward the pickup. Nell turned off the engine and lowered the tailgate. They sat on it side by side.

Now that he had her attention, Travis wasn't sure where to start. He reached for her hand and held it between both of his; unable to resist, he kissed her knuckles. A heavy sigh worked its way through his chest as he gathered his thoughts.

"Travis?"

"First of all," he said, "I'm sorry I worried you."

She made a small sound as if to say now that he was found, all was forgiven.

"You came looking for me." His respect for her multiplied a hundredfold, especially now that he knew she'd been the one to find her dying husband. She'd had no idea what to expect tonight, but she'd put aside her fears and gone in search of him. "I don't think I've ever met anyone braver than you."

"Me?" She laughed softly. "I'm the biggest coward who ever lived."

"Not true."

"If I was as brave as you suggest, I wouldn't have asked you to stay away from Bitter End."

He smiled, following her thoughts. It didn't surprise him that they aligned with his. "That leads nicely into what I wanted to discuss with you."

"Bitter End?"

He felt her stiffen and searched for the words to reassure her.

"Did you find it?" she asked.

"Unfortunately, no. I got lost. My map-reading abilities leave much to be desired. I haven't a clue how close I was or wasn't."

She made no comment.

"Next time I want you to come with me."

"This is a joke, right?" she burst out.

He shook his head. His hands continued to hold hers. "You came looking for me—"

"Yes, but..."

"Don't you realize how much courage that took?"

"But I couldn't bear not knowing—"

"You also need to know what happened in Bitter End. You and everyone else in this community. The truth is long overdue. It's time to uncover the past, place it in the proper perspective, stop pretending Bitter End doesn't exist. Once everyone knows what happened there, the allure will be gone. You won't need to worry about Jeremy and Emma sneaking away to find it on their own."

"They wouldn't do that," she insisted weakly.

"Didn't you say your own father did? And Grady and the Patterson brothers searched for it when they were kids."

"Who told you that?"

"Savannah," he said. "This afternoon. They aren't the only ones either."

Nell turned away from him.

"Why me?" she asked, her voice weary.

"I need someone who knows the history, someone who'll help me understand it. According to Savannah, your family was among the original settlers. All I know is what Richard Weston told me and—"

"I wouldn't believe a word that snake said!"

"Right. So will you help me?" he asked quietly. "Come to Bitter End with me. Together we can solve this mystery once and for all."

Nell's shoulders rose with a sigh. "I...need some time to think it over."

"All right." He suspected that in the end she'd agree.

"You ready to go home now?" he asked.

"Home," she repeated. "Yes." She glanced at him. "We'll get your car tomorrow."

When they were in the truck cab and Nell had started the engine, it suddenly occurred to him that he'd referred to Twin Canyons as home.

Home. That was how it was beginning to feel.

Ruth sat in her rocker and worked the crochet hook and yarn. While her fingers were busy with their task, her mind sped off on its own course. Nell had been gone more than two hours now, worried sick about that tenderfoot.

The children were upstairs asleep and the house was quiet. Calm. A cat nestled in Nell's chair, and Lucky, Jeremy's dog, slept on the braided rug in front of the fireplace. Yet Ruth's mind raced.

She'd been a youngster herself, about Emma's age, when she first heard the rumors about Bitter End. She remembered a schoolmate had told her about the mysterious ghost town, hidden in the hills. She was convinced it'd all been a lie, a story her friend had concocted. Then, years later, when she was wise and mature and all of thirteen, she'd overheard Edwina and Lily Moorhouse mention a ghost town.

Ruth trusted the Moorhouse sisters and had asked them about it. They, too, had claimed it was real and explained that the history of Promise was tied to the forgotten town. Only a few people knew about it, and even fewer knew where it was situated.

Ruth sighed and her hands went idle in her lap. Only one other person had shared her secret—which was that she'd been to Bitter End herself—and he was long dead. At eighteen she'd decided she would find this town. Cocky and self-confident, she'd gone in search of it.

That was how she'd met Jerome Bishop—her Jerry. He was older and had fought overseas toward the end of the Second World War, coming home a decorated hero.

She remembered how curious she'd been about him, how interested. But he was nearly thirty and she was still in her teens. He'd encountered her riding on his land and asked her a few questions. She didn't dare tell him the truth, so she'd fabricated something and prayed he'd believe her.

He hadn't, but said if she was a cattle thief, she was by far the prettiest one he'd ever seen.

Ruth smiled at the memory. A few days later she was back, certain she wasn't anywhere close to Bishop land. But Jerry found her, and in her rush to get away and avoid his questions, she'd let her horse escape and twisted her ankle as she tried to catch the reins.

In his concern about her injury Jerry hadn't plied her with questions, but carefully examined her foot, his touch gentle for such a big man. She'd been half in love with him following their first meeting, but after this, her heart was forever lost.

Naturally such a romance was impossible. He was older, more worldly; she was just a schoolgirl. He didn't kiss her, nor did he chastise her. Instead, Jerry had rounded up her mare, then escorted her almost the entire way home. She'd been too shy to talk much, giving one-word replies to his questions. Before he'd left her, he asked her to forget the ridiculous notion of finding Bitter End on her own—not that she'd ever admitted she was looking for it. He'd gone so far as to suggest she stay home in the afternoons and read books or talk on the phone with her friends. Ruth had smiled politely and said she'd take his advice under consideration.

The next evening he'd stopped by the house to discuss ranching with her father. Ruth had been involved in helping her brothers with their homework. She felt Jerry's eyes on her, and through the whole evening, she feared he'd mention her afternoon horseback excursions. He didn't.

The next time she ventured out horseback riding, Jerry was waiting for her.

"Are you meeting a lover?" he'd demanded.

"No." She'd been appalled that he'd even think such a thing.

She doubted he believed her, but she couldn't bear letting him think she loved another man. Instead, she'd broken down and told him she was attracted to someone who felt he was too old for her. If he'd guessed she meant him, Jerry never said. When he couldn't convince her to forget about finding the lost town, he'd reluctantly agreed to accompany her.

The day they'd stumbled upon the ghost town was one she would long remember. That was when Jerry had first kissed her. Ruth wasn't sure which had excited her more—his kiss or locating the town.

But it was the only time they'd ever been to the town. High on exhilaration, they'd walked down the center of the deserted main street. Soon they realized something was very wrong. It was spring and the hills were blanketed with bluebonnets, yet Ruth noticed not a single flower in Bitter End.

The place was bleak, dark. A huge blighted tree stood at one end of town. Everything was dead.

But that wasn't what had kept them from returning. It was the ugly feeling, the sensation of dread that pressed against her heart, making it almost difficult to breathe. Jerry had kept her close to his side and mumbled something about the town reminding him of the feeling he'd had when he came upon battlegrounds during the war. It felt like death, he'd said.

Whatever had happened was horrible enough to cry out from the land, from the buildings and everything around them. Whatever it was had killed this town and forever marked it for ruin.

They'd never gone back. Never wanted to. Finding the lost town had been their secret, a silent bond they'd shared. To the best of Ruth's knowledge, they'd never spoken of it again.

Afterward there'd been no reason for them to meet. Ruth had missed Jerry more than she could say, but if he missed her, he didn't let on. They met in passing twice—both times in Promise—and exchanged little more than casual greetings. Ruth was miserable, loving him the way she did, and she was sure he cared for her, too. So she decided to take matters into her own hands. It was a brazen thing she did; she smiled at the memory of it and the shocked look on Jerry's face the day she rode over to his family's ranch. She'd figured she had nothing to lose. Her ostensible reason was that she'd be graduating from high school within a few weeks and needed the advice of an older more experienced person about her best course of action.

He'd asked about her options and she'd mentioned two: marrying him or moving to Dallas with a friend and finding work there. Jerry's face had tightened, and then he'd suggested that marrying him was probably the better of the two ideas, but he preferred to do the asking.

She granted him that much and waited impatiently for him to make his move. The day she graduated from high school he stopped by the family home with a diamond ring. Afterward they'd argued amiably about who'd proposed to whom; it was a private joke between them.

A few years after they were married, Jerry's mother had died and they'd inherited the chest.

The very chest that sat in the attic of this house, Jake and Nell's place. She'd gone through the contents once. To a historian the chest would have been a treasure trove, filled with bits and pieces of life in the nineteenth-century hill country. But it was more than that. Ruth had recognized almost immediately that some of the things packed in the cedar-lined chest had come from Bitter End.

She'd looked them over, then closed up the box and never investigated it again. Ruth supposed it was because she'd been so young at the time, and that one visit to the town had continued to haunt her. She'd wanted nothing more to do with Bitter End. No link to it. If she couldn't throw out the chest—and she couldn't—then she'd hide it away, obliterating from her mind any memory of that horrible place. Jerry must have agreed, because once he knew the contents, he'd never asked about it again.

The time had come, Ruth believed, to reopen that chest. They had to disclose what was known about the town, discover its secrets, undo whatever damage they could. She was too old now for such a task. But it seemed somehow fated that Travis Grant had arrived when he did.

She would talk to him, show him the chest, whether Nell wanted her to or not.

That decided, Ruth picked up her crochet hook and started back to work. The clock chimed nine; Nell would be returning with Travis soon. She had a good feeling about those two. They were well matched, the way Nell and Jake had been.

Yes, the more she thought about it, the more fated Jake's appearance began to seem.

The following morning, Nell was in the kitchen preparing the children's breakfast when Ruth came downstairs.

"I take it you found Travis," her mother-in-law said, with a slight smile.

"I found him," Nell confirmed.

As if to verify her words, the back door opened and Travis stepped inside. He looked fresh from the shower, his hair wet and recently combed. His gaze searched out Nell's and he smiled. "Morning, everyone."

"Morning, Travis," both Jeremy and Emma said at once, and their faces brightened at the sight of him.

"Where were you last night?" Jeremy asked. "I asked Mom, but she said she wasn't sure."

"I wasn't sure, either," Travis replied.

Nell cast him a warning glance. He'd already promised he wouldn't tell the children about Bitter End, but she feared he'd forgotten his word.

"I got...lost," Travis said, keeping his gaze on her. When she stopped stirring the oatmeal long enough to glare openly at him, he winked.

Nell felt the color rush to her cheeks and prayed her children wouldn't notice, but her prayer didn't reach heaven fast enough to include Ruth. She noticed her mother-in-law grinning as she took her place at the table, obviously pleased.

When the oatmeal was ready, she served it with brown sugar and raisins. The toast was from a loaf of the homemade bread she'd baked the evening before. She'd kneaded away her worries about Travis on the dough, and it was some of the lightest, fluffiest bread she'd ever baked.

The grandfather clock in the living room chimed eight, and the children leaped up from the table, grabbed their lunches and dashed out the door.

"You finished with your chores?" Nell shouted after them.

They both assured her they were.

"What are your plans for the day?" Ruth asked, directing the question to both Nell and Travis.

Travis glanced at Nell. She dragged in a deep breath. "I'm driving Travis back to where he left his car. We're taking along a five-gallon can of gas," she explained.

"You going anyplace else?" her mother-in-law pressed.

"I've asked Nell to help me find Bitter End," Travis said.

"Will you, Nell?" Ruth searched her face.

"I'm not sure."

"I think you should," Ruth said unexpectedly.

For a moment Nell was too shocked to respond. "You want me to find Bitter End?"

"That's what I said." The older woman nodded. "And once you've located the town and walked through it, come back and tell me. Don't dawdle, either. There's something I have for you—both of you. Something that's been in the attic all these years."

"Ruth?" Nell asked in hushed tones, bending over her mother-in-law. "What is it?"

"Ruth?" Travis knelt down in front of her.

The older woman smiled and gently touched his cheek. "Find the town," she said softly. "Just find the town."

Travis helped Nell clean up the kitchen, then loaded the can of gas in the back of the pickup. She was already in the cab when he climbed inside.

"Thank you," he said.

The man could unnerve her faster than anyone she'd ever known. "For what?"

"For coming with me."

In the light of day Nell was annoyed for responding

to Travis's kisses the way she had. It was because of her relief at finding him safe; it must be. She simply hadn't been herself—except she'd used that excuse before.

Despite Ruth's encouragement, she intended to tell him she refused to look for the town. She didn't want to know what was there, didn't care to find it.

"Losing your nerve, are you?" Travis asked.

"No," she denied heatedly, then added, "I'm a rancher, not a...historian."

"And a—"

"Coward," she finished for him. Her fingers ached from her death grip on the steering wheel. What it came down to was fear. Everything she'd ever heard about the town rang in her ears—rumors, warnings, advice. And it all seemed to whisper *Keep away*.

"What's Ruth talking about?" Travis asked once they were on the road.

"I... I don't know," Nell said, which was only partially true. The attic was full of forgotten treasures from the Bishop family. Old clothing, furniture, letters and memorabilia. Seeing that Jake's family, like her own, had been among the original pioneers, it was quite possible that something stored in the attic had come from Bitter End. Anything her parents might have had, however, had been taken with them when they retired to Florida.

"Won't you come with me, Nell?" Travis coaxed.

It took a long time, but reluctantly she decided Travis was right. She had to confront whatever was there, not just for her own sake but that of her family. Her friends. The people of Promise. It sounded melodramatic to put it in those terms, but then it was a melodramatic situation. Certainly an extraordinary one.

"All right," she finally whispered.

"Thank you," he said again.

Had they been anywhere else, not tearing down the road in her pickup, Nell was convinced Travis would have gathered her in his arms and kissed her. Had they been anywhere else, she would have let him.

That was quite an admission for her, she realized. Despite her reservations and doubts, she was falling in love with this greenhorn. Every unmarried rancher in the area had asked her out at some point since Jake's death, but who did she fall for? A writer. A man who was going to break her heart, one way or another.

Nell let Travis do the driving after a while, and an hour later, with Savannah's map spread out on her lap, Nell suddenly cried, "Here!" She pointed to a grove of trees on the right.

Travis brought the truck to a stop.

"We go on foot from this spot," Nell said, rereading Savannah's instructions for the tenth time.

"So I was close," Travis muttered to himself.

They left the truck and started out on foot. Nell could already feel her heart pounding, and not from physical effort, either. It seemed to thunder, *Keep away, keep away,* with every beat.

"Are you okay?" Travis asked her a few minutes later.

"Sure," she lied. "What's there to fear?"

"We don't know that yet, do we?" he said, his expression serious.

They didn't speak for a while as they made their way through heavy brush and over rocky, treacherous ground. When they reached a limestone outcropping, Nell paused to look over the small valley below—and gasped.

She pointed a shaking finger at a charred steeple in the distance. The church was the tallest structure, but she could see others, too.

Travis's gaze followed the direction of her finger. "Bitter End," he whispered.

Nell studied the cluster of buildings. From her vantage point she could look down at them, could see the whole town laid out. Bitter End was divided by one main street with buildings on either side. The church and cemetery were at one end of the town, a corral at the other. Some of the buildings were constructed of stone, others of wood. It surprised her how well preserved everything seemed to be.

"So far, so good," Travis said.

Nell wordlessly agreed and breathed in deeply before they scrambled down the hill and into the town. They arrived near the corral. As they progressed, Nell experienced a feeling of heaviness, of being weighed down, that reminded her of how she'd felt those first few months after Jake's death.

She didn't say anything, but wondered if Travis felt the same thing.

"What is it?" he asked in a hushed tone.

They were on the main street now, their hands tightly clenched. With each step they advanced into the town, the feeling intensified. The weight pressing on Nell's heart grew stronger and stronger until she slowed her pace.

"I... I don't know."

"What's that?" Travis pointed to the saloon and the rocking chair that sat in front of it. Something leaned against the building.

"It…looks like Richard's guitar," she said. "He hid here for weeks before he was found."

"How could he have stood it?" Travis wondered, his voice low and hoarse.

"I don't know." Nell didn't understand why they felt compelled to speak so quietly. He squeezed her hand, and by tacit agreement they moved from the street onto the boardwalk. Savannah was right, she thought with a shudder. There was nothing living here—except the ceaseless wind.

She paused and looked inside the mercantile. A half-dozen bloated cans of food were scattered on the shelves. An old cash register stood on the counter, its drawer hanging open.

"Someone was looking for spare change," Travis remarked.

"Probably Richard." Evidence of his presence was everywhere.

They located the room in the hotel where he'd been sleeping and carefully skirted past the area where the stairs had collapsed. The wood floors were stained with his blood. Debris and empty bottles appeared here and there; magazine pages and food wrappings were blown against the sides of buildings.

"What are you thinking?" Travis asked as they neared the end of the street.

"That I want the hell out of here."

He chuckled, but the sound was uncomfortable. "Anything else you want to see?"

"No." She slid her arm through his and stayed close to his side. The oppressive sensation remained, reminding her even more forcibly of the horrific grief she'd suffered after Jake's death. It had become a part of her, something she lived with day and night. When it finally did ease, it went a little at a time. Slowly she could laugh again, then dream again. She was only now discovering she could love again. She stopped, suddenly struck by an idea.

"Hold me, Travis," she said urgently. They were near the church.

"Now?" He seemed surprised.

"Please."

He pulled her into his arms and she spoke into his ear. "I'd like to try an experiment."

"Okay. What do you need me to do?"

"Nothing," she said, then thinking better of it, added, "much."

She felt his smile against her skin.

Easing away from him, she placed her hands on both sides of his face and touched her lips to his. The kiss was deep, involving, as intense as the kisses they'd shared the night before. When she drew back, she studied his face.

"I like this kind of test," he told her flippantly. "Am I being graded?"

"No."

"Why not?"

"Travis, this is serious."

"I am serious."

She sighed expressively. "All right, I'll give you a B-plus."

"Why not an A?"

"Travis, you won't get an A until you answer my question."

"Fine. What's the question?"

"The feelings. Have they lessened?"

"I'm feeling all sorts of things just now. Which feeling do you mean?"

"The one we felt when we entered the town."

"I won't know until you kiss me again."

"Quit joking! This is important."

"I wasn't joking. I can't tell."

"Never mind."

"Why?"

"I have my answer."

"And?"

"It *has* lessened," she said. "I'm sure of it."

He nodded. "You're probably right."

Holding hands, they walked out of Bitter End. As they approached the outskirts, she felt a sudden sense of release, as though the bonds that constrained her had gone slack. A few steps outside the town, the feeling had all but disappeared.

After that, they concentrated on the arduous trek back to the road and said very little for some time.

"Are you okay?" Travis asked once.

"Fine. What about you?"

"Fine."

Travis followed her in his rental car as she drove back to Twin Canyons Ranch. Ruth sat on the porch with the rocking chair positioned to face the road; she stood and put away her crocheting as soon as she saw them.

"Did you find the town?" Ruth asked when they entered the kitchen.

"We found it," Nell told her.

She nodded. "I figured you would," she said softly. "Travis, would you follow me upstairs? There's something I'd like you to bring down."

Eight

Travis had one hell of a time bringing the cedar chest down from the attic. It almost seemed as though it was reluctant to give up its secrets, he thought, knowing how whimsical that sounded. Then he needed all his strength to pry up the lid.

Nell stood back, while Ruth edged close to him, firm and purposeful.

With the chest finally open, the first thing Travis noted was how neatly packed it was. The top layer was folded clothes, which Ruth carefully removed and set aside.

They found an old family Bible beneath the dresses and men's shirts. Ruth held it respectfully with both hands. "It's exactly like the one Ellie has," Nell breathed. "Ellie Patterson—used to be Frasier," she explained to Travis. "Ellie owns the feed store in Promise. Her family came here when mine did, and Jake's."

Travis could picture her easily. Ellie, as he recalled, had judged the chili cook-off.

"Ellie found the Bible while she was sorting through her father's things after he died," Ruth said. "She used the Bible for her wedding ceremony. I was touched that she had, since she was so close to her father." Carefully Ruth folded back the leather binding and examined the title page. "It says this Bible belonged to Joseph Savage."

"Jerry's great-great—there are too many greats for me to remember," Ruth said, "but the family's directly descended from Joseph's, that much I know."

"I'm sure this Bible is identical to the one Ellie owns," Nell said, moving in close and running her finger down the page.

"It wasn't unusual for a salesman to come into town and sell any number of the same item," Travis said. "My guess is that's the case here." In his research he'd come across references to old-time peddlers who rode from one town to the next selling their wares. More often than not, the men who sold Bibles were itinerant preachers, too, performing marriages, conducting funerals and preaching fire-and-brimstone sermons.

The next thing Nell extracted was an aged cardboard box. "Probably more clothes," she suggested. "Someone's wedding dress?"

"Open it," Ruth said.

Nell set the box down and with trembling hands removed the lid. She was wrong; it wasn't a wedding dress, not even an article of clothing, but parts of a quilt made of a cream-colored muslin.

"What is it?" Travis asked.

"The backing and some squares for a quilt, from the looks of it," Ruth said. "Apparently someone started the project years ago and never finished it."

"It's not any pattern I've ever seen," Nell said. "Most quilts have an overall design."

And most were a great deal more colorful than this one, Travis mused. The squares lacked the vivid and varied colors of others he'd seen.

"It looks like each square's a picture of some sort," Nell said, and held up one with an oak tree embroidered in the center. The detail was impressive, the stitches minute. She squinted and stared at the square, then shook her head. "I think there's something carved into the side of the tree," she said.

Ruth looked at it and shook her head. "My eyes aren't what they used to be."

Travis took a turn, as well, and after staring at it intensely, was able to make out the letters. "It seems to say, 'cursed'."

"Cursed?" Nell repeated. "Weird." She set the square back in the box. They studied the other squares, but again didn't find them particularly attractive. Each had a different image, although it wasn't always clear what that image was meant to be.

Nell returned the pieces to the cardboard box and set it aside. Leaning over the chest, she reached in and said, "Doesn't this beat all?"

"What is it?" Travis asked.

"It's a doll." Nell pulled out an obviously old rag doll, stuffed tight with a hand-stitched face. It had been made of white linen that had faded to a dull yellow, not unlike the color of the quilt squares. The red calico apron added a splash of brightness.

"I've seen one like that before," Ruth said, frowning in concentration. "Oh, yes! Dr. Jane had one exactly like that in her office not long ago."

"Dr. Jane?" Nell asked. "That seems odd. Are you sure?"

"Positive. She had it sitting on a bookcase. I remember seeing it the last time I was in for my physical. You remember, Nell? You drove me into town yourself. I needed my blood pressure medication renewed."

"How would Dr. Jane come by something like this?" Nell asked. "She's from California."

Travis listened to the conversation and shook his head. A doll identical to one that had come from Bitter End was owned by a California native? He agreed with Nell; it didn't make sense.

"Let's ask her about it," Travis suggested.

"Can't hurt," Nell said, and Ruth nodded.

The rest of the chest's contents consisted of old newspapers from the 1920s through the assassination of President Kennedy in 1963, army discharge papers and the like. Those, too, were neatly filed in cardboard boxes.

As Ruth carefully repacked the chest, Travis helped Nell finish the chores around the ranch. And then, together, they drove into town.

"This is probably a wild-goose chase," Nell said.

"Probably," he agreed, wondering if she'd had second thoughts about pursuing the significance of their discoveries.

They parked in front of the medical clinic, and once again he noted Nell's hesitation. "Nell," he said softly, "what is it?"

"Nothing," she insisted.

Travis stared at her. Ever since they'd returned from the ghost town, she'd been quiet, withdrawn, speculative. He didn't know what to make of it.

Dr. Jane was with a patient. They sat in the waiting room, and Travis flipped through magazines until the receptionist led them back to Jane's office. Travis glanced around; he noticed no antique doll on her bookcase now.

Jane entered briskly and took a seat at her desk. "Good to see you, Nell," she said. "Hello," she added, nodding in his direction.

Nell introduced Travis and they shook hands. Dr. Jane Patterson's lovely blue eyes revealed a genuine pleasure at seeing Nell—and open curiosity about him.

"Ruth mentioned noticing a rag doll in your office a few months ago," Nell said, getting immediately to the point of their visit.

"Doll?" Jane frowned as if she'd forgotten, but then apparently remembered, because she smiled. "As a matter of fact, I did, but I...no longer have it."

"Would you mind telling us where you got it?" Travis asked.

Jane studied them both. "Is there a particular reason for these questions?"

Nell and Travis exchanged glances. "We found a doll very similar to the one Ruth saw here," Nell explained.

Jane reached for a pen and started making small circles. "Can I ask where you found this doll?"

"Have you been to Bitter End, Dr. Patterson?" Travis asked abruptly. Then he remembered she *had* been. Jane was the one who'd found and treated Richard Weston.

He felt Nell's displeasure with him at the bluntness of his approach. But his curiosity was at a fever pitch. He was looking for answers, and the only way to get them was to ask the right questions. A growing sense of excitement filled him.

The doctor surprised him by asking a question of her own. "Have *you* ever been to Bitter End?"

Nell and Travis looked at each other.

"We were there this morning," Travis answered.

"Did you find the doll there?"

"Not exactly," Travis said. "It was in an old chest in Nell's attic."

"I see." Jane folded her hands and leaned back in her chair. "I don't suppose it would do any harm to tell you how I came to have that doll. Maggie Weston brought it to me."

"Maggie?" Nell sounded shocked.

"This was months ago, before Caroline and Grady were married and he legally adopted Maggie. You might not be aware of this, but Maggie disappeared the same time Richard Weston did. As far as anyone can figure, Maggie must've been hiding in the pickup Richard stole from the Yellow Rose Ranch. For a whole night, Caroline and Grady didn't know where she was. Sheriff Hennessey's the one who put two and two together."

"It must have been hell for Caroline," Nell said in sympathy.

"I'm sure it was. The following morning Maggie reappeared as mysteriously as she'd vanished. She wouldn't say where she'd been, but the sheriff thinks Richard brought her back."

"Thank God!"

"He'd taken her to his hiding place, then—in the ghost town?" Travis asked. His jaw tightened at the thought of a five-year-old in Bitter End.

"Apparently so," Jane said. "No one knows exactly what Richard said to the child to convince her to keep his secret. But considering the type of person he is, it's not too hard to guess."

"Prison's too good for the likes of Richard Weston," Nell muttered.

The more Travis learned about him, the more inclined he was to agree.

"While she was in Bitter End, Maggie found the doll and tucked it in her backpack. Later it worried her that she'd taken something that didn't belong to her. She developed stomachaches, and that was when she brought the doll to me."

"And the reason you had it on your bookshelf," Nell added.

"Exactly! I didn't know at the time that the doll was from the ghost town. I'd hoped the rightful owner would see it in my office so I could simply return it without mentioning Maggie's name."

"Where's the doll now?" Travis wanted to know.

"Maggie has it. Once the truth came out, Grady and Caroline decided Maggie could keep it."

"The memory of how she got it doesn't bother her?" Nell asked.

"It doesn't seem to. She believes she saved that doll. So her feelings about it have become quite positive."

"Good," Nell said. "I'm glad such a horrible experience ended well for her."

Jane smiled, then her gaze swung to Travis. "You're visiting Nell?"

"Actually I'm doing research for a story."

"He's my first guest," Nell explained. "The dude ranch hasn't officially opened, but he needed a room and Mary and Phil suggested my place."

Travis didn't like the classification. A guest—a paying one at that. She'd said it as though there was nothing between them, as though their kisses meant nothing. Despite her tone, Travis couldn't make himself believe it.

"I see," Jane said, sounding a little unsure.

She wasn't the only one. "Nell and I are finding out everything we can about Bitter End," Travis explained. "It's time the mystery of that town was solved."

Jane nodded. "I couldn't agree with you more. My fear is now that the word's out, someone else is going to decide to hide there. If something isn't done soon, there's every likelihood people will get hurt again. Some of those buildings aren't safe for people to explore. It's a wonder they've stood all these years as it is."

"The entire town should be destroyed," Nell said, her voice raised.

Travis disagreed with a sharp shake of the head. "Bitter End is an important part of Texas history. Why would anyone want to destroy it?"

Nell didn't answer.

Cal and Glen took a long-overdue lunch break, letting their horses graze near Gully Creek while they ate their sandwiches. The morning had been spent vaccinating cattle. Cal felt they both deserved a respite while the crew, who'd lunched earlier, finished up.

Although Cal saw his brother every day, they rarely had a chance to talk anymore. Especially now that they were both married. Glen was busy with his life in town; he and Ellie had bought a run-down Victorian that they were fixing up. Cal and Jane were still newlyweds, still learning about each other. A lot had happened in the two men's lives in the past year, more than Cal could adequately take in.

Glen finished his lunch first, then stretched out on the cool grass, shading his eyes with his Stetson.

"Jane mentioned something interesting the other

day," Cal said, leaning back and resting his weight on his palms.

"What?"

"Nell Bishop was in to see her with that city slicker guy from New York."

"I wouldn't say that to his face," Glen said, lifting the Stetson and grinning. "I think he wants to be a cowboy. Besides, the guy's bigger than you."

"So what? Hey—I'm a Texan!"

"He went to see Jane? What's the matter," Glen joked, "is he having trouble with the drinking water?"

"No, he's been to Bitter End."

If Cal hadn't gotten his full attention earlier, he had it now. Glen sat up and looked at his brother. "Is that for real? How the hell did he find it?"

"Grady and Savannah drew him a map."

"You're kidding!"

"Nope."

"What gives *him* the right?"

Cal smiled, remembering that his initial reaction had been similar to that of his brother. "He thinks it's time someone solved the mystery."

"Really?"

"I tend to agree with him."

"Fine, but it should be one of us, then, someone from Promise. Don't you think?"

"Why?"

"Because it's *our* town. Our history. Personally I don't like the idea of some city slicker poking around in affairs that aren't any of his damn business. If he wants to uncover a few skeletons, I say let him open his own closet."

"You willing to do it or not?"

"Dig up the dirt about Bitter End?" his brother clarified.

"Yup." Cal studied his brother. "You know—figure out what went wrong. And why."

Glen expelled a long breath. "I say let sleeping dogs lie. Frankly I don't need to know."

"That's the way I felt, too," Cal told him. "Until recently."

Glen broke off a long blade of grass and stuck it between his teeth. "What changed your mind?"

"Richard Weston."

"What about him?" Glen asked, sounding disgusted.

Cal didn't hold any more affection for Grady's brother than Glen did; Richard had done nothing but embarrass the family and the community. It wasn't common knowledge that he'd stolen from his family not once, but twice—and, as they'd since learned, he'd victimized a lot of vulnerable people in a really nasty scam back East. The news about his arrest and prison sentence had been the talk of the town for weeks. Some people had difficulty believing Richard was capable of committing such crimes. Cal had no such problem. Richard was a lowlife and deserved every day of the twenty-five-year sentence he'd received.

"Richard being airlifted out of Bitter End brought up a lot of questions about the town. Quite a few folks had never heard of it. Others had and wanted to know more. I think it's time we put an end to this speculation and settle the past once and for all."

"Grady agrees with you?"

"He'd planned to personally take Travis Grant there, until his water pump broke. Even then, he had Savannah draw Travis a map. From what Jane told me, Nell's involved in this, too."

Glen continued to chew on the stem of grass. His hands were tucked behind his head and he stared up at the blue sky. "Maybe you're right."

"What can we do to help?" Cal asked after a silence.

"You and me?" Glen seemed surprised.

"We're among the few who've actually been to the town."

Glen closed his eyes. "Don't remind me."

Glen had been there once, Cal twice—most recently with Jane, who'd insisted she wanted to find the town. He'd finally given in and agreed to accompany her, knowing that otherwise she'd search for it on her own.

As it happened, their going into the ghost town precisely when they did had saved Richard Weston's life. The events of that day had shaken Cal considerably. He was accustomed to being in charge, knowing what to do, but if it hadn't been for Jane and her medical expertise, he could have done little but watch Richard Weston die.

"I'm trying to remember what I know about Bitter End," Glen said, cutting into his thoughts. "What do you think Nell and her friend might want to know?"

Nell and her friend. Cal ignored the question and concentrated on the picture that formed in his mind. He'd seen Travis and Nell dancing at the rodeo not long ago. It had been a shock to see her in the arms of a man, especially since she'd always refused dates and invitations. Once the shock wore off, he'd felt pleased. She'd been completely absorbed in the guy, hadn't even noticed him and Jane.

The ribs he'd injured in the rodeo had been hurting like hell, but he'd managed to talk Jane into staying for the dance. The pain was worth it, seeing as Willie Nelson had unexpectedly shown up. Jane still talked about it; she'd been thrilled.

"A penny for your thoughts," Glen teased. "If they're worth that much."

"I was just thinking about Nell and Travis Grant…"

"What about them?"

"There's a romance brewing."

"So?" Glen said.

"So, I think it's a good idea. I liked Jake—he was one of my best friends—but I'd hate to see Nell grieve the rest of her life away. Jake wouldn't have wanted that, either."

"Is she interested in this Travis character?"

"Seems to be." More than that, Travis Grant was obviously taken with her. Whatever was happening there, Cal hoped it would work out for Nell. She was in line for a bit of happiness.

Jeremy liked Travis Grant—so much that it actually worried Nell. Her son was enthralled with him. Several times now she'd been forced to talk to Jeremy about giving Travis time to himself. Like this afternoon, for example. She knew Travis was writing, but the minute her son returned home from school, he'd raced out to see Travis. She didn't know what they'd talked about, but Jeremy had been wearing a silly grin ever since. As if he knew something she didn't.

She'd chastised him soundly for not doing his chores, and he'd left the house in a temper. At dinnertime, when she couldn't find him, she knew where he was likely to be. She hurried over to the bunkhouse and knocked at the door.

"Yeah?" Travis called.

Apparently this was how New Yorkers said, "Come in."

Nell opened the door and was surprised not to see her son there, making a pest of himself despite her scolding. "Have you seen Jeremy?" she asked.

"Not lately." Travis was sitting in front of his computer screen, his brow burrowed.

"I hope I didn't interrupt anything," she said, feeling badly to have barged in on him, considering she'd admonished her twelve-year-old for doing the same thing.

"No problem, Nell." He seemed abstracted and barely glanced away from his work.

She quietly closed the door. Jeremy sometimes liked to escape to the hayloft and read, especially if he was angry with her. She headed in that direction next, hoping to make peace with him.

"Jeremy." She stood in the middle of the barn, staring up at the loft.

"Yeah." Her son peeked over the ledge.

Yeah. Just like Travis. She swallowed the urge to correct him and said, "Time to wash up for dinner."

"Already?" he groaned. He climbed down from the loft and followed Nell back to the house, dragging his feet. He didn't mention the incident earlier that afternoon, and because he hadn't, she didn't, either.

"What are you reading?" his grandmother asked him.

"A book," he said, and set it on the kitchen counter. "When will Emma be back from Girl Scouts?"

Nell glanced at her watch. "Any minute. Kathy's mom is dropping her off. Would you kindly tell Travis dinner will be ready in ten minutes?" She didn't need to make the suggestion twice; Jeremy was out the door as fast as a cartoon character racing across the screen.

"He seems to like Travis," Ruth commented.

"I noticed."

"That worries you?"

It did, Nell thought. Once Travis left—and he *would* leave—her son might well feel abandoned. Initially she hadn't been concerned, but Jeremy's liking for Travis had recently grown into full-scale adulation.

And what about her own feelings? Travis had shaken up her emotions, made her feel all kinds of things she'd shut herself off from. Like attraction. And...desire.

"Yes," she answered her mother-in-law. "I'm worried he likes Travis too much."

"You seem to like him yourself," Ruth added slyly.

Nell bit her lip, unable to explain or confide.

"Something happen you want to talk about?" The older woman studied her closely.

Nell just shook her head. Fortunately Ruth left it at that, giving her a hug before pitching in to set the table.

Dinner consisted of meat loaf, scalloped potatoes, homemade bread, corn, green salad and fresh rhubarb pie. Emma ran in the back door, shucking off her jacket, just as they were about to sit down.

As usual, dinner conversation settled around the children and school. This evening Nell was more than grateful to let her two youngsters do the talking. Particularly since her adventures with Travis in Bitter End wouldn't have been an appropriate subject. Nor did she want to discuss their trip into town and the chat with Dr. Jane.

"What's that book you were reading earlier?" Ruth asked when there was a lull in the conversation.

"*Prairie Gold,* by T. R. Grant," Jeremy said. His gaze briefly flew to Travis before he helped himself to a second slice of bread. "He's a great writer."

"You've read enough of his books," Nell said in a conversational tone as she passed the butter to her son.

"You heard of him?" Emma asked Travis.

Jeremy burst into giggles and Nell quelled him with a look.

"You could say we're friends." Travis smiled at Emma, and Nell wondered if he was teasing her daughter. She certainly wouldn't appreciate it if he was.

"I've read all his books," Jeremy stated proudly.

"Every one of them," Nell testified.

"Do you *really* know him?" Emma asked, returning to Travis's earlier statement.

"Travis is a writer," Nell said. "He probably knows lots of other writers." She didn't want to put him on the spot.

Once more Jeremy burst into giggles.

"What's going on here?" Nell demanded.

"Mom, have you ever wondered what the T.R. in T. R. Grant stands for?"

"No," she said. She hadn't given the matter a moment's thought.

"Travis Randolf," Travis supplied slowly, holding her gaze and refusing to let go.

Nell dropped her fork with a clatter.

"Nell?" Ruth said, her eyes showing concern.

"You're T. R. Grant?" Nell whispered, finding it hard to speak and breathe at the same time.

Travis grinned. "At your service."

Nine

"I told you I was a writer," Travis explained, as though the logic should have been obvious.

"I figured it out this afternoon!" Jeremy exclaimed excitedly.

"But you didn't say *what* you wrote," Ruth said, frowning.

It just so happened that one of the most popular children's authors in the entire country was sitting at this very table, was sleeping in their bunkhouse. Was kissing her senseless every chance he got.

"Nell?" Travis's gaze continued to hold hers. "Maybe you and I should talk about this privately after dinner."

The idea of being alone with him for even a minute was too much. She shook her head vigorously. "That won't be necessary."

Before Travis could comment, Jeremy and Emma immediately bombarded him with questions. At any other time Nell would have cautioned them to mind their manners. But not tonight.

After dinner Ruth went into her bedroom to watch *Jeopardy* on her television set. Protesting loudly, Jer-

emy and Emma were sent upstairs to do their homework, while Nell cleaned the kitchen.

She scrubbed the dishes, rinsed them, dried them.
She didn't turn around, but she knew Travis was still
in the kitchen long before he spoke.

"You might have said something," she told him in a
deceptively mild voice.

"Well, I didn't exactly hide it, but I didn't shout it
from the rooftops, either." He paused. "Does it change
who I am?"

"Yes...no."

"I'd rather you got to know me for who I am first—
without muddying the waters with my success."

Although she understood, it hurt that he hadn't
trusted her with the truth. But it was just as well. This
simply reinforced what she already knew—that she
shouldn't expect anything from him.

"You wanted to ask me something?" she said pointedly.

"I want to go back to Bitter End in the morning."

"Why?"

"We're missing something important there, Nell. I
can feel it, but I can't put my finger on it."

"I don't have time to waste. I've got work to do
around here."

He hesitated. "I need you."

"Why?" she cried again, standing with her back to
him. "You know the way now. You *don't* need me."

"I do," he said softly. "But I'll leave it up to you."
Having said that, he quietly left.

When morning arrived and the children were off to
school, Nell had a change of heart. This, she promised

herself, would be the last time. From then on, Travis was on his own.

"I'm glad you're coming," he said, smiling as she climbed into the sports utility vehicle beside him.

"We ran into a dead end," she muttered. "And if it were up to me, we'd drop the entire project now."

"You don't mean that."

It was true she didn't, but she refused to admit it.

They parked the same place they had before and made their way into the ghost town. Even before they reached Bitter End, Nell could feel the sensation approaching. Gradually it descended on her, the intensity mounting with each step she took.

"What are we looking for?" Nell asked in a whisper, standing close to his side. She'd prefer to keep her distance, but the town frightened her.

"I don't know yet," he said, his voice low.

As they stood in the center of the street in the middle of Bitter End, Travis surveyed the buildings. "Does anything strike you as familiar?" he asked after a moment, his voice slightly raised.

"No." Nothing had changed from the day before except her anxiety to leave, which had only increased.

"The tree!" he shouted, pointing down the street. He started for it, leaving her behind.

He stopped some yards from the large dead oak with its gnarled, twisted limbs.

"Wh-what about the tree?" she asked, breathless from running after him.

"Nell, don't you remember the quilt? That's the tree! You can tell by the trunk."

Travis walked slowly toward it. "Look. Nell, look."

He ran his finger over the rough crude letters in the dead wood.

Nell's swift intake of breath was the only sound.

There, carved into the side of the tree, was the word "cursed."

It came to Travis then, in a blinding flash. The quilt squares they'd found so puzzling held the key to whatever had happened in Bitter End.

"The quilt," he said. "The squares tell what happened to the town."

"A story quilt! I hadn't even thought of that." Nell's eyes went bright with excitement. It was all Travis could do not to kiss her right then and there. He resisted, with difficulty.

He might have kissed her, anyway, if he hadn't felt her withdrawing from him. The fact that he was a successful novelist had come to light at the worst possible moment. In retrospect, he realized he should have told her much sooner, but he'd enjoyed the anonymity. He appreciated being accepted and liked for the man he was and not for what he'd achieved.

Then, too, her unawareness of his identity, his success, had given him a chance to know her. His career hadn't intruded on their relationship. They'd simply become friends. Well, more than friends if he had his way.

Unfortunately he'd felt Nell retreating emotionally as soon as she'd learned the truth about him. She believed he'd misled her and he supposed he had, although he hadn't meant to. He'd planned to tell her in his own time. And now...

"Think," Nell said, biting her lower lip. "What else was on those quilt squares?"

Travis tried to remember, but his thoughts were on Nell, not on the quilt. There'd only been a handful, five or six squares. Obviously they weren't enough to complete the entire quilt, which meant some squares were missing, maybe forever lost.

"Okay, the oak tree. And one of the squares showed a grave marker," Nell said, counting them on her fingers.

"One of them showed something that resembled a dry riverbed," he recalled. "But there's no river around here."

"Gully Creek isn't far," she said with a thoughtful frown.

"It isn't unheard of for creeks to run dry," he added.

"What else?" Nell asked.

"A frog?"

"Yes, but a frog doesn't make sense," Nell said.

"If there was a creek here, there could have been frogs."

"Yes, but…" She shook her head. "The quilt sounded promising at first, but I'm beginning to have my doubts—especially about the square with a hangman's noose. What could that possibly mean?"

"I don't know," Travis admitted. Like her, he was feeling some reservations. "You said one of the squares was a grave marker, right?"

She nodded.

"Do you remember what it said?"

"Yes." Nell answered and took a deep breath. "It said Edward Abraham Frasier and there was a Bible reference."

"I don't suppose you remember the Bible reference."

She nodded. "Matthew 28:46."

It didn't mean anything to Travis. They'd have to

wait until they were back on the ranch and had access
to a Bible.

"'My God, my God, why have you forsaken me?'"
Nell quoted in a soft voice.

Travis was impressed. "Great," he said, and reached
for her hand, squeezing it gently. He intended to check
out the cemetery next to see if they could find the grave
marker.

"I…read that passage frequently after Jake's death,"
she whispered.

Travis remained silent, knowing this was a difficult
moment for her.

"Let's go look at the markers in the cemetery here
and see if we can find that name," she finally said.

The graveyard was behind the church, surrounded
by a sun-bleached cedar-rail fence. Several markers still
stood, crude crosses, a few headstones.

Travis wandered among the graves, but found nothing.

"It's impossible to read the names," Nell protested.
"Something might have been etched into the wood, but
you can't read it anymore."

Travis knelt in front of one headstone, choosing it
randomly. A rosebush bloomed nearby. The irony of it
didn't escape him—the only living plants in this town
were in the cemetery. God had a great sense of humor.

He could see that a name had once been visible on
the simple stone marker, and not knowing what else to
do, he ran the tip of his finger gently over it. After a
moment he could make out the first letter.

"W," he said aloud.

"Did you say something?" Nell asked, strolling to-

ward him. She stood at his side while he continued to
kneel in front of the marker.

"A," he said, his enthusiasm growing. "L... T, I
think... E... R."

"Walter?"

"That was his name." Travis glanced up at her. "Try
pressing your finger over the inscription," he said.

Nell did as he suggested, kneeling in front of another
grave, close to Travis. It wasn't easy; her hands were
callused from ranch work while his were more sensi-
tive. The most strenuous activity he used his hands for
was tapping computer keys.

"A!" she shouted triumphantly.

"Wonderful," he said. He removed a small notebook
and pen from his pocket. Walter E. Bastien was the first
name he entered. If he read the dates correctly, Walter
had died at age three.

"D... E... L... E," Nell completed excitedly. "Adele!"

Travis moved on to the next marker. They were able
to read nine names before they found Edward Abraham
Frasier. He'd died at age five. Of the ten names they'd
recorded, Travis noted that eight were children, who'd
all died before the age of seven.

"Life was hard in those days," Nell said soberly. "My
great-grandmother was one of ten children and only five
survived to adulthood."

"A fifty percent mortality rate."

"I couldn't bear to lose a child, not after..." She
didn't need to complete the thought.

"Well," Nell said abruptly, sitting back on her
haunches, "this is all very interesting, but what does
it mean?"

Travis didn't know and merely shrugged.

"How can we solve anything? We need to know what happened! Okay, so the quilt is somehow tied in to the town's history, but what does it tell us? Bitter End does indeed have a tree with the word 'Cursed' carved in the wood. And we found the grave marker for Edward Frasier, who's got to be an ancestor of Ellie's but it doesn't mean anything if we don't know all the facts."

"The tree's dead," Travis murmured.

"What else is new?" she said, sounding almost flippant. "Everything in this town is dead."

"I want to know why. What happened here? At one time this was a prosperous enough community, but something went very wrong. Something that no one's ever written about, so we're stuck with no documentation. Except…what about old newspapers?"

"If Bitter End ever printed a newspaper, whatever copies were published disappeared a long time ago."

"We don't know that." His research skills were beginning to kick in. "I'm thinking that if something horrendous happened, it would be reported elsewhere."

"Like where?"

"Perhaps in the Austin newspaper. Maybe San Antonio. It wouldn't do any harm to check it out."

"But how in heaven's name would we ever find that? Travis, it would take weeks of looking through microfilm."

"My dear," Travis said, slipping his arm around her waist, "haven't you ever heard of the Internet?"

Ellie was busy reading a cookbook when Glen walked into the kitchen, fresh from the shower. He skidded to a stop when he saw her and pretended to be terrified, shielding his face with both arms.

"All right, all right," she said dryly. "Very funny. But I'm not planning to poison you, if that's what you're thinking." Ellie's limited culinary skills had become a shared joke. She'd learned a few recipes but rarely ventured into new territory.

"Honey, I don't mind cooking."

Ellie knew that was true, but Glen's repertoire consisted primarily of roast beef, beef stew and spaghetti with meat sauce, except that he added ingredients not generally associated with those dishes—jalapeños, green olives and walnuts. He was also inventive when it came to salads.

"Where did you get the cookbook?" he asked.

"The library," Ellie said. She couldn't see investing a lot of money in the project until she was sure she was up to the task.

"Do I dare inquire what's for dinner?"

"Tamale pie, cooked in a kettle." She had all the ingredients assembled on the kitchen counter. Her sleeves were rolled up and she'd tucked a towel into her waistband. If she *looked* capable and in control, she figured she might *feel* that way.

"That's your first mistake," Glen said knowingly.

"What?"

"Following a recipe. Use your instincts."

"I don't have any," Ellie muttered. Her upbringing hadn't been traditional. From early childhood, it was understood that she'd be taking over the family business. Instead of spending time in the kitchen with her mother learning the conventional domestic skills, she'd been with her father learning about types of feed and tools and deworming medications.

"You've got instincts," Glen insisted. "You just don't know it yet. Here, let me read the recipe."

"Glen…" she protested, but knew it would do no good. In the months since their marriage, she'd managed to acquire a few skills. Dovie had given her cooking lessons and taught her the basics. Still, Glen continued to tease her.

"Tamale pie," he read over her shoulder. "Look at this," he said with disgust. "There's no mention of jalapeños."

"There's chili powder in the sauce."

"Instincts, Ellie, instincts."

"I'll add jalapeños as soon as I develop some," she said. "Instincts, I mean." She booted him firmly out of the kitchen. "Scoot. Go read the newspaper. Watch television. Worry about the price of beef—whatever—but leave me to my own devices."

He gave a disgruntled shrug, then did as she requested. She'd purposely chosen this recipe because it looked simple enough even for her. If all else failed, she had a frozen entrée tucked away in the freezer.

After reading the recipe twice, she started her task, remembering what Dovie had taught her. One step at a time. Everything went smoothly and she was beginning to think that there might be some Martha Stewart in her, after all. She'd actually enjoyed this, although the kitchen was a disaster. For now, she planned to bask in her success and leave the dirty dishes for later.

The beauty of this recipe was that the entire dinner was cooked on the stove. The cookbook warned against removing the lid and checking on the cornmeal topping until the required time had passed. While she waited, she glanced through the other recipes, finding three or four casseroles that looked tempting. Glen would eat his words, or more accurately, he'd eat her tamale pie and rave about it.

"How much longer?" Glen shouted from the living room.

"Not long."

"Are you making a salad?"

"I was thinking about it."

"Want any help?"

"Oh, all right." She sighed as though she'd made a major concession. In truth, she was pleased. Glen used his much-vaunted instincts to concoct salads, and tossed together the most amazing creations. He started with the traditional lettuce and tomatoes, then added whatever else he could find, including cheddar cheese, shredded carrot, sliced Bermuda onion and even seedless grapes.

"Cal mentioned something interesting the other day," her husband said, his head stuck inside the refrigerator. He reappeared, loaded with ingredients, both plain and exotic.

"Cal is always interesting."

"He said Nell and that reporter friend of hers are looking into solving the mystery of Bitter End."

This was news. "How?"

"He didn't say. At first I was opposed to the idea and said so."

"I'd rather they bulldozed the entire town and set it on fire," she said, not realizing until now that her feelings ran this strong. She'd been there once with Richard Weston, and that had been enough to last her two lifetimes. Never, ever would she return. Of course it didn't help that her companion had done his best to scare her half to death.

Richard had started by blindfolding her for the drive so she wouldn't be able to find the way on her own—as if she'd want to. When they arrived, he'd promptly disappeared. Then he'd popped up in front of her, frightening her so badly she'd nearly fainted.

"At first I felt it was best just to let things be," Glen said.

"You've changed your mind?"

He washed the lettuce and patiently tore it into small pieces. "Cal's right about Bitter End." His tone was thoughtful. "Ever since Richard was airlifted from the town, there's been plenty of speculation about it. Not many people had heard of it, before, but more and more have learned it's there. Because of Richard."

"So we have another thing to thank Richard Weston for," Ellie said sarcastically. It infuriated her to remember she'd actually dated that lowlife. He'd pretended to be enthralled with her, had even proposed marriage. On the other hand, though, if it wasn't for Richard, Ellie doubted she would have recognized how much she loved Glen.

Her husband had been equally blind. When he did finally figure out he was in love with her, he'd managed to humiliate her in front of the entire town. Naturally Richard had encouraged that. Even worse, he'd succeeded in convincing Glen that Ellie was going to marry *him*. That Glen actually believed it was a huge affront to her pride. But in the months since, he'd more than made it up to her.

Glen was a good husband, and when the time came, he'd make a good father. She loved him immensely, and her love grew stronger every day.

"In this instance," Glen said, "I do think we should

thank Richard. Bitter End has been a blight on our history for a lot of years."

"Something horrible happened there." One trip to that awful town had proved it. Just thinking about it made her skin crawl.

"But what?" Glen asked in challenge. "Isn't that the real mystery?"

"Yes," she agreed, but stopped herself from saying more. The timer on the stove went off, signaling dinner was ready. She cast an eye to her husband and sincerely hoped this meal turned out to be as appetizing as the cookbook had promised.

Glen finished preparing his salad, adding last-minute touches of almond slivers, cilantro and goat cheese, tossing everything together with a panache she'd never possess. They carried the meal to the kitchen table, and for a while were too busy eating to bother with conversation. Her tamale pie was pronounced an unqualified success and Ellie was thrilled.

"Aren't you the least bit curious about Bitter End's history?" Glen pressed.

"Yes," she admitted with some reluctance, "but at the same time I'm afraid."

"Of what?"

"Unearthing skeletons I'd prefer remained buried," she murmured. "Suppose it was my ancestors who were responsible? I'd never be able to hold up my head again."

"No one's going to blame you for something that happened over a hundred years ago."

"Don't be so sure."

"It could have been my family," Glen said, resting his fork beside his plate. "Or the Westons. Whatever made Richard the kind of person he is—well, that had to come from somewhere. There could be a whole lot of dirt disclosed."

"You still feel Nell and her...friend should go ahead with this?"

"Yes," he said, "for a lot of reasons. I'd rather deal with some embarrassment than have a kid get hurt out there because he's curious about the mystery." His voice grew uncharacteristically serious. "Secrets are dangerous, Ellie. They lead to fear and repression. Remember what the Bible says—'The truth shall make you free.'"

"The Bible," Ellie repeated. She'd found one among her dad's things. When she opened it, she'd read the names handwritten in the front. She'd studied the births and deaths that had been listed. One death had occurred in Bitter End. A boy of five, Edward Abraham Frasier. It was what had drawn her to the ghost town. She'd wanted to find his grave, but the markers had been impossible to read. Richard had lost patience and she'd given up, eager to escape the town and the dreadful feeling that had come over her while she was there.

"I found something else in my father's things," she said. "I don't think I showed it to you. A six-inch square of material fell out of the Bible."

"What kind of square?"

Ellie shrugged. "At first I thought it might be part of a quilt, but no one would make a quilt with this picture on it."

"What was it?"

"A giant grasshopper," she said. "Huge. The stitching was all very tiny and neat, but frankly it was quite ugly. For a while I thought of having it framed, seeing as it's so old, but eventually I decided against it. A grasshopper isn't something I want hanging in our bedroom."

"I don't know," Glen said, with a teasing glint in his eyes. "I find it rather romantic."

"Romantic?"

"I'm buggy over you."

Despite herself, Ellie laughed.

Glen laughed, too, but then his expression sobered. "I wonder if you should tell Nell and her writer friend about this."

Ellie wasn't sure yet if that was something she wanted to do.

Nell squinted at the computer screen, amazed that something smaller than a board game was capable of such magical feats. Travis had brought his laptop into the house, and by plugging in a few wires had connected it to her kitchen phone. Afterwards he'd reached the web site for one of the state universities and begun reviewing the files on state history.

After an hour she'd taken over the task. Sitting at the kitchen table, she'd become fascinated by what she was reading. So much information available with such little effort! It astonished her. She had to force herself to remember what they were looking for. She feared that even if she did find the answer, she wouldn't recognize it.

"Mom." The back door swung open and Jeremy appeared. He stopped short when he saw Travis, his delight unmistakable. "Travis!"

"Jeremy, my man, how's it going?" Travis held out his palm, and Jeremy slapped it.

Nell rolled her eyes. Before she could comment, the door opened again and Emma burst in. Seeing Travis, she squealed with pleasure and raced toward him. He lifted her into his arms and hugged her.

In less than three weeks' time, Travis Grant had worked his way into their hearts. And hers.

"I told my teacher who you really are," Jeremy announced on his way to the refrigerator.

"And?"

If Jeremy didn't notice the hesitation before Travis spoke, Nell did.

"She didn't believe me. That's the thing about teachers," her son said with all the wisdom of his years. "They get jaded because so many kids lie these days."

"Give me her name and address, and I'll have my publisher mail her an autographed book."

"Would you?" Excitement flashed in Jeremy's eyes.

"Will you mail one to me?" Emma asked.

"Sure," he said, putting her down.

Jeremy tossed her an apple, which Emma deftly caught. "You want a cookie?" he asked Travis. "They're some of Mom's best."

"Of *course* I want a cookie."

Emma brought a pitcher of milk from the refrigerator.

Soon the three sat at the table, chatting. They were so involved in their conversation, Nell thought she might as well be invisible. She smiled to herself. Despite her fears about Travis's leaving, she'd learned something this afternoon. A lesson from her own children.

Both Jeremy and Emma accepted that eventually he'd return to New York. Instead of fretting about it or complaining that he'd disrupted their lives, they were grateful for his visit. Grateful to have met him.

Nell, too, had plenty of reasons to be grateful to Travis. Not only had he pulled her out from her protective shell, he'd also warmed her heart. She knew what it was to feel passion again, to feel that quickened interest in life. To feel what a woman felt when she was falling in love with a man. Nell didn't flinch from the thought.

Another thing: her children's reactions to him revealed how much they needed a father figure, a male role model. For years she'd been bogged down in her grief and refused to see what should have been directly in front of her.

Dinner that night was an informal affair. Ruth was in town with friends playing bridge, and the kids were content with leftovers. While she assembled sandwiches, Travis showed Jeremy how to play a couple of computer games.

"I want to learn, too," Emma insisted impatiently.

"Wait your turn," Jeremy muttered, not removing his gaze from the screen.

Nell thought to remind both kids that there would be no computer after Travis left, in case they thought she'd run out and buy them one. Fortunately she stopped herself in time. Perhaps in a year or two, when the dude ranch was successful, she'd be able to afford a computer. The technology was fast becoming part of everyday life, and she would need one as her business grew. That, and a dishwasher.

Following dinner, Jeremy and Emma, with their usual protests, went upstairs to do homework. Nell was left alone in the kitchen with Travis. He sat at the table with the laptop while she washed up the few dishes they'd used.

"I owe you an apology," she said, surprising herself.

He lifted his eyes from the screen and she gave him a feeble smile. "I've had a rotten attitude recently."

"I need to apologize myself," he said. "I should've mentioned sooner exactly what kind of writer I am."

"That's your business, Travis, and none of mine. As you said the other night, it doesn't make any difference to who you are as a person." She turned and reached for another dish, drying it by hand. "I want to thank you for being so good with the kids. It's no wonder they enjoy your books so much."

"They're delightful kids."

"I think so," she said.

He pushed back his chair, scraping it against the floor. "You're delightful, too," he said, coming to stand beside her. He removed the plate and dish towel from her hand.

"Travis?" She looked up at him, not knowing what to expect. Then again, she did.

He kissed her just the way she knew he would and she allowed herself to be consumed by it. His hands were in her hair, his fingers buried in her braid.

He sighed heavily when he lifted his lips from hers. "Kissing you could become addictive."

"That's what you said about my cookies earlier." Her small attempt at humor was a gentle reminder that this kiss—in fact, everything between them—was to be taken lightly. As soon as they had the information they needed, they'd be able to work out the details regarding the events in Bitter End. And once the mystery was solved, Travis would return to New York.

And she'd return to life as she knew it, a little smarter and a little more capable of coping with the future.

He continued to hold her until they heard the sound

of footsteps racing down the stairs. They broke apart like guilty teenagers.

Jeremy walked into the kitchen, stopped and looked at the two of them. "Am I interrupting anything?"

Nell denied it with a shake of her head.

"I came for a glass of water," he said. A minute later he was gone.

Travis sat in front of the computer again. Nell sat next to him, reviewing the notes he'd taken and rereading her own. They'd found a number of references to Bitter End, but nothing concrete that pertained to the mystery.

Not yet, at any rate. Nell had a positive feeling, though; she was really beginning to enjoy this.

"Nell," Travis said, holding his finger against the computer screen.

"What is it?"

"This newspaper article from the *Brewster Review*—it's from 1879."

"But that's a year before Promise was founded."

"My point exactly." He got out of his chair. "Read it for yourself."

Ten

Nell slid onto the chair Travis had vacated and stared at the computer screen. Excitement bubbled up inside her. Was it possible Travis had stumbled onto the answer already?

As she scanned the first paragraph of the newspaper article, her spirits sank. Travis was looking too hard for a connection. She hated to be discouraging but could see nothing relevant.

"All this reports is the wrongful death of sixteen-year-old Moses Anderson in Bitter End."

"Continue reading," Travis said.

Nell returned her attention to the screen. "It says Moses was defending a saloon girl from an abusive drunk." Nell glanced up at him, a puzzled expression on her face.

"Read on."

Nell did so, mumbling a couple of lines aloud. "And the other men in the saloon sided with their friend." She gasped as she read the next paragraph. "The drunk and his friends dragged the young man outside and—" she looked up at Travis "—hanged him." Nell sighed at the brutality of such a deed. The boy was only sixteen. Nevertheless she didn't see how this one act of mob rule was connected to the troubles in Bitter End.

The question must have shown in her eyes because Travis asked, "Did you notice the teenager was a preacher's son?"

"Yes, but what makes you think this has anything to do with what happened to Bitter End?"

Travis's smile was wide. "The quilt. We were right, Nell—the mystery is linked to those quilt squares. Who better to curse a town than a man of God? The tree had the word 'Cursed' carved into it, remember?"

Of course she did. "Wasn't there another square with the hangman's noose? Maybe that's the connection— Moses being hanged." Nell's enthusiasm mounted. "Let's look at those quilt pieces again!"

"Good idea."

Travis followed her into the living room. She opened the cedar chest and removed the cardboard box. Nell set aside the folded sheet of muslin and placed the squares on the coffee table.

"What in heaven's name do a frog and a word carved in an oak tree have in common?"

Jeremy came down the stairs. "What are you doing?" he asked.

"Unraveling a mystery," Nell explained absently as she continued to study the quilt pieces.

"Why not put Moses Anderson's name on the tombstone, instead of Edward Abraham Frasier's?" Travis added, as though he was beginning to doubt his own theory.

"Who's Moses Anderson?" Jeremy asked, leaning forward to get a better look at the embroidered squares.

"Travis found a news article about him in an old newspaper," Nell murmured, concentrating on the squares.

"Off the Internet? Mom, I'm telling you, we gotta get a computer."

"Someday."

"Aw, Mom…"

"The river scene without a river," Nell muttered listening with only half an ear to her son's pleas.

"Did you notice that the stitching on the riverbank's sort of a rusty red?" Travis asked.

"Soil in the area is iron-rich," Nell explained, dismissing any significance in the choice of color.

"Moses turned the water into blood, remember," Jeremy commented. "We read about it in Sunday School last week."

"Moses did indeed," was Nell's vacant reply.

"Moses and his brother Aaron."

"That's it," Travis shouted, and threw his arms in the air. "Jeremy, you're a genius, a living breathing genius. That's it, that's the key." He gripped the boy's shoulders to hug him wildly. Then he reached for Nell, laughter spilling from him like water.

Jeremy and Nell stared at him as if he'd suddenly gone weak in the head.

"What are you talking about?" Nell demanded.

"The curse!" he shouted.

"What's Travis so excited about?" Emma asked from halfway down the stairs.

"I don't know how we could have been so blind." Now that Travis had stopped laughing, he clasped Nell around the waist and danced her about the room. Jeremy and Emma clapped and laughed.

"Travis, for the love of heaven, stop! Tell me."

Breathing hard, he draped his arms over her shoulders and rested his forehead against hers. "I can't believe we didn't see it sooner."

"See *what?*" she cried, growing more and more frustrated.

Travis turned her around so that she faced the coffee table. "Look at the quilt pieces again."

"I'm looking."

"What was the preacher's son's name?"

"Moses," she said.

"After his son was murdered, the preacher cursed the town."

"Yes." Her gaze went to the square with "Cursed" carved in the tree.

"Now look at the frog."

"I'm looking, I'm looking."

"Jeremy, bring me your Bible," Travis instructed.

The boy raced out of the room.

As soon as Travis mentioned the Bible, Nell understood. "Moses and the plagues."

Jeremy returned with his Bible and handed it to Travis, who started flipping pages in the Old Testament.

"Somewhere in the first part of Exodus," Nell said, fairly certain that was where the story of Passover was told.

"Here," Travis said, running his finger down the seventh chapter. First there's all this business about turning staffs into snakes, then Moses and Aaron did as the Lord commanded and hit the surface of the Nile with a rod, and the river turned to blood."

"Gully Creek became bloody?" That sounded a bit far-fetched to Nell.

"Maybe the water went bad and they couldn't drink it," Jeremy suggested.

"Or dried up," Travis said.

"What else happened in the Bible that ties to Bitter End?" she asked, eager now, reading over his shoulder. Travis skimmed through several chapters, listing the plagues that had befallen Egypt. The death of cattle, flies, hail and lightning, locusts, boils, crop failures were the ones described first.

"What was the one that came after the river turning into blood?" Jeremy asked.

"Frogs," Travis said triumphantly. "The land was covered with frogs."

"Not if the creek dried up." Someone had to show a little reason, Nell thought.

"I don't think we'll ever completely understand the dynamics of what happened."

"The grave marker," Nell said excitedly. "The five-year-old boy, remember?"

"Abraham Edward Frasier."

"Remember, it was the death of the firstborn sons that convinced Pharaoh to let the Israelites leave Egypt," Nell said.

"The children." Travis's voice was low. "Of the ten graves we were able to identify, eight were children." He paused. "The last plague was the death of the first-born sons," he said slowly.

As a widow, Nell knew she could survive any financial trial, bad weather or crop failure, if she still had her home and her land. The one thing she wouldn't be able to stand was losing her children. If *they* were at risk, nothing else mattered.

"That's why everyone left the town," she said confidently. "Their children were dying. The community had withstood everything else—the river drying up, the pestilence, the other trials. But no land, no town, no community was worth the loss of their children."

The phone rang just then and Emma ran to answer it. "Mom," she shouted as though Nell was in the barn, instead of the next room. "It's Ellie Frasier."

Wade McMillen sat at the desk in his study and tried to ignore the bright sunshine flooding the room. The most difficult part of his week was writing the Sunday sermon. While he enjoyed preaching, even enjoyed the research demanded in his work, he wasn't particularly fond of the effort that went into composing his sermons. Especially on a day as glorious as this one.

Putting aside his notes, he rose and walked over to his study window, gazing at the tree-lined streets of Promise. It was a changed town from the one he'd come to serve five years ago. And this past year had seen the most dramatic of those changes.

There'd been a number of weddings, sure to be followed by a rush of births. Just last week he'd been out to visit the Smiths' baby girl for the first time. Wade had watched Laredo, as the new father, rock Laura to sleep, crooning cowboy songs, instead of lullabies. The memory of that scene brought a smile to his lips even now.

Recently Grady Weston had proudly told him Caroline was pregnant. Wade was pleased; this was exactly the kind of happy news he'd been waiting to hear. Maggie would make a wonderful big sister. It would be nice, too, for the Smiths' daughter to have a cousin around the same age. Wade recalled how close he was to Les McMillen, a cousin only three months younger than he was. They'd been inseparable. In many ways he was closer to Les than his own brother, who was four years his junior.

It wouldn't surprise Wade any if Ellie and Jane, the wives of the Patterson brothers, showed up pregnant— and soon. He knew from the hints he'd heard Mary and Phil give their sons that the boys' parents were more than ready to become grandparents. Wade didn't think they'd need to wait much longer.

With his thoughts full of weddings and babies, Wade didn't realize he had visitors until he heard the voices outside his door. His secretary buzzed him on the intercom.

"Nell Bishop and Travis Grant are here to see you," Martha announced.

"Show them in." Wade knew Nell had a paying guest staying at Twin Canyons. Nell had briefly introduced him after service a couple of Sundays ago. Jeremy and Emma had been full of chatter about their guest the past few weeks, as well, but Wade hadn't met him yet.

His first sight of Travis Grant revealed a large man with a kind face.

"Wade McMillen," Wade said, and the two men exchanged handshakes. Wade gestured for Nell and Travis to sit down, which they did. Maybe he was getting to be an old hand at such things, but Wade felt he knew the reason for this unexpected visit.

One glance told him they were in love; he knew the signs. It was early, probably too early, for them to think about marriage. If that was what they were here to discuss, he'd feel obliged to suggest a long engagement. Nevertheless, Wade was pleased for Nell, very pleased indeed.

"What can I do for you?" Wade asked, leaning back in his leather chair.

"We've come to talk to you about Bitter End," Nell said.

Wade frowned. That was the last subject he'd expected her to mention. The ghost town that had been the cause of so much trouble lately, what with Richard Weston having holed up there. Sheriff Hennessey and the town council had combined their efforts to keep things quiet, but information always seemed to leak out, anyway.

"You do know about the ghost town, don't you?" Travis asked.

"Yes. Have you been there?" The question was directed at Travis, but Nell answered.

"We both have. Twice," she added.

"Actually three times."

Nell nodded. "Three times."

Good grief, they already sounded like an old married couple.

Nell looked at Travis and her eyes sparkled with excitement and happiness. "We think we've solved the mystery of why everyone left Bitter End."

"The town was cursed," Travis explained.

"Cursed?"

"By a preacher whose sixteen-year-old son was hanged when a mob of rowdy drunks got out of hand."

Wade hated to discourage them. In the Wild West it wasn't uncommon for a preacher to be credited with the ability to rain fire and brimstone down upon the backs of sinners. There were usually logical reasons for these supposedly supernatural events, but they were cheerfully overlooked.

"His name was Moses," Nell supplied.

"The preacher's?"

"No, the teenager who was hanged."

The violence of the Old West never ceased to distress Wade, but then all he had to do was take a walk through an inner-city slum to appreciate that, in certain ways, humanity hadn't advanced much.

"When the mob of drunks hanged the boy, the preacher came to the town and cursed it with the plagues of Egypt," Nell said.

"That's our theory, anyway," Travis added.

Wade was willing to listen, but he didn't hold out much hope that this was really the reason the town had been abandoned all those years ago. "How do you know about the plagues?"

"From the story quilt."

Nell and Travis glanced at each other as if to decide who should explain the role played by this quilt. Apparently it was decided that Nell would, because she continued. "Ruth had a cedar chest in the attic that was given to her after her mother-in-law died almost fifty years ago. Inside it, we found the makings of a quilt. The backing was intact, but there was only a handful of completed squares."

"We found only six, but we knew there had to be others."

"There were," Nell said, her face glowing with enthusiasm. "Ellie Frasier phoned and told us about an embroidered square she'd found in her father's Bible."

"One with a giant grasshopper," Travis explained.

"Locusts," Wade murmured.

"Exactly."

"We're convinced," Travis said, pausing to look at

Nell, who nodded eagerly, "that the final plague, the one that drove the families away from Bitter End was some kind of epidemic that killed their children. By now, the residents had endured one tribulation after another— bugs, weather problems, failed crops…"

"The quilt told you all this?" Wade asked.

"Yes," Nell said, "it explained everything. Well, almost everything."

"Go on." Wade motioned to Travis. "I didn't mean to interrupt you."

"When the children started dying, the people who were left panicked, packed up everything they owned and moved. Canned goods still remain on the store shelves, so my guess is they had a big meeting and made the decision to get out together immediately."

"Drought, disease, pestilence," Wade murmured. "I'd leave, too."

"It's an incredible story," Nell said, and glanced at Travis, her pride evident. "Travis is going to write about it."

"This is exactly the type of story I've been waiting to find. For years I've been writing for juveniles and I've searched for the right vehicle to cross over from children's books to adult fiction."

"You aren't going to stop writing for kids, are you?" Nell asked, looking distressed.

"No, they're my audience, and I'll always write for them. But the story of Bitter End gives me an opportunity to make my mark with another readership."

This exchange was lost on Wade. He knew Travis was a writer, but had assumed he wrote for a newspaper. Rather than ask a lot of questions, he narrowed it down to one. "Was there something you needed from me?"

The two of them stared at him as though they'd forgotten he was there. "We want you to bless Bitter End," Nell said.

"Bless it?"

"That's what the town needs," Travis interjected. "And according to what Nell tells me, Promise will benefit from it, too."

Wade wasn't sure there was anything to this curse business. All the disasters Travis and Nell had described were probably nothing more than an unfortunate set of coincidences. Superstitions ran deep back then, and people put credence in matters they shouldn't. But it wouldn't hurt to bless the town. He'd be happy to do it.

Three days later, Wade stood in the middle of Bitter End. With him were several members of the town council, Sheriff Frank Hennessey, the Patterson brothers and their wives, Grady and Caroline Weston, Nell Bishop and her writer friend, and Laredo Smith. It was unlikely this many people had congregated here in more than a hundred years. Each had come for his or her own reasons. And almost everyone who'd accompanied Wade was related to the original settlers in one way or another.

Bitter End. Not exactly a promising name for a frontier settlement. As Wade remembered it, the town had gotten its name from the first settlers, who'd arrived by wagon train. The journey had been long and arduous, but eventually they'd reached the land of their dreams. Unfortunately, due to the hardships they'd suffered on the journey, many of their dreams had turned bitter.

As soon as he set foot in the town, Wade had felt a gloom and a darkness settle over him, even though the day was bright and sunny. He tried to ignore it and proceeded with the ceremony.

Once everyone was gathered around him, he opened his Bible and read a passage. As he spoke the words, he felt the oppression loosen its grip on him.

If the preacher a hundred years ago had used the Old Testament, filled with its judgments and laws, to curse the land, then he'd bless it from the New Testament. Freedom from bondage and judgment would be his prayer.

Wade's voice rang loud and clear down the lifeless streets. When he'd finished reading, he bowed his head. The others followed his lead. Wade prayed that God would smile down on this land once more and make it a place of love, instead of hate, a home of joy, instead of sadness.

A chorus of amens followed when he finished.

Laredo Smith stepped forward, carrying a bucket, shovel and a budding rosebush. "Savannah couldn't be here today, but she wanted me to plant this close to the tree where the boy was hanged."

"That's a wonderful idea," Nell said. Then she pointed to the charred marks on the church steeple. "That was one of the plagues—lightning and hail."

Wade was fast becoming a believer of this incredible tale. He'd studied the quilt pieces—including a seventh one that had been found by Dovie, an illustration of lightning striking a church. And he'd checked out the Internet sites identified by Travis. The more he read and heard about Bitter End, the more everything added up.

"The feeling's not as strong," Wade heard Ellie Patterson murmur to her husband.

"I noticed that, too," Dr. Jane added.

Wade smiled to himself as the assembled group headed back to the highway where the cars were parked.

Wade enjoyed the way these friends talked and joked with each other, but he noted that Nell Bishop and Travis Grant appeared strangely quiet. They were the ones who deserved the credit for solving this mystery. Over the past few days, they'd been the center of attention, and while Nell seemed to be uncomfortable in the limelight, Travis was clearly in his element.

It was often that way with couples, Wade had observed. One shy, the other outgoing. One sociable, the other private. The law of opposites—the wonderful balance that brought stability into a relationship.

As they approached their vehicles, Travis stepped up to Wade. "I'd like to thank you again for all your help."

"The pleasure was mine," Wade said, and meant it.

"I'll be leaving Wednesday morning, and I wanted to take the opportunity to say goodbye," Travis went on.

That explained Nell's dour look. Travis was returning to New York City, a city far removed from this land of sagebrush and ghost towns and tales of the Wild West.

"The best of luck with your book," Wade said. "Keep in touch."

Travis glanced in Nell's direction and responded with a noncommittal shrug.

Wade couldn't help wondering what had happened between the two. Whatever it was, he felt saddened that they didn't have more of an opportunity to explore their love. Although he was far from an expert in the area of romance, Wade had sensed they were well suited.

"You're leaving?" The question came from Grady Weston.

Travis nodded. "I've been away far longer than I expected as it is."

"You're not going to let him drive off into the sunset, are you?" Caroline pressured Nell.

It seemed every eye turned to the widow. "As Travis said, he needs to get back." Her tone was stiff. Then she turned away.

Travis stuffed a stack of shirts in his suitcase, not showing any particular care. He was a patient man, but he'd been tried to the very limits of his endurance. Beyond!

Nell acted as though his return to New York was cause for celebration. She'd gone so far as to throw him a farewell dinner party. She'd invited her friends, and the last he heard a dozen people had promised to show.

All day she'd been in the kitchen, cooking up a storm, baking, chopping, sautéing. His last hours in Texas, and the woman he loved had her head buried in a cookbook.

Not that he didn't appreciate the effort. It was a kind gesture, but spending the evening with a crowd wasn't how he wanted it. He'd hoped to have a few minutes alone with Nell, but that wasn't to be. In fact, she'd made it quite plain that she *didn't* want to be alone with him. Fine. He was a big boy; he knew when he'd worn out his welcome.

"Do you need any help?" Jeremy asked as he came into the bunkhouse.

Travis zipped up his bag. "Thanks, but I've got everything packed."

The boy at least had the common decency to show some regret at Travis's departure. Emma, too, had moped around the house from the moment she walked in the door. She followed her brother into the bunkhouse.

"Hey, Emma," Travis said. "Why the sad face?"

Her lower lip quavered. "I don't want you to go."

"He *has* to go," Jeremy answered on his behalf.

"Do you?" Emma asked, her eyes wide and forlorn.

Travis opened his mouth to answer, but Jeremy beat him to the punch. "That's what Mom said, remember? His work and his whole life are in New York." Jeremy sounded as though he'd memorized his mother's response. A very reasonable response, he had to admit— but it wasn't what he wanted to hear.

"Mom said we're going to have lots of guests in the next few weeks," Emma told him.

"She's right," Travis said. Nell would have the dude ranch in full swing before long.

"We're bound to get attached to lots of folks," Jeremy said, again echoing his mother's words, Travis suspected.

Attached. Nell thought the relationship he shared with Jeremy and Emma was just one in a long list of attachments. The woman didn't have a clue, he thought angrily. He loved those kids! Her, too.

And all she saw him as—or *wanted* to see him as— was a paying customer at Twin Canyons Ranch. Which made him the first of many wannabe cowboys.

All he needed was some encouragement from Nell. Then he'd stay. Just one word of encouragement. Two at the most. *Don't go* would have sufficed. Instead, she was so pleased to see him off she was throwing a party. It was hard for a man to swallow.

The dinner guests started arriving at five. Nell had

the front yard set up with tables and chairs. In addition to all the food she'd been cooking, her friends and neighbors bought over a variety of tasty dishes—salads and casseroles, pies and cakes.

Once dinner was served, they seated themselves at the tables and ate. Ruth sat next to Travis. He almost had the impression that she was waiting for him to do something—but what? After the meal Travis went around to pay his respects to the people he was just beginning to know. He seemed to hit it off with Grady Weston best. It was a shame to call a man a friend in one breath and tell him goodbye in the next.

Travis didn't know what Nell found so all-fired important, but he didn't see her the entire meal. As far as he could figure, she'd hidden herself in the kitchen where she'd been all day.

Before he could do anything about it, Grady joined him, and they exchanged pleasantries for several minutes. Then Grady grew strangely quiet. "What time are you going back to New York?"

"First thing in the morning," Travis said. His flight was late in the afternoon, but he had a three-hour drive ahead of him, plus the rental car to return.

"Do you…anticipate seeing Richard again?"

So that was where this conversation was headed. "I don't expect I will."

Grady nodded, his look grave.

"Would you like me to check up on him now and again?" Travis offered.

"He's a criminal and he's paying for his crimes, but dammit all, he's still my brother." Grady's voice dropped.

"Hey, no problem, and I don't need to say I'm there on your behalf."

"It isn't on my behalf, so to speak," Grady was quick to correct him. "I just want to be sure—I guess I'm looking for a change in him."

"Is it possible?"

"I pray it is," Grady said. He stood, patted Travis on the back and left the table to return to his wife.

The laughter and chatter continued for a while, and then people packed up their leftovers and were gone. Travis was grateful. Nell couldn't avoid him forever. He gathered up the serving dishes and carried them into the house.

Nell was washing dishes, her arms elbow-deep in soap suds.

"That was a wonderful dinner," he said.

"Thank you."

"I don't think anyone's gone to so much trouble to send me off." He realized he must have sounded a little sarcastic, but if she noticed, she ignored it.

"It wasn't any trouble," Nell countered. "Besides, the community owes you a debt of thanks. If it wasn't for you, no one would know what happened in Bitter End."

"You worked just as hard."

"You dragged me kicking and screaming into this project, remember?"

That wasn't *exactly* how Travis recalled it. She'd been reluctant, true, but had willingly enough accompanied him. They'd made a great team.

"I'm going to miss you," he said, and wished to hell she'd turn around so he could look at her. Instead, she stood with her back to him and revealed none of her thoughts.

"Me and Emma got all the trash picked up," Jeremy called from the living room.

"It's bedtime," she told them. "Go upstairs and wash."

"Aw, Mom."

"You heard me."

Nell must have removed the plug from the kitchen drain because he heard the water swish and gurgle. She turned to reach for a towel and beamed him a smile so dazzling it startled him.

"What time are you leaving?" she asked.

"Around six."

She nodded. "I probably won't see you, then."

He was hoping she'd suggest they have coffee together before he left. Just the two of them. No kids. No Ruth. Just them.

She didn't offer.

Travis forced himself to smile. "I guess this is it, then."

"This is it."

They stood and stared at each other for an awkward moment.

"It's been…great," Nell said at last.

He nodded. "I'd like to kiss you goodbye, Nell," he said.

She hesitated, then floated easily into his arms. When their mouths found each other, the kiss was a blend of need and sadness, of appreciation and farewell.

When she slid out of his arms, Travis was shocked by how much he missed her there. He might as well get accustomed to it, for she gave no indication that she cared to see him again. Not one word, not one sign.

"You'll keep in touch?" he asked, hoping she'd at least be willing to do that.

"The kids would love to hear from you."

Her words hit their mark. "But not you?"

"I didn't say that."

"Would *you* enjoy hearing from me?" It was damn little to ask.

She lowered her gaze and nodded.

"Was that so hard, Nell?"

She looked up at him and he was surprised to see tears glistening in her eyes. "Yes," she whispered. "It was very hard."

Eleven

It did no good to pretend anymore. Nell sat out on her front porch, watching the sunset. Travis had been gone a week and it felt like ten years. She'd fallen in love with a greenhorn. Travis Grant might know everything there was to know about computers, but he'd barely figured out which side of a saddle was up.

"A writer," Nell muttered, staring at the sky. She was thoroughly disgusted with herself. Everything she'd ever wanted in this life she'd had with Jake. But he'd died, and she was so lonely. She hadn't even realized *how* lonely until that New Yorker kissed her. All the men who'd pestered her for a date in the past couple of years and she hadn't felt the slightest interest. Then Travis came into her life and before she knew it she was in love. It felt like she'd been sucker-punched.

"Are you thinking about Travis again?" Ruth asked, standing just inside the screen door.

"No," Nell denied vehemently, then reluctantly confessed. "Yeah." *Yeah.* Now Travis had her doing it. If he'd stayed much longer, she'd sound just like a Yankee.

"You gonna write him?"

"No." Of that much Nell was sure.

"Why not?"

"I can't see where it'd do any good."

"Oh, Nell."

"He's from New York. He wouldn't be happy in Promise and this is where the kids and I belong." The situation was impossible, and the sooner she accepted that, the better it would be for everyone. Travis Grant was a writer who lived in the center of the publishing world. He'd come to Texas to research a book, not find himself a wife and take on a ready-made family.

She was convinced that in time she'd fall in love with someone from around here. Someone who stirred her heart. Travis had shown her it was possible; now all she had to do was find the right man.

"Nell, dear, I still think you should write him a letter." Ruth sat in the rocker next to Nell and took out her crocheting.

Even if she did write Travis, Nell mused, she wouldn't know what to say. Really, what was there to write about? Bedsides, he might misread her intent and assume she was asking something of him.

Eventually she'd get over him and her heart would forget. Any night now she'd stop dreaming about him. Any day now he'd fade from her thoughts.

No, she most definitely wasn't going to write. If he wanted to continue the relationship, then he'd have to contact her first.

Well…maybe just one letter, she thought. Just to be sure he arrived home safe and sound. And she could always ask him about the book. One letter, but only one.

That couldn't do any harm.

* * *

Travis squinted at the computer screen, then yawned and pinched the bridge of his nose. He'd been home all of eight days and he'd already written the first fifty pages of his new book—the book for adults. The words seemed to pour out of him. He couldn't get them down fast enough.

But then, he'd always been able to escape into a story when his life was miserable. It was one of the blessings of being a writer—and one of the curses. His stomach growled in angry protest and he realized it'd been twenty-four hours since his last meal.

He walked barefoot in the direction of his kitchen, surprised to realize it was morning. It was 6:00 a.m. according to the clock on the mantel. From the view through the windows in his high-rise apartment, he saw that the city was just waking up. In Texas Nell would be— He stopped, refusing to think about Nell, or Jeremy or Emma. They were out of his life and that was the way it had to be. The way *she* wanted it. That had been made more than clear before he left Promise.

Promise. Yeah, right. They should have named the town Heartache.

His stomach growled again, more insistently this time, and Travis headed toward the refrigerator. It shouldn't have come as any surprise to find nothing he'd seriously consider eating. He was rummaging through his pantry shelves when the apartment intercom buzzed. He muttered under his breath as he heard his ex-wife's voice. Still muttering he waited at the door to let her in.

"You've been home for a week and I haven't heard from you," she said accusingly. "I thought I'd stop by on my way to work to greet the prodigal son." She'd always been an early riser, like him, and generally got to the office before seven.

"I've been working." He might not have been as friendly if she hadn't come bearing gifts. She carried a sack from his favorite bakery and a takeout latte. At the moment he would have thrown his arms around a terrorist offering food.

"You eating?"

He reached for the sack. "I am now."

Valerie chuckled and followed him into the kitchen. She was a lovely-looking woman, but Travis was now immune. Unfortunately she was cold and calculating, and about as different from Nell Bishop as a woman could get.

"So what'd you find out about that ghost town?" Val asked.

Travis quickly devoured two jelly-filled doughnuts, pausing only long enough to inhale. His stomach thanked him, and he settled back with the latte. Between sips, he filled in the details, casually mentioning Nell. He acknowledged her help in solving the puzzle and said nothing about his feelings toward her.

Valerie might have remarried, but she tended to believe that Travis remained stuck on her. He couldn't be bothered setting her straight.

"Who's this Nell?"

Damn, but it was impossible to hide anything from her! "A woman I met."

"You in love with her?"

Leave it to Val to get directly to the point. "Maybe." He licked the jelly from his fingertips rather than meet her gaze.

"Travis," she chided. "I know you, and 'maybe' isn't in your vocabulary."

"She was a…nice diversion," he said, evading her question. If he was truly in love with Nell, he'd walk on hot coals before he'd admit it to his ex-wife. The one who deserved to know first would be Nell. However, at this point, it seemed unlikely that their relationship would go any further.

"Did you meet Richard Weston's family?" Val asked.

Travis nodded. "They're good people."

"Actually Richard's not half-bad himself."

Travis's gaze narrowed. He was surprised she didn't recognize Weston for the kind of man he was. He'd credited her with better judgment. "What's going on?" he asked.

Val shrugged. "Nothing. How can it? He's behind bars."

"You actually like this guy?"

Val crossed her legs and smiled. "I know what he did, and while he isn't exactly a candidate for a congressional medal of honor, I find him rather charming."

Snakes could be charming, too. Frankly Travis didn't like hearing her talk this way. Recently Val had implied that she and husband number two weren't getting on, but surely she wouldn't get mixed up with a prisoner. "Time for a reality check, Val."

Her eyes flared. "You're one to talk," she snapped. "You're in love with some cowgirl widow."

"I didn't say I loved her."

"You didn't have to. It's written all over you."

Travis exhaled sharply. He had better things to do than get involved in a useless argument with his ex-wife. "All I'm saying is be careful with Richard, all right? He's a user."

"Of course," she said, and gave Travis a demure smile. "We both know I'm too self-centered to do anything that's ultimately going to hurt me." She stared at him. "You, on the other hand, might be tempted to do something foolish about this cowgirl of yours."

"She isn't mine." Travis didn't want to talk about Nell.

"Have you heard from her since you left?"

He sighed. "Do you mind if we talk about something else?"

Val's delicately shaped eyebrows lifted. "You really are taken with her, aren't you?"

"So what if I am?"

"Are you going to leave it at that?"

"Probably," he said, his control slipping.

"You could always write her. Or call."

"And say what?"

"Don't look at me—you're the one who works with words. Seems to me you should have plenty to say." She glanced at her wrist and leaped to her feet. "Gotta run. Court this morning. 'Bye darling." She kissed his cheek and was out the door.

He wasn't going to write Nell, he decided. He would if there was anything to say, but there wasn't. It'd be a cold day in hell before he let another woman walk all over his heart. And really, when it came right down to it, he and Nell didn't have a thing in common. Not one damn thing.

Well…maybe one letter to ask about the kids and Ruth. And he did plan to send Jeremy and Emma autographed books. He'd keep the letter short and sweet, thank her for putting him up, that sort of thing. One letter wouldn't hurt. But only one.

Nell's gaze fell on the calendar hanging on the bulletin board by the phone. If she'd calculated right, her letter to Travis should arrive in New York City that day. She'd agonized over what to say and in the end had made it a chatty friendly letter. At least that was what she hoped. Her one fear was that her real feelings shone between every line.

Ruth walked into the kitchen. "I picked up the mail while I was in town," she said as she set down her purse and a shopping bag. "Do we know anyone in New York City?" she asked coyly.

Travis. Nell's heart thumped. Because she didn't want Ruth to know how excited she was, she casually reached for the stack of mail, sorting through the various solicitations and bills until she found the envelope. It *was* from Travis.

She stared at it so long Ruth said, "Well, for heaven's sake, girl, open it."

Nell didn't need to be told twice. She ripped open the envelope, her hands shaking with eagerness. Her eyes quickly skimmed the first typed page and glanced at the second. Once she saw how much he'd written, she pulled out a chair and sat down. She read slowly, wanting to savor each word, treasure each line. Like her, he was chatty, personable, yet slightly reserved.

"Well?" Ruth said.

"You can read it if you want."

Ruth looked downright disappointed. "Are you telling me he didn't say anything… personal?"

"Not really." Then again, he had, but it was between the lines, not on the surface. His letter really said that he missed her. That he was thinking of her, working too many hours, trying to get on with his life. Nell identified all this because she'd conveyed identical things to him—in what she'd written and what she hadn't.

"There's a package here, as well, for Jeremy and Emma," Ruth said.

In her rush to read Travis's letter Nell hadn't noticed.

"Are you going to write him back?" Ruth asked.

Nell nodded, but she'd wait a couple of days first. It might look as if she'd been anxious to hear from him if she replied too soon. Despite that, she sat down at the dinner table that night and wrote him a reply. The kids each wrote a thank-you note for the autographed books, and it didn't seem right to delay those. Since she was mailing something to him anyway, and her letter was already written, she sent it off the next morning. It wasn't a special trip into town; she had other errands so it worked out conveniently. Or so she told herself.

Ruth was standing on the porch grinning from ear to ear when Nell returned. "You've got company," Ruth called when she climbed out of the pickup. She glanced at the dark sedan parked near the bunkhouse.

Ruth's smile blossomed as Travis opened the screen door and joined her on the porch.

"Hello, Nell," he said, grinning.

He wore a Stetson, faded blue jeans and rich-looking cowboy boots. He might not be a working cowboy, but he was the best-damn-looking one she'd seen in a very long while. It took all the restraint she could muster not to run straight into his arms.

"Are you surprised?" he asked.

She nodded, afraid she couldn't say anything intelligible.

"I'll leave you two to sort everything out," Ruth stated matter-of-factly, and started toward the house.

Her eyes pleaded with Ruth not to leave her, but the older woman was oblivious to her silent cries for help.

Nell didn't know what to think, what to say. Her heart raced, but she was afraid to read anything into Travis's unexpected visit. Maybe he was in the area for more research or for business or...

She walked over to the porch and sat down on the top step.

"Mind if I join you?" he asked before he sat down next to her.

"Of course not."

"You look wonderful," he said softly.

She nodded her thanks for the compliment. "Were you in the area...?" She had to ask.

"No."

"I... I got your letter." She wanted to tell him how excited she was when she saw it, but couldn't manage the words.

"I got yours, too. That's the reason I'm here."

"My letter?" He must have booked the flight out of New York a minute after he'd read it.

"You love me, Nell, don't you?"

She nodded slowly.

"I love you, too," he whispered, and reached for her hand.

"But—"

"Hear me out," he interrupted. "You're about to list all the reasons it's impossible for us to be together, but there's nothing you can say that I haven't thought of myself. We're different, but it's a good kind of different. We're good together, a team."

"But—"

"Together we solved a hundred-year-old mystery. There's a lesson in it, too. The people who left Bitter End were looking to make a new life, a new start, and put the pain of the past behind them. I'm offering you the same opportunity—and taking advantage of it myself. We belong together, Nell. You and me and Ruth and the kids."

"But—"

"I'm almost finished," he promised, and drew in a deep breath. "It'll be a new life for all of us. I love you, Nell. I want to marry you."

"I can't live in the city," she blurted.

"You won't have to."

"You mean that?" It was almost more than she dared believe.

"Not if you don't want to. I can work anywhere, you know. One of the benefits of being a writer." He paused. "So?"

"I'll marry you." She'd known that the minute she saw him standing on the porch.

"You don't have any questions?" He seemed almost disappointed that she wasn't going to argue with him.

"Yeah. One." She smiled. "Just how much longer do I have to wait for you to kiss me?"

Within a single beat of her heart, Travis had wrapped her in his arms. His mouth was hard and hungry over hers, and Nell let herself soak in his love. He loved her, really loved her! And he was right that it was time to put aside the past and start again.

"How soon can we arrange the wedding?" he whispered against her throat.

"Soon," she said.

Travis chuckled. "But not soon enough to suit me." Then he kissed her again.

* * * * *

LONE STAR BABY

One

Amy Thornton was out of money, out of luck and out of hope. Well, she had a little cash left, but her luck had definitely run out, and as for her reserves of hope—they were nonexistent. When the Greyhound bus rolled into the bowling-alley parking lot in Promise, Texas, she stayed in her seat. Disinterested and almost numb, she stared out the window.

Promise seemed like a friendly town. June flower baskets, filled to overflowing with blooming perennials, hung from the streetlights. People stopped to chat, and there was a leisurely, almost festive atmosphere that Amy observed with yearning. Smoke wafted from a barbecue restaurant, and farther down the street, at Frasier Feed, chairs were set up next to a soda machine. A couple of men in cowboy hats and boots sat with their feet propped against the railing; they appeared to find something highly humorous. One of them threw back his head, laughing boisterously. His amusement was contagious and Amy found herself smiling, too.

A couple of people boarded the bus. As soon as

they'd taken their seats, the bus doors closed. "Next stop is Brewster," the driver announced.

"Excuse me!" Amy cried, and surprised herself by leaping to her feet. "I want to get off here."

"Here?" The driver looked at her as if he thought he'd misunderstood. The bus had sat there for fifteen minutes without her saying a word.

"Yes," she said, as though Promise had been her destination all along. "I'll need my suitcase."

Muttering irritably under his breath, the driver climbed out of the bus, opened the luggage compartment and extracted her travel-worn case.

Five minutes later, choking on the bus's exhaust, Amy stood in the parking lot, wondering what madness had possessed her. She was homeless, without a job and nearly six months pregnant. She didn't know a soul in this town, yet she felt compelled to start her new life here. Away from her mother. Away from Alex. Away from all the unhappiness that had driven her out of Dallas.

Austin had been her original destination. Her mother's cousin lived there—not that Beverly Ramsey was expecting her. But she *was* the only other family Amy had. Moving to Austin had seemed preferable to staying in Dallas, and despite the pregnancy, she'd felt confident she could find employment fairly quickly, if not in an accounting office, then perhaps as a temp. Anything would do for now, as long as she managed to meet her expenses until she located something more permanent. Naturally she'd hoped that Beverly would invite her to stay until she found an apartment. Two weeks, she'd promised herself. No longer. Just until she was back on her feet. Yet the thought of calling her mother's cousin mortified Amy. Her mother had sponged off Beverly's kindheartedness for years. It went against everything in Amy to ask for help. She'd rather make it on her own.

If only she knew what to do.

Promise, Texas. Holding her suitcase with both hands, she glanced down Main Street again. If ever she'd needed a promise, it was now. A promise and a miracle—or two.

The baby kicked and Amy automatically flattened her hand against her stomach. "I know, Sarah, I know," she whispered to her unborn child. She hadn't had an ultrasound but chose to think of her baby as a girl and had named her Sarah. "It's not the smartest move we've made, is it? I don't know a soul in this town, but it looks like the kind of place where we could be happy."

Her stomach growled and she tried to remember the last time she'd eaten. A small poster advertising $1.99 breakfast special showed in the bowling-alley window. Apparently there was a café inside.

The small restaurant was busy; almost all the seats were taken, but Amy was fortunate to find an empty booth. A waitress handed her a menu when she brought her a glass of water and glanced at her suitcase.

"You miss the bus, honey?" she asked. "You need a place to wait?"

"Actually I just got off," Amy said, touched by the other woman's concern. "I'll take the breakfast special."

"It's the best buy in town," the woman, whose name tag identified her as Denise, said as she wrote the order down on her pad.

Seeing that the waitress was the friendly sort, Amy asked, "Do you happen to know of someone who needs a competent bookkeeper?"

Denise gnawed thoughtfully on her lip. "I can't say I do, but I'm sure there's a job for you in Promise if you're planning to settle here."

The news cheered Amy as much as the welcome she felt. Already she was beginning to believe she'd made the right decision. Promise, Texas, would be her new address—the town where she'd raise her baby. Where she'd make a life for them both. "I can do just about anything," Amy added, not bothering to disguise her eagerness, "and I'm not picky, either."

"Then I'm sure all you need to do is ask around."

A rancher sitting at a table across from Amy caught Denise's eye and lifted his empty coffee mug. "Be right with you, Cody," she said, then looked back at Amy. "Tex will have your meal out in a jiffy."

"Thanks for your help," Amy said, grateful for Denise's encouragement and kindness. As she waited, she found herself fighting the urge to close her eyes. She staved off a yawn as her meal arrived.

The eggs, toast and hash browns tasted better than anything she'd ever eaten. She hadn't realized how hungry she was and had to force herself to eat slowly. When she'd finished the meal, Amy left her money on the table and included a larger than usual tip in appreciation for Denise's welcoming helpfulness.

As she stood up to leave, the rancher Denise had called Cody sent her a curious glance. He smiled in her direction until he noticed the slight rounding of her abdomen, then his eyes widened and he abruptly turned the other way. Amy shook her head in amusement.

Taking Denise's advice, she walked down Main Street and looked for Help Wanted signs posted in store windows. She saw none, and it occurred to her that it might not be a good idea to apply for a position, suitcase in hand. Her first priority was finding a place to live. Besides, her feet hurt and the suitcase was getting heavier by the minute.

That was when Amy saw the church. It could have appeared on a postcard. Small and charming, it was built of redbrick and had wide, welcoming steps that led up to arched double doors. They were open, and although she felt silly thinking this, the church seemed to be inviting her in.

Amy soon found herself walking toward it. Lugging her suitcase up the stairs, she entered the vacant church and looked around. The interior was dark on one side, while rainbow-hued sunlight spilled in through stained-glass windows on the other.

Silently she stepped inside, slipped into a back pew and sat down. It felt good to be off her feet and she gave an audible sigh, followed by a wide yawn. She'd rest a few minutes, she decided. Just a few minutes…

The male voice that reached her came out of nowhere. Amy bolted upright. Her eyes flew open and she realized she'd fallen asleep in the pew.

"I beg your pardon," she said, instantly feeling guilt. It took her a moment to discern anything in the dim interior. When her eyes had adjusted, she saw a tall rugged-looking man standing in the church aisle, staring down at her. He resembled a rancher, not unlike the one she'd seen in the café, except that he wore a suit and a string tie.

"Is there a problem?" he asked, his voice gentle.

"No." She shook her head. "None." Flustered, she stood clumsily and grabbed for her suitcase.

"My sermons might be boring, but people generally wake up before Thursday afternoon." His smile unnerved her.

"I didn't mean to fall asleep. I closed my eyes and the next thing I knew, you were here." She glanced at her watch; she'd drifted off for at least twenty minutes, although it felt more like twenty seconds.

"You don't have anything to apologize for," the man told her kindly. "Are you sure there isn't anything I can do to help?"

"How about a miracle or two?" She hadn't meant to sound so flippant.

"Hey," he said, dazzling her with a wide Texas grin, "it just so happens miracles are my specialty." He held his arms open as if to say all she needed to do was ask and he'd direct her request to a higher power.

Amy looked more closely at this man, wondering if he was real.

"Wade McMillen," he said, offering her his hand. "Reverend Wade McMillen."

"Amy Thornton." She shook hands with him and withdrew hers quickly.

"Now, what kind of miracle do you need?" he asked, as if rescuing damsels in distress was all part of a day's work.

"Since you asked," Amy said, slowly releasing her breath. "How about a place to live, a job and a father for my baby?"

"Hmm." Reverend McMillen's gaze fell to her stomach. "That might take some doing."

So he hadn't noticed the pregnancy before, but he did now. "Some miracles are harder than others, I guess." Amy shrugged, figuring it was unlikely he'd be able to help her. But she got into this predicament on her own, and she'd get out of it the same way.

"But none are impossible," Wade reminded her. "Come with me."

"Where are we going?"

"The church office. I'll need to ask you a few questions, but as I said, miracles are my specialty."

Dovie Boyd Hennessey stepped back from the display she'd been working on and studied it with a discerning eye. The pine desk was a heavy old-fashioned one. She'd placed a book next to the lamp, with an overturned pair of old wire-rimmed spectacles on top. A cable-knit sweater was casually draped over the back of the chair, as if someone was about to return. The knickknacks, a quill pen and ink bottle along with a couple of framed pictures gave it a well-used comfortable feeling.

The effect was all she'd hoped for. Her shop had enjoyed a rush of business in the past few months, and the antiques were moving almost as fast as she could get them in the door. Just last week she'd sold a solid cherry four-poster bed that had been in inventory for the better part of eighteen months. Dovie was thrilled. Not just because of the sale, but with the bed gone, an entire corner of the shop would be freed up, allowing her to create a brand-new scene.

Designing these homey nooks was what she loved best. If she'd been thirty-five years younger, she'd go back to school and study to be an interior decorator. Her skills were instinctive, and she loved assembling furniture and various bits and pieces to create the illusion of cozy inviting rooms. But with Frank talking about retiring and the two of them traveling, she probably wouldn't be as involved in the running of her store as she'd been in years past.

As if the thought had conjured up the man, the bells above her door chimed and Sheriff Frank Hennessey walked into the shop.

"Frank!" She brightened at the sight of him. They'd been married nine months now—and he could still fluster her! He was a striking man for sixty, handsome and easy on the eye.

"Travis Grant come for that cherry bed yet?"

"Not yet," Dovie told him, wondering at the question.

Frank smiled—and it was a saucy sexy smile she knew all too well. "Frank, don't be ridiculous."

"We're married, aren't we?"

"It's the middle of the afternoon—good heavens, someone could walk in that door any minute." She edged protectively to the other side of the desk.

"You could always lock the door."

"Frank! Be sensible."

He walked toward the desk.

Giggling like a schoolgirl, Dovie moved beyond his reach. "What about the display windows?"

"Draw the shades."

He had an answer for everything.

"Frank, people of our age don't do this sort of thing!"

"Speak for yourself, woman," he said, racing around the desk.

Dovie let out a squeal and fled with her husband in hot pursuit. He'd just about caught up with her when the bells above the door chimed. Frank and Dovie both froze in their tracks.

Louise Powell, the town gossip, stood just inside the doorway staring as if she'd caught them buck naked on the bed. Her head fell back, her mouth dropped open and her eyes grew round as golf balls.

"Well, I never," she began.

"Maybe you should," Frank suggested. "I bet Paul would appreciate a little hanky-panky now and then."

Dovie elbowed her husband in the ribs and heard him swallow a groan. "Is there something I can help you find?" Dovie asked with as much poise as she could muster. A loose curl fell across her forehead and she blew it away, then tucked it back in place.

"I… I came to browse," Louise muttered. "It's Tammy Lee's birthday next week and…"

Dovie couldn't imagine there being anything in this store that Tammy Lee Killenborn would find to her liking. The inventory included classy pieces of jewelry, subtly elegant clothing and delicate figurines. Nothing she sold had sequins—which was more Tammy Lee's style—but Dovie would never have said so.

"I think it might be best if I came back another time," Louise said, mouth pursed in disapproval. She marched out of the store.

Dovie turned to glare at her husband. "You can bet that five minutes from now everyone in town is going to know my husband's a sex fiend."

Frank grinned as though nothing would please him more.

"Have you no shame?" she asked, but had a difficult time holding in a smile.

Her husband took one look at her and burst out laughing.

Dovie soon joined him.

He locked his arms around her and hugged her close. In all her life Dovie had never been loved like this. For twenty-six years she'd been married to Marvin Boyd; while she'd loved him she hadn't experienced this kind of happiness.

"I don't think you need to worry that Louise will return," Frank assured her. "She isn't going to find something for Tammy Lee here—because, my beautiful wife, you don't sell Texas trash."

"Frank, be kind." Dovie's own opinions made her no less guilty, but she was unwilling to confess as much.

"Hey, I'm just being honest."

Dovie went to the small kitchen off the Victorian Tea Room and reached for two mugs. "Do you have time for coffee?"

Frank nodded. "Actually, I have a reason for stopping by."

"You mean other than seducing me in the middle of the day?"

His grin was full of roguish humor. "Wade McMillen phoned a little while ago."

The pastor was a favorite of Dovie's, and Frank's, too. It'd been Wade who'd suggested a solution to their dilemma. As a lifelong bachelor, Frank had feared he was too set in his ways for marriage, but Dovie had found it impossible to continue their relationship without the emotional security and commitment of wedding vows.

Wade had come up with the idea of their getting married but maintaining separate households.

In the months since their wedding Frank had been gradually spending more and more of his evenings with her. In recent weeks the nights he slept at his own house had become few and far between. He'd lived exclusively with her for most of a month now and showed no signs of leaving, although the option was available to him. Once or twice a week, he'd stop off for his mail or an item of clothing, and he'd check on the house, but that was about it.

"Wade's helping an unwed mother who needs a place to live and I think we can help out."

"Us?" Dovie asked. Frank was by nature generous, although few people realized it.

"I had an idea," he said with a thoughtful look, watching her, "but I wanted to talk it over with you first."

"Of course."

Frank carried their coffee to one of the tables, and she followed with a small plate of freshly baked peanut-butter cookies. She noticed her husband's hesitation.

"Frank?"

"I did a background check on this woman. She's clean. I was able to talk to her landlord and her former employer. From everything they said, she's responsible, hardworking and decent. Her employer said her ex-boy-friend was a jerk. Apparently he hounded her day and night, insisting she get an abortion. From the sound of it, he made life so uncomfortable she quit her job and told everyone she was moving in with family."

"Where's her family, then?"

Frank's gaze held Dovie's. "From what I could find out, she doesn't have anyone to speak of her. Her mother's a flake, her father's dead and apparently that's just about all there is."

"The poor thing."

"I was thinking…" Frank hesitated. "My house has been sitting empty the last month and, well, it probably wouldn't hurt to have someone house-sit. I don't need the rent money, and it'd be a help to me, too."

It took Dovie a moment to understand what he was telling her. "You want to move in permanently with me?"

"For all intents and purposes, I'm living with you now," he said. "There's fewer and fewer of my things at the house. Some old clothes and my furniture. But I won't do it, Dovie, if you object, although I'd like to help Wade and this woman if I could."

"Object?" She all but threw herself into his arms. "Frank, I'm positively delighted!"

"You are?"

She couldn't have hidden her happiness for anything. "I love having you live with me."

"I'd like to keep my house."

"Of course."

"But if it's going to sit empty ninety percent of the time, it makes sense to have someone living there."

"I couldn't agree with you more." This was better than she'd hoped, better than she'd dreamed.

"Naturally, it's only on a trial basis."

"You could move back to your own place anytime, Frank, you know that."

"I wanted to talk to you about it first, but it does seem that letting this young lady stay at the house would help her *and* me. It's a win-win situation."

"It does seem like that, doesn't it?" He sounded as though he'd thought this through but wanted her either to concur or talk him out of it. "Are you sure you're comfortable having a stranger live in your home?"

"Why not? Anything of value has long since gone to your place."

"Our place," she corrected softly. "My home is your home. You're my husband." She said the word with pride and a heart full of love. For eleven years they'd dated and during that time he'd come to her back door. Twice a week, regular as taxes. As her husband, there was no need for him to worry about avoiding gossip, no need to conceal his love. No reason for her to pretend, either.

"And you're my wife." He clasped her hand and squeezed gently.

"Do you want to call Wade now?"

"I think I will." He scooped up a couple of peanut-butter cookies and headed toward her office in the back of the store.

Dovie took a cookie and relaxed in her chair. She had yet to meet this young woman of Wade's, but she liked her already. This unwed mother had helped Frank make a decision he might otherwise have delayed for months—if not years.

Wade had been joking when he told Amy Thornton he was a miracle worker. But it was clear from the moment he saw her that she was in serious distress. Her face was drawn and her large dark eyes were ringed with shadows. When he found her in the church, she'd looked embarrassed and apologetic. Before he could stop her, she'd grabbed her suitcase and clung to it like a lifeline.

Wade persuaded her to come into the office, where he introduced her to his secretary, Martha Kerns. While the women talked, he made several discreet phone calls from his study. He heard Martha suggest a cup of herbal tea, and a few minutes later her footsteps as she left the room. Interrupting his phone calls, Wade peeked out the door to see how Amy was doing. To his surprise, she was sound asleep, leaning to one side, head resting against her shoulder, eyes closed.

As unobtrusively as possible, he lifted her feet onto the sofa and she nestled against a pillow. He paused to study her. In the short walk from the church to the office, she'd told him she was twenty-five, a full eight years younger than he was. Never had eight years seemed so wide a gulf. She was pretty, with thick shoulder-length auburn hair, pulled back and clipped in place. Her skin was naturally pale and wonderfully smooth. Had he touched her cheek, he was certain she would have felt like satin.

Martha returned from the kitchen with two mugs and set them down on the corner of her desk. "She looks a little like an angel, doesn't she?"

Wade didn't answer, but not because he didn't agree. Amy did indeed look angelic. Removing his sweater from his closet, he covered the sleeping woman's shoulders.

While Amy continued to doze, he made a few more phone calls and finally managed to reach Frank Hennessey. Within the hour Frank called him back.

"I'm over at Dovie's," the sheriff announced. "We think we've come up with a solution to the housing problem."

"You know of someone willing to give her a place to live for a few months?" Wade's original thought had been to hook her up with one of the local ranchers as a cook or other part-time helper, but he'd soon realized that her pregnancy would restrict her activities. From there his thoughts moved to the idea of her working as a live-in nanny. In March Savannah Smith had delivered a beautiful baby girl, and Caroline Weston was due in three or four months. Weddings and babies. Wade had been witness to them all.

"Actually I was thinking she might be willing to house-sit for a while."

"Excellent idea." Wade wished he'd thought of that himself. "But who?"

Frank cleared his throat. "Uh, Dovie and I talked it over, and we were thinking maybe she could watch my place."

It didn't take Wade long to understand the implications. "That's an excellent idea," he said again.

"I did a background check on her," Frank said. "Talked to her former employer, too. From everything he said, she's a good person who's been put in a difficult position."

"I don't know what she can afford for rent."

"I don't plan on charging her any," the sheriff said. "She'd be doing me and Dovie a favor. Besides, she has other expenses to worry about."

"That's very kind of you," Wade said. So Frank had made inquiries concerning Amy. It was all Wade could do not to interrogate him. Sleeping Beauty was in his outer office, and he wanted to know more about her. *Much* more. She didn't fit the homeless helpless mode. He wondered why she'd decided to come here, where she had no friends or relatives, no prospects of work or accommodation.

"I have a line on a job for her," Wade said, feeling downright proud of himself.

"Wonderful. Who?"

"Ellie Frasier," he said, forgetting that the feed-store

owner was a Patterson now. Glen and Ellie were married last September; he'd officiated at the ceremony himself.

"The feed store?" Frank didn't sound as if he approved of the idea.

"As a bookkeeper," Wade told him. "I told Ellie up front that she's pregnant, but she didn't seem to mind. Ellie said she'd like to meet Amy first and interview her. She's been looking for someone to come in part-time and take up the slack. She could occasionally use help in the store, too." Wade was beginning to feel like the miracle worker he'd confidently proclaimed himself to be. He grinned, thinking all his miracles should be this easy.

"Dovie and I would like to meet her, too."

"Of course." It stunned him that Frank would open his home to a stranger like this. Frank and Dovie knew next to nothing about Amy Thornton, other than what her former employer had said. Yet they felt comfortable enough to invite her to live in his house. Wade wasn't sure he would've been as generous or as trusting. However, Frank was a lawman—a sheriff who'd seen plenty of reason to distrust his fellow man—and if he trusted Amy, Wade could do no less.

They ended the conversation by arranging that Wade would bring her over to the shop in an hour or so.

Wade returned to the outer room. Amy stirred then and sat up, looking disoriented, as if she wasn't sure where she was. "Oh, my," she whispered, pushing the hair away from her face. "I'm so sorry. I don't know what's wrong with me. I... I can't seem to get enough sleep."

"Don't worry about it," Wade said, and Martha added, "You need extra sleep right now."

"There are some people I'd like you to meet," Wade told her.

"I don't mean to cause you a lot of problems, Reverend McMillen," she said as she handed him his sweater.

"You're not a problem, Amy. Besides, didn't I tell you miracles were my specialty?"

"Fortunately Mr. Miracle Worker here has a lot of helpers in the community," Martha said with a smile.

Wade couldn't have agreed with her more. He led Amy out of the office and to the curb where he'd parked his Blazer. A soft breeze rustled the leaves of maples and oaks, the faint scent of roses and jasmine perfumed the air.

"I'm taking you to Dovie's place first," Wade said, starting the engine. "Frank and Dovie wanted to meet you—and discuss an idea."

"An idea?"

"I'll let them explain."

The Hennesseys were waiting for them. He watched Amy's face when she walked into Dovie's antique store. She paused as if it was too much to assimilate. He'd felt much the same way when he'd first seen the sheer *number* of things in her store. He'd been impressed by Dovie's displays, though. They were so attractive he couldn't help feeling they belonged in a magazine. When she opened her Victorian Tea room, it'd fast become the gathering place for women all around town. Dovie used only the finest linens, the best crystal and bone china from her stock. At first Wade had felt as awkward in her store as he would in a lingerie shop, but Dovie had quickly put him at ease.

"You must be Amy," Dovie said, crossing the room to greet them. "Welcome to my shop."

"It's...beautiful." Amy couldn't stop looking around.

"I've made us tea," Dovie said, and they followed her to a table at the far side of the room.

Frank watched Amy carefully and Wade saw her meet his gaze without flinching or visible discomfort. He sensed she had nothing to hide, and for that Wade was grateful. Situations such as this held the risk of problems; one of his fears was that Amy was running away, possibly from the father of her unborn child. But despite the potential for trouble, he wanted to help her.

Frank waited until everyone had a cup of tea before he mentioned his idea.

"You mean to say you'd let me live in your home?" Amy sounded incredulous. "But you don't even know me."

"Are you hiding something? Is there anything in your background we should know?" Frank asked.

"No," she was quick to inform them, her eyes wide and honest.

"I didn't think so." Frank's features relaxed into an easy smile. "Actually, having you stay there helps us, too. I won't need to worry about the house sitting empty, and you'll have a place to live until you've sorted out your life and made some decisions."

"I... I don't know what to say other than thank you."

Wade could see that Amy was overwhelmed by the Hennesseys' generosity and trust.

"I won't disappoint you," she said as if making a pledge.

"Just so you'll know exactly what's expected of you, I thought we should sit down and put everything in writing. I don't want there to be room for any misunderstanding."

"I'd like that," Amy concurred.

"Do you want to see the house?"

"Please."

Wade stood and checked his watch. "Give us thirty minutes. Amy needs to talk to Ellie first."

"Fine, I'll see you then."

Wade escorted Amy out of the shop and down the street to Frasier Feed. Ellie's father had died the year before, and Ellie had taken over the business. He knew that Glen had been helping her with the paperwork, but it had become an increasingly onerous task. Ellie was finding that it required more time than she could spare.

Ellie met them on the sidewalk outside the store.

"This is Amy Thornton," Wade said, introducing the two women. "Amy, Ellie Patterson."

"Hi," Ellie said, her greeting friendly. She gestured to the chairs by the soda machine. They all sat down, although Wade wasn't sure he was really needed for this interview.

"If you don't mind, I have a few questions," Ellie said.

"All right." Amy stiffened a little, as though unsure what to expect.

Ellie asked about job experience and Wade was glad of the opportunity to listen in. He was pleased to learn Amy had worked for the same employer for almost seven years. She'd started with the company as part of a high-school training program and had stayed on after graduation.

Wade remembered Frank telling him that her former employer had given her a glowing recommendation.

"Seven years." Ellie seemed impressed. She asked a series of other questions and took down references and phone numbers. Wade watched in amazement as almost instant rapport developed between the two women.

"Could you start on Monday?" Ellie asked.

"You're offering me the job?" Amy's voice quavered. "Now? Already?"

"Does that surprise you?"

"I'm…shocked. And thrilled. Thank you. Thank you so much." Tears gathered in her eyes and she stopped for a moment to compose herself before she continued. "Your store," she said, having a hard time getting the words out. "It's one of the reasons I got off the bus."

"I don't understand," Ellie said.

"It looked so friendly, like your customers were also your friends."

"My customers *are* my friends," Ellie said. "I'm hoping we can become friends, too."

A smile lit up Amy's face. "I'd like that very much."

Wade grinned in delight. This was working out perfectly. Within hours of arriving in Promise, Amy Thornton had a job and a place to live. Frank, Dovie and Ellie reaffirmed his belief in the basic goodness of most people.

Once they were back in the car, Wade drove to Frank's house and pulled into the driveway.

Amy glanced at him. "This is the house?"

Actually it was more of a cottage, Wade thought. Cozy and comfortable-looking.

"You really are a miracle worker, aren't you?" she said in apparent awe.

"A place to live and a job. Hey, no problem," he said, snapping his fingers like a magician producing a rabbit in a hat. "No problem at all."

"I don't think finding a father for my baby is going to be as easy," she said, climbing out of the vehicle.

A father for her child. Wade had forgotten about that.

Two

Dr. Jane Patterson had a gentle way about her, Amy thought as she dressed. The examination had been her most comfortable to date. From the moment she learned she was pregnant, Amy had faithfully taken her vitamins, made regular doctor's appointments and scrupulously watched her diet. Her one fear was that her baby would feel the tension and stress that had been her constant companion these past six months.

There was a light tap on the door, and Dr. Patterson entered the examination room.

"Is everything all right with the pregnancy?" Amy asked immediately.

"Everything looks good. From what I could tell, the baby is developing right on schedule," Dr. Patterson said. "I don't want you to worry. Continue with the vitamins and try to get the rest your body needs." She sat down across from Amy, leaned forward and gave her a reassuring pat on the hand. "I'm going to be starting a birthing class in the next couple of weeks and was wondering if you'd care to join."

Amy bit her lip. She'd like nothing better than to

attend this class, but it probably required a partner, someone who'd be willing to coach her through labor and birth. Unfortunately, being new in town, she didn't know anyone she could ask.

"There are several women in the community who are entering their third trimester," the doctor went on.

"Will I need a partner?"

"It's not necessary," she said, and Amy saw compassion and understanding on the doctor's face. "You don't need to decide just yet," she added. "As I mentioned, the class won't start for a couple of weeks, but if you're looking for a partner, I suggest you ask Dovie Hennessey. She took me under her wing when I first arrived in Promise. I didn't know anyone and had trouble making friends."

"You?" Amy could hardly believe it.

Dr. Patterson laughed lightly. "Oh, Amy, you wouldn't believe all the mistakes I made. I felt so lost and lonely. Dovie made me feel welcome and steered me toward the right people. She's wonderful."

Amy lowered her gaze, embarrassed that she was reduced to accepting charity and relying on the kindness of strangers. "Did you know I'm staying in Sheriff Hennessey's house?" she asked.

"I heard you're house-sitting, if that's what you mean."

It puzzled Amy that she could have stepped off the bus in a town she didn't know existed and be welcomed as though she were long-lost family. Half the time she was left wondering when she'd wake up to reality. Wade McMillen had jokingly said he was a miracle worker, and so far, he'd proved himself to be exactly that. A week later, her head still spun at the way he'd gone about finding solutions to her problems.

"Would you like me to put your name down for the birthing class?" Dr. Patterson pressed.

"Yes, please," Amy said. It seemed that the people of Promise, Texas, had made room for her in their community and in their hearts. "I'll think about asking Dovie…" She hated to request yet another favor. Besides, she couldn't see what would prompt a busy woman like Dovie to agree, especially when she and her husband were already doing so much for her. Dr. Patterson seemed to think it was a good idea, though, and Amy wouldn't mind becoming friends with the older woman. Everyone she knew was back in Dallas. Her friends, her colleagues and of course her mother. Alex hadn't liked her seeing anyone else, even girlfriends, and over time she'd lost contact with quite a few people.

"Dovie will be thrilled if you ask her," the doctor was saying.

Amy stared at her. "Dr. Patterson, I don't know—"

"We don't stand on formality here," the other woman interrupted. "You can call me Jane—Dr. Jane if you prefer." The accompanying smile was warm.

"You'll let me know when the classes start?"

"Jenny has the sign-up sheet out front. Give her your name and she'll make sure you're notified before the first class. And while you're speaking to Jenny, go ahead and schedule your next appointment for two weeks."

"Two weeks?" The doctor in Dallas had seen her only once a month. "There's something wrong you're not telling me about, isn't there?"

"Relax, Amy, everything looks perfectly fine. You're healthy and there's nothing to indicate anything's wrong with the baby."

"Then why?"

"You're entering the third trimester, and it's normal procedure to see a patient every two weeks until the last month, when your visits will be weekly."

Amy relaxed. Generally she didn't panic this easily, but so much had already happened that she couldn't help worrying.

"I'll talk to Jenny on my way out," she promised.

"If you have any questions, I want you to call me day or night, understand?" Jane wrote the office phone number on a prescription pad and handed it to Amy. "This is my pager number if the office is closed and it's not an emergency."

"Thank you." Amy's voice shook. She felt overwhelmed by the fact that strangers cared about her and her unborn child when her own mother's reaction had been just the opposite. She'd called Amy ugly horrible names. Alex, the man she was convinced she loved beyond life itself, had shown exactly the kind of person he was when she told him about the baby. He didn't want his own child! People she loved, trusted, had turned their backs on her, and instead a community of strangers had welcomed her with open arms, taken her in, given her the help she needed.

"You'll talk to Dovie then?" Jane said as Amy prepared to leave.

Amy inhaled a stabilizing breath and nodded. "I'll do it right away." Before she lost her nerve or changed her mind.

Since she wasn't expected at the feed store until noon, Amy walked over to Dovie's after she'd left the doctor office. She tried to convince herself that what

Jane had said was true—that Dovie would be delighted to attend the classes with her.

Birthing classes. In three months Sarah would be born. Three months! This shouldn't have come as any shock. But it did. She had so much to do to get ready for the baby. She hadn't even begun to buy the things she'd need. Baby clothes, a crib, a stroller. Her heart started to pound at the thought of everything that had to be done and the short time left in which to accomplish it all.

Amy pushed open the door to Dovie's store and the bells above the entrance jingled lightly.

"Well, hello, Amy," Dovie greeted her from across the room. She was arranging freshly cut red roses in a crystal vase. "Aren't these lovely?" she murmured, pausing to examine one bud more closely. "Savannah Smith came by with Laura earlier this morning and brought me these."

"They're beautiful." Amy swore that if Dovie hadn't been alone just then, she would have abandoned her mission.

"How are you feeling?" Dovie asked.

"Great. I'm enjoying working with Ellie."

"From what Ellie said, you're doing a fabulous job."

Amy was unable to stifle a smile. She'd started her job that Monday afternoon and had spent the first two days organizing Ellie's desk. It was abundantly clear that Ellie had been putting off too much of her paperwork. This job wasn't a fabricated one; Amy was convinced of that. Frasier Feed genuinely needed a bookkeeper and more. Her organizational skills had given her the opportunity to show Ellie how much she appreciated the job.

"Ellie's a wonderful employer."

"After your first day she told me she wondered why she'd delayed hiring someone."

Amy had wondered that herself, but didn't think it was her place to ask. If anything, she was grateful Ellie had waited; otherwise there wouldn't have been an opening for her.

"I just finished seeing Dr. Patterson for the first time," Amy said.

"Isn't Jane terrific?" Dovie's question was asked in an absent sort of way, more comment than inquiry. She added another perfectly formed long-stemmed rose to the arrangement.

"Yes… She mentioned she's starting a birthing class in a couple of weeks."

"Caroline Weston's due around the same time as you."

Amy wasn't entirely sure who Caroline was. A friend of Dovie's, apparently.

"I'm going to need a birthing partner," Amy blurted out, thinking if she didn't ask soon, she never would. "Dr. Patterson… Dr. Jane assured me I could attend the class alone, but then she suggested I ask you to be my partner." She dragged a deep breath into her lungs and hurriedly continued, "I realize it's an imposition and I want you to know that I…" She let her sentence drift off.

Dovie's hand stilled and she glanced up, her eyes wide. With astonishment? Or perhaps it was shock; Amy didn't know which. Her initial reaction had been accurate. Asking something this personal of someone she barely knew, someone who'd already helped her so much, was stepping over the line.

"An imposition," Dovie repeated. "Oh, no, not to me. Not at all. I'd consider it an honor."

"You would? I mean, Dovie, you and Frank have done so much for me and the baby. Letting me stay in his house… I can't tell you how grateful I am. Thank you. Thank you." If she didn't leave soon, Amy feared she'd embarrass herself further by bursting into tears.

"Just let me know when the first class is scheduled, all right?"

Amy nodded. "Jenny said she'd have all the information for me at my next appointment."

"We'll make a great team." Dovie's eyes gleamed with confidence; she gave every indication of being delighted that Amy had asked her. Just like Dr. Jane had said.

Amy had almost stopped believing there were good people left in this world, and then she'd stumbled on a whole town of them.

Denise Parsons had never been friendly with Louise Powell. The woman enjoyed gossip and meddling far too much. The minute Louise entered the café, Denise could tell she wanted something—and she sincerely doubted it was the French-dip luncheon special.

Sighing with resignation, Denise filled a glass of water and reached for a menu, then approached the booth.

"Hello, Denise," the other woman purred.

Yup, she was after some juicy gossip all right, but Denise hadn't a clue what it might be. Well, whatever Louise hoped to learn had brought her into the bowling alley on a Thursday afternoon, which was highly unusual.

"Hello." She returned the greeting with a certain

hesitation. She didn't enjoy being a party to Louise's type of friendship. "What can I get you?"

"Coffee would be great."

"Would you like anything with that?" Tex had been after her to push desserts. With one of the ranchers she might have suggested a slice of rhubarb pie, but personally she preferred to have Louise in and out of the café in record time.

"I understand you were the first one to speak with that new gal in town," Louise said, instead of answering Denise's question.

Denise wasn't sure who she meant.

"The pregnant one."

So Amy Thornton was the reason for this visit. Denise hadn't noticed Amy was pregnant until she'd stood up to leave. Louise stared at her, anticipating an answer. "Yes, I talked to her." She couldn't see any point in denying it. "Did you say you wanted anything with the coffee?" she asked again.

"Nothing." Louise righted her mug and gazed up expectantly.

Denise wasn't about to let the town busybody trap her into a lengthy and unpleasant conversation; she promptly disappeared. She was back a minute later with the coffeepot and a look that suggested she didn't have anything more to add.

Oblivious to anything but her own curiosity, Louise was ready and waiting. "What did she say?"

"Who?" Denise asked, playing dumb.

"That unwed mother," Louise snapped.

"She asked about the breakfast special."

Louise's eyes narrowed. "Did she mention the baby's father?"

Setting the coffeepot down on the table, Denise leaned closer as though to share a secret. "She did say something interesting."

The rhinestones in the older woman's hat sparkled as she scooted closer to the end of the booth. "What?"

"She asked…" Denise paused and looked both ways. *"What?"*

"If we served sourdough bread."

The keen interest in Louise's eyes changed to annoyance. Her back went stiff and she straightened, moving away from Denise, implying that it didn't do her image any good to be seen associating with a waitress. "I can see we have nothing more to discuss," Louise said primly. "And furthermore, this coffee tastes burned."

"I made a fresh pot less than thirty minutes go." Denise had a son in junior high, a kid with attitude. If she wanted someone to insult her and question her abilities, she could get it at home; she didn't need to go to work for it.

With her lips pinched, Louise scrambled out of the booth. She slapped some change down on the table and walked out the door, leaving it to swing in her wake.

"What'd that old biddy want?" Tex shouted from the kitchen.

"She's trying to make trouble, is all." Denise put the coffeepot back on the burner. "Asking about Amy." The unwed mother was fair game in Louise's eyes, Denise realized sadly. The poor girl was doing the best she could and Denise hoped everything would work out well for her and her baby.

"Did you tell her to leave the kid alone?" Tex demanded, none too gently.

"I did," Denise shouted back. In her own way she'd

given Louise as good as she got, and she felt a small but definite sense of triumph.

Wade had known Amy was scheduled to visit Jane on Thursday morning, so he waited until later that evening to visit her. The last time they'd talked had been Sunday morning.

He'd be lying if he didn't admit how pleased he'd felt when Amy showed up for church services. Frankly he'd been more than a little surprised. In his years of serving as a pastor, he'd learned a number of lessons about human nature, not all of them positive—and as a result he'd suffered his share of disappointments. He sincerely hoped Amy wouldn't turn out to be one.

Richard Weston had certainly tested his faith in people. The youngest of the Weston family had shown up in Promise after a six-year absence and taken advantage of the kindness and goodwill of the community. Just when his underhandedness was about to be exposed, he'd disappeared. Eventually he was found—hiding in a nearby ghost town—and returned to New York to stand trial on charges stemming from a scheme that had involved cheating and abusing immigrants. Wade had spent many an evening with Grady Weston and his sister, Savannah Smith, helping them come to terms with what their brother had done—to them and to others. Richard was serving a twenty-five-year prison sentence, and it was unlikely he'd ever come back to Promise. Not that anyone wanted him to.

His experience working as a pastor had given Wade a sixth sense about people. He'd seen through Richard Weston almost immediately, but unfortunately had been unaware of the man's schemes until too late.

Even knowing Richard for what he was, Wade had been shocked by the extent of his perfidy and the horror of his crimes.

He liked Amy and trusted her, not that he was looking for her gratitude. Actually he'd done little more than point her in the right direction. Ellie hadn't hired her simply because she needed a job. And rightly so. She'd hired Amy because of her qualifications.

Home and job—everything had fallen neatly into place. Then on Sunday morning Amy had arrived in time for the morning service, looking almost afraid. Her expressive brown eyes told him she was expecting someone to tell her she should leave. Expecting someone to tell her she didn't belong in a house of God. Wade swore if anyone had so much as tried, he would... He stopped, not realizing until that very moment the depth of his feelings.

He was proud of the way his flock had welcomed Amy Thornton into the fold. Proud of each and every one of them, even Louise, who—so far, anyway—had shown more curiosity than malice.

Wednesday morning Ellie Patterson had phoned Wade to thank him for finding such a whiz of a bookkeeper. Wade couldn't accept full credit; he'd had no idea Amy was a gifted organizer. He smiled, pleased that everything was working out so well.

He rang the doorbell and waited. It might have been best had he phoned first, but he'd learned early on in his pastoral career that if he did phone, most people invented excuses to keep him away. He'd never understood what they feared. Women seemed convinced he'd march right into their kitchens and inspect the inside of their ovens. Men seemed to worry that he might catch them enjoying a bottle of beer—when in reality he'd have been happy to join them.

Involved in these thoughts, Wade stepped back in mild surprise when the door opened and Amy stood on the other side.

"Hello," she said, brightening when she saw who it was.

He wasn't accustomed to people actually being pleased to find he'd unexpectedly dropped by. "I thought I'd see how the doctor's appointment went this morning," he said.

Amy held open the screen door for him. "Come in, please. I just finished making a batch of sun tea. Would you care for a glass?"

"Sure."

Amy had been living at Frank's house for only a week, and already Wade saw subtle changes. She'd draped a shawl over the back of Frank's shabby recliner, and a vase of fresh-cut flowers rested in the center of the coffee table. The wooden floors shone, the windows sparkled; the books were dusted and straightened. A women's magazine lay open on the sofa.

"Make yourself comfortable," she said, and disappeared into the kitchen. She returned a couple of minutes later with two glasses of iced tea. She explained that it was a lemon herbal tea to which she'd added a sprig of fresh mint.

"I hear you were in to see Dr. Jane."

Amy nodded, then sipped from her glass. "She's wonderful."

"We think so."

"I was a little worried, because I was a couple of

weeks overdue for an exam, but she assured me the pregnancy is progressing nicely."

Wade noticed how she pressed her palm against her abdomen as she spoke. It was an unconscious movement, he suspected. If he hadn't known about the pregnancy, he probably wouldn't have even guessed her condition. The swelling was slight and could almost be attributed to body type.

"I've signed up for birthing classes and Dovie has agreed to be my partner."

"Dovie," Wade repeated. "That's great." She was a perfect choice. Dovie loved children; a couple of months ago she'd surprised him when she volunteered to teach Sunday-school class for two-and-three-year-olds. What amazed him even more was that Frank had joined his wife one recent Sunday. It'd been difficult enough to get Frank Hennessey to darken a church door—but teaching Sunday school to a group of preschoolers? That had left Wade with his mouth hanging open in shock. Frank Hennessey seemed full of surprises lately, attributable, no doubt, to Dovie's influence. She'd be good for Amy, too, he mused. And vice versa...

"It all seems so real now," Amy was saying. "Dovie seemed pleased about going to the birthing classes with me."

Wade sat back on the sofa. "Have you decided what you're going to do about the baby?" he asked. This was a difficult subject, but one that needed to be addressed.

"How do you mean?" Amy asked.

"Have you made any decisions about the baby's future?"

"Are you asking me if I've decided to put my child up for adoption?"

He was pleased she understood his intention without his having to spell it out. This was such a delicate subject. Emotions could be volatile and he wasn't trying to steer her in one direction or another. At twenty-five Amy Thornton was perfectly capable of making up her own mind.

"I'm not here to pressure you in any way," he told her.

"In the beginning I considered all my options." She paused and he saw the muscles in her throat work as she struggled within herself. "The man I loved...who I thought loved me...wanted me to end the pregnancy. My mother, between calling me names, wasn't willing to offer any type of support. She said she wanted nothing to do with me again." Amy regarded him steadily. "Thank you, Wade."

"You're thanking me?"

"You're the first person in nearly six months to ask what I want for my child."

He noticed the sheen in her eyes. "So, what have you decided?"

Her hand went back to her abdomen. "I'm an adult and I have good job skills. Ellie seems to think the part-time position will develop into full-time employment. While I don't have a lot of discretionary income and finances will be tight, I've decided to raise my baby myself."

The decision hadn't been easy, Wade knew. He could tell from the look on her face. She was afraid, vulnerable and alone, but she seemed to have found peace with that. It was everything he needed to know.

"I left Dallas because of my baby," Amy said. "The baby's father...well, let me just say that he's out of my life and there's no possibility we'll get back together."

She paused and then, unable to hide the pain in her voice, she whispered, "My mother has disowned me." Her voice grew stronger. "The baby and I are a package deal, and seeing that I've already made two rather unpleasant stands on Sarah's behalf, I figure I'll stick it out for the long haul. I'm very much looking forward to being a mother." This part was added with a smile and something more. Inner peace.

Amy Thornton hadn't come to this decision without struggle, Wade realized. It wasn't one she'd made lightly.

"I don't understand the question, though," she said, her mood abruptly shifting into amusement.

"What do you mean?"

"I thought you were the miracle man, Reverend Mc-Millen."

"Well, yes… I suppose, but…"

"Don't go backing out on me now," she said, placing her hand on her hip in mock outrage. "The first time we met, you made it quite clear that you were capable of producing whatever I needed."

"Hey, I found you a house and connected you with Ellie, didn't I?"

"Yes, you did and don't think I'm ungrateful. But if you'll remember, you also promised to find me a father for my baby."

Dovie posted the notice for the big Grange dance in her shop window. Next to the rodeo and chili cook-off, this function, sponsored by the Cattlemen's Association, was one of the biggest social events of the year.

At the dance the previous summer Glen Patterson had made a fool of himself over Ellie. It was one of the incidents that had led—indirectly—to their marriage. Glen had been a little slow to figure out how he felt about Ellie, and Richard Weston had leaped into the breach. Which had helped Glen clarify his own feelings. Certainly Richard was none to happy when Ellie chose to marry Glen, but Dovie strongly suspected Ellie's recent inheritance had been the key to Richard's interest.

Vulnerable as she'd been at the time, it was little wonder Ellie hadn't seen through Richard the minute he started showering her with attention. Eventually she had of course—with no help from Glen, Dovie mused.

She finished taping up the notice for the dance, then stepped outside to make sure it was positioned straight. The day was lovely, the midmorning still cool with a slight breeze. The reader board at the bank alternated the time and the temperature, and Dovie noted it was seventy-four. By late afternoon it'd be close to ninety.

A great many changes had come about since last year's dance. Several marriages, births, including Savannah and Laredo's daughter. Caroline Weston, the town's postmistress and Grady's wife, was showing nicely now and was as pretty as Dovie had ever seen her. She all but glowed with happiness. It wouldn't have surprised Dovie if Ellie or Jane decided to start their families soon, too. Those stubborn Patterson men had waited until their midthirties to get married. Better make up for lost time, Dovie thought with a wicked grin.

"What's that?" Amy Thornton asked, startling her as she walked up behind Dovie and read the sign.

"The Cattlemen's Association puts on a big dance at the Grange hall every year."

"Oh." Amy sounded sorry she'd asked.

"You're going, aren't you?"

Amy shook her head. "Not like this."

"Like what?" Dovie challenged.

The younger woman cradled her protruding stomach. "In case you hadn't noticed, Dovie, I'm six months pregnant."

"What's that got to do with anything?"

Amy shook her head. "I couldn't attend a dance."

"Why not, in heaven's name?"

"I...just couldn't."

"If you're worried about having something appropriate to wear..."

"I don't have anything appropriate, but that's only part of it. I realize these are modern times, but I'd still need a date."

Dovie smiled. "No, you wouldn't. My heavens, plenty of ranchers attend the dance without a partner, and gals, too. Don't you worry, you'll have more men buzzing around you than a can of fresh cream."

"I wouldn't feel...right."

"And why not?" Dovie demanded.

"I...don't know anyone," Amy said.

Dovie studied her for a long minute. "I can't think of a better way for you to get to know the people here, and for them to know you."

Still Amy hesitated.

"Will you at least think on it?" Dovie pressed. Going to the dance was the best way for Amy to meet other people close to her in age. It'd help if she did have someone to escort her, but she was too new in town.

"I'll think about it," Amy said, "but I'm not making any promises."

Dovie patted her elbow, pleased Amy had agreed to at least consider it. "Good girl."

Amy flushed and looked slightly embarrassed. "I wanted you to know that the birthing class starts a week from Monday. We're meeting at the health clinic between seven and eight-thirty."

"I'll be there with bells on," Dovie promised. Excitement bubbled inside her at the prospect of sharing the moment Amy gave birth to her baby.

They exchanged a few more pleasantries, then Amy continued down the street. Feeling motherly, Dovie wandered back into her shop. She'd bonded with Amy Thornton, she thought, nodding in satisfaction. The girl was like a lost waif, in need of love and nourishment. Not physical nourishment, but emotional. Even as little as a week had shown a vast improvement in her appearance. She wasn't nearly as pale, and the dark shadows under her eyes had all but disappeared.

Dovie strongly suspected this was the first time since she'd learned she was pregnant that she was getting proper rest. In thinking over Amy's story, Dovie was appalled. The young woman had hastily gotten off the bus without knowing a soul in Promise. When questioned, all she'd say was that she'd looked down Main Street and thought it might be a friendly town.

While Promise was indeed friendly, it wasn't unlike a dozen other communities Amy had traveled through on her way to Austin.

Dovie wouldn't say anything to Frank, and possibly not even to Wade, but she had the distinct impression that Amy was *supposed* to get off that bus when she did. There was a reason she was in Promise. Dovie wasn't sure what it was just yet, but time would eventually reveal it.

"I can't believe the dance is almost here."

The deep male voice behind her took Dovie by surprise. She gasped and placed her hand over her heart. "Reverend McMillen!"

"Sorry, Dovie, I didn't mean to frighten you."

"I was lost in thought and I didn't hear you sneaking up behind me. Didn't even hear the bell!"

He laughed and handed her the Sunday-school material he'd promised to deliver at the beginning of the week.

"The big dance is scheduled for the twenty-seventh this year," Dovie said. "You're going of course."

"Of course."

Not that Dovie remembered him doing a lot of dancing in years past. Mostly Wade hung around with the ranchers. The thing was, he fit right in. Tall and broad-shouldered, the preacher looked and acted as though he'd be at home on a horse or roping a calf. It often took people aback when they learned the only herd Wade managed was a church full of stubborn humans.

"Remember last year?" Wade asked.

"I'm not likely to forget," Dovie told him.

"Glen was fit to be tied when he found Ellie dancing with Richard."

Dovie had been thinking the same thing herself only a few minutes earlier. "It was a turning point in their relationship."

"Not that the road to romance was smooth for either of them," Wade reminded her.

"The dance was a turning point for Caroline and Grady, too."

This small bit of information appeared to surprise the reverend. "What do you mean?"

"Savannah and I were the ones who encouraged Caroline to ask Grady when Pete Hadley announced a ladies' choice."

"She did, too, didn't she?"

"Yup, and I think that was what woke Grady up to the fact that she's a woman."

Wade rubbed the side of his face. "Seems the dance is responsible for a lot more romances around here than I realized."

That was when the idea hit Dovie—and hit her hard. Actually it was the perfect solution and she wondered why she hadn't come up with it sooner. My, oh my, it *was* just perfect.

"You've got that look in your eye, Dovie," Wade said, and he stepped back warily.

"I do?" she asked, feigning surprise. She'd already concluded that it was no fluke Amy had chosen to settle in Promise, and now she thought she knew why. She blurted out her idea. "I think you should take Amy to the dance."

"Me?" he cried. "Oh, no, you don't! My job description *doesn't* include escorting lonely hearts to dances!"

Three

Amy stopped at Dovie's house to pick her up for the birthing class far earlier than necessary. She'd been looking forward to this ever since Dr. Jane had first mentioned it. Waiting another fifteen minutes seemed more than she could stand.

Dovie was in her garden when Amy approached.

"Oh, my, is it that time already?" Dovie asked the instant she saw her. Flustered, she glanced at her wrist.

"I'm early," Amy apologized.

"Don't let her kid you," Frank said, joining his wife. "Dovie's been on tenterhooks all evening. I don't think I've ever seen her more excited about anything."

It warmed Amy's heart that her friend was looking forward to coaching her through labor and birth. The thought of having to go through the birth alone had weighed on her mind for months. The wrenching sense of loneliness had virtually disappeared since her arrival in Promise. She marveled anew at these wonderful people.

"I'll just be a moment," Dovie promised, and rushed toward the house.

"There's no hurry," Amy called after her.

Frank sauntered over to the gate and opened it for Amy. "You might as well sit a spell." He led her past the large well-groomed garden toward the wrought-iron table and chairs on the brick patio.

"Dovie's got quite a garden, doesn't she?"

"It's like this every year," the sheriff said. "Heaven only knows what she's going to do with twenty-five tomato plants, but she always seems to know someone who could use them."

Fresh tomatoes were a particular favorite of Amy's. One day she'd like to plant her own garden... Perhaps next year.

"Do you think Dovie would mind if I looked at her plants?" Amy asked, noticing the small herb garden next to the tomatoes.

"Go right ahead. Dovie's garden is her pride and joy. If you want to wait a few minutes, she'll give you the grand tour herself." It seemed to Amy that Frank was just as proud of her accomplishment.

Dovie appeared almost immediately afterward, wearing pressed navy blue trousers and an attractive cotton knit sweater in a lovely rose. Just as Frank had predicted, she was more than willing to walk Amy through her garden. "I seem to have a green thumb," she remarked, shrugging in an offhand way.

"She could coax orchids into blooming in the Arctic," Frank murmured.

"Now, Frank, that's not entirely true," Dovie said, as she slid her arm through Amy's. They strolled down the narrow garden rows, commenting on this plant and that one. The corn was almost knee-high, and the pole beans and other vegetables were well under way.

"I've always wanted a garden," Amy said, and realized how wistful that must have sounded.

"Well, I could certainly use help in mine." Dovie smiled. "Of course it'd be a little awkward for you this year, but perhaps next."

"I'd like that," Amy said. She'd never known people could be this open and generous.

"Shall we head on over to the health clinic?" Dovie asked.

The walk didn't take more than a few minutes. Amy's hands had grown damp with nerves by the time they arrived. She suspected she'd be the only pregnant woman attending without a husband, and she was right. Three other couples were already inside the clinic waiting. Dovie played hostess, greeting each one and then introducing Amy. Caroline Weston looked to be about six months pregnant, as well, and she and Amy were soon talking comfortably. She was pretty, Amy thought, with her dark brown eyes and soft brown hair. Until now they hadn't been formally introduced, but Amy had chatted with her at the post office when she'd gone to apply for a post-office box.

"Dovie was thrilled you asked her to be your birthing partner," Caroline told her. She sat next to her broad-shouldered rancher husband, Grady Weston.

"I'm the one who's grateful." Amy didn't mind saying so, either. "Being new in town, I was afraid I'd be going through labor alone."

"That would never have happened," Caroline said with confidence. Their eyes met and briefly held. "I wasn't married when I had Maggie," she said softly. "My mother was my labor coach. Jane would have made sure someone supportive was with you."

Caroline was telling Amy far more than the words themselves conveyed. She was saying that at one time she'd walked in the same shoes as Amy. She understood what it meant to stand alone and was offering her encouragement and support. Caroline was married now, and from the tender looks she shared with her husband, it was obvious they were deeply in love.

The class lasted ninety minutes, and the time flew. During the first half hour, everyone spoke for a few moments; Amy, feeling shy, said very little. Then Dr. Jane showed a thirty-minute video of a birth and answered questions. The film had been an eye-opener for Amy. Unlike the others, she hadn't been raised in a ranching community and had never been around farm animals. The baby stirred and kicked as she watched; and Amy felt a surge of pure excitement. The final thirty minutes were spent explaining the breathing techniques used during the early stages of labor.

The key, Amy discovered, was finding a comfortable position. Caroline sat on the carpeted floor and leaned her back against Grady's bent knees and pressed her hands against her stomach. The most comfortable position Amy found was lying flat on her back, knees drawn up. She stared at the ceiling and concentrated on practicing her deep breathing.

Dovie sat by her head and brushed the hair from Amy's brow. Surprisingly Amy discovered that she'd relaxed to the point of nearly drifting off to sleep.

Grady and Caroline offered Dovie and Amy a ride home, but Amy preferred to walk. Dovie did, too.

"Thanks for the offer," Amy said. She was looking forward to the next class—in part because she felt that she and Caroline could easily become friends.

"If I don't see you before, I will at the dance Saturday night," Caroline told Dovie as she climbed inside the car. As if she'd forgotten something important, she poked her head out the open window and gestured to Amy. "You're coming to the big dance, aren't you?"

Amy froze. Dovie had mentioned it earlier, and she'd hoped to avoid the subject altogether. Perhaps—like planting a garden—next year would be better timing.

"Amy?" Dovie urged, apparently waiting for her to respond to Caroline's question.

"I...don't think so," she mumbled, flustered and unsure. She longed to go, but it was impossible. Next year, she thought, when she felt confident again. When she felt like a contributing member of the community. When she was slim again. No man would find her attractive now with her rounding stomach and her ankles swollen by the end of the day. When the time was right—well, she had a man in mind... It was, admittedly, much too soon to be thinking along those lines, but Wade McMillen was by far the kindest man she'd ever met. Not to mention one of the most attractive!

Caroline waved when Grady pulled the car away from the curb, and Amy waved back.

"So you've decided not to attend the dance," Dovie said, and did nothing to disguise her disappointment.

"I can't," Amy insisted.

"And why's that?"

"A number of reasons."

"The decision is yours, of course," Dovie said, but it was plain the older woman wanted her to reconsider. "However, I think it would do you a world of good to get out and mingle with people your own age. The dance would be the perfect opportunity to do that."

"Next year," she said, but if she'd hoped to appease Dovie, she failed.

"I want you to give me one good reason you feel you should wait."

Obviously Dovie wasn't about to drop the subject with her usual grace. If anything, she sounded more adamant than she had earlier.

"Oh, Dovie, I wish I could go, but—"

"That does it," Dovie interrupted, cutting her off even before she could complete the thought.

"Does what?"

"You're attending the dance, and I refuse to take no for an answer."

Amy laughed at her friend's stubbornness. "You seem mighty sure of yourself."

"I am." Dovie flashed her a smile that could only be described as smug. "Since I've taken on the role of your fairy godmother, all I need to do now is find the dress and the prince. The dress is simple, and as for the prince—" she giggled with sheer delight "—I know just where to look."

Wade didn't generally avoid people, especially members of his own congregation, but Dovie Boyd Hennessey had been after him all week to take Amy Thornton to the big dance. He'd given Dovie a flippant response when she first proposed the idea, but the truth of the matter was he *did* like Amy. He admired her courage and determination, her grit. And it didn't hurt any that she was easy on the eyes. When he was with her, Wade forgot he was a pastor and remembered he was a man. He wasn't sure he liked that feeling. He happened to enjoy his life exactly the way it was. Besides, if he was going to ask Amy out, then it would be when he felt ready and not because Dovie Hennessey thought he should. He didn't appreciate being pressured; no one did. So he avoided her.

"I'm not asking you to take Amy as her pastor," she muttered the one time she did manage to catch him— outside the post office. "For the love of heaven, open your eyes, Wade McMillen! Amy's a beautiful young woman."

"My eyes *are* open," Wade said. Far wider than he cared to admit.

Dovie's face relaxed into a knowing grin. "Then the matter's settled."

"Dovie, it isn't a good idea." Wade wasn't about to let her maneuver him into this craziness. At least not without putting up a struggle. "I'm sure once people meet Amy there'll be plenty of men wanting to date her. It wouldn't be fair to saddle her with me so soon after she's arrived."

"That's just an excuse and you know it!"

"I'll tell you what," he said, willing to bend, but only a little. "If no one else has asked her by Friday, then I'll take her myself."

"And insult her like she's some…some castoff. I think not."

There was no satisfying the woman. "Someone else will ask her," he muttered, and left it at that.

Dovie's eyes grew hot enough to cause a nuclear meltdown, but she said nothing more.

Wednesday morning Wade had just ordered the breakfast special at the café in the bowling alley when

Sheriff Hennessey slipped into the booth across from him. He righted a coffee mug and motioned to Denise.

"I take it you're avoiding my wife," Frank Hennessey said.

"Can you blame me?" Wade asked.

Frank's tanned face broke into a grin. "I tell you, when Dovie's got a bee in her bonnet, nothing distracts her from getting what she wants." He paused. "I actually feel sorry for you."

Wade had gone over the last conversation with Dovie a dozen times and didn't see how he could do more than he already had. He'd given her his best offer and the woman had insisted he was insulting Amy. This was what made dating hazardous. He saw offering to escort Amy to the dance if no one else invited her as a gesture of kindness. According to Dovie, that wasn't the case. Well, as far as he was concerned, the best thing to do was avoid the dance issue entirely, avoid Dovie, avoid the attraction he felt for Amy—avoid it all.

Denise brought over his breakfast and filled Frank's mug with fresh hot coffee.

"Dovie's talked Amy into attending that dance without a date, so you don't need to worry about her chasing you down any longer."

Wade was relieved and he suspected he had Frank to thank for this unexpected reprieve. "Amy isn't going to have a problem attracting men," Wade said. She was attractive and sweet, and he had no doubt others would soon notice that, too.

A part of Wade, one he didn't want to face, was pleased no one had asked her. He wasn't sure how he'd feel about Amy dating one of the local ranchers, and yet…that was exactly what he wanted, wasn't it?

"Amy's *real* pretty," Frank agreed with him.

Wade didn't appreciate the reminder. "It's just that…"

"Yes?" Frank urged.

Wade longed to explain himself, but he couldn't seem to do it. He didn't understand his own reluctance to invite Amy to the dance, so he said the first logical thing that popped into his head. "I just don't think it's a good idea for a pastor to be romantically linked with an unwed mother. People might get the wrong idea."

Frank held the mug with both hands. He nodded slowly. "I suspect you're right. People are funny about that kind of thing."

Perhaps there was more truth to his words than he realized; Wade no longer knew. Rarely had he felt so confused. It made sense not to complicate his relationship with Amy. For one thing, some folks were sure to make more of a simple date than was warranted. Louise Powell, for instance.

Frank relaxed, leaning back against the red vinyl upholstery, and continued to sip his coffee. "This reminds me of a situation I read about not long ago."

"What situation?" Wade asked.

Frank chuckled. "Dovie's got me reading the Bible these days. She said if I was going to be helping her teach Sunday-school classes, I'd better know what I was talking about."

Wade reached for a slice of bacon, his attention more on his meal than on Frank. "Good idea."

"That's what I thought, too. But there are definite similarities."

Wade was afraid to question too much.

"Between you and that man named Joseph." Frank leaned forward and rested his elbows on the table.

"Joseph?" The bacon had yet to touch his lips.

"You remember him, I'm sure. The one who was engaged to a virgin named Mary. It must have been embarrassing for him, too, don't you think? Here's the woman he's agreed to marry, and she unexpectedly turns up pregnant. Now he loves Mary, but he knows that kid in her belly doesn't belong to him. He also knows that if he continues with the engagement, everyone will believe the worst of him and his bride-to-be."

Wade set the bacon back on his plate.

"Not that I'm suggesting Amy's any virgin, mind you," Frank said.

Wade's appetite had been keen five minutes earlier; now, what little breakfast he'd managed to swallow sat like a lump of day-old oatmeal in the pit of his stomach. He glared across the table at the sheriff.

"Something wrong, Pastor?" Frank asked. His face broke into a grin. A wide one.

"That was below the belt, Frank."

"How's that?"

"Quoting scripture to a pastor."

"I didn't quote scripture."

Wade pushed his plate aside, appetite gone. "You didn't need to."

"You taking Amy to the dance?"

And Wade had thought that Dovie was less than tactful. He was beginning to understand that husband and wife made one hell of a team. "All right, all right," he said ungraciously, "but I want you to know right now that this is the end of it, understand?"

"Fine. If that's the way you want it."

"I do."

Frank's eyes flew to his. "I do? Isn't that what a

groom says when he speaks his vows?" Chuckling, Frank slid from the booth and swaggered out of the café.

Wade was still glaring.

Amy would have been kidding herself if she said she wasn't excited about her date with Wade McMillen.

"Date" might be too strong a word. Two days earlier Wade had phoned and invited her. Amy strongly suspected it was a pity invitation, but at this point pride was no longer as important as it had been. Rather than question what had prompted the invitation, she'd simply accepted.

The instant she got off the phone, Amy had phoned Caroline Weston. While she barely knew her, she felt Caroline was someone she could speak to openly.

Within an hour Amy had received two phone calls. The first one was from Dovie, who promised to bring her the perfect dress. Almost immediately, another call came from Savannah Smith, who was delighted to hear that Wade had asked Amy to the dance. More than delighted. She said it was about time Reverend McMillen realized he was a man, as well as a minister.

The afternoon of the dance, the three women descended on Amy like a swarm of bees.

"Dovie says she's your self-appointed fairy godmother," Caroline remarked as she walked into the house.

"Just consider us Dovie's assistants." Savannah Smith followed her into the living room, carrying a sleeping baby in an infant seat.

Dovie was the last one to enter the house. She carried a lovely antique white gown in her arms. "Ellie and Jane are coming, too, but they might be a few minutes late."

Amy wasn't sure what to make of all this.

"The way I figure it," Caroline said, studying her watch, "we have approximately two hours."

"Two hours for what?"

Caroline looked at her as though the answer was obvious. "To help our dear pastor realize something he's chosen to ignore for too long."

"Oh…" Amy recalled Savannah's words about Wade. But she didn't understand what, exactly, it had to do with her.

Before Caroline could explain further, the doorbell chimed again.

"Are we too early or too late?" Ellie Patterson asked. Dr. Patterson—Jane—was with her.

"Your timing's perfect," Caroline assured them both.

"What's going on?" Amy asked, still wondering what Caroline and Savannah had meant about Wade. While she appreciated all the attention, it certainly didn't take five women to deliver a dress. Then, suddenly, Amy understood—these women were here to give her a makeover. Apparently she looked worse than she'd realized.

Sagging onto the sofa, she brushed her shoulder-length hair back from her face, using both hands. "I'm hopeless, aren't I?" she said, staring up at the women who crowded her living room.

"Hopeless?" Dovie repeated.

The five women burst out laughing.

"Oh, Amy," Dovie said gently, "it's just the opposite." She sat down next to her and reached for Amy's hand, holding it between both of her own. "We're not here to make you beautiful. You already are."

"Then why…?"

Caroline and Savannah exchanged glances as if to decide who would say it.

"We're here to bring Wade McMillen to his knees," Caroline said.

"But he's been wonderful to me!"

"He'll be more than wonderful once we get finished with you," Ellie insisted.

The other women appeared to be in full agreement.

"What do you think of this hairstyle?" Savannah flipped open a magazine for Amy to inspect. The picture revealed an advertisement for cosmetics with a pencil-thin model wearing a black evening gown. There was a slit in the dress that stretched all the way up her thigh and her hair was a mussed flock of red curls. She clutched a strand of diamonds to her nonexistent breasts and threw back her head in laughter.

Not in two lifetimes would Amy resemble this model.

"Do you like the hair?" Savannah pressed.

"The flat stomach appeals to me a whole lot more."

"In time," Savannah promised.

If Laura's mother was an example, then Amy had hope. The infant, asleep in the portable carrier, wasn't more than three or four months old, and Savannah was as trim as a teenager. Amy had begun to wonder if she'd ever get her shape back.

Every day she discovered that more clothes no longer fit. She wore her jeans with the zipper open and a large sweatshirt pulled over them. Even the elastic bands around her two skirts had been stretched beyond recognition.

"I brought a few maternity clothes I thought you might need," Savannah whispered. "I figured we're about the same size. Unfortunately Caroline's too tall to wear anything of mine. Use them if you want and pass them on when you're through."

Then the transformation began. While Savannah brushed her hair, Ellie did Amy's nails and Caroline applied her makeup. When she'd finished, she started on her own.

Amy felt her eyes smart with tears and quickly blinked them away. "Why would you all do something so kind for a stranger?" she asked.

"A stranger?" Ellie squeezed Amy's hand. "You aren't a stranger."

"But I could rob everyone blind," she said, tossing out her arms. "I could run away in that dress."

"But you won't," Dovie said confidently.

"What makes you so sure?"

Dovie paused and gave a casual shrug. "After all these years, I think I've become a good judge of people. You, Amy, are one of the special ones."

"Don't you even think about crying," Caroline said, waving a mascara wand in her right hand. "You'll ruin your eye makeup."

Amy blinked furiously and the six of them broke into peals of laughter.

"Actually," Jane said, flopping down on the sofa, "let's be honest here and admit the truth. We like you, Amy. You haven't lived here a month, and already you're one of us."

Amy smiled, because that was the way she felt, too.

"Now let's be even more honest," Jane said. "We're here on account of Wade."

The others were quick to agree.

"Wade?" Amy repeated.

"Wade," they said in unison.

"I'm afraid," Dovie said kindly, "that our dear pastor needs to be brought down a peg or two, and we've decided you're the one to do it."

"What has he done?"

"He's gotten…" Jane searched for the right word.

"Smug," Ellie supplied. "Set in his ways and too damned sure he's got everything in his life all figured out. He needs a bit of shaking up."

The others nodded. "He's a little too arrogant," Savannah said.

"About the church?" That didn't sound anything like the Wade Amy had come to know.

"No, not with the church," Savannah replied, looking thoughtful.

"We're talking about…"

None of her friends seemed to want to say the word. They glanced at one another.

"Romance?" Amy finally suggested.

"Exactly," Dovie said, rubbing her palms together. "He's gotten rather…stodgy when it comes to matters of the heart. He's a little too sure he doesn't need love and marriage—that they don't fit with being a pastor."

"And we felt it was time someone opened his eyes."

"You think I'm the one to do that?" Amy found the suggestion highly amusing.

"You're not taking us seriously, are you?" Caroline asked.

"How can I?" Amy giggled. "Have any of you happened to notice I'm pregnant?"

"All the better," Ellie muttered. "Wade McMillen is about to get a crash course."

"You ready, girls?" Savannah asked, and pulled a hair dryer from deep inside the diaper bag.

"Ready," came a chorus of replies.

For the next while Savannah worked endlessly getting Amy's thick hair to curl like the redheaded model's in the magazine. Amy wasn't allowed to look in a mirror. While Savannah worked on her, Caroline painted her own nails and Ellie stood in front of the living-room mirror and tested a new brand of eyeliner.

"I don't think Frank ever dreamed his house would turn into a women's dressing room," Dovie teased.

They laughed again. When Laura awoke and wailed for her mother, Amy was sure the infant hadn't been asleep more than a few minutes. She was astonished to realize it had been two hours.

"My goodness, where did the afternoon go?"

"Are you ready to take a look in the mirror?" Jane asked.

Amy considered the question and nodded. The others instructed her to close her eyes, then the six of them trooped into the bedroom. Jane guided Amy to a spot in front of the full-length mirror.

"Okay, open your eyes."

The first thing Amy saw was the five women gathered around her, all smiling gleefully. Her own reflection stunned her. The transformation was complete. She'd never looked more glamorous, more lovely. Amy felt like Cinderella.

"What do you think?" Caroline asked.

"I...don't know what to say."

"You're gonna knock him for a loop," Jane said confidently.

"And the best part is," Ellie said, standing next to her sister-in-law, "we're all going to be there to see it happen."

* * *

Wade McMillen muttered under his breath as he slipped the string tie with the turquoise clasp over his head. He adjusted it and headed for the front door.

He wasn't sure how he'd gotten roped into this date. This would be the first time he'd taken anyone to the big dance. He wasn't sure it was a precedent he wanted to set. Not only that, he'd been finagled into the date and it didn't sit well with him.

Amy was a sweet kid. *But that's exactly what she is,* he reminded himself. *A kid.* Twenty-five was far too young for a man of thirty-three. If he was going to become romantically involved, then it would be with... Unfortunately no one came to mind.

He blamed Frank for this whole thing, right along with Dovie. The two people he'd helped out when they'd reached an impasse several months back. And this was the thanks he got.

Wade closed his eyes and groaned. Amy was young and pretty. Young enough and pretty enough to set Louise Powell's tongue wagging, that was for sure. Well, let the troublemaker talk all she wanted. She would, anyway, and anything he said in his own defense was sure to be misconstrued.

So he'd take Amy to the Grange hall tonight, and he'd dance with her, too, if that was what she wanted. But he fully intended to introduce her around. Charlie Engler might be interested. Steve Ellis, too. Both owned smaller spreads seventy or eighty miles outside Promise. They usually drove into town on Friday afternoons and split their time between the feed store and drinking beer at Billy D's. Lyle Whitehouse was often with them, but Wade wanted to steer Amy away from him. Lyle had a temper and tended to enjoy his liquor a little too much.

What Charlie and Steve needed, Wade figured, was a stabilizing influence. A wife and ready-made family would go a long way toward setting either man on the right path.

That decided, Wade reached for his Stetson, then locked the front door. He whistled as he drove toward Frank's old house. He hadn't thought to get Amy a corsage and stopped at the local Winn-Dixie on his way. Nothing fancy. He couldn't see investing a lot of money in a bunch of dyed blue carnations that were sure to get squashed when she danced. Besides *he* wouldn't be the one to smell their fragrance. Charlie would. Maybe Steve.

He parked his Blazer at the curb and hopped out. His smile was already in place when he rang the doorbell. Knowing Dovie had helped Amy find a decent dress, he wanted to be sure he complimented her on how pretty she looked.

He pressed the doorbell with one hand and held the flower in the other.

An inordinate amount of time passed—at least two minutes—and Wade pressed the bell again. The door opened just then and a fashion model stood before him. His mouth must have dropped open; all he could do was stare. This had to be a joke and if so he wasn't amused.

"I'm here for Amy," he said, wondering who was behind this scheme.

"Wade, it's me," she said, and laughed softly.

Four

Nell Bishop felt like an entertainment director aboard a cruise ship. Her dude ranch was in full operation now, and the second group of cowboy wannabes had thought it would be great fun to end their adventure by attending the dance put on by the local Cattlemen's Association.

There were four men and two women, all gussied up in their finest Western gear. She'd driven them to the festivities in the used minivan she'd bought at the first of the month. So far, her plan to turn Twin Canyons into a dude ranch, complete with a trail drive and sleeping under the stars, had been an unqualified success.

Of course Nell had gotten plenty of help along the way. Her mother-in-law, Ruth, and her children, Jeremy and Emma, had been indispensable; so were the two hands she'd hired.

The crazy part was that after spending a year and a half planning and developing her idea, she was ready to abandon everything—for love. Travis Grant was to blame for this sudden change of heart.

Nell remained on the edge of the dance floor, watching old Pete Hadley, who stood on the stage, a fiddle tucked under his chin, accompanying a country-and-western band. Couples formed uniform rows and performed the latest in line dances.

Men and women alike slid across the polished wood floor, looking like a scene out of a 1930s Hollywood musical, and all Nell could think about was how much she missed Travis. The engagement ring on her finger was testimony of his love. Although they spoke daily by phone, it wasn't enough. They were eager to marry, eager to start their lives together.

Unfortunately planning a time for their wedding wasn't a simple matter. Nell had obligations, and so did he. Because of the dude ranch, she was forced to stay in Texas. A summer in New York would have been a fabulous cultural experience for Jeremy and Emma, but it wasn't possible. Not this year.

Nor could Travis just pack his bags and move to Texas. Not yet. Like her, he had commitments. Speaking engagements, an author tour, followed by a research trip that had been booked for more than a year. Being apart like this wasn't what he wanted, either, but it couldn't be helped.

Three months, he'd told her, and then they'd be together for the rest of their lives. It hadn't sounded so bad when he first outlined his schedule. The weeks would fly by, he'd said, and they had. It was almost July now, and soon August would arrive and before she knew it, September. On the first Saturday of September Travis and Nell would become husband and wife.

"Nell." Caroline Weston stopped in front of the punch bowl beside Nell. "My goodness, I can't remember the last time I saw you. You look fantastic. How are you?"

"Wonderful," Nell told her friend, which was the

truth. But if anyone looked fantastic, it was Caroline. Her pregnancy was obvious now and she literally glowed with an inner contentment. "You must be so happy." Nell was pleased that Caroline had found her cowboy at last. Grady Weston might be stubborn and quick-tempered, but he was a man who would love and honor his wife.

Caroline's face flushed with pleasure as she rested her hands on her stomach. "I've never felt better."

Grady joined his wife. He stood behind Caroline and caressed her shoulders. "Good to see you, Nell. How's the dude ranch going?"

"It's keeping me busy," she said. Her gaze wandered to the dance floor, and she was gratified to see that her guests were enjoying themselves. Two couples and two male business executives made up her current group. They were a good mix; everyone had gotten along well. Nell didn't expect that to be the case with every two-week session and considered herself fortunate.

"My feet need a rest," Caroline announced, and Grady led his wife to a row of chairs that lined one wall. A number of spectators sat there, visiting with one another.

Nell watched as Grady and Caroline joined them. Once she was comfortable, Grady brought his wife something cool to drink. Nell smiled absently and tapped her foot to the music. A year earlier, Grady had unexpectedly phoned and invited her to this very dance. She'd gotten two invitations, in fact—one from Glen Patterson, as well—and now, a brief twelve months later, both Grady and Glen were married.

The ache of loneliness inside Nell increased. Travis Grant was a city slicker, her first guest on the dude ranch, and she'd fallen head over heels in love with him. And he with her. Both had been married before. Nell was a widow, and Travis was divorced. Neither had any intention of falling in love again. But they'd been thrown together working to solve the mystery that surrounded Bitter End, the ghost town situated outside Promise. Eagerly on Travis's part, reluctantly on hers. But after research and much conjecture, they *had* solved it. In the process they'd fallen in love.

At first a lasting relationship between them had seemed impossible. Travis had returned to New York, and she'd resumed the business of her life, starting a new venture and raising her two children. But she'd been miserable. Travis, too. It wasn't long—less than two weeks—before they both realized they belonged together. They'd intended to get married right away. So much for best-laid plans. September had never seemed as far away as it did right that minute.

The music slowed and couples moved into each other's arms. Nell missed Travis so much that watching the dancers was almost painful. She was about to turn away when someone tapped her shoulder.

"I believe this dance is mine."

She instantly recognized the rich resonant voice. *Travis.* But that wasn't possible. He was touring on the East Coast and not due back in New York until Sunday. Not due in Texas until right before their wedding.

Nell whirled around, convinced her heart was playing tricks on her. "Travis?" Her shocked afraid-to-believe gaze met his. After a second of stunned wonder, she hurled herself into his arms.

Travis clasped Nell around the waist and, in his joy, half lifted her from the ground. Without caring about an audience, she spread kisses all over his face. "Travis, oh, Travis."

She didn't know how he happened to arrive in Texas for this dance or how long he could stay. None of that was important just then. Being in his arms was.

"Let's dance," he whispered, and reached for her hand.

Numb with happiness, she blindly followed him onto the floor.

Dancing was little more than a convenient excuse to continue holding each other. Nell closed her eyes as she moved into his embrace, listening to the slow mellow music. With her arms around his neck and her face against his shoulder, she clung to him and he to her. All too soon the dance ended, long before Nell was ready, and from the reluctant way he released her, she knew Travis wasn't ready, either. With no other choice they broke apart and applauded politely.

"How... When?" she asked as they walked off the dance floor. In her shock, she had trouble getting the words out.

Travis took her hand and led her to a quiet corner, away from the festivities. They sat facing each other, so close their knees touched.

"I phoned late yesterday afternoon," he began. "You weren't there. I was feeling miserable without you and exhausted from the tour. I was scheduled to fly back to New York last night."

Nell knew that much already.

"All at once I realized I didn't give a tinker's damn if I ever saw the New York skyline again. Everything that's important to me is right here in Promise."

"Why didn't you let me know...?"

He grinned and touched her cheek as if he couldn't believe, even now, that they were together. "Ruth answered the phone and we talked. She told me you'd been working too hard."

"I haven't, it's just that— Oh, Travis, it's so wonderful to see you." If they'd been anyplace other than a crowded dance with half the town looking on, she would've kissed him senseless. She had so much to tell him, so much she wanted to ask in the little time they had before he left again. His promotional tour might be over, but he was scheduled to leave almost immediately on a research trip deep in the interior of Mexico.

Travis touched her face and his eyes brightened with intensity. "I'm not taking that trip."

"But Travis, you've been planning it for so long."

"I'll go someday, but when I do it'll be with you. I didn't know it was possible to feel this strongly about someone. As far as I'm concerned, the entire book tour was a waste. My publicist said that next time the publisher plans anything like this, they'll gladly pay to have you fly with me. I wasn't worth a damn. Look what you've done to me, Nell."

She smiled. "How long can you stay?" she asked.

Travis glanced at his watch and Nell realized he'd probably need to be back on the road by morning.

"Does the next forty years suit you?"

"What?" His response completely unsettled her.

"I want us to get married."

"Now?"

"As soon as we can set it up with Wade," he said. "We'll leave on our honeymoon right away. Somewhere wonderful, anywhere, I don't care as long as we're together."

"But I can't go now." Nell's heart sank. "I can't leave

the ranch." Although her guests were due to depart the next morning, a fresh batch was scheduled to arrive first thing Monday.

"It's all been arranged," Travis insisted.

"Arranged? What do you mean?"

"Actually this was all Ruth's idea. She asked me to remind you of a surprise birthday party you threw for her last year. Well, this little surprise is her doing." Travis grinned. "Ruth's got your bags packed and says she refuses to listen to any excuses."

"What about—"

"It's covered, sweetheart. Ruth got two of her retired friends to come in and ride roughshod over the next bunch of greenhorns. Everything's under control, so don't worry."

"But—"

"We're getting married, Nell, no ifs, ands or buts!"

"Yes, oh, Travis, yes." Nell was overcome with gratitude—and with joy—that he was here and she was in his arms...and they were getting married!

"I knew you'd agree once you heard my plan."

Smiling through her tears, Nell hugged the greenhorn who'd captured her heart. Ruth had said that one day she'd give her a surprise as big as the birthday party Nell had thrown for her. Nell had never dreamed it would be something this wonderful.

"I'm crazy about you," Travis whispered.

Wonderful, indeed.

After acting like an idiot at Amy's front door, Wade had quickly recovered his composure by making some ridiculous comment about the sunlight blinding his eyes.

He'd been blinded all right, but it wasn't by the sun.

Just then he suspected it had been his own stupidity that had done him in.

The Lord had quite a sense of humor, Wade reflected. He considered what happened a sort of a divine-induced attitude adjustment. From the way he'd behaved, anyone might have thought that taking Amy to this dance was a burden. An unpleasant chore. He'd done everything but hide in an effort to avoid it. In reality, he was so calf-eyed over her it was all he could do to keep the drool off his chin. What he'd needed was a good swift kick in the rear. And Amy had provided it.

The minute they'd arrived, Amy had received more attention than a Smithsonian exhibit. Single ranchers had immediately flocked around her; two hours later, they still did. Wade had never seen anything like it.

No sooner had they stepped into the hall than Steve Ellis had asked for a dance. The guy had his nerve! Wade hadn't seen any of the other men stopping and requesting a dance from someone else's date. What really stuck in his craw was that the evening was half over and he had yet to dance with Amy.

He couldn't get close enough to ask.

Okay, okay, so this was probably what he deserved. He was the first to admit his attitude had been all wrong. He'd made a mistake in not owning up to the way he felt about her. A big mistake—but it seemed he wasn't going to get the opportunity to undo it.

This sudden interest was due to more than simply the fact that Amy was a beautiful woman. Anyone looking at her could see that. On the drive to the dance he'd struggled to keep his eyes on the road and not on her. So, okay, he was attracted to her. He liked her, too. Really liked her, and had from the first.

But he'd been afraid of what people would say if he pursued a relationship with her. A romance. Fear had dominated his actions.

Sheriff Hennessey had tried to talk sense into him. Unfortunately Wade's stubborn pride had prevented him from hearing the message. He resented being manipulated, and he'd focused on that, instead of his feelings for Amy.

From this point forward he refused to allow what others thought to dictate his decisions. He wanted to get to know Amy better. If she wasn't ready to date, then he'd start by being her friend. She was a generous person and he hoped she'd be willing to give him a second chance. That was, if he could manage to break through the throng of men vying for her attention.

At social events such as this, Wade made a point of dancing with the older single women, widows and the like. Women his mother's and grandmother's ages. Tonight, however, he couldn't make himself do it. The only person he wanted to hold in his arms was Amy Thornton—his date. So far, unfortunately, he'd only seen her from a distance.

"Are you enjoying yourself?" Dovie sneaked in the question as she danced past him on Frank's arm. The smile in her eyes told Wade she was well aware of how miserable he was.

Dovie Boyd Hennessey had a mean streak in her, he thought grimly. One that cut to the bone.

"Pretty as a picture, isn't she?" Frank asked as they glided past him a second time.

Wade didn't need to ask who they meant, either. But then he'd made it fairly obvious. He hadn't been able to take his eyes off Amy all night. He was about to turn away and bury his sorrows in a plate from the buffet when the dance ended. Whether by luck or design, Amy stood next to him. She slid her arm through his and gave a deep sigh.

"I've got to sit down for a bit," she said to him. "My feet are killing me."

Here she was, the woman he'd been patiently waiting to dance with all night, and for the life of him, Wade couldn't think of a sensible thing to say.

She gazed up at him as though she'd been anticipating this moment the entire evening. "I hope you don't mind."

"No, ah...sure." His tongue refused to cooperate and work properly. He glanced over his shoulder and saw Grady and Caroline seated close by. Caroline's feet rested in his lap and Grady was rubbing her nylon-covered toes. The scene was intimate, the husbandly gesture loving and thoughtful. The ache inside Wade caught him unawares. In the last year a number of his friends had married, and while he was happy for them, he didn't feel the need for a wife and family himself. He'd always seen his life as complete, viewed his pastoral duties as too demanding for marriage. His satisfaction came from his work, and it was enough—or so he believed. In that moment, however—and other moments like it—he felt keenly alone.

"We can sit here," he said, finally clearing his head. He escorted Amy to an empty section of seats and sat down next to her.

"Thank you," she whispered, and sent him a warm smile.

Wade nearly drowned in her beautiful eyes. He saw her slip out of her shoes and wiggle her toes a couple of times. Then, feeling remiss, he asked, "Would you like something to drink?"

She nodded, her eyes grateful. "That would be wonderful, but nothing alcoholic."

Wade wanted to kick himself, convinced that the minute he left someone would take his seat. He'd been waiting for an opportunity like this and now he was going to lose it.

Sure enough, as soon as he reached the punch bowl, Lyle Whitehouse was standing beside her, leaning against a chair. He looked like he was about to sit down when he suddenly stared over at Wade. Then he nodded and after a couple of seconds walked away.

Wade made it back in record time, nearly stumbling over his own feet in his effort to get to her before some other rancher did.

"Here you go," he said, handing her the plastic cup. "Uh, how do you like the dance so far?" he asked, trying to make small talk.

"I'm having a wonderful time."

No doubt, Wade mused darkly, seeing as she'd danced every dance, and each one had been with a different partner. *Not* including him. But when Pete Hadley and the band started a favorite song of Wade's from the movie *Dirty Dancing,* "She's like the Wind," it was impossible to hold still.

"I know your shoes are off," he said, "but would you care to take a spin?"

Wade wasn't sure what he expected, but not such a quick agreement. "I'd like that."

She slipped her feet back into her shoes and he extended a hand to help her up. They walked onto the dance floor and he took her in his arms. She was tiny, eight or nine inches shorter than he was, which put the top of her head level with his shoulder. Yet they fit together nicely.

Wade wasn't exactly light on his feet, but he could manage a simple slow dance. Amy followed his lead as though they'd been partners for years. He hummed along with the song and was surprised when her soft voice joined his, harmonizing. They smiled at each other, and he gathered her closer.

That was when it happened. The baby kicked. Wade's eyes widened at the strength of the movement. "I didn't realize I'd be able to feel the baby," he said with awe. "That's really something."

"I think she likes the music."

"She?"

"Or he, but since I don't know, I decided to call the baby Sarah."

"And what if she's a he? Do you have a boy's name picked out?"

"Joseph."

That was appropriate, he thought, remembering what Frank had reminded him of the biblical story of Joseph and Mary. Appropriate and a little uncanny.

"A good solid name," he murmured, trying not to let his reaction show.

The song ended far too soon to suit him. He hated to ask Amy to dance again, knowing how worn-out she was, but he couldn't resist. "One more dance?"

She looked up and nodded. He might have been mistaken, but she seemed pleased that he'd asked.

Amy knew how Cinderella must have felt the night of the ball when she first danced with her prince, because that was exactly how she felt just then. All evening she'd waited for Wade to ask her; when it seemed he never would, she gave up. Then the minute she sat down he'd asked.

This was quite possibly the most wonderful night of her life, she mused as Wade held her close. The baby had decided to take up marching and was halfway to Pretoria when she did a swift about-face and kicked Wade. To Amy's delight, he'd been fascinated.

Her fairy godmother, in the guise of Dovie Hennessey, caught sight of her on the dance floor with Wade and winked. Amy winked back and managed to stifle a laugh.

Never in all her life had Amy been this popular with men. From the moment she arrived, she'd been bombarded with requests to dance. When she was first approached, she'd hoped Wade would explain to the others that she was his date. He hadn't done that. Amy knew he hadn't been excited about taking her to the dance and so, rather than burden him with her company, she'd accepted. But truth be known, Wade McMillen was the man she wanted to dance with, more than anyone.

He'd stood by most of the evening, watching her with everyone else, and that had been a bitter disappointment. Only she wasn't disappointed now.

Once they were on the dance floor, Wade didn't seem eager to leave. Amy didn't want to, either. If she closed her eyes, she could pretend that the man who held her was in love with her and wanted this baby. It was a silly fantasy, born of her need to create a secure happy world for her child.

She'd loved Alex with all her heart, but she'd been foolishly blind to his selfishness. For most of her life she'd been more parent than child to her own mother. It had come as no surprise that her mother cut herself off from her just at the time she'd needed her most. Disappointed though she was, Amy could handle the rejection because it was such a familiar experience. Even an expected one.

But Alex had lied to her and hurt her. Deeply. That was one reason this attraction to Wade had surprised her. Now that she was in his arms, even if it was on a dance floor, she couldn't make herself think of him as her pastor. He was a man. Vital, real and handsome.

The baby kicked again, harder this time, and Amy heard Wade chuckle.

"She's got good taste in music," he whispered close to her ear.

"Her mommy's fond of Roy Orbison, too."

"Would you mind if I..." Wade paused as though he wasn't sure he should proceed.

"You'd like to feel the baby?" she asked, tilting her head up just enough to look into his eyes.

"If you don't mind."

"I don't." She took his hand and pressed his palm against her stomach, holding it there. Sarah cooperated beautifully and Amy watched as his face took on a look of reverence and surprise.

"My goodness," he whispered. "That really is something," he said again.

"You should feel her from my end," Amy teased.

His expressive eyes brightened and he broke into a full smile.

"What took you so long?" she asked, feeling content. "The evening was half over before you even asked me to dance."

"I'm a fool. But—" he grinned sheepishly "—I'm a fast learner."

"Good."

The rest of the evening passed far too quickly for Amy. She could have danced with him all night, especially those slow, languid dances. What pleased her the most, perhaps, was how comfortable she felt with Wade. For a few hours it was as though all the worries and problems she'd carried alone all this time had been lifted from her shoulders.

Reality would return soon enough, but for now it was easy to pretend, easy to push her troubles aside and concentrate, instead, on the handsome prince smiling down on her.

Then it was midnight and time to head home. Following the dance, Wade and Amy were invited to a party at Glen and Ellie's place. Amy would have liked to go, but realized Wade had church services early the next morning. It didn't seem fair to keep him up half the night simply because she was in a party mood.

They sang along with the radio on the ride back into Promise. The drive out had been spent in silence, and while they'd done little real talking that evening, Amy felt they'd reached a tacit understanding. She felt they'd achieved an appreciation and acceptance of each other that had been missing previously.

Wade parked under the large weeping willow in front of the house. Moonlight filtered through the branches and cast a silvery glow about them.

Amy reflected on her unexpectedly wonderful evening. Her magical evening with Wade McMillen. Dancing with him, being held by him, was everything she'd known it would be. And she knew with certainty that this was the kind of man she wanted as a father to her child, the kind of man she wanted one day to marry. She'd given up thinking men like him still existed.

"I can't thank you enough," she said, leaning back against the seat and closing her eyes. "Oh, Wade, I had such a lovely time."

"I enjoyed myself, too."

She sighed, her heart full of joy and, yes, gratitude.

"The Fourth of July will be here before we know it," he said.

Amy had heard about the annual Willie Nelson Fourth of July picnic. The community faithfully invited Willy every year, but he'd never managed to come—and then he'd shocked everyone by showing up last spring for the annual rodeo and chili cook-off.

"Do you have any plans?" Wade asked.

"For the Fourth? None." Her hopes soared; surely he'd mentioned the holiday as a preamble to inviting her to join him. It was crazy to think this way, for a lot of reasons. She suspected he was reluctant to become romantically involved, because of his work. But she couldn't keep her heart from hoping… And for her, the timing was difficult, to say the least.

"I understand the community has a big picnic every year in the park," she added, encouraging him to continue.

"I've never been."

"You haven't?" Amy couldn't imagine what had kept him away.

"My family has a big get-together every year. It's quite a shindig."

Amy envied him his family.

"I was just thinking," he said, "that maybe you'd like to come this year."

"With you?"

"Unless, of course, you'd rather attend the community festivities."

Amy was afraid to reveal how eager she was to go with him. "No, I'd rather... I—thank you." She smiled tentatively. "I'd enjoy meeting your family." The baby stirred and Amy bit her lip. In retrospect, perhaps now wouldn't be the best time to meet Wade's parents. She could only imagine what they'd think when their preacher son arrived with a pregnant woman. That gave new meaning to the words "family outing."

As a child Amy used to wonder what it would be like to be part of a traditional family. A real family, where people cared about each other, where they shared things and celebrated together. A mother and father, brother and sister, grandparents. She'd experienced none of that, and she longed for it.

"Are you sure you want me to meet your parents... like this?" she felt obliged to ask.

"I wouldn't have asked you otherwise," Wade told her with a sincerity that couldn't be questioned.

They sat side by side, talking quietly for another five minutes before Amy yawned. She didn't want this incredible evening ever to end, but her eyes were closing despite her resolve.

"Let's get you inside," Wade suggested. He had his car door open before she could protest.

Reluctantly Amy straightened and let him help her out of the car. At the beginning of the night she'd felt young and full of energy. Six hours later, her feet hurt, her legs were weak and shaky, and she was more exhausted than she could remember being in her entire life. Exhausted…but happy.

Wade placed his arm around her as they walked up the sidewalk toward the small house. Until they reached the front porch, Amy hadn't given the matter of a goodnight kiss a single thought. Now she turned to Wade, wondering what he'd do. He seemed as uncertain as she was.

"Well," he said, taking a step back. "I had a great time."

So he'd decided against it. That was fine; she understood. Perhaps next time, even if she felt a little disappointed now.

"Thank you for taking me to the dance," Amy said formally, opening her handbag to search for the key.

"Amy?"

She glanced up, and when she did, she realized that he intended to kiss her. And she intended to let him.

Five

Wade had officiated at a few hurried weddings, but none in which the bride had less than forty-eight hours to prepare. The bride and the entire community. The first Wade had heard of Nell and Travis's wedding was Sunday, after services. Travis announced they'd be applying for the license Monday morning and would greatly appreciate it if Wade could marry them that same evening.

Sure enough, Monday evening the couple stood before him, surrounded by family and friends. In his years as a minister, he'd performed dozens of marriages. Most engaged couples attended several weeks of counseling first. Generally he hesitated to marry people who were in too much of a rush. Nell and Travis hadn't taken his counseling sessions, but he'd talked extensively with them both when they became engaged. They showed all the signs of making their marriage strong and lasting. They were committed to each other and to their relationship. While deeply in love, neither was ruled by passion. Both were mature adults who were accepting and encouraging of each other.

Outwardly their differences seemed overwhelming. Travis lived in New York City and Nell single-handedly managed a cattle ranch near Promise. Travis was a well-known author and Nell a struggling business-woman. But Wade soon realized their differences were superficial; what they had in common was far more important. They shared not only a deep love but a goal, a vision for the future. A vision that had to do with creating a supportive and loving home for each other and for Nell's family. Wade didn't have one qualm about this rushed wedding.

Nell might have had only forty-eight hours to prepare for her wedding, but the church was as lovely as he'd ever seen it. The sanctuary had been decorated with roses and candles whose flickering light cast an enchanted glow over those who'd gathered to share the moment with Travis and Nell. Savannah Smith had supplied armloads of red roses, arranging them in glittering crystal vases. Wade couldn't recall seeing any roses lovelier than the ones from Savannah's lush garden, certainly none with a more glorious scent.

Wade smiled at the couple. Given that the wedding was being held with little prior notice, no invitations had been mailed. But word had been passed on the street. It surprised Wade that so many people had come tonight to share in Nell's joy. Then again, it didn't. The folks in Promise admired Nell, so they wanted to stand with her as she pledged her heart to Travis. Grateful for the role he'd played in resolving the mystery of Bitter End, the town had accepted Travis as one of their own. People were happy for the couple and looked to show their support.

After a few introductory words Wade opened his Bible. When he'd finished, he glanced up, prepared to ask Nell and Travis to repeat their vows. As he did, he noticed Amy sitting next to Dovie and Frank.

He'd seen her briefly following the Sunday service, but she'd slipped away before he was able to seek her out. The night of the dance had been a revelation to him; he'd finally acknowledged how he felt about her. Finally acknowledged that he felt an attraction to Amy—that he wanted to pursue a relationship with her, even if it threw his whole life into chaos. Which it would.

When they danced, he'd felt her baby move against him and an unfamiliar emotion had stirred deep inside him. Later, he'd placed his palm over her extended stomach and it was as though her child had leaped to greet him. Then, he'd brought her home and kissed her goodnight. The moment had been fleeting, but her kiss had stayed with him for hours afterward. Was with him still. In the two days since, he'd thought of little except Amy and her child. He wondered if she'd been thinking of him, too. And hoped she had. Even now, in the middle of a wedding, it was all he could do not to stare at her.

He hadn't expected Amy to be here tonight, but he was glad she'd come—if for no other reason than he could see her again.

"Travis, do you take…" Wade continued speaking, the words as much a part of him as the scripture passage he routinely read in the marriage ceremony. Yet, again and again, his attention wandered back to Amy, as if drawn to her by an invisible force.

After the ceremony the congregation applauded loudly. Travis kissed Nell, and when they broke apart, Nell's face was flushed with happiness. She hugged her children as Ruth, her mother-in-law, dabbed at her eyes with a handkerchief.

Beaming, Travis pumped Wade's hand, then hugged Jeremy and Emma, Nell's son and daughter. Wade laughed outright when Travis kissed a flustered Ruth on the cheek.

Dovie had baked a wedding cake and that, along with coffee, was being served in the church hall immediately afterward.

Wade waited until the church was empty, blew out the candles and followed the crowd to the reception. He found himself standing next to Amy, who was eating a thin slice of cake.

"That was a beautiful ceremony," she said.

"Weddings and baptisms are my specialties."

She patted her stomach. "Sarah's pleased to hear that."

"Has she been marching around much today?"

"Like a drum majorette."

Wade chuckled. He finished his cake and set the paper plate aside. "I wanted you to know how much I enjoyed the dance on Saturday night."

"I did, too." Her cheeks went pink. "I'm looking forward to spending the Fourth of July with you and your family."

There was no further time to talk; Travis approached them, thanking Wade jubilantly. He also thanked Amy for coming to share in their happiness.

Forty minutes after the ceremony Nell and Travis were gone and the hall had emptied. Dovie and a couple of other women from the church had stayed behind to clean up. Amy was with them, ready to pitch in and do what she could.

Wade made his way back to the sanctuary to turn out the lights and lock up the church for the night. The peaceful silence was a distinct contrast to the noise and merrymaking of the reception. He slipped into a pew; he liked to check in with the "Boss" now and then when something was weighing on his mind.

Wade leaned forward, bracing his elbows on his knees. "Okay, okay, so I'll admit it, I'm attracted to her. There, I said it, are you happy? If you were sending me a wake-up call, then I received it loud and clear. I like her—and I liked kissing her. You've got my attention." He raised his head. "Now what?"

Why a scene from the church dinner nearly a year ago would flash into his mind just then, Wade couldn't say. It was one of the biggest social functions held by the church, and he remembered how difficult it'd been to find a place to sit. His friends were all busy with their wives or lady friends. It was one of the only times Wade could remember feeling alone. Shortly afterward he'd given some thought to seeking a romantic relationship. He'd gone so far as to make up a list. He'd completely forgotten that or where he'd placed it.

His Bible.

He reached for the leather-bound volume at his side and found the tattered slip of paper tucked under the fly leaf. What he read was:

1. A woman who loves God as much as she does me.
2. A woman as interested in a family as I am.
3. Long legs.

He laughed out loud at the last request. His smile slowly faded and it seemed as if the voice in his heart wasn't as still or as small as it had been in the past.

"Amy?" he said aloud. God had sent Amy for him?

Sighing deeply, Wade leaned back against the wooden pew. An argument rose fast and furious within him, then died just as quickly. The strength of the attraction he felt for her had overwhelmed him the night of the dance. Afterward, too.

Questions crowded his heart. "I don't mean to complain, Lord, but are you sure you sent me the right woman?"

Silence.

"All right, all right, I get the message. I asked. You sent. I shouldn't complain. It's not that I object to Amy, mind you," he whispered, "it's just that…" What? "Just that…" he began again, and realized he was afraid. Not of falling in love. He was ready for that; he'd come to terms with the prospect of upheaval in his life—had even begun to look forward to it. But he was afraid of what he didn't know. He didn't want to demand answers or pry into her life, but it wasn't as if he could ignore the pregnancy, either.

He was afraid of making an emotional commitment to her and her baby, and then watching her walk out on him. Afraid of loving her and risking his heart.

Amy Thornton had come into his life, looking for a few miracles. What he hadn't understood at the time was that she might accomplish a few miracles of her own.

Grady Weston's long hard day had been spent driving his herd of stubborn cattle from one range to another. The sun beat down on him with an intensity that was a prelude of what would come later in the summer.

He felt good. About life. About love. About his family. In about three months he and Caroline would be parents for the second time. Maggie was his daughter in every way that mattered. The father's name had been left blank on the birth certificate, so he'd been able to adopt her shortly after he married Caroline. But this pregnancy would be the first time he'd experienced all the emotion and joy that came before the actual birth.

Boy or girl, as far as Grady was concerned he'd be happy with either. Even without knowing, he loved this child with a fierceness that was equaled only by his love for Maggie.

He recalled the night his sister had given birth to Laura Rose. Laredo had been hopeless, barely able to function. Grady had found his brother-in-law's actions somewhat amusing, but as Caroline's time drew near, Grady suspected he wouldn't be much better. Already he worried about her. He wished he could talk her into quitting her job at the post office early, but she was determined to work until the last minute. Whether or not she'd return to work after the baby was born was entirely up to her. She'd mentioned she might take a few years off and go back once their youngest had reached school age. He hoped she would; for her own sake more than his.

Grady looked up and was surprised to see someone approach. He strained his eyes, not recognizing the rider until he came closer. It was Wade McMillen. He couldn't imagine what the reverend might want, unless it was to announce some kind of trouble. Studying the rider, however, told him that wasn't the case. Wade rode with an easy grace, instead of the urgency a crisis would demand.

"Howdy," Grady called out, touching a finger to the brim of his hat.

"Howdy," Wade returned. "Laredo said I'd find you

out here. Hope you don't mind that I borrowed one of your geldings."

"I don't have the slightest objection." Wade was a fine rider; if he hadn't become a preacher, Grady figured he would've made one hell of a rancher.

"Have you got a few minutes?" Wade asked.

"Sure."

Wade regarded him seriously. "What I wanted to discuss is private. I'd prefer that it stayed between you and me."

Grady nodded. "If that's the way you want it, then that's how it'll be."

"I appreciate it." Wade met his eyes. "This is difficult to talk about," he began. "I never asked Caroline about the father of her child."

Grady felt his anger rising. "For all intents and purposes, I'm Maggie's father. That's all anyone needs to know."

"I realize that, Grady, and I certainly don't mean to imply anything by asking—but she has a birth father."

"Yes," Grady admitted reluctantly. He couldn't love his six-year-old daughter any more than he already did.

He remembered his initial shock when he'd learned his no-good brother, Richard, was her biological father—when he'd learned that Maggie was the result of a liaison Richard had apparently forgotten. But none of that mattered. Maggie truly was the child of Grady's heart.

There was a time when she wouldn't even look at him, preferring to hide her face in her mother's skirts. Having little experience with children, he'd been unintentionally gruff and impatient with her. But eventually Maggie had been won over—not without determined effort on his part and not without a crisis first. In retrospect he was pleased that winning Maggie's heart had been so difficult. When they'd finally made their peace, he'd experienced a sense of exhilaration and triumph.

"Why all these questions about Maggie?" Grady asked.

Now it was Wade's turn to grow silent for a long moment. "Did you meet Amy Thornton at the dance Saturday night?"

"Amy Thornton," Grady repeated. He frowned. "Isn't she the gal taking the birthing class with Caroline and me?"

"She's the one," Wade said, nodding.

"Dovie's her partner?"

"Yes."

Grady eyed the reverend. "The pretty little gal."

Wade nodded again.

Grady understood now why Wade had come to him. "Are you planning to ask her to marry you?" he asked bluntly.

Wade eyes widened at the directness of the question. "I can't answer that…"

"But you're thinking about it?"

"Not yet, but…well maybe," he admitted.

For a man contemplating marriage, Grady noticed that Wade didn't seem too pleased. Time for a man-to-man discussion, as his father used to say. That being the case, they might as well sit down and let the horses rest. He headed Starlight in the direction of the creek.

A silent and obviously troubled Wade followed him over the crest of the hill. Willow trees bordered the slow-moving water, their long supple branches dipping lazily in the cool water. Grady dismounted and led Starlight to the creek's sloping bank. He sat on a large rock and waited until Wade was comfortable before he resumed the conversation. "Okay, let's talk this out," he suggested.

"The thing is," Wade said, "I don't *know* anything about Amy."

"Do you love her?" It was a bold question, but Grady couldn't see skirting around the subject when that was all that truly mattered.

Wade's head came up. "I think so... Yes." He closed his eyes. "I don't know why I do or how it happened. A week ago I was doing everything I could, short of leaping off a bridge, to get out of taking her to the dance."

Grady laughed. "I seem to recall Caroline mentioning a certain reluctance on your part."

"You mean Amy knew?"

"I think she might have."

Wade groaned aloud.

"What caused this sudden change of heart?"

The question went unanswered for a moment. "I'd tell you straight if I could. When I went to pick her up for the dance, I felt as if...as if someone had stuck me with a cattle prod. I'd noticed her before, plenty, but I don't know... I was afraid, I guess. Afraid of exactly what's happening now. She's beautiful, but I don't want you to think that's the only reason I'm attracted to her."

"Well, it doesn't hurt any."

"True, but it's much more than that," Wade said. He reached for a long blade of grass and peeled off a strip. "I've only kissed her once, and as far as kisses go, it was pretty chaste."

"But you enjoyed it."

Wade's tight face broke into a grin. "I damn near blew a fuse."

Grady laughed, remembering the first time he'd kissed Caroline. It had left him reeling for days. All he could think about was kissing her again. Judging by the desperation and yearning on his face, Wade was obviously experiencing the same reaction.

"Then Monday night at Nell's wedding…"

"Yes?" Grady prodded the minister.

"I… I had the strongest sense—" he glanced at Grady, then quickly averted his gaze "—that Amy and I were meant to be together." He paled slightly. "I barely know her and I know almost nothing about her past."

"You mean, who's the father of her baby and why isn't she with him?" Grady believed in plain speaking.

Wade shrugged, and again he hesitated. "It's just that…"

"Just what?"

Wade tossed the blade of grass aside and then, as if he needed something to do with his hands, removed his hat and held it by the brim, slowly rotating it. "I'm worried," he admitted.

"Falling in love isn't always easy," Grady said, feeling adequately knowledgeable on the subject. "Especially when there's a child involved. That complicates things. But you have to be willing to love the kid as if she's your own—or he, of course. And you have to trust the woman you love…" His own romance with Caroline had gone through its share of difficulties. In truth, he'd been a stubborn fool, and it'd probably help Wade if he shared that, but Grady preferred to let Wade think him wise and perceptive.

"There's a lot of unknowns with Amy."

That would worry Grady, too. It'd been different with

Caroline. Grady had known her almost all his life, not that he'd paid her any heed until recent years, when she'd become friends with Savannah.

"You might just ask her," Grady said. "I find the direct approach less confusing and troublesome myself."

"I could do that," Wade agreed, but he didn't sound confident about it.

"You don't want to ask her a lot of questions," Grady said.

"I'd rather she volunteered the information."

Grady didn't blame him for that. They sat there a good ten minutes without either one of them speaking. Grady was a patient man; he didn't mind waiting.

But when Wade continued to brood in silence, Grady finally asked, "What can I do to help you?"

Wade seemed to slowly shake himself free of his thoughts. "I guess I want you to tell me I'm not acting like a fool," he said in a low voice. "And that there's a chance for me with Amy—and her baby. That I'll say and do the right things."

Grady stood and slapped the minister on the back. "You'll know what's right when the time comes."

Wade exhaled. "I expect I will. Thanks for the pep talk."

"No problem. Come to me for advice anytime you want. I'm not exactly an expert on romance, but I'm willing to help." He actually felt sorry for the poor guy. He'd known Wade for a long time now and had never seen him looking so confused and unsettled.

Falling in love wasn't all starlit nights and picnics and romantic moments; it was also pain and uncertainty and risk.

Wade had just found that out.

* * *

Amy awoke before dawn on the Fourth of July, excited about spending this day with Wade McMillen.

Admittedly part of her excitement was due to the fact that she'd been invited to join his family's celebration of the holiday. In their brief conversation she'd learned that Wade was the oldest of three. His younger brother and sister were both married and each had two children. His mother apparently doted on her grandchildren.

The thought produced a small stab of pain. Amy's mother had wanted nothing to do with *her* grandchild. With effort Amy pushed away all thoughts of her. Alicia Thornton's life had been ravaged by drugs, alcohol and an endless series of disastrous relationships; she'd never functioned with any adequacy as a parent.

From the time she was able to make sense of her own life, Amy had been determined not to make the same mistakes her mother had. Until recently she'd done a good job, behaving responsibly. Then she'd met Alex.

He was another person she preferred not to think about.

Wanting to contribute something to the festivities, Amy tied an apron around her nightgown. "Okay, Sarah," she said, "we're going to bake Wade an apple pie." Dovie had told her Wade had a sweet tooth and one of his all-time favorites was apple pie. She'd even provided Amy with a recipe from her grandmother's cookbook. A crust made with buttermilk, and a few chopped dates added in with the apples.

Feeling ambitious, Amy baked two pies. One apple and one strawberry-rhubarb. Both turned out beautifully. She left them on the kitchen counter to cool, then showered and dressed for the day.

Her wardrobe was limited, but Savannah had given her a few clothes that fit perfectly. She chose a pair of shorts and a sleeveless top, then glanced at herself in the full-length mirror on the bedroom door.

"Oh, my, Sarah Jane," she whispered when she viewed her reflection. "We look *very* pregnant."

Well, there was no help for that. It wasn't as if she could hide the pregnancy; anyway, Wade was well aware of her condition when he invited her. If he'd had second thoughts, he would have said something before now.

No sooner had she finished curling her hair and applying her makeup than the doorbell chimed.

Wade stood there, looking about as handsome as a man had any right to be. She felt a jolt of pleasure at the sight of him.

"Come on inside," she said, unlatching the screen door. "I'm almost ready."

"I'm a few minutes early."

Amy hadn't noticed. "All I need to do is load up the pies."

"Pies?" He quirked one eyebrow.

"Strawberry-rhubarb and apple."

He groaned. "Apple's my favorite."

"That's what Dovie said."

"Did she also tell you what she discovered with Frank—that the way to a man's heart is through his stomach?"

Amy unsuccessfully hid a smile. "She might have mentioned something along those lines." She found a cardboard box in which to transport the pies. Wade moved to help her, and before she understood what he was doing, they bumped into each other.

His arm went out to balance her and she froze when his skin touched hers. Slowly she raised her eyes to his. Her breath jammed in her throat at the look of naked longing on his face. And she realized that same longing was reflected on her own.

Without conscious decision—Amy was convinced of that—they reached for each other. Her arms circled his neck and she stood on her toes, offering him her mouth. Wade kissed her with a thoroughness that left her grateful she was supported by his embrace.

"I've been dreaming of kissing you again since last Saturday."

"I...have, too," she whispered. Her eyes were closed. She was afraid to open them, afraid reality would ruin the moment and she couldn't bear that.

"I've thought of nothing but you all week."

"Oh, Wade, are we crazy? I hardly know you. You hardly know me. And yet...it's as though we're...supposed to be together."

She felt his chest lift with a sharp intake of breath and instantly regretted having spoken. It was true; she'd thought of him all week. But it'd been more than that. Something had changed the night of Nell and Travis's wedding.

Something had happened. Even though Amy didn't really know the couple, she'd let Dovie persuade her to attend the ceremony. Dovie had explained how Nell and Travis had met and fallen in love, and she'd mentioned the ghost town. Amy had found their story inspiring and romantic. She had to admit she was intrigued by Bitter End, too. To think the town had been forgotten all those years!

But as she sat in the church, her attention focused on

Wade, and she suddenly had the most intense feeling of *connection*. She was going to love Wade McMillen, she knew it, and he was going to love her. She couldn't explain where this certainty had come from, but she'd definitely felt it. And so, she thought at the time, had he.

However, having recently demonstrated her poor judgment when it came to men, Amy wasn't inclined to believe in what had happened. Later she'd managed to convince herself that it had been a form of self-hypnosis. Dr. Jane had said that because of the pregnancy, her emotions might be off-kilter.

That was it, Amy was sure. All these mixed-up feelings had been a fluke. Until now, she'd been able to believe that.

"I'm sorry," she whispered, mortified to the very marrow of her bones. "I didn't mean…"

Wade cradled her face between his hands and gazed into her eyes. "You felt it, too, didn't you?"

She lowered her lashes rather than admit the truth.

He kissed her as though to remove all doubt. This time their kisses were neither patient nor gentle, but fiery. Urgent. She wasn't sure if those kisses were meant to deny what they felt, to prove it false—or the opposite.

The baby stirred and Wade must have felt the movement because he abruptly broke off the kiss. Speechless, they clung to each other.

"We'd better go," he finally said. "We have a long drive ahead of us, and Mom and Dad are waiting."

Amy envied him his fast recovery. By the time the effect of their kisses had worn off, Wade had loaded the pies into his vehicle. Amy grabbed her purse and a sweater and locked the house.

Once they were on the road, Wade turned on the

radio and they sang along to a Willie Nelson ballad at the top of their lungs. There was something exhilarating about speeding down the highway on a perfect July morning. Amy felt a delicious sense of anticipation, a quivery excitement.

"Tell me about Bitter End," she said when the song was over.

He seemed surprised that she knew about the abandoned town. "It was settled, oh, about 130 years ago, after the Civil War, by families hoping to make a better life for themselves," he said. "Then...there was some kind of crisis. Nell and Travis found out there'd been an unjust hanging. A preacher's son. Afterward the town was said to be cursed by the preacher, and everyone moved away."

"I'd like to see it."

"I'm sure you will someday."

"It must be an incredible sight," she said, remembering what Dovie had told her, although her friend hadn't actually been to the town herself. Ellie had, but wasn't inclined to speak of it. "Perhaps we could explore it together," Amy suggested.

"Perhaps," he said noncommittally.

"Tell me more about your family," she said next.

"Mom's a housewife-turned-shop-owner," he told her. "After all the years of staying home for us kids, she started her own yarn shop when Janice Marie went away to college. She's always loved to knit, and this seemed a perfect outlet for her creativity. I don't think anyone's more surprised at Mom's success than she is."

"I don't know how to knit."

"Then my mother would love to teach you—whether you want to learn or not," he said with a chuckle. "Dad's a retired insurance broker, but he's busier now than he ever was working. He volunteers at the grade school tutoring children at risk. Last I heard, he was coaching Little League, too. He told me he simply hasn't got time to work, not when he's having this much fun."

"It sounds like you have a wonderful family."

"Just wait until you taste the barbecue. That's Dad's real specialty. He won't let anyone near the grill, not even my mother. He takes real pride in his slow-grilled ribs." Wade went on to describe the apron and hat his father would be wearing. A complete wardrobe reserved for the Fourth of July.

Amy's laugh was carefree. "Now what about your sister?"

"She's mean and ugly."

"Wade!"

"Well, she was when she was twelve and if she's changed I haven't noticed."

Amy didn't believe him for a minute.

"I can't understand what prompted André to marry Janice Marie."

"It might've had something to do with love."

Wade snickered. "It might, but I doubt it. Janice Marie bakes the world's best applesauce cake, and André has a weakness for it."

Amy rolled her eyes.

"Hey, he confessed it to me himself."

"What about your brother?"

"Larry? He's spoiled rotten. Both him and Janice. I'm the only one who turned out decent."

"Yeah, right." She grinned. "I can't wait to ask your mother the *real* story. You know, I'm so looking forward to meeting them." She paused. "What did they say when you told them you were bringing me?" She leaned back, patting her rounded stomach.

"They don't know you're coming."

Amy's amusement died. "What do you mean, they don't know I'm coming?"

Wade didn't appear to notice how upset she was. "I didn't tell them. Hey, it's no big deal."

"Yes, it is," she said, her panic rising. "Take me back to Promise," she demanded. "I can't—I *won't* meet your family. Not like this. Not without them knowing…"

Six

Wade pulled over to the side of the road. Amy looked as if she was about to burst into tears. And he had no idea what he'd done wrong.

"Amy?"

She was breathing hard and tears welled in her eyes. She opened the car door and leaped out.

"What is it?" He followed her, not sure what to do.

"You didn't even tell your parents you'd invited me to the family get-together?"

He gave her a puzzled look. "We often invite impromptu guests. Mom prepares enough food to feed a small army. You're welcome with or without my parents' knowledge."

"Then they don't know I'm pregnant, either." She folded her arms and glared at the sky. "That was a stupid question, seeing they don't even know I exist!"

"My parents aren't going to judge you," Wade promised. "They'll be thrilled I'm bringing you."

She didn't seem convinced.

"All right, all right," he said. "If it's that important,

then I'll use my car phone and we'll call them from here."

He watched her shoulders rise and then fall with a deep troubled sigh. "Are you going to tell them I'm almost seven months pregnant, too?"

"Ah…" He hesitated, not sure how to answer. If he admitted he was, Amy might find fault with him for warning his parents. If he reassured her he wasn't going to say a word, she might accuse him of setting them up for a shock. Either way, he feared he'd end up with just enough rope to hang himself. "What would *you* like me to say?" he asked.

"Tell them," she said, then chewed on her lower lip.

"Okay." He sat back in the car and reached for the phone.

He'd punched out four numbers when she cried out, stopping him. "No, don't!"

Wade replaced the receiver. "Maybe we'd better go over exactly what you do want me to say. Rehearse it in advance."

Amy climbed back into the Blazer and sat there, arms crossed. After a long tense moment she glanced at him. "Do you have any suggestions?"

"I could tell them we met in church."

"Well…" Her beautiful eyes smiled once again. "Isn't that a bit deceptive?"

Wade grinned. "It's the truth—sort of."

The amusement fled from her face. "Oh, Wade, I don't know what we should do."

"Couldn't we simply enjoy the afternoon?" That seemed the obvious solution to him.

"But I'll be self-conscious the entire time."

"Because you're pregnant?"

Amy covered her cheeks with both hands. "I can only imagine what your family will think of me."

"What makes you assume they're going to think anything?"

"Because people do. It's only natural."

"Then they'll think I'm the luckiest man alive to have convinced such a beautiful woman to share the Fourth of July with me." His mother and father were kind-hearted generous people, but she wouldn't know that until she'd met them. Never in all his life had he seen either of his parents intentionally shun or hurt anyone. They just weren't like that. He wanted to tell Amy, but feared she wouldn't believe him.

"They'll think I'm one of your charity cases," she muttered.

Wade didn't mean to laugh, but the idea was so ludicrous, he couldn't help it.

"I'm glad you find this funny," she said. "Unfortunately, I don't."

His laughter died, and Wade turned to grasp her by the shoulders. "Oh, Amy, you're about as far from being a charity case as it's possible to get."

She blinked. "How do you mean?"

"Every time I look at you, I have to remind myself that I'm a pastor."

She frowned, and he released her.

"Don't you know?" he asked. "Every time I'm with you, I end up fighting with myself because I want…" He dared not finish the sentence, afraid he'd reveal the depth of his feelings. "Every time I'm with you I want to kiss you again," he said, his voice dropping to a whisper.

"Oh, Wade, how can you find me attractive with my stomach like this and…and my feet swollen?"

He smiled, wondering if she honestly didn't know. She was beautiful, so damned beautiful—inside and out. "I've never been more attracted to a woman than I am to you right this minute," he confessed. Gently he brushed the hair from her cheek.

Not to kiss her then would have been a travesty. Before he could question the wisdom of it, he leaned across the seat and pulled her forward for a slow, deep kiss. Amy sighed, and her arms went around his neck and she melted against him. Kissing Amy was pure emotion, pure sensation...pure ecstasy. Because he was a minister, he sometimes forgot he was a man, with a man's needs and desires. That was the real reason Dovie had wanted him to start seeing Amy. He understood that now, although he hadn't appreciated her interference at the time. At the moment, however, he didn't need any reminders of his humanness. None whatsoever.

They kissed again and again, until he felt his control slipping. "Amy..." he groaned, needing to break this off while some shred of sanity remained. Already his thinking had become clouded by desire. He pulled away and cleared his throat. "I'm taking you to meet my parents," he said.

Amy didn't argue and Wade was grateful. He started the engine, and after glancing in the rearview mirror, edged the Blazer back onto the highway. "You don't have anything to worry about," he assured her, reaching for her hand. "Mom and Dad are going to love you."

Amy said nothing, but gave him a worried look.

"All I ask..." He hesitated.

"Yes?" she prompted.

"Just remember this is my mother. She's proud of me..."

"Then she won't appreciate someone like me mess-ing up your life. That's what you're trying to tell me, isn't it?"

The pain in her voice hurt him. "No, I was about to ask you not to listen to her tales of how well I took to potty training. That kind of thing."

Obviously relieved, Amy laughed. "She wouldn't say anything like that, would she?"

"I'm afraid so."

The tension eased from her face, and the beginnings of a smile took over.

"Mom dragged out my baby book the last time I brought a woman home for her and Dad to meet. You can't imagine how embarrassing it is to have a woman I'm dating examine naked baby pictures of me."

Amy cast him a skeptical glance. "You do this often, do you? Bring women home for your family to meet?" Her eyes held a teasing glint.

He'd walked into that one with his eyes open. "Well...not exactly."

"When was the last time?"

This was a test of Wade's memory. "It must be four or five years ago."

She raised her eyebrows as though she wasn't sure she should believe him.

"It's true," he insisted. "You can ask Mom yourself if you like." He wanted to let her know how special she was to him.

After almost three hours' driving, they reached Wade's hometown just outside Houston, a small community not unlike Promise.

The second Wade pulled into the driveway, the screen door opened and both his parents came out. His nieces and nephews, whom he loved beyond measure, followed right on their heels.

Wade squeezed Amy's hand. "You're going to be great. You don't have a thing to worry about."

Her smile was brave as Wade helped her out of the car. His parents hugged him briefly, then stepped back and waited for an introduction. Wade scooped up his two nieces and hugged them both, then gave his attention to the two boys.

"Mom, Dad, this is Amy Thornton," he said, his hand on her shoulder. "Amy, my parents, Charles and Karen McMillen."

Both his parents smiled and at precisely the same moment, as though rehearsed in advance, they lowered their eyes to Amy's stomach.

"That's either Sarah or Joseph," Wade continued.

"Good classic names," his mother said, recovering first.

Maybe he should've given them some warning, after all.

"Amy, this is Peter, Paul, Margaret and Mary," Karen McMillen said, gathering her grandchildren around her. "Welcome to our home."

Amy's hands trembled with nerves, Wade saw, but she smiled politely and extended her hand.

"We don't stand much on ceremony here," his mother said. Putting an arm around Amy's waist, she led her toward the house. "Come on inside and I'll introduce you to the rest of the family. Janice and her husband and Larry and his wife are already here."

Wade couldn't remember a time he'd loved or appreciated his mother more. As soon as his mother and Amy were out of earshot, his father cornered him.

"She's pregnant."

Wade grinned. "So I noticed."

"Does someone intend to make an honest woman of her?" his father asked.

Wade's gaze followed Amy and he experienced a rush of emotion. "She's already honest—but I think I'm going to love her and her child."

His father nodded his head vigorously. "Good answer, son. No need to say more."

Amy had never known a family like this, so close and fun-loving, generous and expressive. Because she was new here and still self-conscious, she felt most comfortable observing their interactions from a distance. Everyone treated her in a warm, genuinely friendly way. The kids were full of questions about her and Wade. She answered the ones she could and referred the ones she couldn't to him. Amy immediately liked his brother and sister, especially Janice, who was quick to point out that her name wasn't Janice Marie but Janice Lynn. Apparently only Wade called her Janice Marie. As a six-year-old allowed to help choose a name for his baby sister, he'd been adamant that his parents use Marie. Lynn, he'd insisted, sounded too much like a last name. Wade's younger brother didn't look at all like Wade. He was shorter and heavier set, while Wade was tall and lean. Larry was an insurance broker like his dad had been, and Janice ran a graphic-design business from her home.

More than once Amy found herself drawn into the family's activity, not because anyone tried to persuade her but because of the sheer fun they were having. Karen's grandchildren couldn't wait for dark before lighting their fireworks, so she gave them each a sparkler. Mary, who was just five, was terrified of the sparks and the sputtering, but refused to allow her brother and cousins to know it. She held her arm out as far as possible and squeezed her eyes shut as if she expected the sparkler to explode any second.

Midafternoon Charles McMillen donned his apron and chef's hat and began his stint at the barbecue. He was definitely in charge and very serious about it, too. But he allowed Amy to assist him with basting the ribs and the chicken. She had a wonderful time as they exchanged outrageous jokes and silly remarks. To have had a father like this…

Once dinner was ready, it lasted a full hour. Wade hadn't been exaggerating when he claimed his mother prepared enough food to feed an army; they needed two picnic tables to hold it all.

What amazed Amy most was the laughter and the noise. She didn't know families had this much fun together. The kids raced around the backyard, chasing each other, and if not each other, then butterflies. Games followed, croquet and a hotly contested game of basketball between Wade, his brother and brother-in-law.

"They used to play as boys," Janice said, sitting next to Amy. "Mom used to have to drag them off the court when it was time for supper."

Late in the afternoon Wade and Larry set up a badminton net and insisted everyone had to participate. Amy wasn't sure she'd be an asset, but Wade convinced her to join in.

"But I'm not any good at this." It was too humiliating to confess she'd never played.

"It's easy," he insisted. "Besides, I'll cover for you." He winked as he said it, as though he could actually manage to be in two places at once.

"All right, but don't be mad if I lose the game for us."

"Not to worry, I won't let that happen."

"What line of bull is my brother feeding you?" Janice shouted from the other side of the net.

"My advice is not to listen to him," Wade's brother declared.

Once the game started, Amy was delighted by how much fun it was. They played a sort of free-for-all style, with the children running furiously after each serve, shouting and laughing. The birdie apparently had a mind of its own and flew in every which direction except the one intended. It wasn't long before everyone dissolved into giggles.

At one point the birdie came right toward Amy. Every time it was anywhere close to her, Wade stepped forward and returned it with surprising ease.

Not this time.

"Get it, Amy," he shouted from behind her.

"Me? You want me to get it?" Even as she spoke, she raised her racket. Her shoe must have slid in a damp spot on the grass because her foot went out from under her and she dropped to her knees. Nevertheless, she returned the birdie, but in her enthusiasm lost her balance and fell forward, landing on her chin. The shock was softened by the soft ground, but it jarred her for a moment.

"Amy!" Wade was at her side in an instant. "Are you all right?" He dropped his racket on the grass and helped her sit up.

Amy was shocked to see the fear and concern in his eyes. "I'm fine…really. There's nothing wrong."

"What about your chin? The baby?"

"Everything's fine, Wade." Using his shoulder for leverage, she got back to her feet and reached for her racket.

"I think we should call it quits," Wade said.

His words were followed by a loud chorus of objecting voices, Amy's included.

"We're not going to quit," she insisted. "Not when we're down by two measly points."

"Yeah," ten-year-old Peter said. "I'm not a quitter."

"Me, either," Paul added.

"We're actually ahead?" Larry asked as if this was news to him. "Maybe it isn't such a bad time to quit, after all."

Janice and Larry's wife started swatting him with their badminton rackets, but it was all in fun. The game ended in a tie a few minutes later, and they all stopped when Karen called them back to the table for dessert.

"Who brought the apple pie?" Larry asked. Everyone turned to look at Amy in response to Larry's question. She wasn't sure what to say or do.

"It's the best apple pie I've ever tasted," he said, saluting her with his fork. "The crust is fabulous."

"You're eating my pie!" Wade accused him. "Amy baked that for me."

"You aren't going to eat a whole pie," his brother said confidently.

"Who says?"

"Boys, boys," their mother chided.

"I'll bake another," Amy offered.

That seemed to appease Wade. "All right," he said, and sat back down.

"For Larry," Amy added, and the entire family burst out laughing.

All too soon the day was over. Because of the long drive back to Promise, Wade and Amy left before the big fireworks display.

Amy hugged both of Wade's parents on her way out the door. Neither one had asked her embarrassing questions. Instead, they'd opened their home and their hearts to her without making judgments, with acceptance and love.

"Well?" Wade asked, once they were on the road.

She knew what he was asking. "Your family's...wonderful." No single word adequately described the experience of being with such warm gracious people.

"I told you so, didn't I?"

Amy rested her head against the back of the seat. "You're one of those, are you? An I-told-you-so guy."

"Hey, when a man's right, he's right and he deserves to make sure everyone knows it." He growled a he-man sound that made Amy laugh. She felt content and utterly relaxed.

An easy silence fell between them.

"I love it when you laugh," he said after a few moments.

Amy smiled at his words. There'd been precious little laughter in her life. She wanted to tell him about her childhood, about the things she'd seen, the ugliness she'd experienced. The bare cupboards and drunken men... But the day was too beautiful to ruin with talk of such memories.

"I like your sister," Amy said, instead.

"Janice Marie..."

"She said that isn't her name."

"Well, that's the name I'd picked out if Mom had a girl. When they decided against it, I was downright insulted. What kind of name is Janice Lynn, anyway?"

"It's lovely," she said, thinking how pleased she'd be to have a friend like Janice. "Your dad's a hoot, too."

"He takes after me," Wade teased.

They chatted for the next hour, laughing frequently. The ride home was punctuated with plenty of washroom breaks—which Amy found she needed these days. They were stopped at a rest area when she first noticed a flash of color in the night sky.

"Look!" she cried, pointing.

"That's the fireworks from Brewster," Wade commented. "Would you like to watch for a while?"

"Please."

Wade helped her onto the hood of his Blazer and joined her. Before long the heavens were bright with bursts of color and exploding stars. Amy oohed and aahed at each one. Wade tucked his arm around her shoulders and she leaned against him. They stayed there watching the fireworks until the very end.

It was almost midnight by the time Wade pulled up in front of her house. She struggled to keep her eyes open, yawning as he escorted her to the door.

"That was the most marvelous day of my life," she said. It was the plain and simple truth, although he had no way of knowing that. "Oh, Wade I'm so glad you insisted I meet your family. They're wonderful."

"Hey, what about me?"

"You're not so bad yourself."

Moonlight dimly lit the small porch, and when Wade smiled down on her she realized how much she wanted him to kiss her. How much she needed his touch. It would be the perfect ending to a perfect day.

It seemed he was thinking the same thing, because he reached for her. Amy closed her eyes and sighed. His kisses were slow and leisurely, expressions of comfort and contentment rather than passion. When it was time for her to go inside, Wade unlocked the door and handed her back the key. Then he smiled at her in the moonlight.

"Thank you, Amy, for spending the day with me."

"No, thank *you*," she said. He'd given her so much.

Dovie loved attending the birthing classes with Amy. She'd learned to breathe right along with her younger friend, and they occasionally practiced together in the evenings or on a slow Sunday afternoon.

"You're getting mighty close to Amy and her baby, aren't you?" Frank said one night after dinner. He carried the dirty dishes to the kitchen counter, then poured them each a cup of freshly brewed coffee.

"Does that worry you?" Dovie asked, joining him at the table. She doubted she could hide the truth from her husband. He knew her far too well. Besides, he was right. If she'd had a child of her own, she would have wanted a daughter like Amy. As the weeks went on Amy had come to trust Dovie more and more. Slowly she'd revealed bits and pieces of her past life; this trust had been extended to others, as well. Wade McMillen had a lot to do with the transformation in the young woman, Dovie felt. They were falling in love and it was wonderful to behold.

Poor Wade, Dovie mused. She almost felt sorry for

him. He was so enthralled with Amy he could barely think straight. Amy was no different.

"How many classes do you have left?" Frank asked.

"Just a couple more." Dovie knew he found it difficult that she was away every Monday night, but he'd been a good sport about it. She put dinner in the oven and he ate alone, but when she returned from class, she was eager to share her experiences. He listened patiently while she chatted on and on about what she'd learned.

"When's the baby due?"

"Middle of October," Dovie told him. "And you know that as well as I do."

"Everything's fine with the pregnancy, isn't it?"

"According to Jane, everything appears to be normal. Fortunately Amy's young and healthy."

"Good."

Dovie grinned. Frank had taken a liking to Amy, too, although he wasn't as prone to discuss his feelings as she was.

"It seems to me that Amy should start thinking about getting the nursery ready."

"She's doing the best she can," Dovie said, quick to come to her friend's defense. "Denise Parsons is lending her a bassinet."

"What about a crib?"

"Wade's got that covered."

"Wade's buying her a crib?" Frank sounded shocked.

"Not exactly. He found a used one at a garage sale a couple of weeks ago and he's refinishing it."

"Our pastor?"

Dovie couldn't have disguised her delight to save her soul. "Although when it comes to Amy, I sincerely doubt

Wade is thinking of her in terms of being her pastor."
Dovie finished her coffee. "And I, for one, am thrilled."

"Uh, Dovie, not everyone appreciates Amy the way
you and I do," Frank said, not looking directly at her.

"You mean there's been talk about Amy and Wade?"

Frank gave a noncommittal shrug. "Some."

Dovie was furious. "I can just imagine who's responsible for *that*," she muttered. No one got her dan-
der up faster than Louise Powell. Try as she might to
maintain a Christian attitude toward the other woman,
Dovie was confronted again and again by her vicious
tongue. "What's Louise saying?"

"Well, according to her, there are plenty of women
without a questionable past. Wade could be dating
them."

Dovie rolled her eyes rather than dignify such a statement with a response.

Frank grinned. "What's fun is watching Louise try
to turn folks against Amy. People refuse to listen. They
change the subject or make comments like how nice it
is to see Wade so happy."

Dovie was proud of their townsfolk, too. "I'm having a baby shower for Amy next week." Everyone she'd
called had been eager to participate. "It's a surprise,
Frank Hennessey, so don't you let the cat out of the
bag, understand?"

"My lips are sealed."

Dovie stood, and her husband grabbed her around
the waist and pulled her into his lap.

Dovie put up a token protest, which he ignored.

"Is Amy going to ask us to be the baby's godparents, Dovie?"

"That's up to her." But Dovie strongly suspected she

would. Twice now Amy had asked Dovie about the responsibilities entailed and hinted that Dovie and Frank would make wonderful godparents.

Dovie loved Amy's unborn baby as if Sarah or Joseph were her own grandchild. The closer Amy's due date drew, the more excited Dovie became. Already she'd knitted two blankets and one cap-and-bootie set. Her fingers weren't as nimble as they'd once been, but that didn't stop her.

"Sometimes I think…" Dovie paused.

"What?"

She wasn't sure she should say it aloud, but she'd ventured this far. "Sometimes it feels as if Amy is *our* child. She needs a family, and we have all this love to share."

Frank's arms tightened around her waist. "I'm beginning to believe the same thing."

Wade had never been good at carpentry. He still recalled his school shop project—a birdhouse. It had been a disaster. Give him a textbook and a room full of students any day of the week. He could teach them the principles of architecture, but he couldn't tell a screwdriver from a wrench.

He didn't know what had made him think he could refinish a crib, but he'd taken on the task with enthusiasm. Amy only worked part-time at the feed store, so once she'd paid her utility bills and bought groceries, she didn't have a lot of money left. The crib was his contribution. His own personal "welcome to the world" gift.

While the refinishing job might not win any awards for skill, he figured he should get an *A* for effort. He'd originally intended to give the crib to Amy at the surprise baby shower Dovie was throwing that afternoon.

But it didn't make sense to haul the crib over to Dovie's and then back to Amy's place.

So he did the logical thing. He pretended to know nothing about the shower and dropped it off at her house directly.

Fortunately the contraption folded and fit in the back of his Blazer. Amy was busy washing dishes when he arrived. She wore the same shorts outfit she'd worn the Fourth of July, which produced a rush of warm memories.

"Hi." He kissed her lightly, then followed her inside. "I've got something for you."

"You do?" She smiled with anticipation.

"Sit down and close your eyes." He nudged her into a living-room chair.

Amy sat there quietly, eyes closed as he requested, and while she waited, he returned to the Blazer and carried the crib into the house.

"Okay, you can look now," he said, standing proudly by his work.

Amy stared up at him and then at the crib. Her eyes grew huge. "Oh, Wade." Her hands flew to her mouth.

"I refinished it myself." He realized he sounded like a Cub Scout boasting about his latest achievement badge, but he couldn't help it.

"Now all I need is a screwdriver to, uh, finish tightening the rails." Did that make any sense? He wasn't sure.

"I...don't know if I have one," she said.

Wade let her go through the motions of searching. He'd made darn sure she *didn't* have one before he'd brought the crib over. It was all part of the elaborate plan to get Amy to Dovie's place for the shower.

"Frank must have a screwdriver," he said, reaching for the phone. He went through a little performance at his end—quite convincing if he did say so himself—then hung up. "He wants us to come over."

"When?" Amy asked.

"Now."

She sighed, and he was afraid she might decline with some excuse. "Come on," he urged. "It'll do you good to get out of the house."

She didn't seem to believe him, but finally she nodded and got her purse from the bedroom. At almost eight months pregnant, Amy didn't move around as quickly or comfortably these days.

He helped her into the Blazer and closed the passenger door. He wanted to suggest that she run a comb through her hair or add a touch of lipstick, but didn't dare for fear she'd guess something was up.

"What are all the cars doing at Dovie's house?" she asked.

"I think one of her neighbors is having a Tupperware party," Wade said. Okay, so he was known to stretch the truth now and then. Hey, he wasn't perfect.

He rang the doorbell and stepped aside so Amy would enter the house first.

The instant she did, a loud chorus of "SURPRISE!" greeted her.

She gasped and stumbled back, crashing into him. "You knew?" she asked, twisting around to look at him. Shock and delight flashed from her eyes.

She shook her head. "No one's ever done anything like this for me before," she said, and burst into tears.

Seven

Four weeks. One month. And then, this tiny being in Amy's womb would be in her arms. It didn't seem possible.

Dressing for her appointment with Dr. Jane, Amy rubbed body lotion over her extended belly. It seemed to stretch halfway across the room. Studying her reflection in the mirror, Amy felt grotesque and misshapen, barely able to believe that this would soon be over. That soon, she'd be holding her baby.

She'd just finished pulling on a dress and slipping into her shoes—she'd long since lost sight of her feet— when the doorbell rang. Wade had wanted to take her to the doctor's appointment. He was even more attentive now, more solicitous. Increasingly Amy had come to rely on him. He was so gentle with her. Lately when they kissed, he restrained himself with two or three chaste kisses. If it wasn't for the yearning she read in his eyes, she might have assumed he no longer found her attractive. His gaze told her otherwise.

"You ready?" he asked, and walked into the living room.

"I'll only be a moment," she promised. "I want to put on some lipstick."

"You're perfect just the way you are."

Amy found his words touching. "You must be at the age where you need glasses, Wade McMillen."

"My eyesight is twenty-twenty," he countered. "I happen to recognize a beautiful woman when I see one."

Amy didn't know what she'd done to deserve someone like Wade in her life. She knew she'd fallen deeply in love with him, and it had become more and more difficult to hide the depth of her feelings. They hadn't spoken of love. Not once. And seeing that she was about to give birth to another man's child, Amy didn't feel she was in any position to discuss her feelings.

"Mom phoned last night," Wade told her. "She wanted to see how you're feeling. She asked me to give you her love."

"I hope you gave her mine," she said on her way into the bathroom.

"I did," Wade called after her.

Amy stood in the front of the mirror and applied a pale rose shade of lipstick. It never ceased to amaze her that a woman who was little more than a stranger would send her love, while her own mother had abandoned her. At no time in the past three months had Alicia Thornton made any attempt to contact Amy. Her mail continued to be forwarded and other than a couple of cards from people at her old job, there'd been nothing. No one had tried to reach her. Not her mother. Not Alex.

Which was just as well. She'd left Dallas wanting to escape their influence and make a new life for herself and her child. She liked the people of Promise and they had welcomed her with kindness and generosity. In only a few months Promise felt more like home than any place she'd ever lived.

* * *

Dr. Jane Patterson's office had grown steadily busier over the past two months; today the reception room was almost full. Jenny asked Amy to have a seat and Wade sat with her, holding her hand. Her free hand rested on her stomach.

"Would you like to go for lunch later?" he asked.

As often as they saw each other, they rarely went out on what would be considered a date. "I'd like that," Amy said.

"Any cravings?" he murmured. "Pickles? Ice cream?"

"Cheese enchiladas."

"Done. The Mexican Lindo has some of the best."

Amy didn't realize how hungry she was until he'd mentioned food, and then it was all she could think about.

Jenny appeared a minute later. "Amy, Dr. Jane will see you now."

Amy stood. "I'm sure this won't take long," she told Wade.

Jenny took her blood pressure and pulse and entered the numbers on her chart. Amy sat on the end of the examination table and waited.

Dr. Jane came into the cubicle and read the chart. "How are you feeling?" she asked.

"Ambitious," Amy said. She'd gotten the bedroom ready for the baby in the week since her last visit. The gifts from the baby shower had spurred her into activity. Everyone had been so generous.

"Ambitious," Jane repeated. "That's a promising sign. Are you experiencing any problems?"

"You mean other than rolling over in the middle of

the night? I feel like a turtle who's been flipped onto its back and can't get up."

Jane grinned. "Other pregnant women have told me the same thing." She checked the swelling in Amy's ankles and after a brief physical exam asked her to make an appointment for the following week.

"Everything okay?" Wade asked Amy once they were outside.

"Perfect," she assured him. Other than feeling ungainly, she'd rarely been in better shape. This could be attributed to the care she'd taken with diet and the number of hours of sleep she seemed to require every night. In addition, Wade and Dovie had pampered her at every turn. Their emotional support and friendship had made a world of difference to Amy, and to the pregnancy.

"You've got my mouth watering for Mexican food," he said, holding her hand firmly in his.

"Mine, too."

They entered the restaurant in a festive mood, and the proprietor himself escorted them to a table. Amy barely had time to open her menu when the waiter appeared with chips, salsa and glasses of water.

"I don't know why I'm bothering to read this," she said. "I already know what I want."

For a moment Amy didn't think Wade had heard her. His attention was focused on the booth directly across from them. Amy's gaze followed his to two middle-aged women, both of whom were more than a little overdressed for the restaurant. One wore a shiny silver running outfit with high heels and star-shaped sunglasses. The other seemed decked out for the beach, in a halter top, panama hat and short shorts. She recognized the woman in silver by sight. Louise Somebody. Dovie had pointed her out; she'd said little, but Amy could tell from her tight-lipped expression that this Louise was not a person she liked or respected.

The waiter returned, ready to take their order and it seemed no time at all before he was back with their meals. Amy forked up a mouthful, for her first taste. The enchilada was full of spicy refried beans and melted cheese. Mmm. She took a bite, expecting to be transported to culinary heaven. But as soon as her mouth closed around the fork, those expectations were shattered by the conversation at the booth across the aisle.

"It doesn't seem fitting, does it, Tammy Lee, to have our pastor—a man who's supposed to be above reproach—dating an unwed mother."

"Yes, I would've thought Reverend McMillen would show a bit more discretion," the other woman said.

Amy saw Wade stiffen.

"This food is wonderful," Amy said, hoping to distract him and at the same time hide how much those cruel words hurt.

Wade's attention returned to her. "Ignore those two."

"I will if you will," she whispered back.

He nodded.

"She looks like she's about to pop any minute," the one in the beachwear said, just loudly enough to be heard.

"Personally I think Wade's involvement reflects poorly on the entire church." The woman in the running suit didn't bother to hide the fact that she was staring in their direction.

"I'm sure more than one person has questioned his priorities lately."

"Just who is she, anyway?"

Amy set her fork aside, certain she wouldn't be able to swallow another bite. The food that had been so appealing had little flavor now. What the woman said was true—and something Amy had chosen to overlook all these many weeks. Wade was a minister, a man of God; he had a reputation to consider, and his affiliation with her was hurting him in the eyes of his community.

"It's just not what you'd expect from a pastor."

"It makes you wonder…"

Wade slammed his fork down on the table. "I've had enough," he told Amy.

"No, please!" She was embarrassed enough. Anything he said or did would only add to her humiliation. And his own.

Amy had never seen him angry, not like this. His face was white, his fists clenched, as he got out of the booth and approached the two women.

"Good afternoon, Louise. Tammy Lee."

Both women nodded coolly.

"I couldn't help overhearing you just now."

"You heard?" Louise murmured as though she felt shocked by that—although she'd obviously intended it all along. But why? Amy wondered. Why would she purposely set out to embarrass Wade?

"You were talking about Amy Thornton and me. Have either of you met Amy?"

Amy felt their eyes shift to her. She smiled weakly and nodded in their direction.

"No…" one of them said.

"I can't say I've had the…pleasure," the other said.

"I already knew the answer before I asked," Wade confessed wryly, "because if either one of you had made the effort to know Amy, you'd realize something very important."

Both women stared at him.

"Amy is one of the kindest women I've ever known. She'd never go out of her way to embarrass someone—unlike certain others I could mention."

Louise pursed her lips at this.

"Furthermore," Wade continued, "I happen to be very much in love with Amy Thornton."

The shocked gasp, Amy realized, came from her.

"It hurts me that two women who are part of my church family would be this thoughtless, this judgmental. I hope that, in time, you'll both come to know and care about Amy, too."

Amy didn't hear the rest of the conversation. Her thoughts whirled around in her head. *Wade loved her.* He'd admitted it to those two women. But it troubled her that his love for her was damaging his reputation.

She folded her arms beneath her breasts, cradling her child, protecting him or her from the harsh judgments of the world. This matter of seeing Wade socially had worried her before, but they'd never discussed it. She'd been afraid to confront the issue, afraid that once she did, everything would change. Now she saw that her selfishness had hurt him. These women, gossipmongers or not, were members of his church, and it wouldn't be long before word spread throughout the congregation, possibly the entire town.

Reverend Wade McMillen was in love with an unwed mother.

Her thoughts distracted her, and she didn't even notice that Wade had returned to the booth.

"I apologize, Amy," he murmured. "I wish I could have spared you that."

She tried to reassure him with a smile, but was unable to muster even a token effort.

"I'm the one who should apologize."

"Nonsense."

She couldn't stop looking at him, couldn't stop hearing his words. "You love me?" she asked, her voice more breath than sound.

He reached for her hand. "Funny I should admit how I feel about you to someone else first, isn't it?"

"No." Her throat felt thick, clogged with tears, making it difficult to speak. She lowered her head, trying to clear her thoughts.

"I didn't intend to ask you to marry me like this."

Amy slowly raised her head. "Marry you? But…you don't know anything about me, about my family—about my background."

"I know everything I need to know."

"What about… Sarah? You don't know about her—about the man who fathered her." Amy hadn't mentioned a word about Alex, not to Wade, not to Dovie. Not to anyone. As much as possible, she tried to push every thought of her ex-lover from her mind and heart. One night just recently she'd found herself pretending Wade was Sarah's father, but decided that was a dangerous game.

"I love you, Amy."

"No." She shook her head vigorously. "You don't know what you're saying. You… We've been seeing too much of each other," she said, struggling to hide the panic rising inside her.

"I've never been more certain of anything in my life."

"Oh, Wade." She took her napkin and crumpled it with both hands.

"I want us to get married. Soon, too, so I can be Sarah's daddy."

Amy gave up the effort. She covered her face, reminding herself that her hormones were all askew and not to worry if she was more emotional than usual.

"Is that a yes or a no?" he asked with such gentle concern it made her want to weep.

Fighting for composure, Amy swallowed back tears and inhaled deeply. "I don't know what to say," she managed once her throat muscles had loosened enough for her to speak.

"Say you'll marry me."

"I...need time."

"Darling, I hate to pressure you, but all we've got is a few weeks before we're parents."

She'd love Wade McMillen to her dying day, Amy decided right then and there, for declaring himself Sarah's father.

"I promise to think about it," she told him. For now, that was all she would do. Think. Try to figure out what was best for her and for the baby.

And what was best for Wade.

Grady, Cal and Glen met on the border of Grady's property and the Patterson's ranch, in the same spot they'd often congregated as teenagers. Those days were long behind them now.

"What's this all about?" Cal asked, dismounting as he spoke.

"I assume there's a *reason* you wanted us to meet

you here," Glen added, sliding down from his horse, a high-spirited gelding who pranced in place.

While he might sound like he was complaining, Grady could see that his eyes were alight with interest.

Grady grinned at his two best friends. "Actually there *is* an important reason. I want the three of us to return to Bitter End."

"But why? We were there not long ago. Wade was with us, remember? We had a little ceremony, prayed and everything. I'd hoped that was the end of it."

"This is a joke, right?" Glen said irritably.

If Grady hoped to get his friends' attention, he'd achieved his goal.

"No joke," he insisted. "The three of us need to go back."

"I'd like to remind you again that we were just there," Cal muttered.

Grady knew what his friends were thinking, because the same thoughts had been going around in his mind for a number of weeks now.

"Prayer or no prayer, I've seen enough of Bitter End to last me a lifetime," Glen said. "Far as I'm concerned, someone should burn that place to the ground before anyone else gets hurt."

"Then cover it with sulfur," Cal put in.

No one had come away from Bitter End with pleasant memories, not in more than a hundred years. Through research and a good deal of luck, Nell and Travis had uncovered the source of the trouble. Together they'd learned that Bitter End had been cursed by a preacher whose son had been wrongfully hanged. No one had paid much attention to the preacher, but then the town was beset with plagues of the sort brought down on

Egypt thousands of years before. The citizens of Bitter End had endured it all—drought and locusts, sickness and hail—until the death of their firstborn children, and then they'd scattered in panic. A number of families from Bitter End had become the founders of Promise.

"Bitter End is a piece of Texas state history," Grady told his friends. "It's a part of who *we* are, as well."

Neither Cal nor Glen was as quick to argue now, and Grady knew it was because they recognized the truth of what he'd said.

"You want us to go back and…and confront the past, don't you?" Cal asked.

"That's my thought," Grady admitted. "I want us to stand in the center of that town and face whatever's there." Grady felt instinctively that this was necessary, although he couldn't really say why.

"We stood there with Wade," Glen pointed out.

"I know…but this is different."

"How?" Cal demanded. Even as he argued, he remounted Thunder, ready to follow through with the idea.

"I want to declare this land free of the curse."

"Like anyone's going to listen to us," Glen said.

"Any*thing,* in this instance," Cal added.

"Whatever." Grady had thought long and hard about this moment. He'd been one of the people who stood with Wade McMillen in the center of Bitter End. One of the men whose roots were buried deep in the history of this forgotten settlement. He wanted whatever was there, the curse, to leave.

They rode in silence, the three of them, like gunfighters heading for a high-noon shoot-out.

The town lay nestled in a small valley below a series

of limestone outcroppings. Buildings, both stone and wood, stretched on both sides of the main road. The tallest structure was the church with its burned-out steeple. The wooden two-story hotel, rotting from years of abandonment, leaned precariously to one side, as if the next windstorm would send it toppling. His brother had nearly died in that hotel not many months ago. A sadness came over Grady when he thought of Richard, but he refused to allow his plans to be sidetracked.

By tacit agreement the three men stopped outside the building that had once been the mercantile. The horses shifted restlessly, their acute senses responding to the mysterious atmosphere.

"It's dead here," Glen commented. Nothing grew in town. Bitter End had died all those years ago.

"Do you feel anything?" Cal asked, whispering.

"I'm not sure," Grady said in a normal voice. He refused to give in to whatever was here, refused to bow to his fears.

Glen just looked around, his horse making an abrupt circle as if to check behind himself.

As boys, when they'd first happened upon Bitter End, they'd felt a sense of great sadness, a sense of unease, a tension that manifested itself in the physical. The oppressive silence had frightened them so badly it'd taken them twenty years to venture down these streets again.

The horses seemed incapable of standing still. All three men had trouble restraining them.

"I don't know what I feel," Grady reported. The first time around there'd been no question. The sensation had been overwhelming, unmistakable.

"That feeling of…grief. It's still here," Glen said,

glancing over his shoulder. "But not nearly as strong as before."

"I feel it, too." This came from Cal.

"Are you ready to go back now?" Glen's question was directed at Grady.

He nodded, wishing he knew what to do. He'd hoped...hell, he wasn't sure what he'd been hoping for. He supposed he'd wanted to find something different, discover that the town had miraculously changed. That it had—somehow—come back to life.

Wade had been looking forward to this for two weeks. Grady and Caroline had invited Amy and him to dinner at the Yellow Rose Ranch. Unfortunately he suspected that if they hadn't already agreed to this, Amy would've found an excuse to decline.

She hadn't been herself since the confrontation with Louise Powell and Tammy Lee Kollenborn in the Mexican Lindo. For the past few days, she'd been quiet and withdrawn, and he knew she was disturbed by what had happened. He didn't blame her.

It didn't help that his marriage proposal had come about the way it had. He'd been trying to work out the best approach all week, but then the incident at the restaurant had forced his hand. It wasn't how he'd wanted to ask her—and he couldn't help feeling some resentment, unchristian though he knew that was, toward those two meddling women.

He glanced at Amy as he drove to the Yellow Rose Ranch. She looked half-asleep, and while he knew she was tired, he also knew she was using her fatigue as an excuse to avoid a certain subject. His proposal. He'd waited a long time to find the woman he wanted to marry, and now he had, he wanted to marry her. The sooner, the better, for the baby's sake, as well as his own.

He wouldn't pressure her into a decision. When she was ready, she'd tell him; until then he'd be patient.

Amy straightened when he turned off the highway and into Grady's long drive. "We're going to have a good time tonight," he promised, leaning over to squeeze her hand.

Amy smiled. "I hope Caroline didn't go to a lot of trouble."

Wade knew Amy's due date was only a week earlier than Caroline's. The two women had become friendly and often met for lunch. He was well aware that Amy admired Caroline and relied on her advice, which Wade saw as a good thing.

Grady stepped onto the porch when Wade steered the Blazer into the yard, and Caroline appeared at her husband's side almost immediately afterward. She hugged Amy, then greeted Wade with real warmth. He gave her the flowers he'd brought in appreciation for the dinner. No wine, not until after the babies were born. He hoped there'd be many more such evenings—some of them at his house. His and Amy's.

It would be just the four of them tonight, since Maggie was spending the night with Savannah.

"Everything's ready," Caroline told them, "so we can eat anytime."

"I'm dying to see your nursery," Amy said.

The two women disappeared, but Wade wasn't fooled. Amy might want to look at the baby's room—he was sure she did—but the real reason she'd gone off with Caroline was to talk to her, perhaps seek out her advice about his marriage proposal.

Wade trusted Caroline to encourage Amy to marry him. If she mentioned what had happened with Louise and Tammy Lee, then Caroline would tell her those two didn't speak for the community. With few exceptions, the entire town had rallied around Amy. Caroline knew that as well as anyone.

In every problem is a gift, his grandfather had told him years ago, and Wade remembered it now. The gift Louise and Tammy Lee had given him was the courage to admit, openly and publicly, that he loved Amy.

Dinner proved to be both relaxing and fun. Caroline was an excellent cook and the prime rib, accompanied by garden fresh broccoli, a green salad and mashed potatoes, was one of the best Wade had tasted. This night out was exactly what he and Amy needed. Conversation was mostly light and entertaining, although they talked about Bitter End and answered Amy's questions. She asked about visiting the town, but both Grady and Wade discouraged that.

While Caroline and Amy cleared the table, Wade and Grady had time to talk privately on the porch.

"Speaking of Bitter End, I was there this week," Grady surprised him by saying.

"What made you go back?" Wade asked, taking a sip of his coffee.

Grady shrugged. "I don't know, but I felt I had to— that there's something unfinished there."

"What?"

"I don't know," Grady said. Then he changed the subject abruptly. "How are things between you and Amy?"

"I love her." Wade had already admitted it once and found it easier the second time.

Grady gave him a slow satisfied smile. "I guessed as much."

"Oh, yeah?"

"'Fraid so, Preacher."

"I've asked her to marry me," Wade confessed.

"Is she going to?"

"I don't know." Wade had promised himself he wouldn't pressure her, but he had a feeling deep in his gut that told him the longer she kept him waiting, the less likely she was to agree. His chest ached at the thought of what his life would be like without her. Every conscious reflection included her. She'd become a big part of his world, of the way he planned his future.

Grady commiserated, but had no advice to offer other than "Don't give up."

At the end of the evening, Amy hugged both Caroline and Grady to thank them for dinner. "I've enjoyed myself so much," she said with such sincerity that no one could doubt her. Least of all Wade.

"Dinner was superb," Wade told Caroline. "Great food, terrific company." Because he was single, he was invited out to dinner quite a bit. No fool he, Wade often accepted. But this evening had shown him what his life would be like if—when—he was married.

Wade waited until they were back on the road before he broached the subject of marriage. "I wasn't going to say anything," he began, keeping his eyes on the road.

"About what?" Amy asked, then turned to him, eyes filled with alarm. "If you let me sit through the entire evening with a piece of broccoli stuck between my teeth, I swear I'll never forgive you."

Wade chuckled. "It isn't that." His humor quickly faded. "I wanted to ask if you're still thinking about…"

"If I'll marry you," Amy finished for him. "That's what you want to know, isn't it?"

"I love you, Amy. I want to marry you."

She was silent for so long he wondered if he'd blown it entirely. "Say something," he urged, trying not to sound as anxious as he felt.

"His name's Alex Singleton," she said, her voice low. "We met, of all places, in the grocery store."

Wade gripped the steering wheel hard. He wanted to tell her it didn't make a bit of difference who'd fathered her baby. It wasn't a detail he considered necessary. He loved her and he loved her baby. That was the only fact she needed to consider.

It hurt, too, to hear about another man wanting her, making love to her. But he kept his mouth shut, knowing Amy needed to tell him. In some ways this wasn't for him as much as it was for her.

"He asked me out for coffee. I said no, but he was charming and funny and persistent, so I agreed. The store had a deli, and we sat there. We…talked so long that the ice cream in my cart melted." She smiled at the memory. "He was sophisticated and wonderful. I thought I was in love that first day."

Wade found that listening was more difficult by the minute.

"Because he often went away on business, we weren't able to see each other more than once a week. I… I lived for those weekly dates. Regular as clockwork, he arrived every Wednesday evening and took me out to dinner. We ate at the most wonderful restaurants. Small upscale places."

"So he had lots of money."

"Oh, he had more than that, Wade." Her voice hardened. "He also had a wife and two children."

Eight

Thursday afternoon, Ellie Patterson left the feed store early. George, her assistant, would close up and Amy would help him. Amy had been taking on more responsibilities of late, and Ellie was grateful. She hadn't been feeling well the past couple of afternoons but suspected she knew why—especially since the home pregnancy test had been positive. Seeing her sister-in-law would confirm what she already knew.

Jenny Bender, Jane's receptionist, was just leaving when Ellie entered the health clinic.

"Jane's in her office," Jenny told her, motioning beyond the reception area.

"Thanks."

Sure enough, Jane sat at her desk making notations on a chart. She glanced up when she heard Ellie come in, and her tired face brightened. "Hi, there."

"Hi." Ellie threw herself into the chair nearest Jane's.

"Long day?" Jane asked sympathetically.

"Exceptionally long."

"You're looking a little peaked."

"I feel a little peaked."

Jane studied her. "Do you think you picked up a bug?"

A slow happy smile came from deep within. "The nine-month variety."

Surprise showed in Jane's face. "You're pregnant?"

Ellie nodded. "The little stick turned blue."

Jane clapped her hands in delight. She closed the chart she'd been working on and relaxed in her chair. "Does Glen know?"

"Not yet." Ellie hadn't meant to keep it a secret from her husband, but she didn't want him to be disappointed if it turned out, for some reason, to be a false alarm. "I thought I'd have you verify my condition first."

They chatted for a few minutes, laughed about the things they always did and made plans to spend a weekend in San Antonio later in the month. They talked with the easy familiarity that had developed between them since they'd married the Patterson brothers. Not until after Jane had examined her did Ellie grow quiet.

Jane didn't press her, but Ellie knew her sister-in-law was waiting for her to speak. "I'm afraid, Jane," she confessed. Her emotions had never been this muddled. Intertwined with the joy were all the fears she'd tried to ignore and couldn't.

"It's normal to be anxious. This is your first child, and your body's experiencing quite a few changes, right now. That can be confusing and stressful. Let's talk about it."

Ellie took a deep breath. "Mostly I'm worried that I'll be like my mother. She didn't have an easy pregnancy with me—that's basically why I'm an only child. And she never seemed to *like* having a kid around." Ellie hadn't been close to her mother, but the bond she'd shared with her father had been strong and special. It was the reason his death the previous year had shaken her so badly.

"You're not your mother," Jane assured her.

Ellie relaxed a little. "In other words, don't borrow trouble?"

"That's a good place to start."

Ellie nodded. "You're right. And I don't think my mother ever wanted a child, whereas I do." She gave Jane a tremulous smile. "Glen and I talked about starting our family soon. That's the reason I went off the pill when I did," she confided, "but we didn't think it'd happen so quickly."

"So you're not sure you're ready for this."

Ellie thought about that for a moment. "No, I'm ready," she said decisively. "I just hadn't expected to be this...fertile."

"I imagine Glen's going to gloat to Cal," Jane said with a manufactured groan.

"Have you and Cal decided when you're going to get pregnant?" Ellie felt it would be nice if their children were close in age. Her own cousins, who'd lived in Brewster, were twins, two years older, and when they were around, it was almost like having brothers. Her mother blamed her tomboy attitudes on Rick and Rob, both of whom had gone on to make the military their career. They'd missed her wedding, but had written to congratulate her and Glen.

"Before Cal and I can think about a family, I need to fulfill my contract here at the clinic," Jane said with a show of regret. "Don't misunderstand me, I love my work. It's just that we're eager to become parents. We're hoping I'll get pregnant about this time next year."

"That'd be wonderful."

"Mary's going to be pleased when she hears your news," Jane said, referring to their mother-in-law.

Glen's parents were looking forward to becoming grandparents, and it went without saying that they'd be ecstatic.

"I want you to start prenatal vitamins right away—"

"Jane, Jane." Ellie held up her hand. "Don't treat me like a patient. I'm your sister-in-law."

Jane laughed. "You're right. Congratulations!" She stood up and hurried over to Ellie to share a heartfelt hug.

Friday morning Wade knew he should be working on his sermon, but he couldn't focus his thoughts. Every time he started to write down an idea, all he could think about was Amy. He worried about her, worried that she wasn't eating properly or getting enough rest. He wished she could take a few weeks off before the birth. He wondered what plans she'd made for child care once her maternity leave ended.

Now that her due date was so close, his worrying had become almost obsessive. If she wouldn't marry him, then he hoped she'd at least allow him to be with her when Sarah was born.

When he'd spoken to her on the phone recently, she hadn't sounded particularly interested in his company. But that could be his own doubts talking, because when he showed up at the house yesterday, she'd seemed genuinely pleased to see him.

Wade stared down at his sermon notes and, feeling uninspired, decided to take a break. His first inclination was to head for the feed store, check up on Amy, but he refused to make a pest of himself.

The one person who was sure to understand how he felt was Dovie Hennessey. Dovie was close to Amy, her birthing partner. He had another reason for visiting Dovie's store; he wanted to buy a gift, for Amy, a robe for after the baby was born. Something lovely and feminine.

He walked from the church into town, stopped to chat with the Moorhouse sisters en route. He arrived at Dovie's to find her, as usual, doing a robust business. She acknowledged his presence with a nod and continued to help Betty Bonney, who was considering an antique bowl and pitcher for her guest bedroom.

Wade was a patient man. While he was waiting, he wandered around Dovie's store, picturing Amy wearing this necklace or that scarf, imagining her on the brocade-upholstered love seat, holding her baby. With him beside her...

A while later Mrs. Bonney left smiling and Dovie turned her attention to Wade. "This is a pleasant surprise," she said. "What can I do for you, Pastor?"

"It's about Amy," he replied, feeling a bit self-conscious. "I wanted to buy her something to wear after the baby's born. A robe. Or whatever you think would be appropriate." Actually this was all mildly embarrassing. He could just imagine what Louise Powell would say if she heard about this. If the woman thought it improper for him to have lunch with Amy, what would she think about his buying her nightwear? It didn't *matter* what Louise thought, he chided himself. She was an uncharitable and narrow-minded woman, and her opinions were of no consequence.

"A robe is an excellent choice." Dovie beamed him an approving look. "It's both practical and luxurious."

He nodded. "I want it to be special—not the type of robe she'd wear every day…if you know what I mean."

"I do. In fact, I have something in mind," Dovie said with a satisfied smile. "I was actually thinking of giving this to Amy myself." She led him to the far side of her shop. A selection of old-fashioned wardrobes dominated one corner. The doors of one wardrobe were open to reveal a number of party dresses and nightgowns on scented hangers. She reached inside and pulled out a soft pink satin robe, its long sleeves and collar edged in lace. It was exactly what he'd hoped for. Simple, elegant, beautiful.

"It's new—not vintage," Dovie explained. "But it's modeled after a 1930s pattern." She watched for his reaction. "What do you think?"

He swallowed hard and nodded. The vision of Amy in that robe did funny things to his insides. "It's perfect."

"I agree," Dovie said. "It's utterly feminine and I know she'd treasure it."

Wade touched the sleeve, intending to look at the price tag, but changed his mind the instant his hand made contact with the rich smooth fabric. His gut clenched. Amy, wearing this. Lying in his bed…

"I'll take it," he said quickly.

"Don't you want to know the price?" Dovie asked.

"Not particularly."

Dovie's grin spread across her face.

Wade took out his wallet as he and Dovie walked toward the cash register. She wrapped the robe in tissue paper and placed it carefully in a gift box, which she tied with a pink ribbon. When she'd finished, she glanced up at him. "Amy told you about Alex, didn't she?" Her gaze held his.

"Yes."

"She only told me this week, you know. She's shared very little about the baby's father."

"It's not important." He wanted Dovie to know he hadn't asked. In fact, he'd almost rather Amy hadn't told him.

"After the birthing class this week, I brought her home for tea. She cried her eyes out."

"Amy was upset?" He wasn't sure what unnerved him more—Amy's being distressed enough to cry or her choosing to weep on Dovie's shoulder and not his.

"Yes. She told me about Alex—and about her relationship with you. She said you'd been wonderful."

That reassured him a little; Amy must still care for him, still trust him. Her story had broken his heart. Yes, she'd been foolish and naive, but she wasn't the first woman who'd learned such lessons the hard way. Not the first woman who'd been lied to by a married man—and fallen in love with him.

"You love her, don't you?" Dovie asked, then laughed at her question. "You must. No man pays 125 for a satin robe otherwise."

Wade gasped in mock outrage. He would gladly have paid twice that.

"Do you want me to keep it here at the store for you until the baby's born?" Dovie asked after he'd paid for the robe.

"Please."

They talked a while longer, and then another customer came in and Wade knew it was time to leave. He walked to the town park and sat on a bench, watching the children at play, listening to the sound of their laughter.

Amy had told him about Alex and what had happened once she learned he was married. It wasn't until after she'd broken off the relationship that she'd discovered she was pregnant. Although she'd only mentioned her mother in passing, Wade surmised that they didn't get along and that her mother had provided absolutely no emotional support.

In the days since she'd made her revelations, he'd forcefully pushed all thoughts of Alex and Amy's affair from his mind. It was just too painful to think about Amy loving another man.

He knew that Alex had been afraid she'd come to him and demand child support, so he'd insisted on an abortion. When she refused, they'd had a horrible fight, in which her mother had somehow become involved. She'd also told him, Wade, her mother had come up with an entirely unacceptable suggestion.

Wade could well guess. Six or seven years back, when he worked as a youth pastor in Austin, he'd been approached by a childless couple desperate to adopt a baby. Because of the limited number of available infants and the high number of applicants through legitimate agencies, Wade had been solicited by this couple, who hoped he could arrange a private adoption. They'd made clear that price was no object; in fact, the husband had bluntly spoken of "buying" a baby. While Wade appreciated how frustrating such situations could be, he referred the couple to an adoption agency with which he was familiar.

He could only assume that Amy's mother saw her daughter's baby as a profit-making opportunity.

Amy had been calm and collected while she'd relayed the details of her unhappy romance. Too calm, he recognized now. From what Dovie had said, she'd gone to a woman friend the following day and wept bitter tears.

It made Wade wonder why she'd remained so stoic with him. She'd spoken almost as if this had all happened to someone else.

Feeling a strong impulse to straighten things out with Amy, Wade walked over to the feed store. It wasn't the ideal place for such a talk, but this wasn't something they could ignore. They had to have an honest no-holds-barred discussion. And soon. Then he had an idea—he'd invite Amy to dinner. Tonight. At his place so they'd have the privacy they needed.

Never mind that he was absolutely devoid of any cooking talent. Hey, he'd barbecue a couple of steaks, throw some fresh corn in a pot of boiling water. Couldn't go wrong there.

Ellie was nowhere in sight and George was busy with a customer when Wade entered the store. A couple of local ranchers were hanging around the place, as well. Clyde Lester and James Ferguson sat on the front porch drinking cold sodas.

"Afternoon, Reverend."

"Afternoon," he returned, and went in search of Amy.

He found her in the back of the store with Lyle Whitehouse. Lyle seemed more interested in talking than in buying. Amy didn't see Wade and he suspected Lyle didn't either. He moved closer, not to eavesdrop on the conversation but… All right, he couldn't help being curious.

"…like to get to know you better," Lyle was saying.

"Thank you, but as I said, this saddle soap is the best one on the market."

Irritation edged her voice. It was all Wade could do not to interfere, but he knew Amy wouldn't appreciate that.

"I noticed you first thing the night of the big dance."

Amy replaced the soap on the shelf. She didn't respond.

"I was thinking you'd be a lot of...fun."

"Is there anything else I could interest you in?" she asked coolly. The minute the words left her lips, her cheeks flushed red. "You know what I mean..."

"Sure thing," Lyle said with a laugh. "And you know what *I* mean."

"If George or I can be of any service, please let us know."

Wade glanced around and wondered what had happened to Ellie; generally, as owner of the store, she was highly visible. He frowned. As far as he knew, Amy had been hired as a bookkeeper, not as a salesperson. He wondered when she'd started dealing with customers and why she hadn't told him about the additional duties Ellie had given her.

"As a matter of fact," Lyle said with a sly grin, "there *is* something you can do for me."

Amy regarded him warily and Wade could see that the ranch hand's proximity made her uncomfortable.

"What's that?" she asked politely.

"As it happens I'm looking for a date Saturday night. Rumor has it you're single."

"I appreciate the offer, but I'm busy."

"Not *too* busy though, right?"

"Yes. Far too busy, I'm afraid."

Amy was about to move away when Lyle placed his hand on her shoulder and stopped her, pinning her against the wall. His oversize belt buckle nudged the mound of her stomach, and Wade felt revolted.

His hackles went up. He couldn't tolerate the idea of any man touching a woman without her consent. As far as he was concerned, Lyle had stepped way over the line. But rather than make a scene, he decided to wait for a few more minutes and let Amy handle the situation herself.

"Ah, come on, Amy," Lyle urged.

"No, thank you."

"What am I missing that the preacher's got?"

"Good manners for one thing," Amy said, trying to get past Lyle. But he held on to her, his grip tightening.

"We could have a lot of fun together," he said. "And once the kid's born you and me could—"

"Let me go!" she demanded.

Wade couldn't remain silent any longer. "I suggest you do as the lady asks," he said, stepping closer.

Lyle snickered and met Wade's look head-on. "What lady?"

Amy closed her eyes as if she'd been physically slapped. Without even knowing what he intended, Wade stormed forward and grabbed Lyle by the shirtfront and half lifted him from the floor.

"I believe you owe the *lady* an apology," he said from between gritted teeth.

"This ain't none of your business, Preacher."

"Wade, please," Amy pleaded.

Wade ignored her. Nose to nose with Lyle, he said, "I'm *making* it my business."

"Is that your bun she's baking in her oven, too?" Whitehouse sneered.

"We're taking this outside, you bastard."

"No!" Amy cried.

"Fine by me, Preacher man. I'll be happy to kick your butt for you."

Wade released him, and Lyle eased his neck back and forth a couple of times. "Anytime, Preacher man," he muttered. "Anytime."

"Right now sounds good to me."

"Wade, don't." Amy grabbed hold of him, her fingers digging into his upper arm. "It's all right, please. I don't want you getting hurt on my behalf."

"I can hold my own," he promised her. He turned and followed Lyle out the front door.

Lyle had his fists raised by the time Wade got outside. He squinted his eyes against the bright sunlight as he rolled up his sleeves.

"What's going on here?" Clyde Lester asked.

"Preacher and I have something to settle man to man," Lyle answered.

"Wade, you wanna fight this guy?" Clyde was clearly shocked.

He raised his own fists. "You're damn right I do."

The older rancher looked flustered and unsure. "George," he shouted, "we got trouble here."

George called out to Wade, who turned at the sound of his voice. He didn't even see the fist coming. Lyle's punch hit him square in the jaw. Unable to stop himself, he staggered a couple of steps sideways.

Clyde and his friend cried out that Lyle had cheated. But Wade figured he'd deserved that sucker punch. It would be the last swing Lyle took at him, though.

Wade let out a roar and surged toward Lyle, tumbling them both onto the ground.

Snatches of speech made it into his consciousness. He heard Amy pleading with someone to stop the fight. Clyde was still yelling that Lyle was a cheat. Then George shouted that he was phoning for the sheriff. Soon afterward he heard Lyle grunt with pain. Or perhaps he was the one grunting. Wade didn't know anymore.

High school was the last time Wade had been in a fistfight, but he was strong and agile, capable of moving fast. And he wasn't a coward. Some things were meant to be settled this way, although he generally avoided physical confrontation. But no one was going to insult the woman he loved.

He got in a couple of good punches; so did Lyle. They circled each other like angry dogs and were about to resume fighting when Sheriff Hennessey arrived.

Frank leaped out of his patrol car and stared at Wade as if he couldn't believe his eyes. "What the hell's the problem here?" he said, pulling his nightstick from his belt.

"This is between Lyle and me," Wade said, pressing his finger to the edge of his mouth. His jaw ached, and one eye felt like it was already swelling. Lyle's face looked as if he'd been put through a garbage disposal. Wade figured he didn't look any better.

"Lyle, what happened?" Seeing he wasn't going to get anywhere with Wade, the sheriff tried the other man.

Lyle held Wade's look. "Nothing we can't settle ourselves."

"Well, I don't happen to like the way you two decided

to settle it. I could haul you both into jail for disturbing the peace. That what you want?"

"It was my fault, Sheriff," Amy cried, stepping between Wade and Lyle. "Wade thought I needed help…"

Sheriff Hennessey glared at Lyle.

"Were you bothering this young lady, Whitehouse?" the sheriff demanded.

A truck pulled up beside the patrol car and Ellie got out. "What's going on here?"

"Seems like the preacher and Lyle here didn't see eye to eye," Frank explained.

"I didn't do anything but talk to the little lady," Lyle muttered. "Seems the preacher thinks he's got squatter's rights with her. He's—"

"Leave it right there," Frank said, stepping closer to Lyle.

"Are you going to arrest anyone?" Ellie asked.

Frank gave Lyle and Wade a hard look. "Is this over or not?"

Wade narrowed his eyes, which caused him more than a little pain. "If he's willing to let Amy alone, then I'm willing to call it quits."

"Lyle?" Frank focused his attention on the other man.

"All right," he growled, reaching for his hat. He shoved it on his head and stalked toward his truck.

"I think we've seen everything there is to see here," Frank said to the small crowd of curious spectators. He glanced at Wade and his expression said he was disappointed.

Wade wasn't particulary proud of himself at the moment, either. All he'd done was embarrass Amy and himself. He rarely let his temper get the better of him like this. It was a primitive response, he thought grimly.

A primitive male response. He'd been in such a rage he hadn't been able to control himself, but damn it all, he was supposed to be an example to the entire community.

"Oh, Wade." Amy gazed up at him with tear-filled eyes. She raised her hand to his mouth.

He winced when her gentle fingers touched the corner of his lips. The taste of blood was in his mouth and his head pounded. His left eye was swollen almost shut.

"I've got a first-aid kit in the back of the store," Ellie said.

Amy and Wade followed her to the office, where she took the kit out of the drawer, then left them. Wade was grateful until he saw the tears running down Amy's face.

"Amy, darling, it doesn't hurt."

Her hands trembled as she tore open a gauze package. "Fighting! Oh, Wade, how could you?"

"I don't know exactly how that happened. Things just escalated. In retrospect, I agree it wasn't the best way to settle this, but I can't change that now."

"I'm perfectly capable of taking care of myself."

"I know, I know." Just then he didn't want to argue the right or wrong of it. He'd much rather Amy held him.

"Sit down," she said curtly. He did, and she dabbed at the cut on his lip. "What do you think people will say when they hear about this?"

"Yeah, well, it can't be helped."

"All I've done is hurt you," she said in a broken whisper.

He wanted to protest, but she touched an especially sore spot just then. He jerked back from her and brought his finger to the edge of his mouth.

"I think you should see Dr. Jane," she murmured.

"I'm not that badly hurt."

"No, but you need your head examined."

Wade laughed and winced anew. "Ouch! Don't make me laugh." He reached for her hand and held it in both of his. His knuckles were swollen, he noted, and the skin torn. "A kiss would make everything feel better," he told her, only half joking.

Very carefully she bent down and tenderly pressed her lips to his.

The kiss left an ache inside him that made Lyle's brutal punches seem insignificant. He loved Amy. He wanted her for his wife, wanted her to share his life and his bed. He stood up and wrapped his arms around her waist, burying his face in her shoulder.

As she hugged him close, he breathed in her warm womanly scent.

"This can't continue," she whispered, and broke away from him.

Wade wasn't ready to let her go. "What do you mean?"

"I'm hurting you," she said, her voice gaining strength.

She didn't seem to understand the joy and wonder that loving her had given him. He wanted to tell her, but she spoke again.

"Your credibility with the people in your church is going to be questioned because of this fight."

"That has nothing to do with you. I'll deal with that myself."

"Your reputation with the community—"

"Amy, stop."

"No. I won't stop. It's over, Wade, right here and now."

He couldn't believe what he was hearing. "What do you mean, over?"

She seemed to have steeled herself, because she didn't so much as blink. "Over, as in we won't be seeing each other again."

Lyle's sucker punch had surprised him less. "You don't mean that!"

"I do. It was inevitable, anyway," she said.

"What do you mean, inevitable?" He barely recognized the sound of his own voice.

"You and me," she whispered. "I'd need to tell you soon, anyway."

"Tell me *what?*" Although he asked the question, he already knew the answer. Amy had decided to reject his marriage proposal.

"I…can't marry you, Wade."

He sank back down in the chair, crushed by the weight of his pain and disappointment.

"The fact you asked me to be your wife is one of the…the greatest honors of my life. I want you to know that. I didn't make this decision lightly. I've been trying to find a way to tell you all week."

He was a man of words. A man who loved language, who knew how to use it and could respond to any occasion; it was part of his job, of who he was. But Amy's rejection left him speechless. All he felt was an encompassing sadness. And bitterness.

"What about Sarah?" he asked, unable to hide his anger. He felt she was being selfish, putting herself first. He'd offered to be more than her husband; he'd wanted to adopt her child.

"I'll raise her on my own. It was what I intended from the first."

He got to his feet. "You need to do what you think is best."

"That's exactly what I am doing. Thank you," she said, and her voice wavered slightly.

Wade ignored the emotion she revealed and struggled to contain his own. "I apologize for the embarrassment I caused you this afternoon."

"Oh, Wade."

"I won't bother you again." Having said that, he walked out of the office.

Nine

Preaching Sunday's sermon was one of the most difficult tasks Wade had ever performed during his entire time in the ministry. Word of the altercation between him and Lyle Whitehouse had spread like wildfire through Promise, gathering other rumors and ugly speculations. As he entered the sanctuary Sunday morning, he noticed that he'd drawn a record crowd. The church was filled to capacity, and the overflow had collected in the rear of the room. He'd certainly hoped to pack the pews, but not for a reason like this.

Curiosity seekers had come to see his cut lip and his black eye. They'd come to hear his explanation. He hated to disappoint all the good people of Promise, but he had no intention of offering excuses or justifications. He stood before them as a man who'd made a mistake. One he deeply regretted. He wasn't perfect and didn't pretend to be, but he was ready to accept the consequences of his actions—if it came to that. He hoped it wouldn't, but the choice wasn't his.

The choir opened the service with a favorite hymn of Wade's, written by Fanny Crosby a century earlier.

Although it hurt his mouth, his voice joined theirs as he sang, *"This is my story, this is my song..."*

Rather than keep everyone in suspense, Wade approached the lectern when the hymn ended. "Good morning," he said, and managed a painful smile.

His words were enthusiastically echoed back. Several people craned their necks to get a better look at him. It was a wonder Louise Powell didn't topple into the aisle, considering how far she leaned sideways.

Wade didn't blame his parishioners for being curious. His reflection in the mirror told him far more than he wanted to know. He was a sight with his obvious injuries. The swelling in his jaw had gone down, although an ugly bruise remained. If his mother could see him now, she'd box his ears but good.

"Before I begin my sermon," he said, gazing out over the faces he knew so well, "I hope you'll indulge me while I take a few moments to discuss the rumor that I was involved in a fistfight with a local ranch hand."

A low hum of whispers followed.

"What you heard is correct. I was in an altercation this week."

Again he heard whispers, as though his ready admission had shocked certain people, although from his face it should have been obvious that at least some of the rumors were true. "I don't have any excuses or explanations." He cast his eyes down. "As members of this church, you have a right to expect—to demand—that your pastor's behavior be exemplary, above reproach. I have failed you. I've failed myself. I can only offer you my sincerest apology." His hands gripped the podium, his fingers white from the pressure.

"Seeing that such an action might raise a question

in your eyes about my suitability as your pastor, I've asked the elders to pass out ballots for a vote of confidence. If you're still willing to have me serve you in the capacity of pastor, then I'll do so with a grateful and humble heart. If not, I'll leave the church. The decision is yours."

He sat down, and the elders moved through the church, passing out the ballots.

Somehow, Wade managed to finish the service. As soon as he'd given the benediction, he retired to his office while the votes were being counted. Alone with his worries and fears, he tried to imagine what his life would be like outside the ministry. With his emotions muddled, his heart broken and his career badly shaken, Wade desperately needed the affirmation of his church family. Without it...well, he just didn't know.

Max Jordan knocked politely on his office door.

"Come in." Wade stood, bracing himself for the news.

Max entered the room and set the ballots on the edge of his desk. "The vote is unanimous. The members of Promise Christian Church want you to stay on as our pastor."

Wade sank to his chair in a rush of relief.

"Quite a few of our members have written you notes we thought you should read. You've done a lot for the people in this town, and we aren't about to forget it."

Wade released his breath in a slow sigh. Even Louise Powell had voted that he stay on. Now *that* said something.

"We're not looking for a saint to lead us, Reverend," Max added. "As you said, what you did was wrong, but you were willing to get up in front of everyone and say so. It's reassuring to know you face the same struggles we do. It isn't always an easy thing, holding one's temper in check. You did the right thing, admitting you'd made a mistake and reminding us that violence isn't a solution.

"Today's the best sermon you've ever preached because we could see you'd reached that conclusion the way we have ourselves. The hard way—through experience."

Wade nodded, in full agreement.

"We want you to stay, Wade. Each and every one of us."

Wade took hold of Max's hand and shook it. "Thank you," he said.

"No, Pastor, thank *you*."

Wade had never felt so humbled. His congregation had taught him a lesson in forgiveness that he wouldn't soon forget.

Dovie had rarely seen two people more miserable than Amy and Wade. It was clear to her that Amy was deeply in love with Wade and he was equally crazy about her.

"We have to do something," she told her husband early Monday afternoon. Frank generally stopped by the shop at some point for coffee. It was a habit established long before they were married and one she enjoyed to this day.

"You mean about Amy and Wade?" he asked, helping himself to an extra cookie. The peanut-butter cookies half dipped in chocolate were his favorites.

"Who else would I be talking about?" she snapped. She reached for a cookie, too, although she'd recently made a resolution to avoid sweets. But the situation with Amy and Wade had bothered her since Sunday-morning service.

"I don't think I'll ever forget Wade standing up in front of the church and apologizing like that." It'd demanded every ounce of self-restraint Dovie possessed not to leap to her feet and shout that she'd have punched Lyle Whitehouse out herself had she been there.

Wade had offered no justifications or excuses. She knew the details of the fight only because she was married to the town's sheriff. Although Frank hadn't been all that forthcoming.

"I respect Wade for doing that," Frank said. "But we can't go sticking our noses in other people's business, Dovie, no matter how much we care."

"But, Frank, this isn't just *anyone*. It's Amy."

Her husband sighed. "I know that, too, sweetheart, but we can't live their lives for them. Amy's old enough to make up her own mind."

"But she's miserable."

Frank hesitated. He and Dovie had grown to love the young woman who'd come into their lives so recently. It was as though they'd been given a daughter to love and cherish. They'd established a closeness that answered needs on both sides; Amy yearned for a family, and Dovie and Frank each had a heart full of love to share. It was almost as though her arrival in Promise had been ordained.

"I love Amy as though she were my own child," Dovie told her husband.

"I know, sweetheart. I do, too."

"Can't we do *something* to help her through this?"

Frank mulled over her question for a moment. "I

don't know what we can do other than give her our support."

Dovie sighed, at a loss as to how to help her friend. She longed to wrap Amy protectively in her arms and keep her safe.

Frank left a few minutes later, and she carried their dishes to the tiny kitchen at the back of the shop. Her gaze fell on the beautifully wrapped gift she was holding for Wade. His eyes had shone with emotion—with love for Amy—the day he'd come into the shop and purchased the robe. He'd been almost giddy with happiness—a far cry from the way he'd looked on Sunday.

Amy had skipped church, not that Dovie blamed her. Under the circumstances staying away was probably for the best. Dovie could well imagine Louise hounding her with questions following the service; at least Amy had been spared an inquisition.

On impulse Dovie grabbed the gift and headed out the front door. She turned over the Open sign to read Closed, and walked toward Ellie's feed store with the purposeful steps of a woman on a mission.

Ellie met her out front and waved in greeting. "Hi, Dovie!"

"Is Amy around?" Dovie asked, breathless from her brisk walk. She felt a certain urgency to give Wade's gift to Amy now, despite the fact that it was early afternoon, Amy was at work and she herself had a business to run.

"She's at home." Ellie glanced down at her clipboard.

"She's not ill, is she?" Dovie was instantly concerned.

"I don't think so," Ellie said. She looked up again,

meeting Dovie's eyes. "Has she asked you about Bitter End?"

Dovie frowned. "Yes, but not recently." The ghost town wasn't an ominous secret the way it had been in years past, but it wasn't a topic of everyday conversation, either. "What makes you ask?"

"She's been openly curious for some time," Ellie told Dovie. "I might be off base, but she was full of questions this morning, and then she asked for the afternoon off. She borrowed the truck for a few hours, too."

"You don't think she'd actually consider going there, do you?"

"I certainly hope not." But Dovie could tell Ellie was worried.

"When I questioned Amy about her plans, she hedged—as though she didn't want to tell me."

"Then I'll find out myself," Dovie said, and headed toward the small house where Frank had once lived, the gift box tucked under her arm. As she'd expected, Ellie's truck was parked in the driveway.

Amy answered Dovie's knock; her eyes widened when she saw it was her friend. "Dovie," she said, "come in."

Dovie took one look at Amy and instantly knew that Ellie's fears were well grounded. She was dressed in loose-fitting slacks, a sweatshirt and ankle-high boots. "You're going to Bitter End, aren't you?" Amy couldn't very well deny it, dressed as she was. "Amy, for the love of heaven, you can't just go traipsing around the countryside!"

"Why not?"

"Well, for one thing, you're pregnant—and...and it's dangerous."

"Then come too."

"*Me?*" Dovie brought her hand to her throat, taken aback by the suggestion.

"Yes, *you.* You've never been, have you?"

"No," Dovie admitted reluctantly. It wasn't because she didn't want to see Bitter End herself. She did, but Frank had put her off for one reason or another. She didn't think he'd purposely kept her away, just that he believed it wasn't anyplace for her. But she had roots there, too, and was curious about the old town.

"Aren't you interested?"

Dovie had to admit she was. "Even if I was willing to join you, I couldn't," she said. "I don't have any directions…"

"I have a map," Amy said, and led her into the kitchen. "Nell drew it up for me some time ago and I've been studying it."

"You're serious about this, aren't you?" Dovie said, as she gazed at the map.

"Very much so."

"But why now?"

"I… I don't know. I woke up this morning and I felt this…this burning need to do something, go somewhere. I need to get away for a while, I guess. I know it's silly, I know I probably shouldn't, but I want to see Bitter End. I'm prepared to go alone, but I'd rather someone was with me."

It went without saying that if things had been different, Wade would be taking her. Half an hour earlier, Dovie had been looking for a way to help Amy and Wade, and now it came to her that this would offer the perfect opportunity to talk. She and Amy would be spending time alone, and if ever Amy would confide her feelings it'd be now.

"I'll go."

Amy stared at her. "Are you *sure,* Dovie?"

She nodded. "I'll close up for the day, then call Frank and let him know what we're doing."

"He'll try to talk us out of it," Amy said, sounding as though she feared he might succeed.

"I won't let him."

"But…"

"I'll tell you what," Dovie said, thinking fast. "I've got a cellular phone and I'll conveniently forget to call him until we're there."

"Oh, Dovie, are you sure? He might get terribly upset with you."

"I'm sure he will, but Frank needs to know I have a mind of my own," she said firmly. "I've been wanting to visit that ghost town myself." If they were going to find it that afternoon, there were several things she needed to do. First she had to close the shop, then change clothes and leave a written message, as well as pack her cellular. "I'll be back in half an hour," Dovie promised. "Oh," she said, almost forgetting the purpose of her visit. "The package is for you."

Amy glanced at the beautifully wrapped box. "Another shower gift? Dovie, people have been so generous already. I don't know how to thank everyone."

"This isn't a shower gift," Dovie said. "It's from Wade."

At the mention of his name, Amy's head went back as if hearing it brought her pain. "Wade?" she whispered.

"He was in last week—before the fight—and bought it for you."

"But he…"

"He asked me to give it to you after the baby was born."

Amy frowned, obviously wondering why Dovie had brought it to her now.

Dovie shrugged. "I thought you might want to open it."

Amy looked at the box for a long time without moving toward it.

"I'll be back before you know it," Dovie said, suddenly excited by this little adventure. She felt that Amy knew her own limitations; if she wanted to visit Bitter End, then far be it from Dovie to stop her.

Amy left the package sitting exactly where Dovie had left it. But not for long. She couldn't resist knowing what he'd bought, or why Dovie had felt compelled to give it to her now.

She fingered the large pink bow. Dovie had specifically said Wade had purchased the gift for *her*. Not for the baby, but for her.

The look in Dovie's eyes had told Amy something else, too. The gift had been purchased with love. Amy didn't know how to deal with the kind of love she'd found in Promise; it was all so unfamiliar. Frank and Dovie had been incredibly generous and kind. Caroline had become a good friend, and Ellie, in addition to giving her a job, was her friend, too. Dr. Jane had been wonderful, encouraging her, befriending her.

And Wade…

She tried to squeeze out the memory of the hurt she'd seen in his eyes when she said she wouldn't marry him.

She placed the box on her lap and carefully removed

the ribbon. When she'd finished peeling away the paper, she set the box on the table, again. She hesitated, afraid that if she opened it, she'd be overwhelmed by a rush of emotion and pain. She hadn't seen Wade since the day of the fight and sincerely doubted she would. He might eventually come to visit her and see the baby, but Amy didn't expect to have more than casual contact with him following Sarah's birth. It hit her then how very much she was going to miss him. How very much she already did. This sudden need to do something, to get out and explore the ghost town, was a symptom of how she'd been feeling since she'd broken off their relationship. Restless, dispirited, lonely. Dovie was right; it was ridiculous to visit the town now, but that wasn't stopping her.

Finally Amy could stand it no longer and lifted the lid.

She gasped.

The robe was stunning, beautiful beyond anything she'd ever owned. She put the lid aside and reached for the robe and held it against her. Burying her face in it, she felt surrounded by Wade's love.

She heard Dovie's car just then, surprised it had taken her so little time. Amy glanced out the window and, sure enough, saw Dovie parked in her driveway. She waved, grabbed a sweater and hurried out the front door, map in hand.

"You ready?" she asked.

"Ready, willing and able," Dovie said with a conspiratorial grin.

Dovie drove while Amy navigated. The instructions were clear and it wasn't difficult to find the spot where Nell said to turn off the highway. The terrain was rough after that, but Dovie drove slowly and cautiously, winding around one hill and then another for what seemed forever.

Luckily a number of other cars had followed the same route in recent months, and their tires had worn a narrow path in the hard ground. It seemed incredible to Amy that anyone had ever found this place. They followed the route as far as it took them and stopped by a high limestone ledge.

"This is where the path ends," Dovie said.

Amy continued to study the map. "Nell says we'll need to go on foot from here."

"Down there?" Dovie questioned, sounding unsure.

"Yup," Amy confirmed. She opened the car door and climbed out, then walked to the edge of the limestone outcropping. Nestled in a small valley below was Bitter End. She saw stone and wood structures lining both sides of a main street. A church with a burned-out steeple and fenced graveyard stood at the other end. A corral and livery stable. A two-story hotel. From this distance, the buildings looked intact, as though the years had stood still. Amy sucked in her breath and glanced over her shoulder for Dovie. The older woman came to stand beside her.

"My goodness," she whispered.

The sight was oddly impressive, Amy had to admit. "Let's go see it up close," she said, reaching for Dovie's hand.

Dovie hesitated, studying the rock-strewn descent. "Amy, do you really think we should?"

"I haven't come this far to stop now."

"I know. Should you be climbing down this bluff in your condition?"

"Probably not."

"But you're going to do it, anyway?"

Amy nodded. "We'll help each other."

"If you're sure," Dovie said, and slipped her arm through Amy's.

The trek down wasn't easy. Not with Amy this close to her due date, and Dovie unaccustomed to this type of activity. But they took it slow and easy. Still, by the time they reached the town, both were breathless from exertion and excitement.

"Wow. We're really here," Amy said, taking her first tentative steps into the town.

Dovie's grip tightened on Amy's arm. "Frank would have a conniption if he could see us."

"Let's check it out," Amy said.

"I don't think it's safe to actually go inside any of the buildings, do you?"

"The stone ones look pretty solid," Amy said, surveying the street. This was an absolutely remarkable experience. She couldn't believe she was actually in Bitter End…and only wished Wade was here, too.

Together they explored from one end of town to the other. They identified the old tree, and after some investigation found the word "Cursed," which had been carved into the wood more than a century ago.

"This takes my breath away," Amy said, marveling anew as she traced the letters with her fingertip.

Dovie explained the curse. "I don't think anyone would have understood how this all came about if it wasn't for Nell and Travis. They were the ones to unravel the mystery."

"It's so…" Amy couldn't think of the right word.

"Barren," Dovie supplied.

"Exactly." Nothing grew in Bitter End. The town and everything around it had died. Bitter End had once held such promise…

Her thoughts skidded to a halt. Her relationship with Wade had been filled with promise, but that was dead now, too, like this town. *Stop it,* she told herself. *That's a ridiculous comparison.* She was annoyed by her self-indulgence and embarrassed that she'd been so melodramatic. Wade deserved better from her. If only he was here…

As if in protest the baby moved. The pain was fast, sharp, sudden. "Ooh," she said involuntarily, wrapping her arms around her stomach.

"Amy?" Dovie's voice rose with concern.

"The baby just kicked," she said, making light of it.

"You're not in labor, are you?"

"No…no. It's three weeks yet. There's nothing to worry about." No sooner had the words left her mouth than warm liquid gushed from between her legs.

Her water had broken.

"Amy, what's happening?"

She heard the panic in Dovie's voice and reached out to take the other woman's hand. "We have a small problem here," she admitted in a shaky voice. "It looks like no one told Sarah she wasn't due for another three weeks."

"Your water broke?" Dovie asked. "Are you in pain?"

"It's not too bad." Amy was more frightened than anything.

"Let's not panic," Dovie advised, although her voice was shrill with nerves. She carefully led Amy to the rocking chair outside the hotel and sat her down. "Let's think this through."

"All right," Amy said, clinging to Dovie's hand.

"Frank. I should call Frank." She said this as if it were divine inspiration.

"What about Dr. Jane?"

"He can phone her," Dovie said. "For now, it's more important that you be comfortable and relaxed."

Amy clasped her abdomen. "I'll be fine as soon as… as soon as this pain passes." She closed her eyes, taking a deep calming breath. After a moment she opened her eyes again to find Dovie gazing at her, lines of worry between her eyes.

"Frank will have my head," she muttered as she punched out the number on the small cell phone and waited. It seemed an eternity before Frank answered. Amy watched Dovie's expression as she explained the situation, then saw her eyes widen. She held the phone away from her ear as Frank's voice gained volume.

"You can yell at me later, Frank Hennessey, but right now there are more important concerns."

The conversation between the two continued, but Amy concentrated on timing her contractions and heard little more of what was said. Dovie started pacing. She'd been off the phone only a minute before it rang, the sound cutting through the still afternoon like a fire alarm. Dovie answered immediately and talked for several minutes.

"That was Dr. Jane," she said when she finished, "but I lost her. My phone's dead. Frank knows exactly where we are, though. He'll see to everything."

Amy was in the middle of a contraction and she closed her eyes, counting the seconds the way she'd learned in class.

"Are you all right?" Dovie asked.

"The pains," Amy whispered.

"They're bad?"

"I didn't think they were supposed to be this intense right away."

Dovie squatted down beside her. "Not to worry. We'll get you to the hospital in Brewster in no time."

"I'm not ready! There's so much to do yet," Amy protested, more confused than frightened. She'd assumed she had three weeks. When she awoke that morning, she'd felt better—physically—than she had in days. But not emotionally. That afternoon she'd experienced almost a compulsion for physical activity. She'd hoped that exploring Bitter End would be an interesting distraction.

Like so much else lately, her adventure had backfired.

"Everything's going to be fine," Dovie murmured.

"I know. It's just that I shouldn't be here… Oh, Dovie, how could I have been this foolish?"

"We both were, but everything's going to be fine," she said again. "Frank's on his way and he'll get you to the hospital in plenty of time."

"Thank you," Amy whispered. She closed her eyes to keep her thoughts focused on what was happening to her and the baby. She tried to remember everything she'd learned in the birthing classes, her breathing exercises and the importance of remaining calm and composed. It had all sounded manageable when she was in class; reality was a different matter. She knew she dared not climb back up the steep incline to the car. With her water broken, it could be dangerous for the baby.

Dovie comforted her and counted with her, encouraging her to breathe through contractions.

Finally, what seemed hours later, she heard the sound of someone approaching.

"Thank God," Dovie said. "It's Frank. And Wade."

"Wade?" Amy's eyes flew open. "You knew he was coming, didn't you?" she accused.

"Frank couldn't have kept him away," she said, pleading forgiveness with her eyes. "He was with Frank when I phoned." Dovie regarded her expectantly, as if seeking absolution for not telling her earlier.

"It's all right," Amy said. In truth she was glad he was there. She was afraid and, heaven help her, she needed him at her side.

Wade raced down the hill and into town well ahead of Frank, slowing down only when he reached the hotel steps. His eyes searched hers, his love visible enough that her chest tightened with pain.

"How are you?" he asked.

She smiled. "I've been better."

He clasped her hand in his and kissed her fingers. "I'm coming with you to Brewster. Please don't say no, Amy."

She smiled weakly and nodded. He knelt down in front of her, brushing the hair from her temples.

"Sarah's doing great, I think," she said, gripping his hand.

"What about you? What's the pain like?"

"Like nothing I can describe."

A contraction took hold of her just then and she drew in a deep breath and bit her lower lip. "Oh, Wade," she gasped.

Her hand tensed in his. She didn't mean to be so dependent on him, but now that he was here, she couldn't help it. She needed him. "Count," she instructed. "Please count."

"One, two, three…"

"Slower."

"One…two…three…" He continued until he'd reached twenty and she told him to stop.

She took several big breaths and opened her eyes. "The pains are much more intense than I expected." If they were this strong now, she couldn't imagine what they'd be like later.

"Let's get her to the car," Frank suggested.

"I'm ready," Amy said, and the two men helped her stand. Dovie stepped back and watched, her face taut with concern.

They'd gone only a few feet when another contraction ripped through her, nearly doubling her over. She moaned and clutched her stomach.

"Stop!" Dovie shouted.

"Stop?" Frank repeated, then stared at Dovie. "What's happening?"

"We aren't going to make it to the Brewster hospital in time, not with her contractions two minutes apart."

"What do you mean?" Wade demanded, although her words were perfectly clear.

Frank Hennessey studied him with a shocked white face. "Tell me, Preacher, how much do you know about delivering a baby?"

Ten

Sheriff Hennessey couldn't have called at a worse time. Max Jordan's pacemaker had gone haywire, and Jane dared not leave him, so she'd sent Frank on to Bitter End with specific instructions to phone the clinic as soon as they arrived in Brewster. The rest of her afternoon had been hectic, with the phone ringing off the hook. When she'd finished sewing up Wiley Rogers's sliced thumb and setting Walt Wilson's broken leg, she sorted through the messages and realized she hadn't heard back from Frank.

She was about to call Brewster Memorial to check when Ellie burst through the door.

"It is true?" Ellie asked, her face bright with excitement as she hurried into Jane's office.

"If you're asking about Amy, yes, it's true," Jane said. She stood in front of her file cabinet and slipped a chart back into place. She felt a rush of excitement herself. "Amy's about to have her baby. It turns out she went into labor in Bitter End."

"Why didn't somebody tell me sooner?" Ellie demanded. "Every tongue in Promise is wagging, and

I'm the last person to hear what's happening with my own employee." Disgruntled, she flopped down on the chair and stretched out her legs.

"How'd you find out?" Jane asked, curious. The nuances of small-town life continued to fascinate her. Having been born and raised in Southern California, she never failed to be astonished at the lightning-quick way word traveled in Promise.

"George."

"Who told George?" Jane asked, shaking her head in wonder.

"Pete Hadley, who heard from Denise down at the bowling alley. According to Pete, Denise has a real soft spot for Amy."

A lot of people had a soft spot for Amy, Jane reflected. The young mother-to-be had captured the town's heart. Sunday, when Wade had stood before the congregation and asked for a vote of confidence, the people had given him their overwhelming approval. But their votes hadn't been cast for Wade alone. They were showing support and approval for Amy, as well.

Jane suspected there was even some sneaking admiration over the fact that he'd been defending her against the likes of Lyle Whitehouse. Given the circumstances, a lot of the men in the congregation would have done the same thing.

She didn't think Lyle would be showing his face round town anymore. Billy, the owner of Billy D's Tavern, had suggested the ranch hand take his business elsewhere. Feelings ran high when it came to looking after one of their own. Wade McMillen was highly respected, and folks tended to feel protective toward Amy, too.

"You know who's kind of a gossip?" Ellie said, waggling her eyebrows as if this was an interesting tidbit of information.

"You mean other than you?" Jane teased.

"Me!" Ellie pointed to her chest in mock outrage. "I'm the picture of discretion."

"If you say so." Struggling to hold in a smile, Jane closed the file drawer and waited. "Well, don't keep me in suspense. Who?"

"Martha Kerns."

"The church secretary?" Jane had trouble believing it.

"How else do you think word got around so fast?"

"Hold on here," Jane said, stopping her sister-in-law. "What's Martha got to do with any of this?"

"She was working in the church office when Wade suddenly rushed in and said he was leaving with Sheriff Hennessey."

"Okay, got you," Jane said. It made sense now. Wade had told Martha and word had spread from there. She opened the small refrigerator in her office and removed two bottles of spring water, holding one out to Ellie. "No caffeine," she said.

"Thanks." Ellie reached for it, popped open the top and sank back into her chair. "Do you think Amy's having a boy or a girl?" she asked after a moment of silence.

"Girl," Jane predicted. "After a while a doctor gets a feel for these things. A sixth sense."

"Really?" Ellie sounded impressed.

Jane hadn't a clue which sex Amy's baby was, and as for any measure of shrewd intuition, well, that was a joke. She didn't think she'd be able to carry on this nonsense much longer and abruptly changed the subject. "Have you told Glen you're pregnant yet?"

Ellie leaned forward and set the bottle on Jane's desk. "From that grin on your face, I'd say he knows."

"He does."

"And he's happy?"

Ellie giggled. "You'd think he was the first man ever to get a woman pregnant. All this strutting around the house like a rooster."

Jane shook her head. That sounded just like her brother-in-law.

Although Cal and Glen were brothers, their personalities were vastly different. Jane's husband was quieter, more intense than his fun-loving brother. When she got pregnant herself and the time came for her to tell him, she could predict Cal's reaction. He'd grow quiet, and then he'd gather her in his arms and tell her how much he loved her. He'd pamper and spoil her, and they'd spend long quiet hours making plans for their baby. Glen might pamper Ellie, too, but he'd joke boastfully about it and be sure folks knew what a great husband he was. His high energy and good humor would make him a wonderful father.

"We're telling Mary and Phil tomorrow night," Ellie said.

"They'll be so thrilled." Jane took a long swallow of her drink. "If this keeps up, Promise is going to have a population explosion," she said. First Savannah Smith, then Caroline, Amy and now Ellie. She knew from talking to Nell that she and Travis hoped to add to their family, too. It'd been ten years since Nell had given birth to Emma, but Jane could find no reason for her to experience any difficulty in getting pregnant again. Because Nell was in her midthirties, Travis had voiced his concerns about the risks to her and the baby, but Jane had reassured them.

"Twins run in my family," Ellie said absently.

Jane couldn't help smiling. She could just imagine how her brother-in-law would react to twins.

"Do you think Amy might have had the baby by now?" Ellie asked. She straightened and leaned forward, anxious to hear the latest word.

"I was about to phone Brewster Memorial when you arrived," Jane told her.

"Go ahead. I'd love to be the one to give George the update."

Jane took another drink and flipped through her Rolodex for the phone number.

Just as she'd punched in the number, Jenny entered the office.

"Jane's phoning about Amy," Ellie whispered.

"Oh, good, I was about to ask."

"Dr. Jane Patterson," Jane announced. "I'm calling to check on one of my patients." She asked to speak to the nurse on the maternity floor, then placed her hand over the receiver. "They're transferring me."

"I have a sneaking suspicion Amy's having a boy," Jenny said.

"It's a girl," Jane said confidently.

"Boy," Jenny whispered back.

Jane rolled her eyes and pointed to her small refrigerator. "Help yourself."

"Thanks," Jenny mouthed.

"This is Dr. Jane Patterson from Promise," she said again, launching into her explanation about Amy.

"We're admitting someone now, but I don't have the

paperwork yet," the on-duty nurse said. "If you wait, I'll get that information for you."

Once more Jane put her hand over the mouthpiece. "She's arrived safe and sound."

"What took her so long?" Jenny asked, checking her watch.

"Frank probably took extra time not to upset her," Ellie suggested.

Jane frowned. According to her brief chat with Dovie before the cell phone went out, Amy's water had broken and she was experiencing some hard labor pains. She'd expected them to have arrived at the hospital much sooner than this.

"Everything's all right, isn't it?" Jenny asked, her gaze holding Jane's. "They got there okay?"

"With Frank driving, did you have a doubt?" Ellie asked, and drank the rest of her water.

In other circumstances Jane would have traveled with Amy, but that was impossible today. Amy was with Frank, Dovie and Wade McMillen. Unless the mother chose a home delivery as Savannah had, most of the babies in the county were born at the hospital in Brewster.

The floor nurse came back on the line. "What did you say your patient's name was again?"

"Amy Thornton."

"She hasn't been admitted yet," the nurse said matter-of-factly.

"Pardon me?" Jane asked. Although she felt an immediate sense of panic, she remained outwardly calm. "I'm sure there's some mistake. Could you check again?"

"Please hold the line."

Ellie stood. "There's an easy way to settle this. Frank drove in his patrol car, didn't he?"

Jane nodded.

"All we need to do is phone the sheriff's office and ask them to radio Frank."

"Good idea." Jane relaxed while Ellie and Jenny disappeared into the outer room to use the second phone.

The nurse from Brewster Memorial returned to the phone. "I'm sorry, no one in Admitting has talked to or seen anyone named Amy Thornton."

Jane replaced the receiver as Ellie and Jenny appeared in the doorway.

Ellie's face revealed her anxiety. "Something's wrong."

"The hospital has no record of Amy," Jane said.

Jenny chewed on her lip. "I phoned the sheriff's office," she explained, "and they radioed Frank."

"And?" Jane asked.

"There's no response. Apparently he isn't in the patrol car."

"Then where is he?" she demanded.

"That's the problem—no one seems to know," Ellie said. "They've been trying to reach him for the last thirty minutes."

"How's she doing?" Wade asked, unable to hide his anxiety. He no longer cared if Frank or Dovie knew how concerned he was. A rain squall had hit them soon after they'd decided not to carry Amy to the patrol car. They couldn't stay outside with Amy about to give birth; they had to find someplace safe and dry.

Bitter End was the last place he felt was safe for Amy. He blamed himself for this situation; she'd asked him about the town and he'd put her off. He didn't like the idea of her in this dead town, and the thought of her giving birth here sent chills down his spine.

With Amy moaning in pain and Dovie calculating the time between contractions, he felt panic rising inside him. All four of them were already soaked to the skin. The only structure in the town where Amy wouldn't have to lie on the floor was the church with its hard wooden pews, and with the two men supporting her, she managed to make her way inside. There were still some provisions from Richard's stay in the town, including towels, blankets and pillows.

Dovie cleaned a pew while Frank searched for anything else that might be of use. She and Wade helped Amy onto the pew, and then Dovie went off to give Frank a hand. Wade refused to leave Amy's side. He hadn't attended a single one of the birthing classes, and he didn't know if he was helping or hindering, but she seemed to want him there, and God knew he had no intention of leaving her. Not then. Not ever.

Again and again he counted the seconds as her body was gripped by contractions. Each one seemed to grow in length and intensity. He felt as if his heart would break at the agony she was suffering.

Then Dovie returned with Frank, each of them carrying a tarpaulin and some other supplies. Rain pounded against the roof and leaked into the center of the church where lightning had once struck. It astonished him that the building had survived the wear and tear of the elements all these years.

"Relax," Frank advised, squeezing his shoulder. "Everything's going to be fine." He'd found a lantern—obviously left there by Richard—and lit it. The immediate warm glow filled the dim interior.

"I'll relax once I know everything's all right with Amy," Wade told the other man, too tense to do anything but worry.

After maybe ten minutes, the rain stopped as suddenly as it'd come. Wade couldn't remember seeing a cloud in the sky, and then all at once they'd been trapped in the middle of a torrent.

Now that they'd made the decision to stay in Bitter End, it seemed fitting that Amy's child be born in a church, even one as dilapidated as this. Someone had been inside recently, and he doubted it was Richard Weston. Probably Travis Grant. He and Nell were back from their honeymoon and apparently he'd made a number of research trips to the old town.

"Is everything all right here?" Frank asked nervously. He pulled Wade aside, and Dovie took his place. Amy lay on a pew, a pillow beneath her head and as comfortable as they could make her.

"As far as I know," Wade assured him.

Frank nodded abruptly. "I'll be right back," he said.

"Where are you going now?" Dovie asked.

"To the patrol car. I want to radio the office. Tell 'em what happened and where we are."

"I wish I'd thought to charge the batteries in my phone," Dovie said with an apologetic expression.

"So do I," Frank muttered as he headed out of the church. "I'll get Amy's suitcase while I'm at it. We picked it up before we came out here."

Amy moaned, and Wade knelt down on the floor next to her.

"Oh, Wade, it hurts so much," she whimpered.

"Do you want me to rub your back?" Dovie asked.

"No...no." Amy stretched out her hand to Wade.

He clasped it in his own. Wanting to help as much as he could, he reached for the cool washcloth Dovie had brought in and wiped her brow.

The pain seemed to ease and so did her fierce grip on his hand.

"Have you ever delivered a baby?" Dovie asked him, looking paler by the minute.

"No," he said.

"Me, neither."

"I'm not exactly a pro at this myself," Amy said weakly in what he sensed was an effort to insert a bit of humor. A pain must have overtaken her again because she closed her eyes and started to moan.

"Do something," Wade pleaded with Dovie, who took her position by Amy's feet.

"The baby's fully crowned," Dovie whispered, glancing up at Wade.

Amy's answering smile was weak. "She's coming, Dovie, she's coming." With that she began to bear down.

"Pant!" Dovie instructed. "Pant."

Amy did, and Wade encouraged her with a stream of praise and reassurance.

"The suitcase," Dovie said. "We'll need the suitcase."

"It's in the car," Wade remembered. "Why the hell isn't Frank back? I'll go get it." He loosened his grip on Amy's hand but she refused to release his.

"No! Wade, Wade, please don't leave me."

Wade met Dovie's look.

"I'll go," she said, and hurried from the church.

Wade held Amy's hand against his heart. "I love you."

"I know. I love you, too. So much." Tears slipped from the corners of her eyes and rolled toward her ears. She sniffled once and started to moan again.

"Wade!" she cried. "The baby's coming!"

A calmness came over him, and he moved to the end of the pew, taking Dovie's role. The first thing he saw was a full head of wet dark hair. Amy panted, and the baby's head slipped free. Wade supported the tiny head, which fit perfectly in his large hands. The baby's small eyes were squeezed shut and she didn't look the least bit pleased with this turn of events.

It seemed that no time had passed before Dovie and Frank burst into the back of the church. Frank carried the suitcase.

"We need a baby blanket," Wade called.

Frank knelt down and opened the suitcase, and Dovie rushed forward just as Amy gave a shout and half rose. As she did, the baby slid into Wade's waiting arms. He gazed down at this perfectly formed miniature human being and experienced such a rush of love and joy it was all he could do not to break into sobs himself.

"Is it a girl?" Amy asked, crying openly.

"No, a boy," Wade said as the infant wailed loudly. The cry pierced through the church and Wade swore it was the most beautiful sound he'd heard in his entire life.

"An aid car's on the way," Frank told them. "I'm going to meet them by the highway."

"Go," Dovie said, and waved him off. She took the baby from Wade and wrapped him in a blanket, then handed the bundle to Wade, while she tended to Amy, who had delivered the afterbirth.

"A boy," Amy said, half sitting to look at her son. Tears streaked her beautiful face.

Tears of his own blurred his eyes as he stared down at the incredibly tiny being. The immediate sense of love he felt for this child was beyond comprehension. It took a real effort of will to hand him to his mother, but at last he laid the baby on her abdomen.

Amy gazed upon her son and lovingly kissed his brow. "Welcome, little Joseph Gair."

The baby screamed, as if he was protesting the rough treatment he'd already received from life.

"Gair—that's my middle name," Wade choked out. It had been his grandfather's first name.

"Your mother told me."

Wade reached out his finger and Joseph immediately clenched it with his hand. The connection was one that would last all his life. Wade was sure of it.

While Dovie finished with Amy, Wade sat at the far end of the pew holding Joseph. The child's eyes opened briefly and he looked up at Wade in the soft light and stopped crying. Within a minute he was sound asleep.

A boy. Not Sarah, but Joseph. "Sleep, darling boy, sleep," Wade whispered, and kissed his brow.

"Is everything all right?" Amy asked, twisting around to see Wade and her son.

"Perfect," he whispered. "Perfect."

Tears glistened in Amy's eyes, and he didn't know how she knew what he was thinking, but she did. He saw it in her look, in everything about her.

"Marry me," he said softly.

"Honestly, Amy, put that boy out of his misery and marry him," Dovie pleaded.

Wade could have kissed Dovie. He'd never been more convinced of anything than the rightness of marrying Amy and making Joseph his son. The moment the infant had entered life, he'd come into Wade's hands—to guide, to love, to support. This was his son, born of his heart. This was the woman he would love and cherish all his life.

"I love you so much," Amy whispered.

"Does that mean yes?"

"Yes." Her whispered response was half laugh and half sob.

This was the way it was meant to be. Amy and Joseph and him, and whatever other children might be born in the years to come.

"The aid car's here," Frank announced from the back of the church.

"Already?" Dovie sounded as though she didn't believe him.

"It was dispatched earlier," Frank said, walking toward them. "Apparently when we didn't show up at the hospital, Jane called the office and they radioed ahead for an aid car."

"It might have helped if they'd arrived ten minutes earlier," Dovie muttered.

Wade knew better. The aid car had arrived right on schedule.

Amy had never slept like this. The hospital room was dark, and she sighed and smiled as she reviewed the events of the day before. It didn't seem possible that she'd actually given birth in Bitter End. Things had gone crazy all at once, but she'd always be grateful for the way they'd happened. Otherwise Wade wouldn't have been there, and she couldn't imagine what Joseph's birth would have been like without him at her side.

If she'd ever doubted his love, he'd proved it ten times over in those few hours. She closed her eyes and recalled the incredible sense of rightness that she'd felt when she agreed to marry him. All her doubts and fears had melted away. Instinctively she knew it was what she had to do.

All her reasons for declining earlier remained, but after Joseph's birth, those reasons didn't seem nearly as important. Her greatest fear was that she'd be a detriment to Wade and his commitment to his church. Wade deserved someone better. It was what she'd sincerely felt, but all that had changed when she realized how much Wade loved her and her child. How much she loved him.

Content, she smiled, and for the first time noticed a shadow in the corner. Sitting upright, she saw Wade sprawled asleep in a chair. He'd stretched out his feet and slouched down, his arms flung over the sides.

"Wade," she whispered in astonishment. "What are you doing here?"

He awoke immediately, saw her and smiled softly. Sitting up, he glanced around the room. "What time is it?"

She looked for a clock but didn't see one. "I don't know."

"Oh." He glanced at his watch. "It's 4:00 a.m."

"Have you been here all night?" she asked.

"Guess so—it sure feels that way." He rubbed the back of his neck and rotated the stiffness from his shoulders.

"You must have been so uncomfortable." Amy couldn't believe that he'd been with her all this time.

"I'll live," he said. "How are you feeling?"

"Starved," she admitted.

He stood and shook out his legs. "I'll see what I can do about scrounging up something to eat."

"Don't go," she begged him, and held out her hand.

He walked over to her side and she lifted her arms to him. They kissed, and it was beautiful, sensual, intense. It felt good to be in his arms again, to recognize that sense of belonging.

"How did you happen to spend the night?" she asked.

She felt Wade's smile against her face. "They let me into the nursery to help with Joseph. I was there, Amy, when they weighed and measured him and washed him for the first time. He doesn't take to baths well." He paused to smile and their eyes held a long moment.

"Oh, Wade, I'm so happy."

"He's a beautiful baby boy," he told her.

"I'm having a little trouble adjusting to the fact that Sarah's a boy!"

"He's got a fine pair of lungs on him, too."

"I heard, remember?"

"Dr. Jane was by, and Ellie and Glen stopped in, too, and there are quite a few floral arrangements. The nurses kept them by their station because they didn't want to disturb your sleep."

"Everyone's been so good to me."

"It's because you're loved."

Amy felt that love. It overwhelmed her that the people of Promise would be this kind. That they would accept a stranger the way they had.

"Everyone was full of questions, too."

Amy could well imagine that.

"I must have been asked a dozen times how you ended up giving birth in the ghost town."

"I guess people think it was foolish of me to go there so close to my due date."

"I don't," Wade countered. "I'm convinced it was exactly where we were supposed to be."

She smiled and understood what he was saying. There was a rightness to her being in Bitter End, as if all this had been ordained long before.

Wade yawned loudly and covered his mouth.

"You must be exhausted," she said.

"I am," he told her. "It isn't every day a man delivers a son and convinces a gal to marry him."

"I should hope not," Amy said, and kissed the back of his hand.

Eleven

"Dovie," Frank called, hurrying from room to room to search for his wife. He could hardly wait to tell her the latest about little Joe.

"I'm in the garden." Dovie's melodic voice drifted into the house from the backyard.

Frank walked onto the back patio to discover his wife picking ripe red tomatoes from her ever-abundant garden. She wore a large straw hat and, in his view, had never looked lovelier.

"I saw Amy and Joseph this afternoon," he said, and laughed at the immediate flash of envy he read in her eyes.

"Frank Hennessey, why didn't you come and get me?"

"I would have, but it was a chance meeting. I'll have you know that little tyke smiled at me."

"He didn't."

"Dovie, I swear it's the truth. He looked up at me with his big beautiful brown eyes and grinned from ear to ear."

Dovie added a plump tomato to her basket. "He was

probably pooping. He's only two months old. That's far too young to be grinning."

"Hey, I'm his godfather. I know these things."

She gave an exaggerated sigh. "And I'm his god-mother and I know about these things, too."

"You're jealous because he didn't smile for you first."

"Well, I have news for you, Frank Hennessey. Little Joe most certainly did smile for me." The moment the words left Dovie's mouth, she snapped it closed, knowing she'd said more than she'd intended. Frank recognized that look of hers all too well.

"You've been to see him again," he charged. "I suppose you bought him another toy."

"I didn't," she denied.

The flush in her cheeks claimed otherwise. "All right, all right, I bought him a designer bib. Oh, Frank, it was the cutest little thing you've ever seen."

His eyes narrowed as though he disapproved, but in reality, he was having the time of his life spoiling this youngster, too. Amy and Wade had made him and Dovie the official godparents—and little Joe's unofficial grandparents. Christmas was a month away, and they'd already bought him more presents than Santa delivered to the entire state. They seemed unable to stop themselves. It was as though an entire new world had opened up to them with the birth of this child. They were crazy about the baby and crazy about each other, too.

"The bib was a policeman's uniform complete with badge," Dovie told him. "You aren't *really* angry, are you, sweetheart?"

How could he be? Frank loved this child as though he were his own flesh and blood. He suspected a great deal of this was the result of being present at little Joe's birth, but that was only part of the reason.

Frank had waited until he was sixty years old to marry, and once he'd committed himself to Dovie he wanted to kick himself for leaving it this late. He recalled with clarity the talk he'd had with his wife some months previously. Dovie had lamented the fact that they would never be grandparents.

He hadn't been much of a churchgoer, but after he'd married, he'd started attending services with her. He remembered one of Wade's sermons about Abraham and Sarah becoming parents well after their childbearing years. In some ways the story reminded him of what had happened to him and Dovie. Amy had arrived in Promise needing a family, and she'd adopted them and they'd adopted her. All the love they had in their hearts was lavished on Amy, Wade and little Joe.

"He's an incredible baby," Frank said.

"Incredible," Dovie echoed.

Frank slipped his arm around her waist. "You're pretty incredible yourself, Dovie Hennessey."

"So I've been told."

He threw back his head and hooted with laughter.

Dovie set her basket of vegetables aside and threw her arms around his middle. Her eyes sparkled with joy as she gazed up at him. "I'm happy, so very happy."

"I am, too." The transition to married life had been much easier than Frank had suspected. He'd fought long and hard, convinced he was too set in his ways to give up bachelorhood—and his stubbornness had nearly cost him the only woman he'd ever truly loved.

Frank hugged Dovie close. "We're going to spoil that baby rotten!" he declared.

"But, Frank, we're going to have so much fun doing it."
Frank could see that once again his wife was right.

Three months after Christmas Savannah Smith ventured into Bitter End. What she found caused her to race back to the ranch and breathlessly inform her husband. Laredo suggested she tell Grady and Caroline that same afternoon, which she did. The news burst from her in a rush of excitement.

"You're sure about this?" Grady asked.

"Grady, I know what I saw."

Caroline and five-month-old Roy came to visit the following day. "You went to Bitter End?" her best friend asked. "Good grief, Savannah, what would ever make you go back there?"

"The anniversary of my first visit. It was two years ago, March twentieth, and I wanted to see if the rose-bush I'd planted in the cemetery had survived."

Savannah's whole life had changed that day two years earlier when she found a weary cowboy walking down the side of a country road and offered him a ride. She'd never done anything like it before and she never would again. For the first and only time in her life, she'd picked up a hitchhiker, and before the year was out she'd married him. She and Laredo Smith had become partners in the Yellow Rose Ranch and partners for life.

"Grady phoned and told Cal," Caroline said, cradling her son in her arms.

"I talked to Nell and Travis, too," Savannah said.

"Someone must have phoned and told Wade."

"Glen and Ellie, I think," Laredo suggested.

"Wade suggested we all meet out there first thing in the morning."

"You're going, aren't you?" Caroline asked.

Laredo and Savannah looked at each other and nodded. "We wouldn't miss it," he told her.

Fourteen of them planned to gather in the ghost town and see the strange phenomenon for themselves. Each one had been to the town at some point or other in the past two years. Each for his or her own reasons.

Savannah felt a certain responsibility to be present, since she was the person who'd started it all two years ago when she'd gone to Bitter End in search of lost roses. She was also the person who'd stumbled upon this latest wonder.

They met and parked their vehicles outside the town. Then each couple walked down the steep incline onto the dirt road that led into the center of town.

Savannah watched and smiled at their reactions, knowing that the same sense of astonishment must have shown on her face twenty-four hours earlier.

Grady's arm was around Caroline's shoulder. Roy was asleep in his carrier. Little Joe, too. Savannah knew that in the years to come these two boys would be best friends. Much the same way Grady and Glen and Cal had been from grade school onward.

"It's true," Ellie whispered. Her pregnancy was obvious now. Glen's hand held hers.

"It's a miracle," Nell whispered, gazing around her.

All around them, in every nook and cranny, against the corral, by the old water trough and even near the large rock, roses bloomed. Their scent wafted about, perfuming the air, their muted colors bringing life and beauty to a once dead place. Pansies winked from small patches of earth—gardens a century ago—and blue-bonnets covered the hillside, waving bright blue petals in the breeze.

Perhaps most incredible of all was the dead tree in the center of town. Up from the trunk had sprung new life, green shoots. In time the new tree would overshadow the old; life would vanquish death.

"Who can explain such a thing?" Frank asked, awestruck.

Savannah understood his awe; she felt the same way herself. Naturally there'd be a logical explanation for what had happened if they sought one. Most likely a freshwater spring had broken free.

"I don't know that I can explain it," Travis said, looking thoughtful. "But I can speculate about what might have caused this."

Everyone turned to him. "Bitter End's come full circle now," he said.

"Why now?" Ellie wanted to know.

"Well, keep in mind that I'm a writer—a storyteller—and I like events to have a structure. I like a sense of completion." Travis smiled at Amy and Wade. "But if my guess is right, we have little Joe to thank for all this."

"Joe?" Amy gazed down on her sleeping son.

"Amy, too," Dovie added, slipping her arm around the young mother's waist.

"A preacher's son died in Bitter End all those years ago," Travis said. "And now a preacher's son has been born here. So, like I said, everything has come full circle."

"Full circle," Savannah whispered, knowing instinctively that this was indeed what had happened.

"The curse is gone."

Savannah smiled. "And in its place is a profusion of beauty."

A town in bloom, filled with promises for the future. Promises for life.

* * * * *

#1 *New York Times* Bestselling Author

DEBBIE MACOMBER

Planning the wedding will be the easy part!

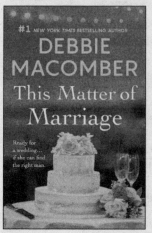

If Hallie McCarthy is going to get married and start a family the way she wants to, she's going to need a plan. And a man. Since Hallie is an organized, goal-setting kind of person, she gives herself a year to meet Mr. Knight-in-Shining-Armor. But all her dates are absolute disasters. Aren't there any nice, normal guys out there?

Too bad she can't just fall for her good-looking neighbor Steve Marris. He's definitely not her type. Anyway, Steve's busy trying to win back his ex-wife, who's busy getting married—just not to Steve. Life would be so much simpler if he could fall for someone else. Like...Hallie.

They are friends, though—and sometimes friends become more...

Available now, wherever books are sold!

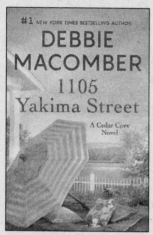

The countdown to Christmas begins now!
Keep track of all your Christmas reads.

Harlequin.com

XMAS0319BPA

Get 4 FREE REWARDS!

We'll send you 2 FREE Books plus 2 FREE Mystery Gifts.

FREE Value Over **$20**

Both the **Romance** and **Suspense** collections feature compelling novels written by many of today's best-selling authors.

DEBBIE MACOMBER

36869	CHOIR OF ANGELS	___	$7.99 U.S.	___	$9.99 CAN.
33125	NAVY FAMILIES	___	$7.99 U.S.	___	$9.99 CAN.
33121	NAVY BRIDES	___	$7.99 U.S.	___	$9.99 CAN.
33032	HANNAH'S LIST	___	$7.99 U.S.	___	$9.99 CAN.
33019	ALASKA HOME	___	$7.99 U.S.	___	$9.99 CAN.
33018	ALASKA NIGHTS	___	$7.99 U.S.	___	$9.99 CAN.
33017	ALASKA SKIES	___	$7.99 U.S.	___	$9.99 CAN.
32918	AN ENGAGEMENT IN SEATTLE	___	$7.99 U.S.	___	$9.99 CAN.
31926	THE SOONER THE BETTER	___	$7.99 U.S.	___	$9.99 CAN
31917	BECAUSE IT'S CHRISTMAS	___	$7.99 U.S.	___	$9.99 CAN.
31913	CHRISTMAS IN ALASKA	___	$7.99 U.S.	___	$9.99 CAN.
31903	WEDDING DREAMS	___	$7.99 U.S.	___	$9.99 CAN.
31894	ALWAYS DAKOTA	___	$7.99 U.S.	___	$9.99 CAN.
31888	DAKOTA HOME	___	$7.99 U.S.	___	$9.99 CAN.
31883	DAKOTA BORN	___	$7.99 U.S.	___	$9.99 CAN.
31860	THE MANNING BRIDES	___	$7.99 U.S.	___	$9.99 CAN.
31624	ON A CLEAR DAY	___	$7.99 U.S.	___	$8.99 CAN.
31580	MARRIAGE BETWEEN FRIENDS	___	$7.99 U.S.	___	$8.99 CAN.
31551	A REAL PRINCE	___	$7.99 U.S.	___	$8.99 CAN.
31535	PROMISE TEXAS	___	$7.99 U.S.	___	$8.99 CAN.
31441	HEART OF TEXAS VOLUME 2	___	$7.99 U.S.	___	$8.99 CAN.
31413	LOVE IN PLAIN SIGHT	___	$7.99 U.S.	___	$9.99 CAN.

(limited quantities available)

TOTAL AMOUNT	$ _____
POSTAGE & HANDLING	$ _____
($1.00 for 1 book, 50¢ for each additional)	
APPLICABLE TAXES*	$ _____
TOTAL PAYABLE	$ _____

(check or money order—please do not send cash)

To order, complete this form and send it, along with a check or money order for the total above, payable to MIRA Books, to: **In the U.S.:** 3010 Walden Avenue, P.O. Box 9077, Buffalo, NY 14269-9077; **In Canada:** P.O. Box 636, Fort Erie, Ontario, L2A 5X3.

Name: _____

Address: _____ City: _____

State/Prov.: _____ Zip/Postal Code: _____

Account Number (if applicable): _____
075 CSAS

★ mira

*New York residents remit applicable sales taxes.
*Canadian residents remit applicable GST and provincial taxes.

MDM0519BL